Also by Claire Kingsley

HAVEN BROTHERS
Obsession Falls
Storms and Secrets
Temptation Trails

BOOTLEG SPRINGS
Whiskey Chaser
Sidecar Crush
Moonshine Kiss
Bourbon Bliss
Gin Fling
Highball Rush

Bourbon Bliss

CLAIRE KINGSLEY
WITH **LUCY SCORE**

Bloom *books*

Copyright © 2019, 2024 by Claire Kingsley
Cover and internal design © 2024 by Sourcebooks
Cover design by Kari March Designs
Cover image © Natalia/Adobe Stock

Sourcebooks, Bloom Books, and the colophon are
registered trademarks of Sourcebooks.

All rights reserved. No part of this book may be reproduced in any form or by
any electronic or mechanical means including information storage and retrieval
systems—except in the case of brief quotations embodied in critical articles or
reviews—without permission in writing from its publisher, Sourcebooks.

The characters and events portrayed in this book are fictitious or
are used fictitiously. Any similarity to real persons, living or dead,
is purely coincidental and not intended by the author.

All brand names and product names used in this book are trademarks,
registered trademarks, or trade names of their respective holders.
Sourcebooks is not associated with any product or vendor in this book.

Published by Bloom Books, an imprint of Sourcebooks
P.O. Box 4410, Naperville, Illinois 60567-4410
(630) 961-3900
sourcebooks.com

Cataloging-in-Publication data is on file with the Library of Congress.

Originally published in 2019 by Claire Kingsley.

Printed and bound in the United States of America.
POD

For all the quirky girls. Stay weird.

Chapter One

George

My knee hurt more than it should.

I was more than eight weeks post-surgery for a torn ACL, and it shouldn't have been this sore. Instead of wandering around the VIP room at Bleu Martini—a favorite club among my teammates in Philly—I was chilling in a plush booth with my leg propped up.

The dim lights cast a bluish tint over the room. I could still hear the club music bumping through the walls, but our private party had mellowed. The smooth R&B sounded like Rex's patented sex playlist. Judging by the way my teammate had his latest groupie backed up against a wall, it probably was his sex playlist.

I adjusted my leg, trying not to visibly wince. I should probably have been home icing it. But Rex had threatened to drive to my place and drag me out tonight if I didn't come. And I hadn't exactly admitted how bad it was.

I'd talked to my agent already. And my coach. My

teammates, however, hadn't heard the news. My career as a pro football player was officially over.

In some ways, it was devastating. Football was the only thing I really knew. I'd been playing since I was five.

But from the moment I'd gone down on the field, my knee screaming with pain, I'd known. It was my second ACL tear in five years. I'd come back from the first one. You didn't come back from two. Not when they were the same knee, and you were a thirty-two-year-old receiver. Despite the way everyone—from doctors to my agent—had tried to make the best of it, I'd known. It was a career ender. No amount of PT was going to save me.

So when my doctor had given me the final verdict a few days ago, I hadn't been surprised. Wasn't happy about it. But not surprised, either.

"Sup, GT." Deacon Phillips, defensive player of the year, five-time all-pro linebacker. He was getting up there in years, just like me. But he'd managed to get through the season without any injuries.

I leaned back, like I wasn't elevating my knee, just relaxing in the club. Like I was too cool to make any effort. "Taking in the scenery."

"Bullshit." He set his beer down on the table and slid into the booth. "Don't mess with me, man. You coming back?"

I looked away. The guys weren't going to like this. I knew they were all holding out hope. They'd made it to the playoffs without me, but lost the first game. A bitterly disappointing end to what had begun as a perfect season. We'd all been hoping I'd pull through and we'd have another shot next year.

"No, man. I'm not coming back from this one."

"Shit," Deacon said under his breath. He shook his head. "Can't they give you a bionic leg now or something? Jesus. This is it for you? Really?"

I nodded, letting it sink in as I said it aloud. "Yep. I'm done. No more football."

"I had a feeling it was coming, but this is brutal, bro. I don't know what to say."

"Don't give me any pity crap. I had a good run. Y'all are gonna be fine without me."

He shook his head, like he didn't believe me.

I took a deep breath, glancing around the room, at a dozen or so of the guys I'd played with for the last few years. The worst part was the feeling that I was letting them down. Not to mention the coaches and staff. They'd pinned a lot of their hopes on me—me and these magic hands. Sticky as my hands were, they didn't do me any good without legs to run on. Without my wheels, I was just another tall guy with big hands.

"Anyone else know?" Deacon asked.

"The organization knows. It's official. I need to start telling the rest of the guys, though."

"Shit."

"Yeah." There wasn't much more to say.

He glanced over his shoulder, and I knew exactly who he was looking at. MacKenzie Lyons. My on-again-off-again—currently off-again—girlfriend. She'd arrived about ten minutes ago, and so far, she seemed to be pretending to avoid me. I wondered if she'd known I'd be here. I'd never figured out how so many women seemed to find where my teammates and I were hanging out. No one ever took credit for inviting them, yet there were always women around.

Wasn't sure how I felt about seeing MacKenzie tonight. This wasn't exactly a high point for me. Kind of a low, really. Did I want her here to witness the end of my career?

Maybe I'd call it an early night and bail now.

As if she could see how close I was to getting up and leaving, MacKenzie broke off from the conversation she was having with a woman I didn't know, set her eyes on me, and walked to my table. Even I had to admit, she looked hot in that tight black dress and heels.

"Trust me, dude," Deacon said as he got up. "Hit that while you still can."

"Deacon," MacKenzie said, and he tipped his chin to her before walking away.

3

I gestured for her to sit. She gracefully lowered herself down next to me.

"How's the knee?"

"It's great," I lied.

"Yeah?" Her face brightened. "I've been worried about you."

We'd broken up—again—at the beginning of last season. To her credit, she'd called to see if I needed anything after my surgery. Considering we weren't together, she hadn't needed to do that, so I'd appreciated the gesture.

"You know me, I'll be fine. I always bounce back."

"Yeah, you do." She gently nudged me and nibbled on her bottom lip.

I'd have been lying if I said I wasn't tempted. Her expression—flirtatious and suggestive—told me she was a sure thing tonight. I could slide my hands up those supple thighs. Lean in and brush my lips across the sensitive skin at the base of her neck. Get her hot for me. Take her back to my place.

Nothing wrong with some good sex. Sounded nice right about now.

But then would come the complications. The questions. I wasn't really a one-night-stand guy, and she knew it. Would she want to get back together? What would she want from me if we did?

I knew the answer to that question and it was enough to stay my hand. Keep me from reaching out to caress the obscene amount of thigh showing beneath her short skirt. She'd want expensive dinners. Gifts, preferably of the designer variety. Vacations. Exclusive locales, first class, five-star hotels. It was why MacKenzie dated athletes. Why she'd dated me.

I'd dated worse before her—women who were brazen and unapologetic in their pursuit of the elusive pro-athlete boyfriend. MacKenzie had at least attempted to give me access to her feelings. To care about more than what I could buy her, or the status dating me afforded her. But it hadn't been enough. There was still the expectation of more. More money, more gifts, more luxury.

A lot of the guys I played with were fine with that. Happy to shower their girlfriends with diamonds and designer purses. Pay for their luxury apartments and expensive cars. To them, it was a business transaction. They provided a certain lifestyle, while the women provided certain comforts. A hot date to be seen with. Kinky sex behind closed doors—or sometimes in front of them.

That wasn't enough for me. I wanted more. I wanted feelings. Something real. The guys gave me shit about my supposedly high standards, but to me it wasn't that the groupies and wannabe starlets weren't hot enough. The problem was, those women wanted me for all the wrong reasons. They wanted GT Thompson, all-pro receiver. They didn't want *me*.

I'd thought MacKenzie might be different. Thought it twice now, and twice I'd been wrong. I wasn't going down that path again, regardless of how insane she looked in that curve hugging black dress.

"What's wrong?" she cooed. She was laying it on thick tonight. Made me wonder what her game was. She reached out to draw her fingernails lightly up my shin, over my pants. "Lonely?"

"Nah, I'm good," I lied. Second time tonight. "Just keeping it mellow."

She kept her fingers on my leg, brushing them up and down. Familiar. Too familiar, but I didn't want to move in case I winced.

"Should we get a bottle of champagne?" she asked. "Have a little celebration?"

"What are we celebrating?"

"Second chances."

I raised my eyebrows. If she was talking about us, we'd blown through a second chance already. "Second chances for what? And do you mean second…or third?"

The corners of her mouth tilted upward. "I mean next season. A second chance at the playoffs."

The words came out before I could stop them. "I'm out, Mac. There is no next season."

5

A cloud of emotion passed across her features. Shock. Maybe horror. Was she really that upset for me?

"What?" she asked.

"I'm not coming back. I'm done with football."

"You're not serious," she said, the shock melting into a false smile, her bright red lips parting over her sparkling white teeth. "Of course you're coming back. You always bounce back."

"Not this time."

Her back straightened and she shifted away. "You're retiring?"

I nodded. There wasn't much more to say.

The curve had gone out of her spine, so she no longer arched her back, emphasizing her boobs and admittedly fantastic ass. She had a wicked resting bitch face and it was out in full force. No more softness. No more compassion.

"I didn't realize." She stood, clutching her small sequined purse to her body. "I'm sorry to hear it."

"Shit happens," I said, spreading my arms wide again. Still playing the part of the guy who was too mellow to let anything faze him.

"Of course," she said, faking another smile. "Good to see you, GT. Take care."

I tipped my chin. "Take care."

She walked away without looking back. It didn't matter that her ass looked great in that dress. The sultry sway of her hips left me feeling nauseated, not aroused.

I wasn't sure why being rejected by a woman I didn't want stung so bad, but it did. The second she'd realized my career was over, she'd been out. Totally uninterested. It shouldn't have surprised me. But I'd thought MacKenzie might care enough to at least ask if I was okay. Maybe be concerned about my future. Ask what I was going to do next.

But she hadn't. And it shouldn't have mattered. But it did.

I looked around at my teammates—my friends. At the girls dressed to kill in their tight dresses and expensive heels. I was surrounded by beauty. Attractive people, beautiful clothes.

But it was hollow. Empty and meaningless. And I realized I was ready to move on. Ready to leave the life of a pro-athlete behind me and take a new path.

My knee still fucking hurt, and MacKenzie's rejection stung. But there had to be more for me out there somewhere. A world that valued me for more than playing a game.

And maybe she was out there, too. The woman who'd see me as more than a guy who was good at catching a ball.

Chapter Two

June

The text from my sister Cassidy came just as I was finishing my work day, her number lighting up my phone. I waited to check while I finished what I was doing. I plugged a few more numbers into the spreadsheet, already knowing the result. I could do the calculations in my head faster than I could create the data sets and tables. But my client needed the numbers to exist somewhere other than my brain. Hence, spreadsheets and graphs.

With that finished, I saved my work and closed my laptop. I worked from my home office eighty-nine-point-two percent of the time. The other ten-point-eight percent was spent in Baltimore, where my company was located. I was an actuary, and a highly-paid one at that. I'd started my career working for a large insurance company, but made the switch to consulting a few years ago. It was a situation that suited me well. I liked my work—and was proficient at it—but staying in Bootleg Springs had been a priority. My current arrangement allowed me to do just that.

Contrary to what my sister seemed to believe, I didn't stay in Bootleg because I was afraid to venture into the wider world. I stayed because it suited me. It was quiet—most of the time, at least. I knew everyone in town. I had a routine. My family was here. I saw no compelling reason to leave.

I picked up my phone to read Cassidy's text.

Cassidy: Girls' night Juney! We're going to the Lookout. Pick you up at 8?
Me: It's Thursday.
Cassidy: So?
Me: We go out on Fridays.
Cassidy: I know but it's spontaneous. Scarlett and Leah Mae are coming, too. It'll be fun.
Me: Okay, but picking me up won't be necessary. I'll meet you there.

I sighed and put down my phone. I didn't particularly want to go out tonight. It was a weeknight, but that didn't mean the Lookout would be any less rowdy than a Friday. It would be loud, and there would probably be a bar fight.

But I liked making my younger sister happy. Not that I had any idea why drinking alcoholic beverages in a noisy bar produced feelings of happiness in Cassidy and her friends. But it did, so I obliged.

There were a lot of things I didn't understand about Cassidy. In fact, there were a lot of things I didn't understand about people in general. I'd accepted that a long time ago. I didn't try to fit in or figure out why humans perplexed me. I didn't understand them, but I didn't have the drive to try either.

People were odd. They said things they didn't mean and did things that bore no relationship to what they said. I found them unpredictable, and therefore uncomfortable.

Numbers, on the other hand, made sense. They were reliable. They obeyed the rules and behaved in a predictable manner. As an example, I could do complex mathematical

9

equations in my head, but I couldn't fathom why my sister and Bowie had failed to engage in a romantic relationship for years, when it had been clear to everyone they had feelings for each other.

Numbers made sense. People did not.

Yet I lived in a world where people existed, and I found that it pleased the people I cared about if I spent time interacting with them. Which sometimes meant joining my sister for a girls' night at the Lookout on a Thursday.

I prepared my dinner, dividing the meal precisely into two portions. One I placed on a plate, while the other went into the refrigerator for tomorrow. Although I generally only cooked for one person—myself—I had a collection of *cooking for two* cookbooks on a shelf in my kitchen. Cooking twice what I needed increased my kitchen efficiency, allowing me to prepare half the number of meals I would otherwise need.

"Hey, Juney." Jonah came downstairs, running a towel over his wet hair. "That smells good."

I stiffened. Did he mean he wanted to share? Or was he simply commenting on the pleasant aroma of my meal?

"It's likely the combination of basil and garlic that produces the scent you're enjoying," I said. Cassidy would say it would be polite to offer him some. "Would you like a portion?"

"Oh, thanks, but no," he said. "I'm doing intermittent fasting, so I'm not eating again until tomorrow."

"Good. I made the second portion for myself to eat tomorrow, so that works out for both of us."

He smiled in a way that made me wonder if he was amused or irritated with me. It was hard for me to tell. "Guess so. Do you have plans tonight?"

"Yes."

"Okay. Um, what are they?"

"Girls' night at the Lookout."

"Sounds fun," he said. "I have to be up early in the morning, so I'm staying in. Feel free to call me if you need a ride or anything, though."

"The chance of me overindulging in alcohol is approximately one percent," I said. "I'm sure I'll be able to drive myself. But thank you for the offer."

He smiled again. "No problem."

Jonah was my first ever roommate. I'd gone from living with my parents and sister to living alone. I'd even lived alone in college. I didn't like sharing my space. Another person meant someone moving things from their rightful places, making messes, and worst of all, failing to understand the importance of football on Sundays.

But Jonah was a pleasant roommate. He was unobtrusive, clean, and cooked his own meals. And he never, ever tried to dictate the television schedule when there were games on. We'd even watched the Superbowl together, although at the time I'd still been mourning my fantasy football league loss.

Jonah went off to do whatever it was Jonah did. I had my dinner, then settled onto the couch with a book. Cassidy, Scarlett, and Leah Mae were no doubt using this time to prepare for the upcoming evening. Women seemed to feel a night out necessitated a lengthy routine of makeup application, the use of various hair products and heated appliances, and a great deal of indecision when it came to clothing choices.

Wardrobe decisions were simple calculations. You took the occasion, time of day, expected attendees, and venue, and accounted for the season and current weather conditions.

Occasion: spontaneous girls' night

Time of day: weeknight evening

Expected attendees: Cassidy, Scarlett, Leah Mae, and various other Bootleg Springs residents

Venue: The Lookout

Season and current weather conditions: early February, cold and dry

Outcome: sweater, jeans, thick socks, boots

It had taken me no more than a few seconds to reach the appropriate conclusion. As for the rest of the primping routine, I saw no need to augment my appearance with cosmetics or spend a great deal of time and effort on my hair. It wasn't as if I was going to the Lookout to attract a mate.

Neither were the other women in my life, of course. They were all firmly ensconced in committed relationships. Which made their desire to spend so much time on their appearance even more perplexing. Who were they dressing up *for*, now that they were no longer single?

I didn't understand people.

At seven fifty-five, I got up and put on my boots and coat. I lived a short drive from the Lookout, and if past behavior served as an accurate predictor of future outcomes—and I knew that it did—the other girls would arrive between five and fifteen minutes after the agreed upon time. In other words, I was not in a rush.

To my surprise, when I arrived at the Lookout at eight-oh-two, Cassidy's car was in the parking lot.

I opened the door to the bar, steeling myself for the assault on my senses. The Lookout was loud, music and voices spilling out into the cold night. Warm air engulfed me when I stepped inside—about two degrees above what I found comfortable.

Pausing, I gave myself a few seconds to find equilibrium in this new environment. It required tuning things out, erecting a barrier between my brain and the sensory input that beat at me. When I felt suitably insulated, I joined my sister and her friends at their table.

"Juney!" Cassidy said with a smile. "I'm so glad you came out with us!"

I smiled and gave her a stiff hug.

Cassidy and I looked quite a bit alike—both with dark blond hair and green eyes. The same upturned, lightly freckled noses. But our appearance was where the similarities ended. Our personalities were remarkably dissimilar, despite our shared genetics.

Of course, when it came to personality, I was remarkably dissimilar to everyone in Bootleg Springs, familial relations included.

However, our differences hadn't inhibited our personal relationship. I'd always maintained a positive rapport with Cassidy. I felt a great deal of affection for my sister. We weren't like other siblings. We'd rarely bickered or argued, even as children. We looked out for each other, each in our own way, and I appreciated that.

"I like your sweater," Leah Mae said, pointing at my clothing choice.

"Thank you. The weather is cold, so a sweater seemed prudent."

"And it's cute, too," she said.

I gave her a small nod. Leah Mae was pleasant. Considered beautiful in the traditional way, she was tall and thin with long blond hair and noticeable gap between her two front teeth. She'd been a model and on a reality TV show, but now she was back in Bootleg Springs and dating Jameson Bodine. They appeared well-suited for each other, and happy in their relationship. That was good. Jameson was my favorite of the Bodine men. He didn't talk a lot, which made spending time with him comfortable.

I'd once heard someone say they thought Jameson and I should date. I didn't have much desire to date anyone, but I'd been particularly surprised by the suggestion. I'd be the first to admit, I didn't understand human relationships. But it seemed to me, from what I did know, that a functioning relationship required a certain degree of communication. Putting two people together who didn't talk very much seemed like a recipe for failure.

Scarlett had also chosen a sweater for her evening attire. Hers hung off one shoulder, leaving her bra strap visible. I didn't know if that was a conscious choice, or if her sweater didn't fit right. Scarlett was petite and I suspected she often found clothing too large for her small frame.

She grabbed her sweater at the neck, pulling it in and out, as if to create a breeze beneath it. "I don't know about you, but I'm getting hot. I might be ditching mine."

"You wearing anything but your bra underneath?" Cassidy asked.

Scarlett held her sweater out and peered in, as if she'd forgotten what she was wearing. "Well, yeah. I'm not going to strip, silly."

"Why not?" Cassidy asked. "Might be fun."

"What's got you so frisky tonight?" Scarlett asked.

Cassidy shrugged. "Nothing. I'm just in a good mood. Want to have some fun."

"Baby, fun is my middle name," Scarlett said. "Let's get you nice and liquored up so you can go home and have wild, drunken sex with Bowie."

I drew my eyebrows in. "Intoxication carries a high probability of nausea and vomiting. I fail to see how that's conducive to engaging in sexual intercourse, especially of the wild variety."

Cassidy patted my shoulder. "You have a point, there, June Bug. But getting a little tipsy is fun sometimes."

That didn't precisely address my point, but it didn't matter. I took a seat on one of the empty stools and set my handbag on the table.

The band started a new song and a few couples moved in front of the tiny stage to dance. It was the oddest thing. The beat was too slow for much movement. They stood together, swaying back and forth, hardly moving their feet. I didn't grasp the appeal of any sort of dancing, but I'd always found slow-dancing particularly inexplicable.

Gibson Bodine strummed his guitar and sang into the microphone while his bandmates, Hung and Corbin, played along. They were an eclectic-looking mix of men. Gibson was tall and bearded, his expression usually some variation of a scowl. Hung was a gray-haired Asian man, and Corbin looked like he still belonged in high school, with smooth dark skin and thick hair.

Cassidy brought me a drink and I sipped it quietly. The girls talked about the men—and cats—in their lives, which didn't leave me much to add to the conversation. But I didn't mind too much. After a while, I pulled a book out of my handbag and laid it out on the table to read.

"Hey, what are you doing here?" Cassidy asked, drawing my attention away from my book.

Bowie Bodine put his arms around her. "I missed you."

"It's girls' night," she said, but there wasn't any conviction behind her words. Even I could tell she was glad to see him.

Which I found odd, considering they lived together. They were in the middle of a renovation, turning their duplex into a single residence. Bowie had likely seen Cassidy less than two hours ago. I didn't understand how that was long enough to miss a person, but I let the question drift from my mind.

To the surprise of everyone but me, Jameson and Devlin weren't far behind Bowie. Scarlett laughed and gave Devlin a playful smack on the chest for crashing girls' night—but then grabbed him by the front of his shirt and gave him a rather inappropriate kiss. Leah Mae didn't even pretend she wasn't happy to see Jameson, throwing her arms around his neck and hugging him.

I found myself smiling as I watched my sister and her friends—our friends. I liked seeing them happy. It reminded me of the way I felt around my parents. They were happy, so I was happy for them.

"Hey Juney." Jameson took a seat across from me. "Good book?"

"It's an analytical look at the history of statistics in American professional sports."

"Sounds right up your alley," he said.

"Can I get you another drink?" Bowie asked me. "I'm buying."

I gestured to my half-finished bourbon. "No thank you. I already calculated the ratio of time to bourbon consumption to ensure I'm in the proper frame of mind to drive myself home."

He smiled. "Well, I wouldn't want to mess with math."

Drinks were passed around and my sister and friends all engaged in lively conversation. I watched, feeling detached. It

15

wasn't their fault. They'd always done their best to include me. It wasn't even the fact that they were all coupled-off, and I was the lone single person at our table. I usually felt this sort of social detachment. It was as if I was a scientist in a lab, observing, but apart.

The vast majority of the time, this state of affairs didn't bother me in the least. It was just the way things were.

But tonight, the separateness I felt did bother me. I wasn't certain as to why.

Finally, I decided I could slip out without eliciting any unnecessary attention. Instead of heading for the solace of home, I found myself driving in the other direction—toward my parents' house.

My mother and father still lived in the same house where Cassidy and I had grown up. It hadn't changed much since I'd moved out. A little more worn, perhaps, although they kept it in pristine condition. And it still smelled the same—a mixture of cinnamon and vanilla that always reminded me of the cookies my mom loved to bake.

I went in without knocking, like I always did, and found my dad dozing on the couch. The TV was on, casting flickers of light across the dim room.

Dad's crossed arms rose and fell as he breathed, his white mustache twitching. I clicked the door closed and he startled, his deep intake of breath vibrating in his throat like a loud snore.

"Oh, June Bug," he said with a smile. "You caught me napping."

"Did you have a particularly tiring day?" I asked as I sat on the couch next to him. "You should be careful not to overexert yourself."

"I'm all right. What brings you here tonight?"

I looked away, the light of the muted TV drawing my gaze. I wasn't sure how to answer his question. I could have gone straight home. Home was comfortable. I liked it there. Had Cassidy not asked me to meet them at the Lookout, I'd have been perfectly content to spend my evening at home.

However, I *had* gone to the Lookout, and something about that had left me feeling unsettled in ways I didn't know how to articulate.

"Cassidy's having a girls' night, so I was at the Lookout. The men appeared to be unsatisfied with their significant others spending the evening without their company."

"So the men crashed your girls' night, and it turned into a double date?"

"Triple. Leah Mae and Jameson were also there."

"Ah yes, of course they were." He paused and appraised me through slightly narrowed eyes. "You feeling a little bit left out?"

"No," I said, and it wasn't a lie, exactly. "They took care to make sure I was included."

Dad smiled. He had the kindest, gentlest smile. "I'm sure they did. But that doesn't mean you didn't feel a bit on the outside."

"I suppose I did. But it's all right. Considering I was the lone single female in the group, it's not surprising."

He picked up the remote. "Should we see if there's a game on?"

This was why I'd come. Dad understood me. I settled back into the couch and folded my hands in my lap. "Yes, I think we should."

Dad patted me on the knee and turned the channel.

Chapter Three
George

The sun filtered through the trees as I sped down the highway. It was cold out there, and I'd felt the tires slip on slick ice in a few shady places. Had to be careful. I'd only passed two, maybe three cars along the highway. This town I was headed to—Bootleg Springs—was in the middle of nowhere. My sister Shelby had said it was remote, but I was starting to wonder if I'd missed it.

Shelby had been in Bootleg Springs since last November. I wasn't sure what she was doing out there. My younger sister always had something cooking. Truth was, I hadn't seen Shelby a lot over the last ten years. We'd kept in touch through texts and Skype calls, and spent a few holidays with our parents down in Charlotte. And I'd taken the whole family on a cruise a few years ago, during the off-season.

But it wasn't just a Thompson sibling reunion that had me headed into the mountains of West Virginia. Apparently this place was known for their hot springs. Some people even said they had healing properties. When I'd chatted with Shelby a few days ago, she'd suggested I come out and stay a while. She'd said the town was nice, and at this point, I'd do just about anything if it would help rehab my knee. It wasn't like I had anything else going on.

There were perks to being unemployed.

The highway curved, leading into a longer straight stretch. A car came toward me, headed in the opposite direction—a gorgeous black Dodge Charger. Bad ass car. I cracked the window to listen to the engine while it passed. I could just hear the faint rumble of that throaty purr. Nothing like a hot muscle car with an owner who knew how to make her sing.

But before I could admire the hum of the Charger's engine, a deer darted across the road, right in front of the other car.

The Charger swerved, narrowly missing the animal. Its tires must have hit an icy patch, and the car spun in a tight circle, veering off the road. I clenched my steering wheel as I watched it happen, as if in slow motion, powerless to help. The driver tried to correct, but the car slammed into a tree with a loud crunch.

I pumped my brakes, careful of the ice, and pulled across the empty highway. As soon as I was safely stopped on the side of the road, I flew out of the car and ran over to see if the driver was okay.

The driver's side door was pinned against the trunk of the tree. I went to the passenger's side and yanked the door open.

Bending down, I leaned against the heavy metal door, and peered inside. "Are you okay?"

The driver looked dazed. He was dressed in a black knit hat and thick coat, his jaw covered with dark facial hair. He had a hand to his forehead, but I didn't see blood. Seemed like a good sign.

"What the fuck," he muttered.

"You okay, man? Need help getting out of there?"

He looked at me and blinked a few times, like he was trying to figure out what had just happened. One hand still gripped the steering wheel, his knuckles white.

After prying his hand open and flexing his fingers a few times, he nodded. I reached in and helped him across the seat, then made sure he was stable on his feet before I let go of his thick forearm.

He put his hand on the car, probably to steady himself. "Holy shit. I didn't hit her, did I?"

"The deer?" I asked. "No, she ran off."

He nodded, still visibly dazed.

"Are you hurt?"

"I don't think so. Hit my head, but that's nothing."

"I don't know, man, a head injury isn't something to fuck around with. Trust me."

His eyes seemed to clear and he straightened. "Right, yeah. Oh fuck, my car."

Now that I was fairly sure the guy was all right, I turned my attention to the Charger. It would have been a damn shame to get even a scratch on this beauty, and this was much worse than a scratch. I couldn't see the extent of the damage from this side, but it couldn't have been pretty.

"You have someone you can call? Or can I give you a ride somewhere? I'm not sure where you were headed."

"Fuck," he muttered again. "Yeah, I'll call one of my brothers."

"Sure. I'll wait and make sure you get where you need to go."

He met my eyes for the first time, like it was sinking in that I was there. "Thanks for stopping. Appreciate it."

"No problem." I held out my hand. "GT Thompson."

"Gibson Bodine." He took my hand in a firm grip and shook. "Really. Thank you."

"Anytime. Looks like you're going to need a tow."

"Yeah, damn it. Fucking deer."

I stepped aside and waited while Gibson made a few calls. He paced back and forth next to his car, his gravelly voice thick with frustration. I cupped my hands in front of my face and blew into them. It was damn cold out here.

When he finished, he slid his phone into the back pocket

of his jeans. "My brother's on his way. He lives in town, so he's only a few minutes away. Tow truck is on its way, too."

"All right. You want me to hang out until they get here?"

"No, man, you can go. It's colder than shit out here." He glanced at his car, his expression pained. "Thanks for stopping."

"Of course. You sure you're all right?"

"Yeah, I'm not hurt. Can't say the same for her." He nodded toward the Charger. "But I'll fix her."

I said goodbye to Gibson Bodine but took my time once I got back in my car. Pretended to look at my phone for a few minutes while the heat blasted. He'd said he was fine, but I didn't want to leave him out here alone, just in case.

It didn't take long before another car pulled up and a guy got out. Only then did I get back on the highway and continue on to Bootleg Springs.

––––––––

The little place I was renting was just outside town, on the shores of the pristine mountain lake. No ice crusted the top of the water. Steam rose from the surface and I remembered the hot springs. Looked like the lake water was warm enough to stay liquid, even through the cold winter.

The sky was clear and white snow coated the trees. The peace and quiet was going to do me some good. Even after witnessing that car accident, I could feel myself relaxing, my stress unraveling.

Felt good. I liked this place already.

My sister was not one to waste time. She wanted to get together the second I arrived, so once I got my things situated in my rental cabin, I drove into town to meet her.

Bootleg Springs was the definition of quaint. Clean streets, fresh paint on many of the building façades. Hand-painted signs announced businesses like Yee Haw Yarn and Coffee, the Rusty Tool, and Moonshine Diner, where I was meeting Shelby.

Warm air scented with a rich mixture of delicious food smells greeted me when I walked inside. My stomach rumbled.

I spotted Shelby at a booth near the back, her face lighting up with a big smile.

She stood as I approached, and I wrapped her in a bear hug. Gave her a good squeeze. She was a lot smaller than me, but then I was six-foot-five, so most people were. Her brown hair was pulled back and she wore a light gray sweater and jeans. We looked oddly alike, considering we weren't biologically related. My parents had adopted Shelby when she was a baby.

"Hey, sis," I said as I slid into the booth opposite her. "Long time no see."

"Hey, GT. You look great. How's the knee?"

I straightened my leg beneath the table and rubbed above my knee cap. "It's good."

"Liar."

"I'm not lying. It is good. Could be better, though."

She nodded. "How are you doing with…you know. Everything else."

"You mean the end of my football career?"

"Yeah, that."

"I'm all right." I put my hands up in protest before she could disagree with me. "Shelby, I swear. I knew it was coming. Besides, I'm too old to keep getting beat to hell like that. I'm lucky the worst of it is my knee."

"True. But this is a big deal. I know you've talked about retiring before, but it must be hard to have the choice out of your hands."

"I've made my peace with it."

She smiled. "Good."

The waitress, a woman with a red beehive hairdo and a name tag that said Clarabell, came to take our order. Shelby chose an open-faced turkey sandwich. I went for the meatloaf and mashed potatoes. My favorite.

"How's little Marshmellow?" Shelby asked after Clarabell left.

"She's adorable, obviously," I said with a grin. Marshmellow, or Mellow for short, was my pet bunny—a Netherland dwarf.

She was tiny, soft, and pure white. "I miss her already, but Andrea's taking care of her for me while I'm away."

"Aw, I need to come visit her."

"You should. This being unemployed thing makes that a lot easier. I have all kinds of time."

"I'm so relieved," she said. "Mom and Dad have been worried about you, but you seem like you're taking everything in stride."

"Doing my best," I said. "But you need to tell me more about this hot spring."

"Right." She got out her phone and started typing. "I'll just text you the directions. It's easier than trying to explain."

"Is it hard to find?" I asked.

"Kind of, yeah," she said. "There are a few places to soak, but I found a really good one. It's more private. I've only been out there once, but it was so nice."

We chatted for a few more minutes until Clarabell brought our food—and holy hell, it was good. Down-home cooking at its best. Now I *really* liked this place. I had a feeling I was going to become a regular Moonshine customer during my stay. I was already wondering how soon was too soon to order another meal. I wanted to dig into that open-faced turkey sandwich next.

I glanced up as I ate and noticed a woman sitting a few booths away. She had dark blond hair that hung carelessly around her shoulders. No makeup. The sleeve of her navy sweater slid down her arm as she tucked a strand of hair behind her ear. She had her phone in one hand, and she picked up a pen with the other. Her eyes darted back and forth between her phone and a notebook as she wrote something down.

She was cute, in a not-usually-my-type sort of way. But it wasn't so much her appearance that made me glance twice. Something about the way she moved caught my attention. She was precise and exacting, her eyes flicking back and forth as she jotted in that notebook of hers. I found myself gazing at her, wondering what she was doing.

And then she spoke.

Not to me. She was sitting alone, and she didn't appear to be talking to anyone. I couldn't make out what she was saying—she was muttering to herself. But for some reason, I found the whole thing fascinating.

"Do you know who she is?" I asked Shelby, nodding my head in the direction of the muttering woman.

"Oh, that's June Tucker."

"Do you know her?" I asked, still gazing at June. Of course Shelby would know everyone in town by now.

"Not really. The locals haven't exactly been welcoming of *my kind*." She didn't sound the least bit upset by that. "But I've seen her around."

"And you see a lot."

She wrinkled her nose. "She's different."

"In what way?"

Shelby raised one shoulder in a slight shrug. "People say she's a little off. She doesn't interact like everyone else. But they still make a place for her. She's interesting."

I looked at June again. She appeared to be having a quiet argument with…herself? I wasn't sure. The phone in her hand indicated she might be on a call, but there wasn't another voice coming from the speaker. And I didn't see ear buds or a headset. Maybe she really was talking to herself.

She seemed…focused. As if unaware that she was in a public place and people might think it odd that she was talking to herself. Or maybe she just didn't care.

Either way, it was hard to take my eyes off her.

"Earth to GT." Shelby snapped her fingers near my face. "Quit staring. You're being weird."

I grinned at her and motioned to her half-full plate with my fork. "Are you going to finish that?"

"All yours." She pushed the rest of her dinner to my side of the table.

I loved eating with my sister. I always got her leftovers.

"So, I know my timing isn't great, what with you having

24

just arrived, but I'm going back to Pittsburgh in a couple of days."

I put my fork down. "What? Why?"

"I got a gig writing some articles for a PR firm there," she said. "It's not my favorite thing, but it pays, and I need to make some extra cash right now."

For half a second, I thought about offering Shelby money. But I knew exactly what she'd say if I did, if she didn't just smack me. I knew if she was in real trouble, she'd let me help, but otherwise, she wanted to make it on her own. I respected that.

"Well that sucks, but you gotta do what you gotta do," I said.

"Exactly. I'll be back. I still have research to do here." She put her napkin down and rose from her seat. "I need to go to the restroom. I'll be right back."

Shelby's dinner was every bit as good as mine. I'd probably need to quit eating so much eventually, since I wouldn't be hitting training camp in a few months and losing any excess weight I'd put on during the off-season. But today was not that day.

Movement caught my eye and I looked over to find June getting up from her booth. She'd put her phone and notebook away—probably in the handbag she slung over one shoulder.

She looked up and our eyes met. Instead of breaking eye contact, like strangers usually did, we stared at each other. Her face was impossible to read—expressionless. But something about her held me captivated. I couldn't look away.

Maybe it was the way she looked directly at me. No batting eyelashes or attempts at acting coy. Her gaze left my face, traveling down to my feet, then back again. It didn't seem like she recognized me, but I couldn't be sure. There was no way to read what might be going on behind those pretty green eyes.

With a little nod of her head—as if she'd just filed away her observations for later use—she left.

I watched her go, feeling dazed, like I'd just taken a hard

hit that had rung my bell. Why had she looked at me like that? Was she a fan of a rival team and hated me? Did she even know who I was?

I had no idea.

But suddenly Bootleg Springs was a lot more interesting.

Chapter Four
George

I hadn't been sure what to think about the claim that the hot springs in some little town in West Virginia might have healing properties. But as I lowered myself into the warm water, I wondered if maybe they were right. I sank down slowly, letting the heat loosen my tight muscles.

The quiet and seclusion were just as relaxing as the water. Patches of snow still sat beneath the trees and the air was chilly against my bare skin. The contrast between the cold air and warm water felt great. The spring itself was a pool of glassy greenish-blue water. Plants crept in along the edges, as if vying for the warmth and hydration, and steam rose from the surface.

This place had been tricky to find—as Shelby had warned me—but there was no one around. I shifted a little to get comfortable, leaned my head back, and closed my eyes.

Oh yeah. This was good.

"Excuse me. You're not supposed to be here."

My eyes flew open at the sound of a woman's voice. It was June, the woman I'd seen at the diner yesterday. Her dark blond hair was in a ponytail and she was dressed in a cream sweater, black leggings, and canvas low-tops. Her piercing green eyes stared straight at me, unblinking.

"Um, what?" *Way to go, GT. Great response.*

She crossed her arms, but her expression didn't change. "You're not on the list."

I glanced around, like I was going to see a bouncer with a clipboard somewhere. "On what list?"

"There's a sign-up sheet. You're in my spot."

"A sign-up sheet to sit in a hot spring?"

"Yes." She blinked once.

It was about then that I remembered I was naked. She probably couldn't see my junk, but if I got out with her standing there, I'd be treating her to quite the show. Inexplicably, I was sporting a semi. Was it her? She probably had a nice body under that bulky sweater, but it was hard to tell. And it wasn't like she was flirting with me. Not in the least. She was probably the least-flirtatious woman I'd ever met. So I had no idea why my dick was trying to cause a scene.

Partial erection or not, this water felt amazing. I didn't particularly want to get out. Maybe I could talk her into letting me have more time.

"Listen, I'm sorry about taking your spot. I honestly didn't know. I'm not from around here, and no one told me there was a sign-up sheet. My sister said try the hot springs, so here I am." I grinned at her, spreading my arms to the sides.

"That doesn't change the fact that it's my time."

"This does present a predicament, doesn't it?" I rubbed my jaw. "I guess you'll just have to get in with me." Obviously she wasn't going to, but maybe she'd offer to come back in an hour.

She set her bag down and pulled off her sweater, revealing a white tank top underneath. My mouth dropped open as I watched her fold her sweater and put it in her bag. Then she hooked her thumbs under the waistband of her leggings and started to slide them down.

"What are you doing?" I asked.

She stopped, bent at the waist, her pants partway down, and looked at me. Her expression still hadn't changed. "I'm getting in."

"What?"

"You just said I should get in with you. I decided your solution is acceptable. I usually prefer to soak alone, but this time, I'll make an exception."

"Why?" It was a weird question, but it was the first thing that popped into my head.

She tilted her head, still bent over. "You weren't aware of the sign-up sheet. Tourists typically can't find this place without someone showing them, and any Bootlegger would know the rules. So either you got bad information, or someone set you up. Neither of those things seem like reason enough to make you leave."

"My sister told me, and I don't think she'd set me up. Not like this, at least. That's not really her style."

She finished taking off her leggings and folded them. I could see the goosebumps raise on her skin from the cold. With a little shiver, she pulled off her tank top and quickly put it in her bag.

There *was* a hot body beneath her sweater. A very hot body that was clad in nothing but a black bikini.

And now my erection was not of the *semi* variety.

I slid forward on the ledge I was sitting on, trying to get lower in the water. I wanted more distance between my crotch and the surface, in case she looked down. She climbed into the pool and settled herself on the ledge across from me.

"I'm—"

"George Thompson," she said, before I had a chance to finish.

I was accustomed to people knowing me, even approaching me in public. I'd signed autographs on everything from dirty napkins to women's boobs. But for some reason, the fact that this strange girl knew who I was surprised me into silence.

And she'd used my full name. No one called me George.

Not even my parents. I'd been GT since I was a kid. But coming from her, I liked it.

"June Tucker," she said.

I leaned forward, reaching out my hand. "Nice to meet you, June."

Her eyes flicked downward once and I almost drew back. But she gave me a businesslike shake.

She reached over the side of the pool and dried her hands on her towel before tightening her ponytail. Something about the way she moved was mesmerizing. She wasn't graceful, exactly, but there was a precision to her movements that was strangely appealing.

"You have an erect penis."

I stared at her for a few seconds longer than I should have before looking down. I did have an erection, and I was well aware of it. But I hadn't expected her to notice. And I really hadn't expected her to mention it like that.

"Um. Yeah, I guess I do."

"Why?"

"Well… I don't really know exactly."

"Are you meeting a lady friend, or did I interrupt you before you could complete your masturbatory emission?"

"I…no."

"I ask because people typically come here to have intercourse. That's the real reason the town created a sign-up sheet, no matter what people say about it. I assume your current state of arousal must have preceded my arrival."

I sat up straighter. If she was going to notice my junk, and be so blunt about it, there wasn't much reason to hide. The water was obviously too clear to give me any cover. If she were anyone else, I'd assume she was trying to make me uncomfortable so I'd leave. But there wasn't a hint of manipulation in her tone.

I liked that.

"No, I didn't come here to have sex with anyone. Or to…"

"Masturbate," she offered.

30

"Right. Not that either."

"Then what's responsible for your erection? In adult human males, it's uncommon to have increased blood flow to the penile capillaries without an external source of arousal. If you were under the age of eighteen to twenty, your physical state would be less surprising."

"You mean if I was a horny teenager, you wouldn't question my hard-on?"

"Precisely."

"I suppose that's fair. I don't know. Maybe it's you."

The first flicker of true emotion I'd seen in her passed across her face. Had I surprised her?

"That doesn't seem to be a likely possibility. Are you taking erectile dysfunction medication?"

I snorted out a very unflattering laugh. "Like Viagra? No. Definitely no need for that."

This was probably one of the weirdest conversations I'd ever had, but even talking in such straightforward terms about the fact that I was sporting a chubby wasn't bringing the big guy down. If anything, I was getting harder the longer we talked.

"Hmm." June settled back against the pool, the water buoying her boobs. That was not helping the hard-on situation. Not at all.

"Is it bothering you?" I asked.

"Your erection? No."

"Okay." I swallowed, trying to think of something to say that didn't involve my man parts. "You knew my name. Do you watch football?"

Another glimmer of emotion passed across her features. Her eyes lit up, but when she spoke, her voice was still monotone. "I follow a number of professional sports, but football is my favorite."

Despite her tone, I could feel something emanating from her—a spark that flared when she said *favorite*.

"Awesome. Are you a Philly fan?"

31

"I don't follow teams, I follow players."

My mouth hooked in a grin. "Do you follow me?"

"I did, prior to your injury."

"Ouch."

"Is your knee still causing you pain?"

"Sometimes, but that's not what I mean. I said *ouch* because you said you don't follow me anymore."

"That's not what I said."

I crossed my arms. "No? You said you followed me prior to my injury. Doesn't that mean you don't follow me now?"

Her eyebrows knitted together. "Since you're not playing, you're no longer generating player statistics. There's nothing for me to follow."

"Oh," I said, understanding dawning. "I feel you. You were into my stats, not so much my personality."

"Precisely. I know very little about your personality."

"But you know my numbers?"

June nodded. "More than ten thousand six hundred yards over your nine-and-a-half seasons. Eighty-two touchdowns, four two-point conversions. Seven fumbles. An additional two thousand eight hundred ninety-four yards in punt and kick-off returns."

My jaw dropped as I listened to her distill my career into a chain of numbers. "Wow. That's…impressive."

"I know."

"You just keep all that stuff up there?" I asked, tapping my own temple to indicate her head.

"Yes. I have a natural propensity for numbers."

"Huh." This girl was fascinating. "All right, June Tucker. Do you know the stats for a lot of players?"

"Yes."

"Who else do you know?"

"Would you like a list?" she asked.

There was no sarcasm in her tone. She wasn't sassing me. I had no doubt that if I said yes, she'd easily rattle off a list of players.

"No, I don't need a list. I'm just curious how that works. How do you remember so many numbers?"

She shrugged, and her tone remained nonchalant. "I have a high IQ and a nearly photographic memory when it comes to numbers."

"What about other things? Do you have a photographic memory for stuff other than math?"

"My capacity for recalling information in a variety of subjects is much higher than average," she said.

"But you're best at numbers."

"Yes."

"That's very impressive."

The corners of her mouth twitched into the closest thing I'd seen to a smile. "Thank you."

I leaned back and rested my head against my hands. I liked this girl. Hoped I'd see more of her—and in a town this size, I had a feeling that was likely.

Chapter Five

June

The ice cream counter in Moo-Shine's Ice Cream and Cheese offered twelve different flavors, but I didn't need to look at the selection. It was February, which meant rocky road. November was chocolate. Peppermint in December. January was strawberry. It was February, so I'd have rocky road.

"Hi there, June." Penny Waverly, the owner, came out of the back. She was my parents' age, and Cassidy and I had gone to school with her children. She'd opened the shop a few years after discovering she was lactose intolerant. She had declared she'd live vicariously through her customers, since she could no longer eat dairy.

"Hello, Penny."

"Hi, June. What can I get you?"

"One scoop of rocky road in a sugar cone."

She picked up the silver ice cream scoop and waved it back and forth. "Of course, of course. I should have known. You want anything else with this? Cheese fondue? It's awful cold for ice cream."

"The ice cream will be sufficient, thank you."

She smiled as she scooped out a round ball of rocky road ice cream and placed it on top of a pointed cone. "Here you go. One scoop of rocky road on a sugar cone."

I took my ice cream and paid, then chose a seat at one of the round tables near a window. No one else was in the shop. She didn't do much business in the winter. Ice cream was much more popular when the weather was hot, although her selection of cheeses did attract customers, particularly on the weekends. But weekdays in the early afternoons were typically quiet in the winter—often just me and one or two other customers—which was exactly why I came in every Tuesday for an ice cream cone when the weather was cold. I liked being where other people weren't.

The door jingled and I looked up from my cone to find George Thompson entering the shop. The former all-pro receiver—and until his injury, star of my fantasy football team—was significantly taller in person than I'd expected. It was illogical, given that I'd known his height and weight—and all his other pertinent statistics—before I'd ever seen him in person. But his size was surprisingly intimidating.

He ran a hand through his thick brown hair as he studied the selection. He hadn't seemed to notice me sitting here. He was indeed tall, and wide. Broad shoulders stretched the limits of his winter coat and his arms looked so long.

When I'd seen him at Moonshine, he'd been seated. I hadn't gotten an adequate assessment of his size. Even in the hot spring, I hadn't realized how big he was. Certain body parts had certainly appeared very large. I felt my cheeks warm as I recalled seeing his erect penis beneath the water. It wasn't the first time I'd seen a man naked, and he hadn't appeared to care that I'd seen him unclothed, so it was curious that I now felt a surge of embarrassment over the incident.

What an odd sensation. My facial capillaries were flushing with blood and no doubt turning my cheeks red. It made me unsure whether I should look away, or perhaps sneak out of the shop before he could see me. I had a strange desire to flee.

But then my eyes traveled down his long arms to his hands.

Those hands that were so adept at catching a football, protecting it from the grasps of opposing players who meant to take it from him. Those hands were so…appealing. Long, thick fingers. Wide palms. They were huge. Much bigger than they appeared on TV.

Of course, that made sense. Typically, players were surrounded by their teammates on televised games. Seeing a large man next to other large men had the effect of disguising their size difference compared to the average person.

There were no other players here. Just George Thompson, with his height, and his broad shoulders, and his huge hands.

And other huge things, currently hidden by his pants.

I tore my eyes away. My heart rate had increased and the blood rushing to my face intensified. I could feel my pulse thumping in the hollow of my throat, beating in my wrists. My stomach tingled with an unfamiliar swirl of sensation.

Was I getting sick? Perhaps I'd eaten something questionable and I was feeling the beginnings of a bout of food poisoning. I looked at my ice cream. The bottom of the scoop near the cone was beginning to soften. A drip was forming, but the odd fluttering in my stomach made me reluctant to eat any.

"You might want to lick that before it drips on you."

"What?" I heard my voice ask the question and a part of my brain scoffed at my own ridiculousness. I knew exactly what he'd said, and what he'd meant. There was no need to ask him to repeat himself. But I just had.

George pointed to the bead of melted chocolate ice cream hovering at the rim of my cone. "Your ice cream is about to drip."

"Oh."

Instead of bringing the cone to my mouth so I could lick it, I watched as the ice cream slid down the outside of the cone toward my fingers.

George's hand moved into my field of vision and one of those impossibly large fingers traced the drip's path up the cone

36

in the opposite direction. He swiped the ice cream with the pad of his finger, then brought it to his mouth and sucked it off.

I looked up at him in awe. If anyone else had touched my food, I would have been unable to continue eating. I had a very strict *no touching my food* policy. But watching George Thompson lick my ice cream drip off his finger did not have the immediate effect of making me want to dump the rest in the garbage.

In fact, I had the oddest experience of briefly imagining it had been *my* mouth sucking that drip of ice cream off George Thompson's finger.

"Sorry," he said and gave his fingertip another quick suck. "It was going to drip on your hand."

I didn't reply. I couldn't. Seeing this man's naked private parts had not rendered me speechless, but watching him lick ice cream off his finger had.

None of this interaction made sense.

"That's okay," I managed to say. I forced my gaze back to my ice cream so I'd stop staring at George Thompson's mouth. And his huge hands.

"Nice to see you again, June."

"It's nice to see you, too," I said, still not looking at him. "Dressed, this time."

"That I am," he said. "Although it's too cold not to be. Still, freezing temperatures aren't enough to keep me from enjoying some ice cream. I see we have that in common."

"Apparently we do."

I looked up again and noticed he'd also chosen rocky road on a sugar cone, although his was piled with two scoops, not one. I was about to point out our similar taste in ice cream as being another commonality we shared when the door opened, letting in a blast of cold air.

Misty Lynn Prosser waltzed in. She wore a puffy pink coat with a thick band of fake fur around the collar and a pair of skin-tight jeans. Cassidy and Scarlett hated Misty Lynn. I didn't waste energy on hating her. She was unintelligent and unnecessarily promiscuous—hardly worth anyone's notice, as far as I was concerned.

Instead of going to the counter to order something, her eyes landed on George. Her lips curled in a predatory smile and she sashayed over to my table. And suddenly I had a feeling I understood more about why Scarlett and Cassidy hated her.

"Well hi, there," she said, her greeting clearly meant for George, not me.

George's eyes darted to me once, then to Misty Lynn. "Hi."

"Aren't you a big hunk of man," she said, openly appraising him. "In town for a visit?"

His brow furrowed and he leaned slightly away from her. "Guess so."

"I'm Misty Lynn." She traced a finger down the zipper of his coat. "Welcome to Bootleg Springs."

A surge of heat poured through me and I dug my fingernails into my palm. My ice cream was still melting, but I didn't care. I did *not* want Misty Lynn to touch George Thompson.

"Are you here for ice cream, Misty Lynn?" I asked. "Or something else? I don't think Penny carries nicotine gum. You'll have to get that at the Pop In."

She finally looked at me, her expression annoyed, as if she'd been trying to pretend I wasn't here, and I'd ruined it by speaking. "No, I have plenty of gum." She patted her coat pocket and turned back to George, her smile returning in an instant. "I was in the mood for something sweet, so I figured I'd stop in."

"That's nice," George said, and I was not unaware that he still hadn't given her his name.

Good.

"What's that you're having?" she asked.

She reached out toward him again and I had the strangest desire to fly out of my seat and claw her eyes out. George deftly side-stepped and sat in the chair across from me.

"I'm just having some ice cream with my friend June," he said. "It was nice meeting you."

His dismissal was so obvious, even Misty Lynn understood

38

it. She stared at me, and her wad of chewed gum almost fell out of her open mouth.

I stared back. I didn't have anything else to say to her, so I just waited for her to leave.

She pulled the gum back into her mouth with her tongue. With a dramatic roll of her eyes, she spun on her heel and left.

"Now you're really making a mess," George said.

"Oh." My ice cream had dripped all over my hand. I hadn't even noticed the cold sticky drips. I quickly licked the excess off the cone, then switched it to my other hand.

Before I could grab a napkin, George had my messy hand in his. It looked so tiny nestled in his huge one. With slow strokes, he gently wiped the ice cream off with a napkin.

Strange things were happening to my body. The feel of my hand touching his elicited a rush of heat between my legs. How very perplexing. George wasn't doing anything overtly sexual. He was cleaning up the mess I'd made while I'd been in the throes of inexplicable jealousy. Why was this making me feel so tingly?

I pulled my hand back. "Thank you. Rocky road ice cream was invented by William Dreyer, one of the founders of Dreyer's Ice Cream. He was reportedly inspired by his business partner's candy. He cut up walnuts and marshmallows with his wife's sewing scissors and added them to chocolate ice cream."

"Really?"

"Yes. It dates to the late nineteen twenties. They named the flavor rocky road not long after the stock market crash in nineteen twenty-nine. Their intention was to give people something to smile about in the midst of the Great Depression."

George licked his ice cream, twisting it across his tongue to get all the way around. "I didn't know that."

"I don't know if it worked. I've never come across data that indicates the name *rocky road*, or the particular flavor combination, increased people's happiness during that time in American history."

"I'd be willing to bet it did, at least for some people."

"Are you making fun of me?"

He held my eyes for a few heartbeats, his brow furrowed. "No. Why would you think I was making fun of you?"

"Because we don't know each other. Usually people who don't know me find me odd."

"I don't find you odd. That was an interesting anecdote about ice cream that I didn't know. And I'd be willing to bet that rocky road ice cream made people happy. Then, and now."

He licked his cone again and I mimicked his movement, swirling the ice cream across my tongue in a slow circle. It was soft and cold in my mouth, the rich chocolate flavor pleasing.

Even more pleasing was watching George deliberately lick his ice cream.

The persistent jumpy feeling in my stomach increased. Perhaps Penny had put something in this ice cream that didn't agree with my digestion. Or it could have been something else I'd eaten in the recent past. I started cataloging everything I'd consumed in the last twenty-four hours. I'd have to throw away the leftovers I'd planned to have for dinner tonight. I couldn't take a chance on making this strange stomach problem worse.

My heart was beating too fast. I swallowed hard, wondering if I was going to be sick. A part of me wanted to stay here with George. Another part wanted to run. I was vaguely aware that I was experiencing an acute stress response. My sympathetic nervous system was activated, releasing hormones into my body that produced the fight-or-flight sensation. But the release of catecholamines, including adrenaline and noradrenaline, was inhibiting my ability to think rationally.

"Goodbye," I said, suddenly standing, and rushed out the door before George could say another word.

Chapter Six

June

George Thompson had invaded Bootleg Springs. Not literally. He hadn't staged a coup to oust control of the town from Mayor Hornsbladt. And he was only one man. He couldn't actually be in multiple places at once, as *invasion* would suggest. But it seemed as if he were. It seemed as if he were *everywhere*.

When I made my weekly trip to the library, I'd seen him walking up the sidewalk on the other side of the road. The next day, I'd come into town to pick up a few essentials at the Pop In. He had come out just as I was about to get out of my car to go in. I'd waited to exit my vehicle until he was out of sight.

I'd started keeping a mental log of George Thompson sightings. Counting the first time I saw him at Moonshine, our encounter in the hot spring, and eating ice cream with him at Moo-Shine, the tally stood at eight. Eight times I had seen or talked to George Thompson in the last week.

He was very distracting.

I drove into town and parked, then did a thorough

inspection of my surroundings. Past incidents were a good predictor of future events, which meant the probability I would see him again was high. It seemed as if every time I left my house, there was a George Thompson sighting. Bootleg Springs was a small town, but how was it possible that he was constantly crossing my path? The numbers indicated it was more than coincidence. Yet I had no reason to believe there was any intent on his part. I needed to do some deeper research into the science of probability and statistics regarding coincidences.

Hesitating another few seconds, I narrowed my eyes and took another hard look around. Gray clouds hung low in the sky, threatening a late winter snow, and the streets were empty. No sign of George. It was probably safe to exit and proceed inside.

It was Thursday, so I was meeting Cassidy at Yee Haw Yarn and Coffee. Her work schedule varied, so we didn't meet every week. But when her shifts allowed, we met here on Thursday afternoons. The fact that she still made time for me when she was busy with not only her career, but her relationship with Bowie Bodine, said a great deal about her character.

But Cassidy had always made time for me. I was the older sister, but I knew that in some ways she felt responsible for me. She and Scarlett had always included me in their social gatherings. I knew it had cost them socially to do so—during our teen years in particular. If people had tried to exclude me, Cassidy and Scarlett had been quick to declare they wouldn't participate. Parties, bonfires, nights out—if I wasn't invited, they didn't go.

As much as I'd always appreciated their loyalty, I'd never wanted to be a burden. I didn't get along with people with the ease of Cassidy and Scarlett. But our peers had come to accept me—for the most part—or at least had grown accustomed to my presence. It was another reason I had stayed in Bootleg Springs. I fit here, as much as I'd ever fit anywhere. Mostly because of my sister.

I went inside, casting a glance over my shoulder on the way

in. No George. I felt a strange mix of things at not seeing him, and I couldn't understand why I was so confused. Shouldn't I have been relieved? I'd been anxious at the thought of running into him when I came into town. Now that I knew an encounter wasn't imminent, why was I experiencing what felt suspiciously like disappointment?

Cassidy was already inside, still dressed in her deputy uniform. I felt a surge of pride for her. She'd worked hard to become a deputy, something she'd wanted her whole life. Upholding the law in a town like Bootleg Springs wasn't always easy, but she was exceedingly proficient at her job.

"Hey Juney," she said when I approached her table. She pushed a mug of steaming hot water toward me. "I got you water for your tea."

"Thank you." I ripped open an Earl Gray tea bag and dunked it in the mug. In my head, I started counting down the seconds from two hundred forty. Letting tea steep too long would result in an unpleasant bitter flavor.

"How's your week going so far?" she asked.

I paused for a moment, considering whether I should tell her about George. What was there to tell? That a football player I'd followed for his impressive statistics had come to Bootleg and now I couldn't stop thinking about his hands? Wait, what did his hands have to do with anything? Surely the important information would be the facts. The George sightings I'd experienced over the past week. Why were his enormous hands relevant?

And yet here I was, imagining those strong hands. And the way he'd licked my rocky road ice cream off his finger.

"Juney? You okay?"

"What?" I blinked, my eyes coming back into focus. "Yes, I'm fine. I was...thinking about something else."

"Yeah? Something good or something bad?"

"Just work," I lied. Why was I lying to my sister? "It's not good or bad. It's essentially neutral."

"All right. You just seem a bit distracted, is all. You sure you're okay?"

"I believe so, yes."

Except I wasn't. I'd lost count of the seconds my tea needed to steep. I looked down at the swirl of tea-brown emanating from the bag, mixing with the clear water. How long had it been? Why had I stopped counting? I could count and think at the same time. What was wrong with me?

I dunked my tea bag a few times and tried to judge by the color whether it was ready. I decided it needed an additional sixty seconds and began the countdown again.

"I heard there's a famous football player in town," she said. "Did you hear about that? Do you know who it is?"

"George Thompson, known as GT Thompson professionally," I said before I could stop myself. "Two Superbowl wins with Philadelphia. Over ten thousand six hundred career yards. Eighty-two touchdowns."

"Wow, I guess you do know." Cassidy's eyes lit up and her mouth turned in a smile. "I thought he was one of your favorites. Have you seen him? You should get his autograph."

"Why would I want his autograph?"

"Oh, you know. Sometimes fans like to get an autograph as a keepsake."

I nodded. Of course I knew that. I had a small sports memorabilia collection at home—mostly things Dad had given me for birthday and Christmas gifts. In fact, one of my favorite items happened to be my Thompson jersey.

But the thought of seeking him out—on purpose—sent a flurry of nerves fluttering through my belly. So far, I hadn't been sick, as one would expect after ingesting a harmful strain of bacteria. Perhaps it wasn't food poisoning after all. But if it wasn't an ailment caused by microorganisms, what was the cause of my intermittent stomach upset?

Instead of addressing the suggestion that I get an autograph from George—or admitting that I'd already met him several times—I decided to change the subject.

"How are things at work?" I asked.

"Mostly great. It's so much better now that Connelly is

gone. I don't feel like I have to defend my ability to do my job every day. But the Callie Kendall investigation is…tricky."

"How so?" I asked. The Callie Kendall disappearance had always been a source of mild interest for me, although I didn't share the town's obsession with the mystery. Statistically speaking, it was unlikely we'd ever find out the truth. Not after nearly thirteen years.

She took a deep breath. "The forensics report on Connie Bodine's car came back. I thought it might shed some light on how she died—whether her accident was really an accident. But Juney, they found fingerprints in her car and I'm terrified of what's going to happen when word gets out."

"They found Callie Kendall's fingerprints, I presume."

Her eyes darted around and she nodded.

I blinked, letting this new piece of information sink in. "That means Callie was in her car."

She nodded. "Most of the prints match the Bodines, obviously—the parents and the kids. But there were some that didn't match the Bodines and on a whim, I asked them to run them against Callie's. There were at least two that were a match."

No wonder Cassidy looked stressed. Her job and her relationship with Bowie Bodine had intersected on the uncomfortable topic of whether Bowie's father—and perhaps, his mother—was involved in Callie's disappearance.

"Where were they found?" I asked.

"Passenger seat."

"Could there be an alternative explanation that doesn't implicate the Bodines in her disappearance?"

"It's possible Connie gave her a ride somewhere. You know how Bootleg parents are—parenting everyone's kids, not just their own, when they need to. But Scarlett doesn't remember her mom driving Callie anywhere. Neither do the others. It's still possible it's a coincidence, but…"

"Unlikely."

"Right," she said. "I talked to Bowie and the rest of the

family. They're concerned, of course. I'm trying to keep this quiet so we don't get a media circus every time there's a bit of evidence that pops up."

"That's a prudent choice."

I took a sip of my tea and nearly spit it out when the door opened and in walked Bowie. But seeing my sister's boyfriend was not the cause of my sudden inability to swallow. Right behind him was George.

My eyes widened and I choked down the hot liquid, trying to suppress a cough. Bowie came straight for our table, his sights naturally set on Cassidy. George wandered up to the counter and appeared to be looking at the menu.

He was so tall. I didn't know why his taller-than-average height kept making such a strong impression on me. But it did. And there were those hands. My eyes lingered on them—on his wide palms and thick fingers. He brought one hand up to his chin and slid his thumb along his jaw. I watched, fascinated, as he rubbed his chin, his attention on the menu above the counter.

With a start, my breath caught in my throat, and I tore my gaze away. He hadn't seen me. I needed to get out of here.

I scooted my chair back and stood, quickly shouldering my handbag. "I have to go."

"Don't leave on my account," Bowie said. He'd pulled up a chair next to Cassidy and had his hand on her thigh. "I just stopped in for a second. I'm meeting the guys to go fishing."

"No apologies necessary," I said, trying to keep my voice low. It took a great deal of willpower not to look at George, but I didn't want Cassidy or Bowie to notice him. "I have a work commitment and need to leave."

"Do you want to take your tea to go?" Cassidy asked.

"No." My heart raced and my palms felt clammy. "I'll see you both later."

Apparently I was doing an adequate job of hiding my distress. Cassidy didn't seem to notice. "All right. We'll see you tomorrow night?"

"Yes."

Bowie leaned in and whispered something that made Cassidy giggle. I was exceedingly grateful for his distraction. I risked a glance at George. He was ordering. He'd turn any second and…

And what? See me? Say hello? He had always behaved in a normal fashion. He would probably be friendly. What was wrong with that?

Something. Something was wrong with it, and I didn't know what, and that made me desperate to leave. I didn't understand why I was so shaky. My hands trembled, my heart beat too fast, and my belly felt like it was doing somersaults.

Moving quickly, and hugging the far side of the shop, I kept my eyes on the floor and made my way to the door. I didn't look back to see if George had noticed me. I wasn't sure what I'd do if our eyes met.

I'd never been so flustered in my entire life. The cold air hit me as I walked outside, soothing my warm cheeks. I took slow, deep breaths as I walked to my car, trying to regain control of myself. What was wrong with me? Was something about George Thompson enough to elicit this dramatic physical response? Was it his fame? His status as one of my preferred athletes that had me so agitated? Or was it something else?

I had no idea.

Chapter Seven
George

The cup of coffee I'd picked up at Yee Haw Yarn and Coffee—this town had the best business names—warmed my hands as I walked up the street. The temperature was up a bit today, as if spring might be finding its way to the mountains out here in West Virginia. Even in town, I could hear birds chirping.

I checked the time. Five oh seven. I had some time to kill before I met Shelby for dinner. Wondered what kind of trouble I could get up to on a Thursday afternoon.

Although, what I really wondered was what June Tucker was doing.

I'd only caught glimpses of her since the rocky road encounter. That was by far my new favorite ice cream flavor. Watching June lick ice cream off a cone? I'd take that any day of the week, thank you very much.

It was fascinating how that brain of hers could hold onto so much information. Who just walked around, living life, storing the origins of rocky road ice cream in her head? She knew my entire career forward and backward, and clearly sports weren't the only thing she could talk about with a tremendous amount of knowledge.

Sexy as hell, that's what it was. I'd dated women I'd considered intelligent. But they didn't hold a candle to June Tucker. She was on another level.

My phone rang, so I pulled it out to answer. It was my assistant, Andrea Wilson.

"Hey, Andrea. What's up?"

"Hi, GT. Sorry to bug you, but I just have a few things."

"No problem. How's Mellow?"

"Mellow? Oh, the rabbit. She's fine."

"You're making sure she has playtime, right? She needs attention."

"Yeah, of course. I check on her once a day."

"Is she warming up to you?"

"Um, I guess so," she said. "You know I'm not really an animal person. But the rabbit's fine."

Talking about my little fluffball made me miss her. "Send me a picture when you go over there tomorrow, okay?"

I decided to ignore the frustrated breath Andrea let out. She could be prickly, but she was good at her job, and she'd worked for me for years. She handled everything from my schedule and travel arrangements to dinner reservations to my finances. A lot of players did without an assistant after they hung up their jersey, but it was hard to imagine life without Andrea making sure my shit was together.

"Whatcha got for me, Andrea?"

"I've worked out a revised budget and financial analysis for you. Yearly projections and so forth. I'll email it to you."

"Can you just bottom line it for me?"

"Sure. Between investments and your pension, you should be fine financially. Just don't go out and buy a Lambo or something."

"Not much chance of that. What else?"

"Your physical therapist wants to schedule a follow-up.

49

When do you think you'll be back in town? I'll get that set up for you."

I scratched my chin. "I'm not sure, to be honest. I kinda like it here. And the hot springs are no joke. My knee feels better already."

"Hmm." The sound of her fingers clicking against a keyboard came through the phone. "Let me know when you have a return date and I'll get an appointment scheduled."

I hesitated, momentarily distracted by a large green tractor lumbering up the road. The driver parked it in front of a store that said Build-A-Shine and jumped down.

"Sounds good."

"Last thing and then I'll be out of your hair."

I paused and leaned against a building. A car drove by, its engine considerably quieter than the tractor had been. "Sure."

"You have a few invites to charity events. One is this week, so I already declined. What about the others? Do you want me to forward them to you and you can decide?"

A loud *clop, clop, clop* caught my attention. A woman on horseback came around a corner. She wore a baseball cap with a big rooster on the front and she rode that horse up the street like it was totally normal.

Then again, I supposed it *was* normal here.

"Um… Sorry, Andrea, I was distracted for a second. Just sit on those for now. I don't want to have to rush home for anything. I need some downtime. And I'd like to keep my options open as far as how long I stay here."

"Okay."

A chicken strutted up the sidewalk, pecking at the ground, like she was looking for a tasty morsel. I laughed.

"Sorry," I said. "There's a chicken walking up the sidewalk."

"Did you say a chicken?" she asked. "Where *are* you?"

I chuckled again. "Bootleg Springs. And yes, a chicken. She seems friendly. Anyway, I'll talk with you later, Andrea. Thanks for checking in."

"You're welcome. I'll email if I have more questions."

"Sounds good."

I pocketed my phone and watched the chicken as she pecked at the ground a few more times, then scratched.

"You finding what you need, there, sweetheart?" I asked. "Are you supposed to be on the street, or did you get out of your coop?"

"She's free range."

A man with a bushy white mustache stood nearby. He wore a sheriff's uniform, complete with a star-shaped badge. His name tag said Sheriff Tucker. I wondered if he was related to June. Looked a bit like her, and in a small town, it seemed likely.

"I guess I won't worry about finding her owner, then."

Sheriff Tucker shook his head. "Nah, no need. This here is Mona Lisa McNugget. She's our town chicken. Doesn't really belong to anyone."

Of course her name was Mona Lisa McNugget. "She's a fine-looking hen, Sheriff."

"That she is. I hope you don't mind me introducing myself." He held out a hand. "Harlan Tucker."

I took his hand and gave it a solid shake. "Pleasure to meet you. GT Thompson."

He cracked a smile as he let my hand drop. "Yeah, I have to admit, I know who you are. There's been a bit of buzz in town about you."

I shrugged. "That can happen."

"Shame about your knee," he said, gesturing to my leg. "You had a good two more seasons in you."

"I'm not so sure about that. One, more likely. But thanks."

"I tell you, that touchdown reception you had against Texas last season was amazing. I think we watched that catch a hundred times."

"Thanks. You follow football?"

"Sure do. I'm a sports fan in general, but there's nothing like some good old-fashioned football."

A man on the street caught my attention, and I watched

him, my mouth partially open. Long white hair spilled out from beneath a black top hat and a white beard hung to his belly. He rode down the street on a skateboard, holding a drink of some kind in a mason jar.

"Sheriff," he said, tipping his hat as he passed.

"Morris," Sheriff Tucker said.

This town was something else.

"I won't keep you." Sheriff Tucker patted his pockets, like he was looking for something. "But if it wouldn't be too much to ask, I was wondering if I might get your autograph. My daughter is a big fan. I'd love to surprise her."

His daughter? Was she June?

"Of course, I'd be happy to."

A pickup truck drove up the street, slowing when it came near. Sheriff Tucker put his hands on his hips, watching as the truck came to a stop. Two men sat in the cab, and three were in the bed. I recognized one of the men in back as Gibson Bodine. The others had to be his brothers, or related somehow. The resemblance was clear.

Gibson tipped his chin to me and I nodded back.

I blinked a few times, wondering if I was seeing things. Did they have a barbecue in the back of the truck? They certainly appeared to. The black contraption stood in the center of the bed, and Gibson held a long metal spatula. They couldn't be grilling while they were driving…could they?

"Afternoon, Sheriff." One of the men in the back nodded to him, looking a little sheepish. I was fairly sure he was the same guy who'd picked up Gibson after he'd almost hit that deer.

"Bowie," Sheriff Tucker said. He nodded to the others. "Boys. What are y'all up to?"

"Going fishing," Bowie said.

"Are you now?" Sheriff Tucker asked. "That grill isn't on, is it?"

The mouth-watering aroma of cooking meat wafted toward us. My stomach rumbled.

"Yeah, it's hot," Gibson said, opening the lid. The meat popped and sizzled.

"Boys, you can't be driving around while grilling," Sheriff Tucker said. "We've been over this."

"It's okay, Sheriff," Bowie said. "Jameson welded the grill to the bed for us, so it won't go anywhere."

The man driving leaned over and tipped his cap. "Hey, Sheriff. Don't worry. It's secure. We learned our lesson last time."

"And here I thought if a few of them had women in their lives, it might settle them down a bit," Sheriff Tucker muttered under his breath.

"Care for one?" Bowie asked, pointing to the meat sizzling on the grill.

Sheriff Tucker's expression softened and his nostrils flared, like he was taking a good, long sniff. "Well, I suppose I might as well."

The third guy produced a paper plate while Bowie got out a bun. Gibson took a patty off the grill and slid it onto the bun.

"Thanks." Sheriff Tucker took the plate. "Horse puckey, where are my manners? Boys, this is GT Thompson. Mr. Thompson, these are…well, the Bodines. Most of 'em are, at least." He pointed to each of the men in turn. "Gibson, Bowie, and Jonah in the back. In the driver's seat there is Jameson." He pointed to the man in the passenger seat—the only one who didn't look like he must be related. "And Devlin McAllister. He's their sister Scarlett's beau."

I held up a hand. "Nice to meet you."

"I thought you looked familiar," Bowie said. "Sorry to hear about your knee. What brings you to Bootleg Springs?"

"The knee, actually. I heard about the hot springs and decided to give it a go. So far, I'm a believer."

"Damn right," Gibson said.

"Burger?" Bowie asked.

I was meeting Shelby soon for dinner, but why the hell not? The food smelled fantastic. And I was a big guy. I could pack away a lot of calories.

"Absolutely."

They got my burger on a plate and handed it over.

"Thanks."

"We best be moving on," Bowie said. "Those fish won't catch themselves."

"Don't be spilling charcoal out the back again," Sheriff Tucker said.

"We're way ahead of you, Sheriff," Gibson said. "We rigged up a propane tank back here."

"Well, in that case…"

I raised my eyebrows. Somehow driving around with a propane tank didn't seem any safer. But I had to admit, a bunch of guys driving around in a pickup truck, grilling hamburgers on their way to go fishing? It was awesome.

I liked this town.

"Nice to meet you," I said. "And thanks for the grub."

"Anytime," Bowie said. "Night, Sheriff."

"You check in with Cassidy?" Sheriff Tucker asked.

"Of course I have," Bowie said, putting a hand to his chest, like he was insulted the sheriff had to ask. "She's with Scarlett tonight."

"Fair enough. Careful with that grill."

The truck pulled out on to the street and drove away.

Sheriff Tucker shook his head. "My future son-in-law. But Bowie's a good kid. Glad he and my daughter finally got their heads on straight."

"Your daughter the football fan?"

"No, Bowie's with Cassidy, my youngest. The football fan is June."

So he *was* June's father. I suddenly wanted very much to be in this man's good graces.

"Well, like I said, I'd be happy to sign something for her."

He pulled a scrap of paper and a pen out of his pocket. "Wish I had something better, but this'll do."

I signed the piece of paper, taking care to make my signature legible for once, and handed it back.

"Thank you, Mr. Thompson," he said.

"GT," I said. "And no problem. Tell your daughter I said hello."

"I'll do that," he said, smiling so his mustache twitched.

I hoped he would. And maybe soon I'd have a chance to see June Tucker again.

Chapter Eight
June

An evening at the Lookout wasn't typically a cause for anxiety. I didn't mind being here. I could always read or browse ESPN.com on my phone if I was bored.

But tonight, I was completely out of sorts. George Thompson was here.

His presence in the bar was palpable. It was as if he displaced the air, leaving what was left to press against me, the molecules all fighting for space.

Grateful I'd chosen to dress in layers tonight, I took off my cardigan. I couldn't decide if the temperature in the Lookout was warmer than usual, or if it was me.

Or George.

Briefly, I contemplated leaving. I'd run out of Yee Haw Yarn and Coffee yesterday to avoid him. But I'd spent the rest of my day in a haze of distraction, trying to unravel the knots in my belly. Confused as to why I'd chosen to flee. Although I was feeling a now-familiar swirl of nerves, I didn't want to leave.

But I wasn't going to go so far as to talk to him, either.

"Is that him?" Cassidy asked as she sidled up next to me. She gestured with her beer toward George. "The football player?"

I was about to answer in the affirmative but he chose that moment—that precise second—to meet my eyes and smile.

It wasn't just a smile. Oh, no. It was a slow spread of his lips, parting across perfect teeth. Dimples puckering his cheeks. It was crooked and sexy and utterly disarming.

I almost fanned myself. *Fanned myself*, which was so ridiculous I couldn't believe the urge had been mine.

"Whoa," Cassidy said.

"Yeah." Was that my voice? So breathy and mesmerized?

"I take it the answer is yes," Cassidy said. "You look a little starstruck. And…oh my god, he's coming over here."

He was, indeed. His eyes were locked with mine, that grin still on his face. George Thompson was walking toward me, his six-foot-five frame all confidence and grace.

I swallowed hard but managed to keep from jumping off my stool and running out the door.

"Hey June," he said. "You look very pretty tonight."

Cassidy's eyes were huge, her mouth open.

I needed to say something. "Hi." That wasn't very good. He'd complimented me—had he called me *pretty*?—so the appropriate response was… "Thank you."

He kept smiling at me, as if he didn't even notice Cassidy. Which was exceedingly odd. Men always noticed Cassidy. She was beautiful and friendly. George didn't know she was in a committed relationship with another man. Why wasn't he turning to her to engage in a stimulating and perhaps flirtatious conversation?

Why was he still looking at *me*?

"Would you like to dance?" he asked.

My lips parted, but I had no idea what to say. No one ever asked me to dance in the Lookout.

"Why yes, she would," Cassidy said.

Before I knew what was happening, Cassidy pulled me off the stool and shoved me at George. I squeaked, my feet getting tangled, and stumbled into him.

And then his hands—those gloriously large hands—were on me, keeping me steady. Holding me by the waist so I wouldn't fall.

I was utterly breathless. Unable to speak. I tilted my head back so I could look up at his face. Instead of stepping away and putting a reasonable amount of distance between us, he moved closer, so our bodies almost touched.

"You all right?" he asked.

I nodded.

"Shall we?"

He led me out onto the dance floor as a new song began. *Tennessee Whiskey.* It was a slow song, and people paired off around us, wrapping their arms around each other to slow dance.

"I don't understand dancing," I said.

"You mean you don't know how?"

"No, this style of dancing doesn't appear to require any particular skill. It's just two people swaying to music. They're barely moving their feet. Other styles of dancing require a great deal of skill and practice. I can see the merit in that. I don't understand the purpose of this."

One corner of his mouth hooked upward. "Are you always so logical?"

"Yes."

"Good to know. Well, I can't speak for everybody, but I can tell you why I like dancing."

I kept my eyes on his face, awaiting his explanation.

"You know what? It'll be easier if I just show you. Come here."

He slid a hand around my waist and pulled me against him. I sucked in a breath. One hand rested on the small of my back. With his other hand, he took mine, and nestled it between us. He started to move, shifting his feet with the slow beat of the music.

Leaning down, he rested his stubbly jaw against my temple and spoke softly near my ear. "Now close your eyes."

"Why?"

"Because I'm going to explain dancing. Trust me."

I let my eyes drift closed. "Okay."

"For starters, the music."

"Chris Stapleton got his start—"

"Hold up there, June," he said. "You're thinking too much. Don't think about the artist or the origin of the song. Just feel it. The beat. The way we're moving to it. Don't think. Just feel."

We were moving in time with the slow but steady rhythm. "I can feel the music."

"Good. Now tell me what else you feel."

Keeping my eyes closed, I focused on the physical sensations I was experiencing. "I feel your hand on my back."

He caressed my back in a slow circle. "What else?"

"You're holding my hand and it's warm."

"Mm-hmm."

Tension melted from my shoulders and I nuzzled my forehead against his scratchy jaw. It was pleasantly rough. "I feel your cheek touching my skin."

He slid his jaw against my temple, down my cheek to my ear. "You like that?"

"It is very nice."

"You seem surprised."

"A little."

I felt him smile. It brought to mind the way his cheeks puckered with those dimples.

"Do you want to know what I feel?"

"Yes."

His grip on me tightened slightly, his strong arm holding me against him. His thumb traced a little line over the back of the hand he held, and he kept his cheek against my temple.

"I feel your body against mine. It's warm and soft in all the right places. I feel the curve of your lower back and the promise of your hips beneath my hand."

I took in a quick breath, my heart beating fast, as he moved his hand down my backside. His palm slid up my hip and returned to its place on the small of my back.

"Do you want to know what else?"

I nodded. I really wanted to know.

He turned his face into my hair and took a deep breath. "You smell fresh and clean, like a meadow on a spring day. I feel your soft skin against my face. Holding you like this makes me wonder what it would feel like if more of our skin was touching."

My breath was shallow and heat pooled between my legs. I didn't dare open my eyes. It was as if he had me under a spell. A spell I didn't want to break.

"Should I keep going?"

"Yes."

His voice was gravelly and low, deep and full of suggestion. His warm breath made my skin prickle with goosebumps.

"I feel your chest pressing against me and I wonder if your nipples are hard. What they'd feel like against my tongue. Should I tell you more?"

I nodded. I didn't want him to stop.

He held me tighter and there was something there. Something hard, and thick, and very, very noticeable. Had I been in my right state of mind, I might have commented on the fact that his erection was pressing against me. But I was not in my right state of mind. I was floating on a pillowy cloud of arousal, mesmerized by his hands on me and his deep voice in my ear. Heedless of our surroundings.

"You smell so good, it makes me think about what you taste like. Your lips and your skin. I feel your body relaxing against mine. This is why I like dancing, June. Because I can hold you like this. I can think about how good you feel and all the dirty things I'd do to you if I had the chance. I can touch you and smell you and if I'm lucky, someday maybe kiss you. Taste you. But to everyone watching, we're just dancing."

"I think I understand dancing," I said, practically breathless.

He smiled against me again. I still hadn't opened my eyes. There was too much to feel. I didn't want the distraction of visual stimulation to get in the way of all this tactile sensation.

His body was hard—masculine and well-muscled. I hadn't even thought about the way he smelled until he'd mentioned scent. Smell had a powerful effect on the brain, and his was lighting up places I hadn't realized were there. I was filled with his woodsy, clean scent. Neurons fired like fireworks over the lake, producing explosions of sensation.

My spine tingled and my heart pounded. We swayed in silence as the song came to an end. His cheek still rested against my head and he held my hand tucked against his chest.

Reluctantly, I opened my eyes. It was like coming awake after a vivid dream. The world seemed hazy and indistinct. Another song began—a song with a faster beat—and George led me to the side of the dance floor.

"Thank you for the dance." He still had my hand in his and he brought it up to his lips. Kissed the backs of my fingers.

"Thank you. That was…"

He raised his eyebrows, waiting for me to finish.

"It was very stimulating."

That grin was back, slow and sexy and distracting. "Good. I thought so too. Can I buy you a drink?"

I blinked at him in surprise.

"Is that a yes, or a no?" he asked.

"Why?"

"Why do I want to buy you a drink?"

"Buying a woman a drink is a customary action in human mating rituals."

"Hmm," he said, tilting his head. He actually looked *interested*. Most people listened to me, then moved on with the conversation when I was finished speaking. "I suppose you're right. Is that a problem?"

"Well…no."

"Don't worry, June. I'm not the kind of man who'll push his human mating rituals too far. I like to feel things out first. I enjoyed dancing with you, and I like talking to you. We're in a bar, so my next logical move is to buy you a drink so we can sit and talk more. That sounds nice to me. If it sounds nice to you, say yes."

"Yes."

He smiled again and it made my legs feel shaky and unstable. "Good. What can I get you?"

"A bourbon bliss."

"I would not have pegged you as a bourbon drinker, but I like it. One bourbon bliss, coming up."

There was a small table with two stools a few steps from where I stood. I sat and waited for George to come back with my drink. Cassidy and Scarlett were across the bar, watching me. They leaned their heads together and spoke, their faces animated. Scarlett pointed at me and Cassidy batted her arm down.

I turned my gaze away from them. I didn't like being the object of their scrutiny, but I didn't blame them. I never danced, and men never bought me drinks at the Lookout. This was wholly uncharted territory for all of us.

A few moments later, George returned with my drink. I noticed Nicolette behind the bar, watching me too. She winked and I looked away, tucking my hair behind my ear.

George slid my drink across the table and sat on the other stool. His drink appeared identical to mine and he brought it to his mouth to sip.

I couldn't stop staring at him. At his mouth, and his dimples. At his broad shoulders and thick chest. His long arms and strong hands.

He set his glass down. "This is good."

I took a drink, needing a second to collect myself. I never drank to excess, but you didn't grow up in a town like Bootleg Springs and not develop an appreciation for alcoholic beverages.

"This is generally my drink of choice. I also appreciate good moonshine, particularly of the apple pie variety."

"I don't think I've ever had the pleasure of apple pie moonshine."

"It's quite remarkable when crafted properly."

"It sounds like it. Does it really taste like apple pie?"

"It does. Moonshine is generally a harsh-tasting beverage. Early on, distillers started adding things to make it more palatable. Apple pie moonshine is generally regarded as the oldest moonshine recipe in this region."

He took another sip. "Interesting."

"Bootleg Springs is something of an anomaly. The majority of West Virginia was in favor of prohibition. In fact, some communities had prohibition laws that predate the Eighteenth Amendment to the United States Constitution."

"Sounds like you Bootleggers prefer to live by your own rules."

"In many ways, that is accurate, yes."

"I like it here. It's a nice town." He reached across the table and traced his finger across the back of my hand. "But tell me more about you."

It was hard to think when he was touching me, even with just the pad of his finger. "Um, what do you want to know?"

"How about, what do you do for a living?"

"I'm an actuary. I work as a consultant for a number of large companies."

"You must work from home, then?"

I nodded, and he didn't stop caressing my hand. "Yes. It's an arrangement that suits all parties."

"And what do you like to do for fun?"

"Watch sports."

That made him smile again. "Like football."

"Yes, although I'm happy to watch a variety of sporting events."

"Because you like to follow the statistics."

"Precisely."

"I gotta tell you, June Tucker, you are simply fascinating."

I wasn't sure how to respond to that. This was a brand of male attention I so rarely received. The last man I'd dated had been much like me. Logical, with an affinity for numbers.

We'd met at work when I'd been in Baltimore for a conference. Although I'd thought we had enough in common to sustain a relationship, things had fallen flat. That was two years ago, and I hadn't bothered with an intimate relationship since.

"Am I being too aggressive for you?" George asked.

"You are touching me a lot."

He kept caressing the back of my hand. "Would you like me to stop?"

"No."

"I told you, June, I like to feel things out. But I figure I can get away with some touching on our second date."

"Second date? We haven't had a first date."

"Sure we did. We had ice cream together."

"I would disagree with your label of *date*."

"On what grounds?" he asked. "We sat together and enjoyed conversation over dessert. That sounds like a date to me."

"A date requires both parties to be in agreement as to the intent of the encounter."

"In other words, I didn't ask you first, so it couldn't be a date?"

I nodded. "Yes."

"All right, so tell me this. Can an encounter that was not agreed upon ahead of time as being a date *become* a date?"

I had to ponder that for a moment. His hand was still on mine—more or less holding it now—and the tactile sensations were vying for attention with the thoughts in my brain. And winning.

"Yes, I suppose that's possible, depending upon the circumstances."

"So one could make the argument that this is now a date."

"This?"

"Yes, this. You and me, here tonight. I didn't ask you ahead of time, but I did buy you a drink."

I had to concede, this was very date-like. "Yes, it could be considered a date. But why the preoccupation with labeling?"

"No reason, really. I'm hoping you'll say yes to another one, though."

"Another date?"

He grinned. "Yes, another date. With me. Are you free tomorrow?"

Was this really happening? Was George Thompson asking me out on an actual date? Tomorrow was Saturday, and under usual circumstances, I'd be—

"I'm free."

"So that's a yes?"

"You really want to go out on a date with me?"

He picked up my hand and brought it to his lips again, kissing the backs of my fingers. "I absolutely want to take you out on a date. I wouldn't have asked if I didn't."

"Then, yes."

I gazed into his brown eyes, feeling a little dazed and dumbstruck. We'd met on several occasions now, and had multiple chances for conversation. And he still wanted to take me out on a date.

Why? I really didn't know. But maybe—just maybe—George Thompson liked me for me.

Chapter Nine

June

My dad was prompt, as usual. He'd texted earlier to ask if he could stop by at six-thirty, and at precisely six twenty-nine, he knocked.

"Hi, June Bug," he said when I opened the door.

He came in and gave me a hug.

"Hi, Dad."

I had thirty minutes before George would be here to pick me up. I felt a little nauseated and wondered if I should cancel. Putting a hand to my forehead, I estimated my temperature. It felt normal.

"You all right?" Dad asked.

"Yes, I'm fine." I led Dad into the living room and we both sat on the couch. "You said you had something for me?"

He smiled and handed me an envelope. "Go ahead."

I opened it and pulled out a piece of paper. Turning it over, I found a familiar signature. GT Thompson. But he'd signed it *George Thompson*.

Dad's grin widened. "I ran into GT Thompson in town.

Did you know he's here in Bootleg? I admit, I might have looked for a chance to approach him. I asked if he'd sign something. Told him my daughter was a fan."

I was touched. Dad had given me autographed memorabilia before, but those were things he'd ordered for me. This was different. Although I'd already met George, Dad didn't know that. And he'd gone out of his way to do this for me. It was very thoughtful. But expressing my emotions was not one of my better skills. I wasn't sure what to say.

"Thank you, Dad."

"I wish I'd had something better, like a football or one of his jerseys. But I figured I ought to get his autograph while I had the chance. I don't know how long he's in town for, or whether I'll run into him again."

"If you stay long enough, you'll meet him again tonight," I said. "He's taking me out on a date."

I didn't think I'd ever seen my dad look so utterly shocked. His eyes widened, his pupils dilating, and his mouth opened. I hesitated for a second, but he didn't speak.

There was another knock on the door. Cassidy came in without waiting for me to answer. Her arms were loaded down with bags and she had clothing slung over one arm.

"Hey, Juney," she said with a bright smile. "Oh hi, Dad. June, what are you doing? You should be getting ready. I meant to be here half an hour ago but…well, let's just say I got held up."

Dad groaned. "Oh, lordy."

"Meant to be here for what?" I asked.

"To help you get ready, of course." She glanced at Dad. "Is he okay? He looks like he swallowed a bug."

"Did she say date?" Dad asked. "You have a date with GT Thompson?"

"She sure does." Cassidy put her load down on an armchair. "Now Daddy, you know I love you, but there's some serious girl stuff that's about to happen here."

"Since when do you know GT Thompson?" he asked, apparently ignoring Cassidy's girl-stuff warning.

"I've met George several times," I said. "Culminating in an encounter at the Lookout last night."

"By encounter, she means he flirted with her like crazy, danced with her, bought her a drink, and then asked her on a date tonight," Cassidy said. "And he'll be here in less than half an hour. That's not much time to get you ready."

"I'll be," Dad said, shaking his head. "All right, girls, I think I'll get out of your way." He muttered something else, but I was starting to feel a little dizzy. All this talk of George and dates and girl stuff was making my heart race.

"Thanks, Dad."

He gave me a quick peck on the cheek, then hugged Cassidy. "Have a nice time tonight, June Bug. Goodnight, girls."

I watched him go, feeling shaky.

"Okay, first, outfit," Cassidy said, apparently unaware of my current state of distress. "Where's he taking you?"

"I actually don't know."

"That's okay. He's picking you up at seven, so that must mean dinner. It's chilly out tonight, but it might be warm wherever you go to eat. We'll do layers." She dug through the clothes she'd brought. "I have this adorable sweater I got from Leah Mae. If you wear a shirt underneath, you could take it off if you get too warm. Or if, you know, you want to get frisky."

"Why do I need to change?" I asked, looking down at my current attire. I was wearing a white blouse and dark gray cardigan with a pair of black pants. It seemed suitable for a date.

Cassidy looked me up and down. "You look fine, but I think we can do better than that."

"Why?"

"Come on, Juney, this is a big deal. When was the last time you had a date?"

It only took me a second to do the math. "It's been seven hundred forty-two days."

Her eyes flicked up to the ceiling, like she was thinking. "So just over two years? Who were you dating two years ago?"

"Michael Morgan," I said.

She groaned. "Oh, I remember him. Although I don't think we ever met him, did we?"

"No. He lived in Baltimore and our relationship never progressed to the point of introducing him to family."

"He was a jackass anyway."

"What leads you to the conclusion that he was a jackass?"

"He broke up with you, didn't he?"

"Yes, the choice to end our relationship was his."

She nodded once. "Then he's a jackass. Most of 'em are. But I don't know, June Bug, I think you might have found one of the good ones."

That made me smile a little, although the pleasant feeling was tempered by the persistent roiling in my stomach.

"I might have to cancel," I said.

"Why?" Cassidy asked. "What's wrong?"

"I think I contracted a viral infection. Or perhaps ingested something that was contaminated with harmful bacteria."

"What makes you think that?"

I pressed my hand to my belly. "I keep experiencing intermittent bouts of stomach upset."

Cassidy grinned. Why was she smiling? Illness wasn't an amusing matter.

"Tell me something. When did you first start getting an upset tummy?"

"Eight days ago."

"Uh huh. And what else happened eight days ago?"

"I'm not sure what you're referring to."

"Is it possible that it has something to do with seeing or thinking about a certain tall, attractive football player?"

I was about to refute her claim, but I found that I couldn't. Every incident of feeling sick coincided with seeing or thinking about George. That was peculiar.

"I'm guessing the look on your face means I'm right," she said. "I think you have a crush."

"A crush? I've never had a crush before."

"No?" Cassidy asked. "No one ever made your knees a little weak and butterflies flap their wings all through your tummy?"

"Butterflies couldn't survive in the acidic environment of the human gut."

She laughed. "I know, silly. It's an expression."

"I realize it's not literal. I'm just pointing out that—"

"Juney. Stop trying to change the subject."

I took a deep breath. "Does having a crush mean your stomach feels like it's turning upside down and your heart beats faster than your level of physical exertion could account for?"

"Yes."

"And your facial capillaries fill with blood, resulting in warmth and redness?"

"You blush, yeah. Have you been experiencing those things?"

I nodded, almost afraid to admit it.

"Then June Bug, you have a good old-fashioned crush on GT Thompson."

Was she right? Was that what was wrong with me? I had a crush on George?

The intense whirl of emotions was too overwhelming for me to process. I pulled away from it, mentally distancing myself from the feelings I was experiencing. It was almost as if I could see them, a jumbled mass of colors, like a thick ball of multicolored yarn.

Part of me couldn't understand why people put themselves through this on purpose. The anxiety and fear involved in the human pairing process was unpleasant.

But it was also exhilarating. Alongside my nervousness for the evening was a sense of anticipation. A tingle of excitement at the thought of seeing George again soon. The memory of his lips brushing the backs of my fingers was still fresh, and I found myself gazing down at my hand.

He'd touched this hand. Held it. Kissed it lightly. And I'd enjoyed it very much.

"June?"

"I'm sorry, what did you say?"

Cassidy smiled again. "I said I know you're probably nervous, but you don't need to be. And you also need to let me do your makeup."

"I don't wear makeup."

"Just a little." She clasped her hands to her chest. "Please, June Bug. Pretty please with a heaping pile of sugar and a cherry on top."

"In most other animal species, it's the males who are expected to impress the females with displays of physical attractiveness. From an evolutionary standpoint, it makes more sense for the male to be adorned with features that render them beautiful as a means of attracting a mate, and for females to possess traits that allow them to better protect their young."

"Well, we ain't peacocks, so how about you let me at you with a little eyeliner."

"All right. But not too much."

She clapped and squealed.

The front door opened, and Jonah came inside. "Hey, what are you girls up to?"

"I'm helping June get ready for her date."

"A date? Good for you, Juney."

"What about you, Jonah?" Cassidy asked, raising her eyebrows. "Plans tonight?"

"No, no plans." He jerked his thumb toward the stairs. "I'm going to go shower."

Cassidy looked like she might say something else, but she closed her mouth. She narrowed her eyes as Jonah walked upstairs. "We need to get that man a date."

"We, as in me and you? Because I think Scarlett is more suited to matchmaking activities than I am."

"I meant generic we," she said. "Scarlett's already muttering about him still being single. Do you think he's out here mending a broken heart or something? Has he said anything to you?"

"He hasn't shared many details of his life before Bootleg," I said.

"Hmm," she said, crossing her arms. "He's a tough nut to crack, that one. We'll get to him, though. For now, sit your cute self down so I can get started."

She sat me down at the dining table and after a lot of instructions—*look up, look down, part your lips, rub them together*—she stepped back and nodded.

"You're gorgeous. Go look."

I went into the bathroom and flicked on the light. Slowly, I looked up into the mirror.

That fluttery feeling in my tummy was back as I looked at myself. She hadn't used very much makeup, and the colors appeared remarkably natural. I still looked like myself. Just…a little fancier. More polished, perhaps.

She stood in the doorway and leaned against the frame. "Well? What do you think?"

I had to push away that big tangle of feelings again before I could answer. "This is quite satisfactory."

"I'm glad you like it. Now let's go upstairs and get you dressed before your date gets here."

Chapter Ten

George

This felt oddly like high school.

I stood on June Tucker's porch, half expecting her father to open the door and ask about my intentions with his daughter. Why, I wasn't sure. June was a grown woman, and I didn't think she lived with her parents. There were three cars parked outside—two in the driveway and one on the street. Maybe she had roommates. Although, from what I knew of her, she didn't seem like the roommate type.

Her house was tidy, with a small front porch and a dark red door. Lights glowed through the cracks in the curtains.

A tickle of nervousness ran up my spine. I cracked a smile at that. When was the last time I got nervous before a date? Maybe that was why this reminded me of being a teenager.

It wasn't Sheriff Tucker who answered my knock, but it wasn't June either. I recognized the man who opened the door as one of the Bodines from the other day. He'd been grilling in the back of that pickup truck. What was he doing here?

"Hey, GT," he said, opening the door and standing aside. "Come on in."

"Thanks."

"Jonah Bodine," he said. "We met the other day. I'm June's roommate."

"Right, the grill in the truck."

He grinned. "Yeah. My brothers are…well, there's never a dull moment."

"It was a good burger."

"Yeah, thanks. I think June will be down in a second. She's upstairs with her sister. Make yourself at home."

Jonah went into the kitchen where he had something sizzling on the stove. Smelled good, like soy sauce and ginger.

June's house was nothing like I'd pictured it. Cozier than I'd expected. The living room had a brick fireplace and a couch with big fluffy pillows and throw blankets. Another chair sat near the window and there were several bookshelves stuffed with books.

I wandered over to the fireplace. She had a few pictures on her mantle. One was her and the woman I'd seen at the bar last night—must have been her sister. Another had the girls with their parents. Sheriff Tucker stood behind June, and a woman who was clearly their mother was on the other side. The third photo was June with her father.

In all of them, June wore the same subdued smile. Just a subtle turning of her lips. It was so distinctly *her*. At first glance she appeared emotionless. But I could see the depth hiding behind those pretty eyes. There was a lot more to June Tucker than one might see at first glance.

And if she'd let me, I wanted to be the guy to uncover it.

Footsteps coming down the stairs made me turn. It was like something out of an eighties flick. June took each step carefully, as if she were moving in slow motion. She was dressed in a black V-neck top that hugged her curves beautifully. Dark jeans with ankle boots. Her dirty blond hair hung in waves around her face. Her green eyes were bright, her lips shiny and pink.

I watched, captivated, as she made her way down the stairs. Her sister followed, but stopped about halfway down.

"Wow," I said. "You look beautiful."

"Cassidy did my makeup." She stood still at the bottom of the stairs, as if her feet had gotten stuck. "I wasn't sure it was necessary, but she made a compelling enough argument that I agreed."

I closed the distance between us. "You look nice all the time, but she did a great job."

June leaned closer to me and took a deep breath through her nose. "You smell extremely pleasant tonight."

From the corner of my eye, I saw Cassidy wince.

"Thank you." I leaned down, putting my face near her hair, and inhaled deeply. "You smell extremely pleasant as well. Have we talked about the impact of scent on the brain?"

"I don't recall that we have."

"We should. It's remarkable." I put my nose in her hair and smelled her again. Her scent went straight to my head, like a shot of good whiskey. "I read once that our sense of smell is directly connected to the limbic system."

"The oldest part of the brain," June said, her voice breathy.

"The primitive part of the brain." Since she wasn't moving away, I took another deep breath. God, she smelled good.

It was about then that I remembered we weren't alone. Jonah stood in the doorway to the kitchen and Cassidy was still on the steps. Both were staring at us, open-mouthed.

I kept my attention on June. "Shall we?"

"Yes."

I offered my arm, but she hesitated, drawing her eyebrows together and looking at me with confusion. I grabbed her hand and tucked it into the crook of my elbow.

"Oh. Right."

Her hand was small against my arm, her fingernails cut short and unpolished. She was as natural as a woman came, this one, and I loved that about her. No games. No agenda. So different from the women who'd always surrounded us when I played football.

75

I tipped my chin to Jonah and Cassidy. "Have a good evening."

"Night, you two," Cassidy said with a smile. She wiggled her fingers at her sister.

I led June to my car and opened the passenger side door, closing it after she got in. She sat with her back stiff, her hands clasped in her lap. I couldn't quite tell if she was nervous, or if that was just how June sat when she was in a car.

She'd relaxed quickly enough when we'd danced last night. Feeling her melt into me as we'd swayed to the music had been enormously gratifying. I could tell June was going to be a bit of a mystery. She wasn't like most girls, and if I wanted to get to know her better, I was going to have to play by her rules.

I didn't mind. She was intriguing. A little awkward, and often blunt. But intriguing nonetheless. A challenge. I was a competitive guy. I couldn't resist a good challenge.

We pulled into the parking lot of the Bowl and Skate. It was packed full of cars, but I found a spot off to the side.

June glanced at me. "Bowling? Or roller skating? I should warn you, I'm not proficient at either of those activities. And it appears to be busy."

"We're not here to bowl," I said. "Or skate. There's a bowling tournament tonight. I figured we could be spectators. It's not exactly a football game, or even baseball for that matter. But it's the best I could do on short notice."

June smiled. Her lips parted, the corners turning up, in an honest-to-goodness smile. It lit up her face, making her eyes sparkle. Made me feel like I'd just scored a game-winning touchdown.

"We're here to *watch* bowling?"

"That we are. Sound good?"

"Yes. It sounds great."

I got out of the car, but she was out before I could get around to open the door for her. I made up for it by holding the door open when we went into the bowling alley.

The rumble of bowling balls rolling down the lanes and the

crack of falling pins filled the air. Every lane was full, a color-ful motley of people in garish bowling league shirts. The scent of onion rings, fries, and beer mingled with the disinfectant the attendant sprayed into the rental shoes to keep them clean. Someone bowled a strike in lane four, and the team erupted with cheers.

I put my hand on the small of June's back and led her through a knot of people. Most of the crowd was down near the lanes—there weren't a lot of spectators—so we found a small table near the shoe counter.

Several laminated menus were stacked on one end of the table. I handed one to June and took a look at the selections. Pretty standard bowling alley fare. It all sounded good to me. Onion rings were definitely happening.

"What looks good?" I asked.

She tilted her head as she studied the menu. "I'm partial to just about everything they offer. Particularly onion rings."

Onion rings? Damn, I liked her. "I'm with you there."

There wasn't a wait staff, so I got up and ordered at the bar. I brought back a pitcher of beer and poured two glasses.

June watched the bowlers, her eyes roaming across the scoreboards. I wondered what was going through that sharp mind of hers. The bartender brought our food—it smelled greasy and delicious—and we both dug in.

I never would have thought watching a bowling tourna-ment could be this enjoyable. But just watching June have fun—listening to her calculations and predictions—was fasci-nating. She knew things about the origins of bowling—because of course she did. Her eyes were bright and her smile lit up the room as she scarfed down fried food and watched the tournament.

Made me think back on other dates I'd had. Expensive restaurants with fancy menus. Exclusive clubs. VIP treatment. Those days had held a certain appeal. It was fun to be treated like you were a big shot; even I could admit that.

But I'd never been so relaxed on a date before. I could kick back, stuff my face with onion rings and fries, and just chill. No pressure. No wondering if my date was only with me for my status or my money. June was a fan, but she didn't seem to give two shits about my fame. And it was one more thing on a growing list of reasons I liked her.

"Have you picked a winner yet?" I asked, gesturing to the teams.

"It's likely to be *I Can't Believe It's Not Gutter*."

I glanced at the scoreboards. "Looks like they're in third. You think they'll pull ahead?"

"Their strongest players bowl last in the rotation, so I suspect their score will improve considerably in the later stages of the game."

"Can't argue with that logic."

We watched a bit longer, finishing our meal. I needed to use the restroom, so I excused myself, leaving June at our table.

When I came out of the restroom, the thunder of bowling balls had been replaced by loud voices. An argument had broken out between the teams in lanes six and seven. A group of players in bright fuchsia bowling shirts—the *Pin Pushers*—squared off with the *Ball Busters* in neon green.

Most of the other bowlers had stopped playing, their attention on the altercation. I glanced around, wondering if there was a league official or a manager who could step in. Did bowling tournaments have refs?

"He was over the line," a man in fuchsia said, jabbing his finger at one of his opponents in green. "It's a foul. No points."

"Bull honkey! He was not over the line. It's a spare."

A woman walked straight into the fray. A woman who looked disturbingly like June. I shot a quick glance at our table. Empty. It *was* June.

Oh hell no. I was *not* letting my woman get in the middle of a throw-down at a bowling tournament.

Wait, when had I started thinking of June as *my woman*?

I didn't have time to contemplate that now. Seeing her stride into the middle of what looked like a fight waiting to happen had me ready to hurdle over the barrier to get to her. I was hit with a surge of adrenaline and I balled my hands into fists as I followed her onto the bowling floor.

The man in green's face was red and his voice shook. "Now you listen here—"

"I'm done listening to this nonsense." The man in fuchsia jabbed his finger at the opposing team again. "You try to get away with this every year. I'm not having it."

June got right between them. I wanted to grab her by the waist and haul her out of there. Keep those crazy bowlers from touching her. What was she doing?

"Gentlemen," June said, her voice filled with authority. She held out her arms as if to keep the two teams away from each other. "Let's look at this logically. If the *Pin Pushers* did indeed have a spare, the relative results of the game won't change. They're currently in fourth place, and a spare won't move their score high enough to take third."

"But if they get another strike, that spare could kick them over the edge," the man in green said.

June rolled her eyes as if she couldn't understand why she was having to explain something so simple to these people. "The points differential is already too high. The spare in question isn't significant to the overall scores. Not this late in the game."

"But—"

"As long as none of your team members deviate from your current average, your position in third is secure," June said.

The man in fuchsia crossed his arms, his brow furrowing.

I grabbed June's hand to pull her out of there. "She means don't mess up and they can't beat you."

That seemed to pacify him. He shot the man in green one last glare, then both teams went back to their lanes.

I put my arm around June and gently led her back to our table. "Well, that was some unexpected excitement."

"And kids think math isn't important."

I laughed. This girl was something else. "You showed them, didn't you?"

Chapter Eleven

June

George certainly knew how to take a woman on a date. Although my dating experience was limited, it wasn't non-existent, and this had been the best date I'd ever had.

I'd assumed he'd take me to dinner, which would have involved a need for a great deal of conversation. Looking back on how I'd felt prior to George's arrival at my house, much of my anxiety had stemmed from the fear that I'd be unable to maintain a mutually satisfying conversation for the duration of a meal.

But he'd chosen an alternative that had not only been more comfortable, it had been exceedingly enjoyable.

He offered me his arm again as we departed from our table near the shoe counter. This time, he placed his other hand—that large, strong hand—over mine and squeezed. His skin was warm, but not uncomfortably so, and his touch made me want to lean closer. Feel more.

It was odd that despite George's size, his presence in my personal space didn't feel intrusive. In fact, since I'd settled the scoring dispute between the *Pin Pushers* and the *Ball Busters*, he'd become increasingly physical. He'd led me away from the bowlers with his arm around my shoulders in a gesture that had felt protective—maybe even possessive.

I'd liked it.

We left the Bowl and Skate and drove home. He pulled up in front of my house and turned off the engine. A wave of disappointment crashed through me as he got out of the car. This was it. The date was over, or on the verge of being so. In mere moments, I'd be back inside my house and George would be gone.

I couldn't explain why I found the notion of saying goodnight so depressing. There was nothing logical about the cascade of negative emotion that washed over me. It was just a date. It wasn't as if we had to say goodbye for an extended period of time. My brain seemed to understand the reality of our situation. It was very likely I'd see him again as early as tomorrow.

But there was another part of me—a part that seemed to reject logic and reason in favor of the power of all these *feelings*—that hated the idea of our night together ending.

Gram-Gram had always said that when faced with an unpleasant situation, it was best to just pluck the whole chicken. In this case, there weren't any actual chickens involved, but I understood what she'd meant.

I got out and walked straight for my porch, trying to fish my house key out of my handbag as I went. George was right behind me. I could practically feel his presence at my back. My heart beat faster and I once again felt vaguely nauseated.

"Thank you for taking me on a date," I said as I fumbled for my key. "I had a nice time."

"June?"

His voice brought me up short and I tilted my head back so I could look up at him.

"Yes?"

"Are you all right?"

"I'm fine. Why wouldn't I be?"

He shrugged, just a subtle lift of his shoulders, and didn't break eye contact. "I don't know. I guess that's why I'm asking. You seem like you're in a hurry to go."

"The date's over."

"Is it?"

Realization dawned on me and the roiling in my stomach intensified. He expected me to invite him in. He'd taken me out on a date and believed it would end with sexual intercourse.

It felt as if the blood was draining from my face. I had no problem with people—women or men—who chose to have sexual relations on a first date. Or second, if that's what this was, and last night's drink at the Lookout counted as our first. But physical intimacy was complicated for me. And that wasn't something I wanted to have to explain to George tonight.

Was that why he'd taken me out? Was his primary aim to get in my pants, as Scarlett would say?

He blinked once, his eyes still on mine, his gaze intense. I expected him to move closer. To crowd me with his large size. But he didn't. His expression softened and one corner of his mouth twitched, as if he were about to smile.

"I told you, June Bug, I'm not a man who'll push his human mating rituals too far. I know you're going inside without me tonight."

Hearing him use my favorite nickname did strange things to my insides. It made me feel warm and melty. But the gooey feeling warred with guilt over making the assumption that he'd only taken me out on a date for sex.

I glanced down. "I'm sorry I had the wrong impression."

He touched my chin with his fingertip and brought my gaze back up to his. "Don't be. We're still getting to know each other."

"If you've not already become aware, I think it's only fair that I inform you of something."

His brow furrowed and I'd never realized how intensely sexy that looked on a man. "What?"

"I'm not very good at this."

"Not good at what? Saying goodnight?"

I shook my head. "Dating."

He smiled, running the pad of his finger along my jaw. "I think you're doing just fine."

"Thank you. You as well. You're clearly quite proficient."

"At human mating rituals."

"Yes."

"I'm not sure I am." He traced that magical finger from my forehead, down my temple, and tucked my hair behind my ear.

"Why not?"

"It's our second date, and I haven't kissed you yet. Or is it our third? Even worse."

"Well, one could argue—"

He put his finger against my lips. "Yes, we could argue about whether we've had a date before tonight. But I'd much rather just kiss you. What do you think?"

Kissing on my front porch did sound appealing. My eyes traveled to his mouth. His lips were full, the corners lifting.

I nodded and he moved his finger from my lips.

My heart beat furiously. If not for my solid understanding of human anatomy, I'd have wondered if it could bruise itself against my ribs. My fingers and toes tingled, and I couldn't take my eyes off George's mouth. Those lips. That rugged square jaw and those dimples in his cheeks.

He brushed my hair back from my face again, tucking the other side behind my ear. What a mysteriously charming gesture.

Instinctively, I tilted my chin up, angling my face to better receive his lips against mine. Judging by his incoming trajectory, it seemed the optimal angle would be...

And then our mouths touched, and my mind went blank.

Soft, wet lips exerted gentle pressure against mine, and my eyes fluttered closed. His hand moved around to the back of my head, his fingers sliding through my hair. A tingling sensation spread across my skin, intensified by the scratchiness of his stubble.

Without conscious thought, I reached for him, letting my hands rest against his torso. My fingertips and palms discovered ridges of muscle beneath his shirt. The combination of rough and soft—hard and warm—made a shiver race down my spine and heat pool in my core.

He sucked my lower lip into his mouth and traced it with his tongue. I clutched his shirt, drawing him closer, and his grip on me tightened. Our tongues touched, first just the tips. Then they slid against each other in a long, languid stroke that practically made my knees buckle.

A low noise vibrated in his throat, a hum that was nearly a growl. He pulled me closer, wrapping his arms around my much smaller frame, enveloping me.

There was skin and movement and the scruff on his jaw. Warm tongues and wet mouths. It was all so overwhelming. Drowning me in a flood of sensation.

His grip on my head loosened as he gradually drew back. I tried to follow; I wasn't ready to stop kissing yet. I felt him smile against my mouth before kissing me again. One last breathtaking, soul-stealing kiss.

As he pulled away from me, I was briefly disoriented. I blinked a few times and reached out to touch the door, as if the solid wood could ground me in reality. The cascade of physical sensations still stimulating my nervous system was almost too much to process.

"Can I call you?" George asked.

"What? Oh. No."

He leaned back slightly, his eyebrows shooting upward. "No?"

"We have yet to exchange phone numbers. It would be impossible for you to call me."

He smiled. "You're right, I worded that question wrong. Can I have your number so I can call you?"

"Yes, of course you can."

We exchanged numbers, my heart still beating so hard it made the blood roar in my ears.

"I'll call you," he said. "Good night, June Bug."

"Goodnight, George."

I went inside and shut the door behind me.

Jonah glanced up from the couch. The TV was on. "Hey, Juney. How was your date?"

"Magical."

Chapter Twelve

June

George did call. The very next day. Cassidy was quite impressed, and to be truthful, I was as well. He didn't seem like the type of man who'd promise to call if he didn't mean it. But from what I knew of men, that was a common problem. And I wasn't very good at reading people.

He asked to see me again, and I certainly harbored no objections. The next thing I knew, an entire week had gone by, and I'd spent time with George every single day.

Saturday evening rolled around, and I needed to make my weekly trip to the Pop In. Normally I would have gone much earlier—it was getting quite late—but I'd been with George all day.

My schedule was in complete disarray after sharing so many meals with him. But I didn't mind. I transferred some unused items to the freezer, reworked my plan for the coming week, and made a truncated shopping list. Problem solved.

Besides, it was worth disrupting my routine for dates with George.

I parked in front of the Pop In, but as I walked in, I almost ran into my sister coming out the door.

"Juney," she said, sounding surprised. She was dressed in her deputy uniform.

"Are you on duty?"

"No, I just got off, but I was about to call you."

"Why?"

She glanced around, then lowered her voice. "Something's happened with the Callie Kendall case. Something huge. Bowie's family is coming over to our place so I can explain."

I glanced down at the shopping bag in her hand. "What's that?"

"Dessert," she said. "I felt like…well, this is big news, and I thought we'd all appreciate some sugar to go with it."

"What's the news?"

She glanced around again. Was she concerned about being overheard?

"There's no one here to listen in on our conversation," I said. "I think you can speak free—"

"I know, Juney." She grabbed my arm and pulled me away from the door. "But this is a big deal. Word's gonna get out soon, but… I can't believe I'm about to say this aloud." She paused, taking a deep breath. "Callie Kendall's been found."

I blinked at her, unsure of what to say. "Is that a joke or sarcasm of some kind? Because you know I don't get sarcasm."

"No, it's not sarcasm. Just come to my house, all right? I'll explain it to everyone all at once."

I wasn't sure how to respond to that—had she really said Callie Kendall had been found?—so I didn't try. I simply went to my car and followed Cassidy to her house.

She and Bowie shared what had once been a duplex. They'd embarked on a remodeling project to join their two halves into one. The new design was spacious and open, now that most of the central wall was gone. It was decidedly less dusty than the last time I'd visited, but there were still power tools and stacks of building supplies and lumber.

Cassidy's cat, Eddie, bounded down the stairs, passing my sister on her way up to change her clothes. My nose tickled at the very sight of him. I was allergic to pet dander, particularly of the feline variety. Usually I came prepared with tissues, but this had been a surprise detour. I sniffed, hoping her two cats would keep their distance.

A hum of anticipation thrummed through me as I waited for everyone to arrive, processing what Cassidy had said. I'd once estimated the chance of the Callie Kendall case being solved at less than four percent, with a rate of decrease of point oh six percent per year.

In other words, I was surprised by this news.

Bowie came down dressed in a waffle knit shirt and jeans. Cassidy was just behind him in a loose-fitting blue sweater and leggings. She pulled her hair up into a ponytail as she walked.

"Hey, Juney," Bowie said.

Cassidy's other cat, George-Cat—I called him George-Cat now to differentiate between human George and feline George—twined around my legs and rubbed his face against my shoe.

"I don't understand why your cats find me so interesting," I said. "It's as if they have an instinctual drive to bother the people least likely to give them attention."

"They're just bein' friendly," Cassidy said. "Come here, George. Leave June alone, you'll make her sneeze."

I took a seat on the couch in their newly expanded living room. Although the chaos of the remodeling project was still in evidence, their house was quite livable. Cozy, even.

It didn't take long for the rest of the Bodines and their significant others—for those who had them—to arrive. Scarlett and Devlin. Jameson and Leah Mae. Jonah was there, dressed like he'd just left the gym. Gibson arrived last, smelling of wood and stain. He must have been working when Cassidy called.

"Thanks for coming, y'all," Cassidy said. She stood in front of the group gathered around her—some seated on the couch or chairs, others on the floor. Gibson stood next to me, leaning against the wall. "There's really no way to take the shock out of what I'm about to say, so I'm just going to go ahead and say it. Callie Kendall was found this morning."

There was a shocked silence, lasting the space of a heart-beat, before the room erupted with noise, everyone asking questions at once.

"Are you serious?"

"Where?"

"Who found her?"

"What happened?"

Bowie held his hands up for quiet. "Come on, now. Quiet down and let her talk."

"It's fine, we reacted the same way at the station when we got the news," Cassidy said. "Here's what I know. She was picked up early this morning on a highway outside a little town called Hollis Corner, about five hours from here. Didn't have anything with her, just the clothes on her back. The trucker took her to the nearest hospital. They contacted local police and her parents."

"Oh my god," Scarlett said through her hands covering her mouth.

Cassidy took a deep breath. I could tell by the way she stood that she was tired. "Once the hospital staff gave the all-clear, the local cops interviewed her. Took a long statement. After that they called us."

"Are they sure it's her?" Devlin asked.

"Judge Kendall came out himself and gave a positive ID," Cassidy said.

"What happened to her?" Scarlett asked. "This is killing me. Why did she disappear?"

"According to the report she gave the Hollis Corner police, she'd met a guy online. He was older, in his twenties, so she didn't tell anyone. He convinced her to run away with him."

"What?" Scarlett shrieked.

Cassidy nodded. "She didn't go home that night because she was running away to be with him. She cut through the woods and hitched a ride out of town, trying to get to Perrinville. The guy she'd met had a bus ticket waiting for her."

"Why in the hell didn't he just come get her himself?" Scarlett asked.

"I don't know," Cassidy said. "The report doesn't answer that. Maybe he didn't have a car."

"She hitched a ride?" Jameson asked.

I could almost hear the unasked follow-up question. Had it been their father who'd picked her up?

"She said your dad stopped and gave her a ride."

"Shit," Jameson said under his breath.

"They didn't make it all the way to Perrinville," Cassidy continued. "About a mile outside town, he almost hit a deer. Slammed on the brakes to avoid it. She hit her face on the dash."

"Blood on her sweater," Scarlett said under her breath.

"Yep. The report isn't clear on what happened at that point, exactly, or why her cardigan was left behind. Only that she continued into town on foot and caught the bus."

"This could explain the presence of her fingerprints in your mother's car," I said.

"It could, although I don't know why he would have been driving our mom's car," Bowie said.

"We know he drove it a few days later," Jameson said. "Maybe his truck was broken down at the time."

Bowie shrugged. "It could have been. I don't remember for sure."

"Wait," Scarlett said. "If Callie ran off with some guy she met online, why'd she disappear for so long? Did she marry him and move to Australia or something?"

"No, I don't think she married him," Cassidy said. "Not legally anyhow. It turns out the guy she'd met was in a cult."

"What?" Scarlett shrieked again, and Devlin rubbed her back as if to calm her.

"Yep. He lured her into running away with him and kept her prisoner at the compound where they lived. Wouldn't let her leave. She finally escaped this morning."

"How?" Jonah asked.

"The report says that a couple of days ago the cult leader decided they had to move. She described the situation at their compound as *chaotic*. Sounds like they were all scrambling to get out of there before they were attacked by demons or something." Cassidy shook her head. "Anyway, Callie hid, and they left without her."

"Did they come back for her?" Jonah asked.

"She didn't know. The Hollis Corner police have been assuring my dad all day that they *have everything under control.*" Cassidy rolled her eyes. "But they don't know either."

Even I could tell Cassidy was being sarcastic.

"Where is she now?" Scarlett asked. "Still at the hospital?"

"Nope," Cassidy said. "Judge Kendall whisked her out of there as soon as she was discharged."

"They just let her go?" Scarlett asked.

"She was a missing person, not a suspect in a crime," Cassidy said. "And she didn't have any injuries that warranted hospitalization. With a positive identification from her father, there was no reason to keep her there. If it had been me on the scene, I'd have done more. Asked more questions. Taken fingerprints. Something."

"Wait—they didn't take fingerprints?" Devlin asked.

Cassidy rolled her eyes again. "The notes in the report say they had a hard time getting her to cooperate due to her *traumatized state*. I think they had to really coax the story out of her. And once her dad showed up, he wouldn't let anyone near her."

"I guess it makes sense for her father to try to protect her," Jonah said.

"I know, and I don't mean to be callous about it," Cassidy said. "I just don't think the Hollis Corner police department did their job as well as they should have."

"I can't believe this," Scarlett said. "Callie's alive."

The room went quiet for a long moment. It seemed as if everyone was struggling to digest this news. This had deep

91

ramifications for the Bodine family. Their father's name would be cleared. Not to mention what it was going to mean for the town as a whole.

Bowie put his arm around Cassidy, and she leaned against his chest. Scarlett shook her head slowly while Devlin rubbed her back. Jameson held Leah Mae's hand in both of his.

Jonah stared at the floor. He'd arrived in town around the time his late father had become a person of interest in the case. I'd always had the impression he didn't think much of the man he'd been named for.

"You all right, Gibs?" Scarlett asked.

All eyes moved to Gibson. His arms were crossed and his icy blue gaze was fixed on something near his feet.

"That's it, then," he said, his voice a low growl. I couldn't tell if it was a statement or a question. He turned and walked out the door and it banged shut behind him.

"Please don't tell me he's mad because Dad's innocent," Scarlett said. "I mean, I know he was involved if he gave her a ride. Don't know what he was thinking there. But he didn't do anything *terribly* wrong. Callie could have told him anything to convince him to drive her to Perrinville."

"Giving a teenage girl a ride out of town ain't exactly good judgment," Bowie said. "But it certainly doesn't seem like he did anything malicious."

"Gibs needs to let go of some of that anger he's so keen on holding," Scarlett said. "It ain't healthy."

"Yeah, well, I don't know if that's possible at this point," Bowie said.

"Why didn't Dad tell anyone?" Scarlett asked. "All those years, he knew the truth and he never told. Why would he do that?"

"Maybe he was afraid he'd be a suspect," Bowie said.

"Or maybe he'd been drinking," Jameson said quietly. "He could have been worried about getting in trouble for that, too."

"Could have been both," Bowie said. "What I don't under-stand is why he kept her sweater."

"Maybe he thought it would be important someday," Jameson said.

Scarlett pounded the couch cushion with her fist. "I'm so angry with Dad right now."

"I suspect he harbored a great deal of guilt over keeping that secret, whatever his reasons," I said.

"Yeah, you're probably right," Scarlett said. "Thanks, Juney."

"That must have been a terrible secret to keep," Jonah said.

Everyone went quiet for a moment. Jonah himself was a secret their father had kept. I was about to point that out when Jameson spoke.

"Do you reckon Mom knew the truth?"

"I bet she didn't," Bowie said. "She'd have made Dad come forward. And we already know he kept things from her."

Jonah cleared his throat.

Bowie patted him on the back. "I think I speak for everyone when I say I'm glad you're one secret that's no longer hidden."

"Hell yes to that," Scarlett said. She reached over and squeezed his arm. "Even if you are yet another brother."

Jonah smiled. "Thanks, Scar. Thanks, y'all."

Scarlett sagged against Devlin. "I feel like I'm in shock. I don't know what to think right now."

"It's gonna take time to sink in," Bowie said. "And we need to talk to Jayme, just to make sure there aren't any more legal ramifications we need to know about."

"I guess Callie's parents were wrong about her," Leah Mae said. "They must be feeling so many things tonight, having her back."

Even I felt a pang of emotion at that. Her parents had not only believed her dead, they'd always maintained that their daughter had committed suicide. To have her suddenly alive must have been both shocking and joyous for her family.

"What do you say we have a toast?" Bowie asked before disappearing into the kitchen. Cassidy followed him, and they returned with a bottle of whiskey and glasses. Bowie poured a small measure of the amber liquid for each of us and Cassidy passed them out.

Bowie raised his glass. "To Callie Kendall. May her return to her family and society be as smooth and happy as possible."

"To Callie," we all said, then swallowed our whiskey.

I turned the glass in my hand, listening as the conversation continued. They speculated about what Callie's life had been like, living with a cult. How the man she'd met had managed to lure her in. Where the cult had gone, and whether the police would ever track them down.

But there was something tickling the back of my mind. Something about Callie's story that poked at me, like a puzzle piece that didn't quite fit. I wasn't sure why, but I had a nagging suspicion that there was more to her story that had yet to be told.

Chapter Thirteen

George

It was late when my phone rang, June's call surprising me. We'd had brunch together and taken a chilly walk down by the lake earlier. She'd told me she was busy tonight, so I was on the couch in pajama pants watching a movie when she called.

The sight of her number on my screen made me smile. "Hey, June."

"I apologize for the unexpectedness of my call," she said.

"No need to apologize. I'm glad you called. What's up?"

"I've been made aware of some surprising news this evening."

"Is everything okay?"

She took a breath. "Yes, it's okay."

"That's good. Do you wanna come over and tell me about it?"

"I think I do, yes."

"Come on over. I'll text you the address."

"Thank you."

About five minutes later, I heard her pull up outside. She knocked, and I let her in.

"Hi there." I took her hand in mine as I shut the door behind her. Brought it to my lips for a kiss.

"Hello. I like it when you do that."

"What, this?" I kissed the backs of her fingers again.

"Yes, that. It feels very nice."

I leaned in to kiss her lips this time, but didn't linger. She'd come over to talk, and I could see the tightness around her eyes. I gestured to the couch and we both sat.

"What's going on? You said everything is okay, but you seem a little keyed up."

"Are you aware of the Callie Kendall case?" she asked.

"Little bit," I said. "She's the girl who went missing?"

"Yes. It will be thirteen years ago this summer. She was found this morning."

My eyebrows lifted. "Found alive?"

She nodded. "Yes, surprisingly. The odds weren't high, but it's important to note that although statistics can predict the probability of outcomes, there are still those instances that make up the minority portion."

"Right. Even if there's a ninety-nine percent chance of something, there's still that pesky one percent."

"Precisely."

"What happened to her? Do you know?"

June went on to explain what she'd learned from her sister. I'd heard a bit about the case from Shelby and seen the missing persons posters around town. The picture June painted was stunning. But stranger things had happened.

"The town is going to...actually, I'm having a hard time predicting what they'll do," she said.

"I expect they'll be happy she's alive. And also want to know every detail they can get."

"Without a doubt. This is arguably the biggest thing that's happened in Bootleg Springs since she disappeared."

I took her hand in mine, mostly just because I liked touching her. "Think it's in the news yet?"

"As of about thirty minutes ago, media coverage was very limited," she said. "I expect that will change in the morning."

"I expect you're right."

Media coverage didn't *change* the next day. It exploded.

Saturday night, there'd been a few news sites reporting on the possibility that Callie Kendall had been found. One even had a few photos taken outside the hospital as she was leaving with her father.

By Sunday morning, the story was everywhere, all the way up to the national news.

At first, reports were short and filled with disclaimers that they were following up on this breaking news story. Monday morning, the Kendall family released a brief statement, expressing their gratitude in having their daughter home, and asking for privacy for their family.

Reporters, however, appeared to be intent on getting their story, regardless of requests for privacy. They'd no doubt camped outside the Kendall home in Richmond to get the few photos of her—mostly entering or exiting a vehicle—that began to circulate.

The media descended on Bootleg Springs, too, although not in the numbers I'd expected. June said something cryptic about having *dealt with those vultures*. And I figured most reporters and bloggers would be trying to get more out of Callie and her family, not so much the residents of Bootleg Springs.

By Wednesday, there didn't seem to be a soul in Bootleg who wasn't talking about the miraculous return of Callie Kendall. People put balloons and banners all over town. Tables were brought out, lining the sidewalks, and by lunchtime, they were filled with casseroles, platters, and piles of desserts. The mayor declared it a public holiday. The bank closed, as did the schools. Outside the Kendall house, people left flowers and tied balloons to the fence post.

The residents of Bootleg bundled up against the cold and shared food and drinks with their neighbors. They toasted and hugged and reminisced and theorized. It was quite the sight. I texted Shelby some photos. She was disappointed she wasn't here, but said she was happy for the town. We both were. Seeing the community come together like this restored my faith in humanity by quite a bit.

The commotion settled down and after a few days, life seemed to go on as normal. I got together with Jonah Bodine to work out a few times. Soaked in one of the hot springs. Not the secret one. I still didn't know how to get to the online sign-up form, and I didn't want to get caught over there again. I turned down an invitation to a charity event in Pittsburgh—asked Andrea to send a donation instead.

I chatted with locals. Had an impromptu drink at the Lookout with Bowie Bodine. Watched ESPN with June. Had her over to my place for a stay-in date night.

All in all, I was settling into a routine here in Bootleg. I'd already stayed longer than I'd planned. I'd originally rented my place for two weeks, and I'd gone well beyond that now. I was doing things that felt suspiciously like putting down some roots. Shallow ones yet, but this had already become more than a vacation.

I looked out the front room window of my rental. I had a partial view of the lake, obscured by some trees. The sky was gray, the water glassy and still. It was pretty out there. Calm and peaceful. Not for the first time, I thought about how much I liked this town.

But it wasn't just the town that I liked, and I knew that wasn't the reason I'd stayed so long.

I hadn't counted on meeting someone out here in the mountains of West Virginia. I certainly hadn't imagined I'd meet someone like June Tucker. How could I have? She was as unusual as the day was long, and damn it, I loved that about her.

Sure, she was blunt and sometimes she looked at me like I baffled her. But her bluntness meant she wasn't a bullshitter. I trusted her, and that wasn't something that came easy to me. Not after ten years playing football, surrounded by groupies. Hell, the cleat chasers had started following me around in college, even before I was getting paid to catch a ball. I'd hated sitting across from a woman, wondering if there was any part of me she liked besides my fame and my money.

There usually hadn't been.

I opened the refrigerator door and winced at the emptiness that greeted me. I had an almost-empty container of half-and-half, a few condiments, and a pepperoni roll I'd brought home yesterday.

When I'd first arrived in Bootleg, I'd had a number of surprise visitors showing up at my door bearing casseroles and desserts. Between that and takeout, I'd kept myself well fed.

However, supplies were running low, and my steady stream of neighbors who seemed interested in feeding me had dwindled. At home, Andrea had ordered my groceries for me. It had been easier that way. She knew my schedule, so she'd planned my meals, and made sure I had what I needed for the days I'd be in town. A part-time cook had prepared everything. I'd never needed to worry about making sure I had food around, just grabbed what was there and heated it up.

Now that I wasn't playing football—and I wasn't home—I probably needed to start thinking about things like grocery shopping and meal planning.

For now, I had one of Clarabell's pepperoni rolls. I took it out and popped it in the microwave.

Before I hit start, there was a knock on the front door. June poked her head in.

"Hello," she said. "Can I come in?"

That girl. My blood ran a little hotter at just the sight of her face peeking inside.

"Hey, June Bug. Come on in."

Her hair was pulled back in a low ponytail and she wore

99

a gray cardigan over a white t-shirt and jeans. She held up a brown paper bag. "I brought food. I apologize for not calling or texting first. Perhaps you've already eaten. But Cassidy said I could be spontaneous if it included food."

"Your sister knows one of the primary ways to a man's heart," I said. "But you can stop by anytime, with or without a meal."

June smiled. Every time she did that, I wanted to do a touchdown dance. I already knew June didn't give that smile to just anyone. I liked being the guy who got to enjoy it.

I liked being the guy who got to enjoy *her*.

She came into the kitchen and I took the bag, setting it down on the counter. I slipped my arms around her and pulled her close. Leaned down and found her lips with mine.

Thoughts ran through my mind. Thoughts about June, and Bootleg, and maybe—just maybe—not going home to Philly anytime soon.

But June and I hadn't had that sort of conversation yet. We hadn't put a label on this, and I wasn't sure how she was feeling about us.

I pulled away, keeping my arms around her waist. "It's good to see you."

"Although it's been less than twenty-four hours since we were together, I was feeling a strong desire to be in your presence."

I kissed the tip of her freckled nose. "You missed me."

"Yes, I suppose that's true," she said, as if the notion surprised her.

Hell, maybe it did.

I gave her another quick kiss and let go of her so I could pull out the food she'd brought. The smell made my stomach rumble.

"What have you been up to today?" I asked as I fished out a container of mashed potatoes.

June got plates out of the cupboard. I noticed she didn't ask where they were—she'd made herself at home—and that little detail made me smile.

"I worked until four. Then I had a meeting with Lula. She's looking to expand her business."

"Are you helping her out?"

She nodded, grabbing silverware out of a drawer. "I often invest in businesses in town. I make more money than I need for myself, and I have an understanding of financial matters that some small business owners lack. It's a mutually beneficial arrangement."

"Sounds like it. What's Lula's business?"

"She owns the best spa in town. I helped her with her business plan last year and the results were even better than projected. She'd like to reinvest the profits."

"That's awesome."

We dished up our plates, heaping piles of mashed potatoes next to slices of fresh-made meatloaf. June poured gravy from a small container over my potatoes, then hers. Then we took our meals to the kitchen table.

"How many businesses have you invested in?" I asked.

She slid a bite of mashed potatoes into her mouth and swallowed before answering. "Seventeen. Jameson Bodine's girlfriend, Leah Mae Larkin, is the most recent. She's opening a clothing boutique. I secured an excellent rental rate on the storefront. What about you? How do you invest the income you earned playing football?"

"My assistant Andrea handles that for me."

June raised her eyebrows. "Does she? Is she a qualified financial planner?"

"Qualified enough for me. She's worked for me for years."

"Interesting," she said and took another bite. "What sorts of investments do you have?"

I shrugged, letting a spoonful of gravy-smothered potatoes melt in my mouth. "A variety of things, I think. Mutual funds and so forth. I think there's some real estate in there."

"You think?"

"Andrea has a handle on it. I pay her very well to take care of things for me."

"I read that it's very common for football players to struggle financially after retirement," she said. "Are you careless with your money?"

June's bluntness didn't faze me. It was an honest question, and at least part of me hoped she was fishing for information because she was sizing me up as a potential boyfriend. "The truth? I was very careless with money my first few years in the league. I was young and went from having not much to having a hell of a lot pretty much overnight. Blew a lot of money on stupid shit. I'm not proud of that."

She took another bite and nodded.

"I got my act together, though. Not all guys do. In fact, I'd venture to guess most of them don't. Especially the ones who stay single. I noticed the guys who seemed steadiest had wives or long-term girlfriends. I think the ones who found a good woman had an easier time being responsible with their money."

"Statistics are clear. Married men live longer than single men."

I gestured with my fork. "Indeed they do."

"But you didn't get married. Did you have a long-term girlfriend who helped…steady you?"

I heard the hitch in her voice, and maybe it made me a bad person, but I liked the idea of June feeling jealous over me.

"No, not really. I dated the same woman off and on for a few years, but she wasn't good for my bottom line. The opposite, actually. Keeping her happy was expensive."

She scrunched her cute little nose. "That doesn't sound like the basis for a good relationship."

"It wasn't. No, I didn't have a woman to keep me in line, but I did see some things that made me think hard about how I was living. Three years into the league, I was playing alongside Braden Santori in Seattle."

"That was the year you had one hundred thirty-seven receptions."

I grinned at that. "Sure was. It was also the year that Braden had a career-ending injury. We were the same age, drafted at the same time. Neither of us were living like football was a short-term career. But there he was, suddenly out of a job. He didn't handle it too well."

"What happened to him?"

"Less than a year later, he was out of money. He'd bought a fancy condo and a big mansion for his mom. New cars for himself and his family. His heart was in the right place, but without his football salary, he couldn't afford all the payments. Poor guy was twenty-five years old and he'd gone from being a millionaire to declaring bankruptcy."

"That's quite the change."

"Yep. I saw that happen to him and it made me take stock of my own life. And my money. I hadn't saddled myself with as much debt as he had, but I was living like money didn't matter."

"Is that when you hired Andrea?"

"She came on board a little later, but more or less, yeah." I took another bite and looked down at my now-empty plate. "Thanks again for the food. I'm not sure where all mine went, but it was delicious."

June grinned. "You ate that very fast."

"It was so good, once I started I couldn't stop." I winked.

Her cheeks flushed a light shade of pink. I couldn't help but think about that blush creeping down her neck to her tits. My dick swelled and I was glad I was wearing sweats.

I half-expected her to comment on my thinly veiled innuendo, but she didn't. She blinked at me a few times and went back to her dinner.

"So, June Bug, I've been thinking about something. I wanted to run it by you."

"Yes?"

"I think we'd both agree we like seeing each other."

"I would agree with that statement, yes."

"Good. Seeing as how I'm no longer playing football, I find myself with quite a bit of freedom for the foreseeable future. Especially when it comes to where I live."

103

"That makes sense. Particularly if you're financially stable."

"Right, exactly. And I was thinking that instead of going home to Philly, maybe I'd stay here in Bootleg for a while."

"Stay here?" She put her fork down. "I don't know why I repeated that as a question. I heard you quite clearly."

"Maybe because what I said surprised you."

"That is accurate, yes."

"So…what do you think?"

She looked down at her plate, her expression unreadable. I could practically see the wheels in her head turning as she pondered my question. As much as I wanted an enthusiastic *yes* out of her, seeing her consider my suggestion felt good. I liked that she was taking me seriously.

"Yes," she said, looking up to meet my gaze. "The question of whether or not you'd remain in Bootleg has been weighing on my mind. I would very much like it if you stayed."

I reached across the table and took her hand—squeezed it, then idly rubbed my thumb across her knuckles. "Good. Then I will. I need to call Andrea and have her bring Mellow out here."

"Mellow?"

"She's my bunny. I didn't tell you about my little Marshmellow?"

"Do you spell it with an *a* or an *e*?"

"An *e*, even though I know it's not the proper spelling."

She shrugged. "It's a name. I'll allow it."

"Well thank you very much, Miss Dictionary."

"I'm not a dictionary, and that sounds like a mockery of a beauty queen title."

I laughed, which made her laugh. I squeezed her hand again. "I was just teasing. But I am serious about bringing Mellow out here. I miss my little furball."

Her brow furrowed slightly. "George, does bringing your bunny to live here with you in Bootleg Springs mean you and I are officially in a romantic relationship?"

I hesitated for a beat, about to say *I'd like to think so*. But

I knew June preferred it when I was straightforward. "Yes, it does."

That smile of hers lit up her eyes. "Okay. I like that too."

"Me too, June Bug. Me too."

Chapter Fourteen

June

Word spread like wildfire in Bootleg Springs. Whether it was good news or bad, nothing stayed quiet for long. Not unless we were all in agreement that we needed to keep our mouths shut, or that one of our own needed protecting. But idle gossip, particularly where anyone's love life was concerned, was fair game.

Within a day of George deciding to stay in Bootleg I found myself at the heart of the second-biggest story in town. The first, of course, was still the reappearance of Callie Kendall. But talk of the famous football player courting June Tucker had tongues running a mile a minute.

I wasn't accustomed to being the center of so much gossipy attention. When I'd come up with the plan to get rid of the media by spreading a false story, I'd received my share of pats on the back, nods, and hat tips. But we'd been keeping that quiet, so the praise had been subtle—the way I preferred.

This was different. Aside from an unfortunate stint with Hank Preston in high school, I'd never dated someone in town.

I'd always kept my romantic interests—such as they were—quite separate from my community. And most people in town seemed to have decided I was destined to be single forever. It was never my name being paired up with someone in the paper. No speculation as to who would show up and sweep June Tucker off her feet.

People had talked about Cassidy and Bowie, especially when word got out that they'd been dating in secret. Jameson had declared his intentions with Leah Mae for the whole town to see by stopping his truck in the middle of the street to kiss her. That had certainly generated a number of conversations. Scarlett had caused a stir when she'd started seeing Devlin. But Scarlett caused a stir all the time, so that hadn't been unusual.

None of that had ever spilled over to me. I'd always been on the sidelines, quietly observing. Now the talk was about me, and it was weird.

I'd been seen with George already. We'd danced at the Lookout, and shared meals at Moonshine. But something about the news that he had decided to stay in Bootleg Springs had set off the gossip wagon. Now it was rolling down the street right through the middle of town. On fire.

I ignored the look Sierra Hayes gave me as I walked to the Bootleg Springs Spa. She glanced around as if wondering why I was out and about alone now that I was part of a couple. If she had asked, I would simply have told her that George was with the Bodine men.

Bowie had invited George to hang out with him and his brothers—and future brother-in-law, but I tended to think of Devlin as one of the Bodines now, despite his having a different last name. They were a unit, and they'd assimilated Devlin into their clan. I wasn't sure what their planned activities entailed. Bowie had deflected by saying *man stuff*. That sounded to me like watching sports, which was something I would have liked to be included in.

But I understood the concept of male bonding—in theory, at least—and Cassidy had invited me for a spa day. Spa treatments had numerous health benefits, and Lula ran the best spa in town.

And I had to admit, Lula's treatments did make my skin look very soft and…touchable. It wouldn't be terrible if it made George more interested in touching me.

I was the only one precisely on time, so I waited in the lobby, thumbing through a magazine I'd brought with me. Lula's waiting area was decorated with soft colors, wispy curtains, and comfortable furniture. Quiet music played in the background—something instrumental and soothing. A hint of citrus hung in the air—just enough to make it smell fresh, yet calming.

Leah Mae arrived, and a few minutes later, Cassidy and Scarlett. When our little group was all accounted for, Lula took us back. We donned fluffy bathrobes in the changing room and took our places in the treatment room.

The air was warmer here, but dressed in just a robe, I was comfortable. I took a seat in a reclining chair, put my feet up, and pulled out my magazine.

"Maybe we should go visit her," Scarlett said out of the blue.

Cassidy settled into a chair. "Who?"

"Callie Kendall," Scarlett said. "I can't stop thinking about her."

"Same here," Leah Mae said. She twisted her long blond hair into a bun and wrapped a hair tie around it. "Her disappearance was one of the defining moments of my life. It seemed like everything changed after that. And now it's just…over."

"Exactly," Scarlett said. "I'm still trying to wrap my head around it."

"I'm not sure what to think, either," Cassidy said. "Seems like we should give them privacy, though. It's not like any of us knew her all that well. Unless you did, Leah Mae."

"Not really," Leah Mae said. "We were in the same grade, but I mostly hung out with Jameson when I was here summers. I didn't run around with Callie all that much."

"Did anyone know about her guy?" Scarlett asked. "Because I sure as hell didn't. Not that I would have. I probably seemed more like a little tag-along kid to her, not someone she'd confide in."

"I didn't know, either," Cassidy said.

Leah Mae shook her head. "Me neither."

Callie was my age, as well, just like Leah Mae. But none of them looked to me to ask if Callie had shared her secret boyfriend with me. I'd socialized because Cassidy had insisted, more than because I'd wanted to—especially back in high school. I'd never sought out friendships with the other girls my age. They were fine—girls like Callie Kendall and Leah Mae Larkin had always been nice to me—but I didn't have the need for a best friend or a *squad*, as they said. I'd had my parents and my sister, and by extension I'd had Scarlett. All the Bodines, really. They'd always been enough. More than enough, sometimes.

"I guess it goes to show, you never know what's going on behind closed doors," Cassidy said. "People can hide all sorts of things, if they have a mind to."

"Maybe all that stuff about her being troubled and depressed was true," Scarlett said. "Her parents kept insisting on it. I suppose they'd have known. We only saw her summers, and some holidays. They were with her day in, day out. Maybe that had something to do with why she ran away."

"She could have been hiding all sorts of things from the rest of us," Leah Mae said.

I didn't have a hard time believing that Callie Kendall had disappeared because she'd run off with a man she'd met online. I hadn't known Callie well enough to judge whether that was consistent with her character. But I'd seen many of the girls I knew make bad decisions when it came to men. A teenage girl getting caught up with a guy who turned out to be trouble was common. Even I hadn't been immune to that.

That wasn't what was tickling the back of my mind every time I thought about Callie. Something was; I'd just been too distracted by George to put much thought into it.

"Something about her story seemed off," I said.

"You think?" Scarlett asked. "What part?"

"I haven't figured it out yet. I've had my mind on other things."

"Like your big sexy boyfriend," Scarlett said.

My cheeks warmed and I kept my eyes firmly on the pages of my magazine.

"Lordy, June Bug, seeing you blush over a guy is both bizarre and adorable," Scarlett said. "You really like him, don't you?"

"Of course I do. I wouldn't be dating him otherwise." I flipped the page, trying to keep my voice passive. But a flare of excitement bubbled up inside me. "He's having his pet rabbit brought to Bootleg in a few days."

"He's introducing you to his bunny?" Scarlett asked. "Things really are getting serious."

"Was that sarcasm?" I asked. I didn't usually understand sarcasm.

"No, I'm being serious," Scarlett said.

"I think it's cute," Cassidy said. "Daddy likes him, too. And not just because he's a football player."

"Was," I corrected. "He's no longer playing professional football."

"How's he doing with that?" Leah Mae asked. "Is he having a hard time adjusting?"

"He's doing well. George is…" I paused, thinking about my answer. "He's a relaxed sort of person. It's one of the things I admire about him. He thinks things through and doesn't get worked up if it isn't necessary. He knew his career was coming to an end, and he accepted the change in his employment with a great deal of aplomb."

"Good for him," Leah Mae said.

"Hmm," Scarlett said. "Sounds kinda boring. No offense intended, Juney."

"Oh, he's not the least bit boring," I said. "He's extremely interesting and intelligent."

"Guess there's more to him than football," Cassidy said.

I wasn't good at reading people, but I could see the warmth in Cassidy's eyes when she smiled at me. She was being genuine.

"Yes, that's correct. There is a lot more to him."

The conversation moved on to other topics as we got our facials and massages. I listened idly, adding a comment or two when I felt I had something to say.

Strangely, I wanted to keep talking. About George, specifically, but I didn't find room in the conversation to interject. And it wasn't his stats that sat on the tip of my tongue. He was so much more than his numbers. I could have talked about the conversations we'd had. The way his huge hands felt when they enveloped mine. I could have told them any number of things that had nothing to do with football, or statistics.

When we finished, we all got dressed and headed outside. Cassidy had a text from Bowie.

"He says they're down at the lake." She frowned at her phone. "What are they doing down there? I thought they'd be at the Lookout or something."

"Didn't they go to Build-A-Shine?" Leah Mae asked.

"Cass, why is Tom Hammond's trebuchet down there?" Scarlett asked, pointing toward the beach.

From here, we had a clear view straight down to the beach. And sitting there at the water's edge was the trebuchet Tom Hammond had built. I'd seen it in action plenty of times. All of Bootleg had turned out for its inaugural toss and since then, he'd launched all sorts of things across his field.

"Oh my god, they can't be," Cassidy said.

Scarlett's mouth hung open. "I think they are."

"They wouldn't…would they?" Leah Mae asked.

"It makes some sense," Cassidy said. "He is too big, even for all of them."

I squinted, trying to see what was going on at the lake. "What are you talking about?"

"Let's go," Cassidy said.

We raced down the street with Scarlett leading the way. The cool air stung my cheeks, my skin sensitive after the facial.

The Bodine men were indeed standing around the big wooden structure. It was on wheels and could be pulled by a tractor, but why had Tom Hammond brought it down here?

And where was George?

My second question was answered when George staggered out from behind one of the wooden supports. He splayed his big hand against the side of the trebuchet and leaned against it, like he was having trouble holding himself up. He had a mason jar in his other hand, and by the expression on his face and the way he leaned to the side, I could tell he'd had his fair share of moonshine.

Bowie slapped him on the shoulder and took the drink out of his hand.

Scarlett stopped at the edge of the sand and flung her arms wide to keep the rest of us from passing her. "Best to just let it happen."

Bowie leaned closer to George as he set down the mason jar and said something too quietly for me to hear. Both men laughed. I narrowed my eyes. Bowie was suspiciously steady on his feet. He was a Bootlegger through and through, so of course the man could hold his liquor. Maybe George had just gotten a little carried away and Bowie hadn't.

"Now!" Bowie shouted.

Gibson, Jonah, Jameson, and Devlin all raced to George, letting their drinks drop to the ground. They grabbed him by the arms and legs while Gibson pushed against his shoulders from behind.

"What's goin' on?" George asked, his words slurring.

They muscled him closer to the replica siege engine and Gibson fastened what looked like a harness onto him.

"Hold still, big guy," Bowie said, his voice strained.

George tilted to the left. "What're you doing?"

"He secure, Gibs?" Bowie asked.

Gibson pulled on a strap. "He's good."

Jameson let go and grabbed a white motorcycle helmet, then forced it down over George's head while the rest of the men held him still.

"What are they doing?" I asked.

"What is this?" George asked, making a half-hearted attempt to grab the helmet. Gibson and Jameson held his arms down.

"Ordinarily, we'd just toss your ass in the lake," Bowie said. "It's a thing that needs to happen if you're going to be courtin' June. I'm sure you understand. But you're too damn big. We didn't think we could get you down the dock, let alone pick you up to toss you in. So we came up with an alternative."

"Cassidy, what are they doing?" I asked again, my sense of alarm increasing.

"Tossing him in the lake." Cassidy's voice was very matter-of-fact.

"That's not tossing," I said. "That machine is going to *launch* him into the lake."

"Sure is," Scarlett said.

Leah Mae covered her mouth with her hand, and her eyes widened.

"Lie down, now," Bowie was saying to George. "Good. Come on. All the way."

"But…" I sputtered, struggling to get any words out. "But…why?"

Cassidy turned to me. "Because, Juney. He made his intentions with you known. That means the Bodines have to dunk him in the lake. It's what they do."

"They did it to Dev," Scarlett said. "Right off my dock."

"But I'm not… He's not… I don't understand." An odd sense of warmth spread through my chest and up my throat. "They're doing that for *me*?"

George was lying down—or at least, on his back beneath the large arm of the trebuchet. The Bodines were still holding him down.

"You bet they are," Cassidy said.

The ridiculousness of what I was seeing seemed to fade, replaced by a simple realization. The Bodines were throwing George in the lake because he wanted to date me.

I hadn't been this happy since George said he wanted me to meet his rabbit.

"We ready?" Tom stepped up, ready to release the rope.

"This is surprisingly elaborate," I said, more to myself than anyone else nearby.

"They've outdone themselves with this one," Cassidy said. "Go!"

The shout came from several of the Bodines—I wasn't sure which—and the men all jumped back. Tom released the rope, the weight on one end went down, and George went up.

And up.

And over.

George yelled as he flew through the air in a tall arc. The trajectory was impressive. The men all cheered as he fell, whooping and hollering and high fiving.

"Wait," I shouted, fear making my heart race. "Is he intoxicated? He'll drown!"

"Don't worry, Juney, we already thought of that," Jameson hollered back. "Nash and Buck are both out there in boats, ready to rescue him."

"He'll be fine," Gibson said, flashing me a rare smile.

George hit the water with a splash and the cheers resumed. I raced down to the edge of the lake, and sure enough, Nash and Buck were both rowing toward the figure bobbing in the water.

His white helmet was visible; he was probably fine.

Chapter Fifteen

June

The trebuchet became a Bootleg lakefront phenomenon—for the rest of the afternoon, at least. A steady stream of people lined up, the cold be damned, to take a turn—until Freddy Sleeth belly-flopped so hard he came out with two black eyes and a broken nose. Then my dad and Mayor Hornsbladt declared it too dangerous for human projectiles and made Tom take it back to his place.

A procession of mourners followed his tractor as Tom towed it back to the Hammond Farm. It looked like a funeral march. Men removed their hats out of respect. Tom managed to turn everything around that night by throwing a big bonfire and launching an old Volkswagen Beetle across his field.

George had not only survived the inaugural lake launch, he'd become even more of a celebrity for it. The story grew in the telling, and within a few days, people were saying he'd been thrown clear to the far bank. Some had him skipping across the surface like a rock. Still others said he'd sliced into the water like an Olympic diver, barely making a splash.

The truth was, he'd come out of the water disoriented, but sober as an entire church choir. And he flinched whenever any of the Bodines got near him.

What he didn't realize was that he was one of us now. He wouldn't get launched into the lake again, as long as he didn't do anything to hurt me. Which was such a strange and archaic thing, I couldn't understand why it made me so happy. What business was it of theirs who I dated, or how our relationship turned out?

For once in my life, I didn't overthink it. This was Bootleg Springs. It was how we did things.

George called the next Friday morning to let me know his assistant, Andrea Wilson, was driving out to Bootleg that afternoon with his pet rabbit. That made me inexplicably happy as well. Although it was clear to me the ideal pet was a pot-bellied pig—for a variety of reasons—George's rabbit was obviously important to him. And his excitement over seeing his small mammal, and introducing me to her, was infectious.

In other words, I was excited too.

A silver SUV was parked outside his rental when I arrived. I went to the front door and knocked.

"Hey, June Bug." He pulled me inside, his hands around my waist, and leaned down for a kiss.

I completely forgot about the fact that someone else was here. George kissing me had a tendency to make my mind go blank. But the sound of a throat clearing made me jump.

George appeared nonplussed. He grinned at me, then led me inside, his hand on the small of my back. "Perfect timing. Andrea just got here. Andrea, this is June Tucker. June, Andrea Wilson."

Andrea reminded me of Leah Mae. Tall and thin with wavy blond hair and expertly applied makeup. Her clothes were stylish—a crisp blouse and pair of dark slacks. High heels. She pursed her red lips and smiled.

"Nice to meet you." I held out my hand to shake. I was an expert hand-shaker. I'd been drilled by Cassidy and my dad on the proper technique—solid grip, but not too hard, shake twice—until I could have done it in my sleep.

"You too." Andrea shook my hand and her eyes flicked over me, like she was sizing me up. Then her gaze moved to George. "I didn't realize you were going to have company. I actually have some things to go over with you. If you have time."

I'd be the first to admit, I was not usually adept at reading non-verbal cues. What Andrea *said* seemed innocuous enough. George was her boss, and he'd been out of town for a while. It made sense that she'd want to take advantage of being in the same place to review any necessary items on her list. But her body language and tone of voice told a completely different story.

This woman did not like me. And she did not want me here.

"That's no problem. June and I don't have plans. Let me just get Mellow situated."

Andrea shot daggers with her eyes in my direction.

I mentally added this to the list of firsts I was experiencing with George. I'd never had a woman look at me with envy before—at least never that I'd been aware of. It was disconcerting.

George went to the kitchen table where a small cage sat. At first, I thought perhaps Andrea had forgotten the rabbit. There didn't appear to be anything inside. He reached in and produced a little scrap of fur, cradling it in the palm of one of his large hands.

It wasn't a *rabbit*. It was a tiny white bunny.

He held Mellow up to his face and her little nose wiggled as it touched his. She was so small she barely seemed real. Her fur was pure white, her eyes icy blue. There was black around her eyes that gave the impression she was wearing eyeliner. But it was her size, and the care with which George held her, that had my insides turning to mush.

"Oh," I breathed. "She's so cute."

George beamed at me. "Isn't she? She's a Netherland dwarf. Hi, my little one. I missed you."

He nuzzled her against his cheek and my ovaries suddenly burst into song, declaring their presence in my body. I'd never in my life felt an urge to procreate. But watching this man snuggle a tiny white bunny made me desperate to have all his babies.

"Do you want to hold her?" He held her out toward me.

"Okay."

I cupped my hands and he gently transferred Mellow into my grasp. She barely weighed anything—just a little tuft of softness. The pads of her feet felt like velvet and her tiny nose wiggled as she sniffed her new surroundings.

"She's used to being handled a lot," he said. "She won't jump out of your hands or anything."

Holding her up so I could see her face, I brought her closer. She inched forward and her sweet little bunny nose tickled against my skin, making me giggle.

"Good girl, Mellow," he said. "I knew she'd like you."

Andrea cleared her throat again. "GT, it's a long drive."

"Sure, sure." He scooped Mellow out of my hands and took a seat at the table, still holding her. "Whatcha got for me?"

Andrea shot me a glare that George didn't appear to see. He was too busy getting Mellow situated in his lap.

I decided to sit at the table with him. He had business to attend to, but he hadn't asked me to leave.

"I need some signatures." She grabbed a messenger bag and pulled out some files, then set them on the table in front of him.

"Sure."

I grabbed a pen off the counter behind me and handed it to him.

He rewarded me with that dimply grin of his. "Thanks."

Another throat-clear from Andrea. She opened a file and flipped through a few pages. "Here."

George signed.

Andrea flipped through a few more. "Here."

He signed again.

I glanced over at Mellow's cage. "She's out of water."

"What's that?" George asked as he signed another document.

"Mellow doesn't have any water." The cage was nearest to me, so I scooted it closer. I wasn't familiar with Mellow's feeding schedule, but there was no sign of food. More bothersome, in my opinion, was the bone-dry water bottle.

"Uh-oh, little one. Are you thirsty?" George held her up to his face again. "Can you get her some water, Andrea? That should be kept full at all times."

Andrea rolled her eyes as she stood. "She's fine."

I unhooked the water bottle and handed it to Andrea. Our eyes met and there was no mistaking the flash of heat in her gaze. She took the bottle to the sink.

George thumbed through the paperwork while Andrea refilled Mellow's water. It bothered me that he wasn't reading what he was signing. That was on my list of things you never do. Right up there with drinking more than one cup of Sonny Fullson's peach cobbler moonshine or sticking a fork in a light socket. The kind of thing *everyone* knows you should avoid.

Andrea got the water bottle reattached and George gently set Mellow in her cage. She scurried to the spout and drank.

"Poor little nugget," George said. "You were thirsty."

It bothered me deeply that Andrea had let Mellow run out of water, although logically, I didn't understand why. Was it simply that the animal's needs hadn't been met? "A domesticated animal should always have a supply of water. They lack the capacity to communicate their needs to the humans responsible for their care."

"I realize pets need water," Andrea said.

"She looks all right," George said.

Andrea collected the files and put them back in her bag. "I have a long drive. Unless you need me to find a pet store to get her food, I should go."

Even I could hear the sarcasm in her tone. But George didn't seem to.

"No, I'll handle it. Thanks for bringing her out, Andrea. Appreciate it."

Andrea's eyes flicked between me and George again. "No problem. It's my job."

George stood and walked her out. I waited at the table, watching Mellow drink. When she finally stopped, she seemed happier. Which was probably a figment of my imagination, as I didn't think rabbits could express human emotions.

"What do you think?" George asked. "Isn't she a sweetheart?"

"No, your assistant exhibits no qualities that would justify calling her sweet."

He laughed. "No, I mean Mellow."

"Oh, then yes, she's exceedingly sweet."

"I let her run around at home, so I just need to bunny-proof a little bit. Then we can let her out."

I followed George into the living room. He started pulling cords off the floor and picked up a scrap of paper that had fallen.

"What did Andrea have you sign?"

He was on his hands and knees, checking around the small TV stand. "What?"

"You signed a number of papers. I'm wondering what they were."

"Oh, I'm not sure exactly. There's been a lot of paperwork as I transition from being on the active roster to retirement. There's the pension, and insurance changes—things like that. Andrea has it all organized for me."

"But you shouldn't sign things you haven't read."

"It's fine, June Bug. I pay Andrea to read it for me."

That seemed like a shockingly terrible idea. "You can't do that."

"Why not?"

"She didn't even make sure Mellow had water."

He paused, still on his hands and knees, and looked up at me. "What are you talking about?"

"Mellow's water bottle was completely dry. Not just out of water. Dry, George. If she can't be trusted to take proper care of that tiny, helpless bunny, how can you entrust her with things like contracts and your finances?"

"June, she's worked for me for years."

I crossed my arms. "I don't trust her."

"You just met her. I don't think you need to be making snap judgments about her based on one little mistake. She's not an animal person."

"I'm simply pointing out that if you're going to put so much of your life, including your money, in a person's hands, they ought to at least have the ability to care for an eighteen-ounce domesticated mammal."

He stood and crossed his arms. "What's this really about? Don't tell me you're going to pull the jealousy thing. I know Andrea's pretty, but you don't need to be like that."

My eyes widened. Hearing him call her *pretty* felt like a blow to the stomach. "I'm hardly envious. The woman's not even smart enough to realize when a water bottle is empty. Besides, of the two women in this room, I wasn't the one glaring."

"Glaring? Andrea wasn't glaring at you."

"She most certainly was."

"Well, you did call her out on the water being empty."

"I pointed out a simple fact, and the well-being of your pet was at stake."

"Oh my god, June," he said. "Chill out about it. Mellow's fine. Andrea wasn't glaring at you. Why would she?"

I paused, blinking at him, and that bright and twisted knot of emotions throbbed deep inside my chest. Mentally stepping back, I separated myself from the tangled jumble so I could think.

It wasn't the fact that Andrea had been giving me unfriendly glances that had my stomach hurting. And I had no reason to believe George was involved in a romantic or otherwise inappropriate relationship with her. Jealousy wasn't the cause of my current state of distress.

I didn't like the way he was brushing my concerns aside, like he didn't value my opinion. And it bothered me that his judgment seemed clouded. Was he so easily distracted by a pretty face? He himself had admitted his last girlfriend—maybe all his past girlfriends—had been with him for his money and fame. Why had he continued to associate with people like that? What did that say about him now?

And why didn't he care that I was worried about him?

My lack of relationship experience felt like a glaring hole, huge and black. I didn't like being in situations that made me feel inept. It was uncomfortable, and when I was uncomfortable, my first reaction was to retreat.

"I have to go."

"Wait, June—"

I was out the door before he could finish.

Chapter Sixteen
George

Curling my hand around my beer, I let the icy cold bite into my palm. I was still recovering from whatever demon concoction the Bodine brothers had let me drink. *Made me drink* was more like it. I should have known that peach cobbler moonshine was far more potent than it tasted. It had to have been. It had mellowed me out enough that they'd coaxed me into being launched into the lake by a fucking trebuchet. Honestly, who did that?

But it was also kind of awesome. I mean, *who did that?* Bootleg Springs, that's who.

I figured they'd done their brand of hazing. I'd not only survived—something I hadn't been too sure about when I'd been sailing through the air—but I'd earned their approval, too. And I was glad for it. I liked June—a lot—and it was clear these were the sort of people who took care of each other, and didn't take too kindly to outsiders being untrustworthy with one of their own.

What I hadn't counted on was getting into an argument

with my brand-new girlfriend so soon. Not just an argument. A fight that had her racing off before we could resolve anything.

I blew out a breath, then took a long pull from my beer.

"Rough day?" Nicolette asked. Her dark hair was pulled back in a ponytail and she wore a t-shirt that said *My Sarcasm is Thicker Than My Thighs*.

"Yeah. Are you the sort of bartender that listens to everyone's problems?"

She shrugged as she wiped down the bar with a white cloth. "Only if you're okay with hearing you're a dumbass."

"How do you know I'm being a dumbass?"

"If you're sitting on that stool sucking down a beer after the hangover you must have from Sonny's peach cobbler 'shine, you were being a dumbass about something."

"Tough crowd."

"I own the best bar in a town where I have to call the cops on a bunch of eighty-year-old bingo players on the regular and a bar fight is just some good fun on a Friday night." She grinned. "You bet I'm a tough crowd."

I tipped my bottle to her. "Fair point."

The door swung open and three of the reasons for my hangover strolled inside. Bowie, Jonah, and Gibson Bodine looked every bit the brothers they were. Tall, dark hair, eyes ranging from blue to gray. I knew Jonah had a different mother, but he had enough Bodine in him that there was no mistaking his parentage.

I liked these guys. Even though they could have killed me the other day.

"GT." Bowie slapped me on the back and hauled himself onto the stool next to me. "Hey, Nicolette. Beers for me and Jonah, when you have a second. Water for Gibs." He turned to Gibson. "Or could she get you a nice lemonade?"

"Piss off," Gibson said. "Sweet tea, Nic."

Jonah sat next to Bowie, and Nicolette handed them their beers. Gibson took his mason jar of sweet tea and plucked out the straw.

"There's a lot of sugar in that," Jonah said, gesturing toward Gibson's drink.

"Beer has carbs," Gibson said with a scowl.

Jonah seemed to concede his point and took a drink.

"Why are you sitting here drinking alone?" Bowie asked.

I took another pull. "Got in a fight with June."

Gibson and Jonah shared a look that clearly said *that poor sucker.*

"Already?" Bowie asked. "GT, I thought we made things clear. Do we need to haul your ass back down to the lake? Because I'm telling you, it took a solid week of planning to pull that off and I don't think we can get away with it again."

"Now hold up, Bodine," I said. "We got into a little argument. That sort of thing has to be allowed. Otherwise you must be tossing your sister's boyfriend into the lake at least once a week. Even I've seen them argue."

Bowie grinned. "We like Dev, but we still have a little fun with him from time to time. But no, you're right. Couples argue."

Gibson snorted. "Don't have to deal with that shit if you stay single."

"Amen to that," Jonah said.

Bowie scoffed. "Ignore those two. They don't understand."

"Like you're some relationship expert," Gibson said. "You haven't been dating Cass that long."

"We've been through our share of ups and downs already," Bowie said, his tone even. "Don't be a dick."

Gibson just shook his head.

"What happened?" Bowie asked.

"My assistant brought my bunny—"

"Hold up," Gibson said. "Did you just say *bunny?*"

"Yeah."

"I don't even know what to say to that."

Jonah stifled a laugh.

"She's my pet."

"That's a surprising piece of information," Bowie said. "I'd have pegged you as more of a dog person."

"I played football for ten years. I traveled too much to have a dog. I needed a pet that could be alone a lot, but still be friendly when I was home. That's my little Marshmellow."

They all stared at me, open-mouthed.

"Judge me all you want." I took a drink. "You'll see when you meet her. She's goddamn adorable."

"Okay, moving on from the bunny," Bowie said. "What does this have to do with Juney?"

"My assistant Andrea brought Mellow, along with some paperwork for me. June met her and it all seemed fine. But when Andrea left, June launched into this thing about how I shouldn't trust her, mostly because Andrea had forgotten to fill up Mellow's water."

"June isn't prone to overreacting," Bowie said. "I have a hard time believing she was that upset over your bunny's water."

"It wasn't just that. She got on my case about not reading through all the paperwork I had to sign, but that's Andrea's job. And she said Andrea was glaring at her or something."

"Uh-oh," the three men said in unison.

"What?"

"*Was* Andrea glaring at her?" Bowie asked.

"No," I said. Had she been? "I don't think so."

"And how'd you respond to June's accusation of glaring?" Bowie asked.

"I said I knew Andrea was pretty, but June didn't need to be jealous like that."

Bowie and Jonah both winced. Gibson shook his head, like he couldn't believe he was talking to such a moron.

"Jesus, GT, you didn't really say that to her, did you?" Bowie asked.

"Something like that," I said. "I should have left out the pretty remark, huh…"

"You think?" Gibson asked.

"All I meant was, June has absolutely no reason to be jealous of Andrea. She's worked for me for seven years. If I was going to mess around with her, I would have done it a long time ago. We have a strictly professional relationship and we always have."

"Look, GT, you have to be straight with June," Bowie said. "She's smarter than half this town combined, but she sees things literally. You gotta say what you mean, not assume she'll figure it out."

"That's not even the real issue," Gibson said.

Bowie's eyebrows winged up his forehead. "What?"

"The issue is that June had a concern and you blew her off. She saw something that she thought wasn't right. She let you know. You told her she shouldn't be jealous of your pretty assistant, which basically sent the message that you weren't taking her seriously. No shit she's mad at you. I wouldn't speak to you either."

Bowie and Jonah stared at Gibson.

"What?" he asked.

"That was very insightful, Gibs," Bowie said. "Although why were you tossing shit my direction? You're aggressively single, but you're qualified to dole out relationship advice?"

Gibson cracked a rare smile behind his thick beard. "Coaches don't play on the field, Bow."

"That's a fair point," I said, tipping my beer to Gibson.

He nodded.

"Coach my ass," Bowie said. "This is from the guy who once dated Misty Lynn Prosser."

"Shut your pie hole." Gibson finished his sweet tea, set down the jar, and stalked off toward the pool tables.

"That was interesting," Jonah said. "Gibs was being oddly helpful just then."

"I know," Bowie said. "And he told us to go easy on you when we were planning the whole lake thing."

"I won't even pretend I understand that guy," Jonah said. "But he doesn't hate you, GT, so you have that going for you."

I knew Gibson remembered me helping him the day he'd almost hit that deer. I didn't like that he'd crashed his car, of course, although he'd already fixed some of the damage. But I didn't mind the fact that it seemed to have put Gibson in the pro-GT camp. I had a feeling not many people got that guy to like them.

But I still had to figure out what to do about June.

"I screwed up, didn't I?"

"Little bit," Bowie said.

"How do I fix it?" I asked. "My last girlfriend would have wanted diamond earrings or a designer purse. I *know* that's not June. Hell, it's one of the reasons I like June."

"First of all, be prepared for her to show you charts and graphs that explain how she's right." Bowie took a drink. "But I have to admit, despite the fact that I'm in love with June's sister, I don't understand Juney too well."

I got the sense that a lot of people didn't understand June very well. Which seemed odd to me. She was different, but in a lot of ways, that made her easy to understand. You knew where you stood with her.

Of course, that didn't mean I magically knew how to handle our first fight. But at least I knew buying her presents wasn't the answer.

I stared at the mouth of my beer bottle. June wasn't like other girls I'd known, but that didn't make her any less a woman. I'd hurt her feelings. Gibson had been spot on. She'd been concerned about me. She cared. And I'd brushed that aside, assuming she was jealous.

Some girls played games. Made you guess. Not my June Bug. She'd said exactly what she meant. I just hadn't been listening carefully.

"I need to go talk to her."

"Good luck," Bowie and Jonah both said.

"Thanks."

I got up from my stool and headed for the door. Gibson caught my eye. Gave me a quick chin tip, which I returned.

Then I went in search of my girl.

Chapter Seventeen

June

I stared into my open refrigerator, wishing it contained something suitable. When I'd first heard about George's injury—back when he'd been nothing but a statistic on my fantasy football team—I'd been upset, and Cassidy had suggested I eat my feelings. An odd concept, to be sure, but it did contain a certain merit. Binging on carbs would spike blood sugar levels and the resulting dip as insulin flooded the body would make one sluggish and tired. Perhaps the resulting sensation of lethargy was preferable to sadness and anxiety.

Regardless of the biological mechanisms involved, I wanted carbs and fat. And thanks to my careful meal planning—and living with health-conscious Jonah—I didn't have anything good.

How was a girl supposed to eat her feelings if there was nothing appropriate to eat?

What would Cassidy do? She'd text Scarlett. They'd do… whatever it was best girlfriends did when one of them was upset about a fight with her boyfriend. And that probably included eating something delicious.

I grabbed my phone and brought up Cassidy's number. If I texted her for assistance, I knew she'd come. If I wasn't mistaken, she was off today.

But what did I tell her? That my boyfriend and I had argued and I was feeling a potent mix of emotions I didn't know how to process? Was he even still my boyfriend? How did I explain it all over text?

I decided to call.

Cassidy picked up partway through the third ring. "Hey, Juney. What's up?"

"Are you currently occupied?"

"No, not really. I just got off my shift and I'm snuggling with George. George-cat, that is."

"Would you be available to assist me with a problem?"

"Sure." The tone of her voice changed. "What's wrong?"

"I need to eat my feelings and I don't have any carbs."

"Juney, what are you talking about? What's the matter?"

I switched my phone to my other ear. "I'm having an emotional crisis. I'm not sure what to do with all the feelings I'm experiencing and I think I need to eat."

"Hang tight. We'll be right over."

We meant Cassidy would bring Scarlett. And maybe Leah Mae. That was fine with me. If they each brought a baked good, I'd have more options.

Twenty-two minutes later, all three women arrived. True to my prediction, all three had a box or bag. Cassidy had opted for ice cream. Scarlett had cinnamon rolls from the Pop In. And Leah Mae had a box of lemon squares her dad's fiancée Betsy had made.

"Okay, Juney," Cassidy said when we'd all settled in my living room with plates and bowls of sugar and fat. "What's going on?"

I spooned a bite of chocolate ice cream into my mouth, not even caring that it wasn't the right time of year for this flavor. "George and I had an argument and I left."

My phone buzzed on the coffee table.

"That him?" Scarlett asked.

"Probably."

"That's all right," Cassidy said, gesturing toward my phone like she was shooing it away. "It's okay to take a little time to sort out your feelings before you talk to him. What did y'all argue about?"

"His bunny. And his assistant."

"You're going to have to elaborate a bit," Cassidy said.

I explained the basics of our argument.

"He called her pretty?" Scarlett asked. "Oh hell no."

"The fact that he mentioned her attractiveness isn't why I'm upset," I said. "He trusts her to handle things like his finances and he'll sign documents she puts in front of him without reading them. But she can't remember to make sure his rabbit has water."

"Could be an honest mistake," Leah Mae said.

"Leah Mae Larkin-someday-Bodine, you are *not* defending her," Scarlett said.

"No, Scarlett Bodine-someday-McAllister, I'm not defending her. I'm just pointing out that June might have jumped to a conclusion."

"I agree with Leah Mae on this one," Cassidy said and held up a hand when Scarlett glared at her. "Don't freak out, Scar, I just mean June doesn't have a lot of evidence to back up her concerns. One mistake doesn't mean she's inept as an assistant."

"He still shouldn't have called her pretty," Scarlett said. "And I don't mean that because a guy can't *think* another woman is pretty. He can, he just needs to keep it to himself. His *very new* girlfriend doesn't need to hear it. That's all I'm saying."

"Agreed," Cassidy and Leah Mae both said through mouthfuls of baked goods.

"Look, Juney, it sounds like y'all just had a spat," Cassidy said. "A little argument. Are you worried you can't get past it?"

I looked at my half-finished bowl of ice cream, considering

her question. "That's part of my current state of distress, yes. Did I ruin things by walking away so abruptly?"

"Of course not," Cassidy said. "Why don't you just go see him and talk about it?"

"No, she should wait for him to come to her," Scarlett said. "Make him work for it."

"If you want to make up with George, bring him food," Leah Mae said, holding up a lemon square.

"You're just saying that because you're dating the second-biggest sugar whore in town," Scarlett said. "I bet you could get Jameson to do anything by offering him cake."

"That's one way," Leah Mae said and licked her fingers.

"That is the upside to arguing," Scarlett said. "Making up."

"Oh yes."

"Mmm-hmm."

I glanced between the three of them. "You're talking about intercourse, aren't you?"

"Oh my god, Juney, stop calling it *intercourse*," Scarlett said. "Especially if you're having it."

My body tensed at the topic. They talked about their sexual relationships all the time. *Girl talk*, they called it. And I didn't mind, as long as it didn't involve me. I didn't want to talk about me and sex. It wasn't something I wanted to face yet. "We're not having intercour—I mean, we're not having sex."

"That's fine, no one's saying you should be," Cassidy said, her voice soothing. "It's up to you to decide when the time is right. But make-up sex is a beautiful thing."

"A beautiful, beautiful thing," Leah Mae agreed.

Scarlett nodded. "Lord, yes. Sometimes I pick a fight with Dev just so he'll blow my mind after we make up."

"Scarlett Rose, you are evil," Cassidy said.

"Just remember," Scarlett said, pointing a chunk of cinnamon roll at her. "I'm the one who told you multiple orgasms were a real thing."

"That they are," Leah Mae said. "And Bodine men are experts at giving 'em out."

Cassidy high-fived her. "Yes, girl."

"I know how to solve my problem," I said, letting my spoon clatter into my bowl.

"Good," Cassidy said. "The ice cream helped, didn't it?"

I glanced at my bowl. It had helped a little bit. As had their conversation. Not directly. But somehow the chat with my sister and her friends had helped solidify my thoughts. I knew what I needed to do.

I needed to show George that I was right.

———

Two hours later, I was prepared with everything I needed. I'd researched twenty different celebrities—from athletes to actors—who'd been taken advantage of by agents, managers, and personal assistants. I'd sorted through their stories for the elements they had in common and charted them on several graphs. Visual aids were often helpful when making a point.

I was determined to show George why I had concerns about Andrea. And I had the data to back my position.

The knock at my door startled me. Who was here? I hadn't called George to ask him to come over yet. I'd only just finished my research, the print outs still warm in my hand. The remnants of my carb-fest with the girls sat untouched on the coffee table of my living room. I hadn't even cleaned up.

"June Bug," George said through the door. "Will you answer, please?"

Invited or not, his timing was satisfactory. I tapped the edges of the printouts, shuffling them into a neat pile, and went to answer the door.

"Hello, George."

He let out a breath and his shoulders relaxed. Was that relief in his expression?

"I need to talk to you." He came in and grabbed my hand, enveloping it in his larger one.

I let him lead me inside. He didn't seem to notice the mess in my living room. Just sank onto the couch and pulled me down next to him, still clasping my hand. I set the stack of papers in my lap.

"I came to apologize," he said, meeting my gaze. His brown eyes were so clear. "I hurt your feelings earlier, and I'm sorry. You were concerned about me and I acted like I didn't care. But I do. I care about you, and I care about your opinion. And I'm sorry I didn't take what you were saying seriously."

His apology was so unexpected, and so sincere, it took the wind right out of my sails. I stared into his eyes, my burning need to be right winking out like a spent match.

I was still concerned about Andrea. That hadn't changed in the minute or so since he'd arrived. But maybe—just maybe—the facts weren't the most important thing in this situation. The data wasn't the point.

He was.

I pulled my hand back from his and grabbed the stack of papers as I stood. George watched as I walked over to the trash and tossed them in.

"I accept your apology," I said, brushing my hands together. "And I apologize for my part in our dispute. I showed a lack of faith in your judgment. You're an intelligent man. One I admire a great deal. I could have expressed my concerns in a manner that wasn't so…harsh."

"What was that you threw away?" he asked.

"I'd prepared documentation to prove my point."

His mouth turned up in a smile. "Let me guess. Charts and graphs?"

"Yes. How did you know? You only saw the cover page."

"You aren't going to show me?" he asked.

"No."

He laughed and shook his head. "Come here."

I joined him on the couch and he kissed me. A deep, slow kiss that had me thinking about what the girls had said regarding make-up sex. We weren't there yet, but I got an inkling of what they'd meant. George and I made out on my couch, and it was incredibly satisfying.

Chapter Eighteen

June

In the weeks since the news about Callie Kendall had broken, most of Bootleg Springs had settled down about it. The balloons, signs, and streamers had all come down. Conversations and arguments that had once centered around the prevailing theories about her disappearance turned to other topics, although there was still a fair amount of boasting from those whose favorite theories had been the closest. Anyone who'd spouted the *ran off with a boy* notion was especially smug.

I heard from my sister that the case files and what evidence there was had been boxed up and put in storage. She grumbled about the Hollis Corner police department being the ones with jurisdiction to look into the cult and the rest of Callie's story. I could tell she didn't like being kept in the dark about it.

People took down the missing persons posters. Some had been pinned to walls so long the paint was faded around them, leaving bright paper-sized rectangles behind.

There was an odd sense of loss mixed with relief. Callie had been found, her mystery solved. Everyone agreed it was a good end. She was alive and well. But it had ended so abruptly, it was hard to shake off over twelve years of speculation, curiosity, and hope.

I had enough to keep me occupied, so that little splinter of doubt about Callie Kendall waited in the back of my brain. I knew it was there, but I didn't turn my attention to it. There was work, and I was brought in to help with a risk analysis and sales plan.

And there was George.

I was falling for George Thompson. The logical part of my brain recognized these strong feelings for exactly what they were. Noticed them, saw their brightness. Their warmth and innate appeal. I liked these feelings, even though I was often confused by them.

Why was an evening snuggling with George and Mellow watching SportsCenter so much better than doing the exact same activity at home? Or with my dad? Why did my heart beat faster when I knew George was coming to pick me up for a date?

And the touching. I'd never been one to relish a great deal of physical contact. I liked my space, and I'd never found touch to be a compelling way to bond with other humans.

Not so with George. Those enormous hands of his roamed across my body—respectfully, of course—and I loved every bit of it. Couch snuggles, hand-holding, arms around my waist. Kissing. Oh, the kissing. His kisses were so distracting, I'd never once thought to ask ahead of time if he'd flossed recently.

I was curious about this newfound emotional resonance I was experiencing. I didn't understand it, but in this case, it wasn't triggering my instinct to shy away. I wanted to dive into it. Experience more. George had told me more than once, *don't think, just feel*. And I wanted to. I wanted to try feeling all sorts of things.

So I did what one should always do when faced with a topic about which they'd like to learn more. I went to the library.

The Bootleg Springs Library was right downtown, housed

in one of the oldest buildings still standing. Its brick façade was a little crumbly, but still inviting. Brand-new wooden steps led up to a landing that Scarlett had fixed just last summer. She'd replaced the worn wood that had been so rotten Millie Waggle had gotten her foot stuck, pulling her shoe clean off.

Inside it smelled like heaven—leather, old paper, and a hint of lemon from the polish the librarian, Piper Redmond, liked to use on the surface of the front counter to keep it shiny.

I stepped inside and took a deep breath. This library was one of my favorite places on earth. It wasn't particularly large, as far as libraries went. Nor was it fancy. I'd been to others that were far more grand, or housed old and important books. This library was simple, but it was home. I'd spent hours of my childhood within these walls, curled up with a book.

My parents had encouraged my love of reading but had always been puzzled by my choices. While Cassidy was reading the *Baby-Sitters Club*, I was checking out books on astronomy and physics. I read Carl Sagan's *Cosmos* when I was eight. I'd devoured anything that had to do with science, and later, math. Cassidy had been dumbstruck when I'd brought home college math textbooks so I could do the problems for fun.

My brain craved that sort of stimulation. Without it, I felt twitchy and restless. As long as I was soaking up knowledge about something, I was happy.

I wandered past the non-fiction area—those shelves I knew so well—and stared at a place of unknowns. Fiction.

I'd expanded my horizons beyond science texts as a young teenager when my dad had hooked me on sports. Then I'd started devouring books on sports statistics and athlete biographies. It had started with baseball—batting averages were easy to calculate and interesting to follow. But football had excited me in a way other sports hadn't. There was an element of chance to the game that numbers couldn't account for. A brutality to it that had made it especially stimulating to follow.

But reading fiction? I'd never bothered unless it had been assigned reading in school.

"Hey, June. Are you looking for something in particular?" Piper asked.

Piper Redmond was nothing like a stereotypical small-town librarian. She had a pixie cut that changed colors every week, more piercings than I could count, and a riot of colorful tattoos all over her body. She was a Bootleg transplant, having moved here to take over the library eleven years ago. Despite her loud exterior, Piper's demeanor was subdued. She spoke softly and had read more books than anyone I'd ever known.

"Yes," I replied. "I need books with lots of feelings."

"Hmm." Piper tapped her finger against her lips. "What sorts of feelings?"

"All of them."

She smiled. "Then I know just what you need."

She led me to the romance section. My first instinct was to scoff, but I knew better than to question her. She'd given me countless recommendations over the years, and she'd never once steered me wrong. If she thought I should read romance novels, I'd trust her.

I waited, holding out my arms so she could deposit her selections in a growing stack for me to carry. She chose six books of varying thicknesses, all displaying passionate couples or attractive men on the covers.

"You can't go wrong with any of these," she said. "Fair warning, they'll rip your heart to shreds, but put it back together quite nicely."

"That sounds like the sort of book I'm looking for."

"Need help with anything else?" she asked, depositing one more on top.

"No, these should keep me busy for a few days."

"There's more where these came from," she said. "If you like one in particular, let me know, and I can suggest more that are similar."

"Thank you."

I followed her up to the check-out counter, but paused when a title in the non-fiction section caught my eye. *Crime*

Statistics in America: Newly Expanded and Updated Edition. I grabbed that too and added it to my pile.

Piper scanned my books and I slid them into my tote bag, satisfied with my selections. I went home and stacked the books on my coffee table, then tucked myself into a corner of my couch. I'd planned to dive into the first of Piper's suggested romance novels, but the crime statistics book was poking at that splinter in my brain. The Callie splinter.

I wasn't sure why. Callie's case was solved. There was no longer a mystery to ponder. But something about her story still bothered me. Maybe it was time to turn my brain on the problem and figure out why.

Bringing up footage of one of the news stories on YouTube, I let it play in the background while I thumbed through the book on crime stats. Nothing was connecting. No flash of insight making my brain light up.

And then, there it was. Neurons fired, connections were made. I knew what had been bothering me. I just needed to do a little digging to see if I was right.

George texted, letting me know he was on his way. We had plans with Cassidy and Bowie to go out on a double date. I sent a quick reply, my thoughts buzzing on the problem at hand.

Twelve minutes later, George arrived. He came in and I looked up, feeling dazed, like I'd just woken from a long nap.

"Hey you," he said. "What has you so focused?"

"I'm sorry." I brushed my hair back from my face. How had it gotten so tangled? I'd only gone from the couch to the kitchen table. "I figured it out."

He pulled out the chair across from me and sat. "Figured what out?"

"What was bothering me about Callie Kendall's story."

"Oh?"

"Callie said she spent the last twelve years living with a cult outside Hollis Corner," I said. "But Hollis Corner has an unusually high crime rate for its size."

"How do you know?"

139

"I find anything that's a statistical anomaly to be interesting. Hollis Corner is a statistical anomaly. It's a rural community with a crime rate not explained by its population density. I first discovered it when I was running risk analysis reports for a client. Today, I saw this book at the library." I tipped the crime statistics book so he could read the cover. "It reminded me."

"Okay, I'm with you so far."

"The higher-than-expected crime statistics extend back at least two decades."

"In other words, Hollis Corner is a crime-ridden cesspool, and that's not new."

"Precisely." My mind whirred, like a well-oiled machine, gears turning smoothly, moving from one conclusion to the next. "Which means one of two things."

"One, the cult is not a cult; it's a criminal organization."

A little jolt of excitement burst through my veins. He understood. "Yes. Or, the criminal activity stems from another source."

"Do you know which it is?"

"Yes." I turned my laptop so he could see. "Hollis Corner is firmly within the territory of the Free Renegades. They're officially classified by the Department of Justice as an outlaw motorcycle club. That means there's significant evidence that they are heavily involved in criminal activity."

"So they're not a bunch of doctors and lawyers who like to drive Harleys and wear leather."

Another zing of excitement made my fingers tingle. "Precisely. The crime rate stems from the fact that local law enforcement is largely ineffective in towns such as Hollis Corner. The Free Renegades are well known for maintaining a mafia-like grip on their locales."

"Okay, I'm still with you. But what does this have to do with Callie's cult?"

"The Free Renegades wouldn't allow a cult to exist in their territory," I said. "They would have run them out of town before they could build their compound. They don't tolerate any perceived competition, and a cult leader would be considered such."

"They'd see him as a threat to their authority."

"Yes."

"Hm." He rubbed his jaw. "And I'm no cult leader, but if I was, I don't think I'd choose to put my compound in the way of a criminal biker gang. Sounds like that would mean a higher chance of the authorities sniffing around, even if the bikers didn't run them out first."

"That was my thought as well."

"But wait." George got up and started pacing. "Let's think this through from another angle. What if the cult made a deal with the bikers? They paid them tribute, mafia style, for protection."

"Your theory is not impossible," I said. "But it is highly improbable. Cult leaders and heads of criminal organizations often have traits that make them prone to self-aggrandizement."

"They have big heads, sure."

"I would imagine clinical narcissism as well, but I don't have statistics on that." I'd have to look that up later. "My point is, I don't think the two groups would have coexisted in the same region."

"What if they were isolated? Maybe the bikers left them alone because they weren't close by."

I shook my head. "The Free Renegades have an established territorial range that includes the outlying areas."

"So what are you saying?"

"I don't have enough evidence to draw a solid conclusion. But I think it's possible Callie Kendall was lying about where she was all those years."

George grinned. "God, you're sexy when you're being smart."

I couldn't help but smile back—a little. "That's... I don't know what that has to do with the topic at hand."

"You just are. I love watching that big brain of yours work. But why do you think she'd lie?"

I closed my laptop, frustration leaving a knot in my stomach. "I don't know. Human motivations are such a mystery to me. On the surface, her story is entirely plausible. The only reason I questioned Callie's story was her mention of Hollis Corner. I knew I'd read something about it before."

George sat back down. "All right. Let's think about her motives. Why would Callie lie and say she was held prisoner by a cult?"

"I was hoping you'd have some ideas."

"Well, maybe she's ashamed of the truth. Maybe she really just ran off with a guy and when it didn't work out, she decided to come back to her life. But she feels bad for staying away for so long, especially when there was so much media attention on her story."

I wished I understood people better. Maybe I should have listened to my sister and tried harder to socialize.

"Or maybe she's doing it for the attention," he said. "I'm very familiar with that sort of thing."

"How so?"

"Groupies. A lot of the reason girls chase athletes is for the attention. They want to be seen. If they're dating someone who gets media attention, they get some by being with them. It's more than that, usually. They want to be spoiled with expensive things. Those designer purses and shoes are like Girl Scout badges to them. They want to collect them and show them off. But the attention is a big deal, too."

"I suspect a desire for attention is a strong motivator. But if she wasn't with the cult, where was she? And why now? Why come forward after all these years?"

"I don't know," he said.

"Regardless of her potential motives, I'm sure about this, George. Something doesn't add up."

"It bothers you when you don't understand an equation, doesn't it?"

"Yes, that's exactly it. This doesn't make sense, and it's more than a statistical anomaly or an aberrant data point."

"Well, do you think you can put it aside long enough for dinner and a movie? We're supposed to meet Cassidy and Bowie in ten minutes."

I closed my laptop. Surprisingly, I could. Even more surprisingly, a double date with George held more appeal than an evening spent looking up numbers and calculating probabilities. Callie's mystery would be waiting for me tomorrow.

Tonight, I had a date.

Chapter Nineteen
George

I was getting awfully handsy with June. But as long as she was letting me, I wasn't stopping.

We sat across from Cassidy and Bowie in a cute little Italian restaurant, Mama Lucia's. It was the sort of place with tablecloths and good wine, but still felt a bit like sitting in someone's dining room for a family dinner. We could hear the owners—a middle-aged couple—arguing in Italian in the kitchen, and the whole place smelled like garlic, fresh bread, and spices.

I had a hand on June's thigh and the little vixen was wearing a skirt. I'd commented on her clothing choice when she'd come downstairs after changing, and she'd calmly stated that she wore skirts regularly, I just hadn't seen her in one.

No shit I hadn't seen her in one. I hadn't touched her in one either, prior to getting my hand on her leg beneath the table as soon as humanly possible once we'd been seated. From the second she'd walked down those damn stairs, my attention had been glued to her legs.

Long, sleek, soft. I rubbed her leg a bit and let my hand

slide higher. Above the table, she wasn't reacting. I didn't think her sister was aware of what I was up to. Bowie wasn't stupid—I was pretty sure he could tell. I was also pretty sure he was doing the same thing—or more—to Cassidy over on their side.

I pretended not to notice. Guy courtesy.

This was the most skin contact I'd had with June since we'd started dating. The physical side of my last relationship hadn't developed this slowly. In fact, none of my relationships had developed this slowly. A date or two, and I'd had them in my bed—or been in theirs. I was a physical guy. Touch and contact were a big deal to me.

But with June, I was enjoying the slower pace. I rubbed her thigh, but didn't push too much. Had she been tipping her knees apart and inviting me in, I would have done so, enthusiastically. I would have found an excuse to skip the movie and taken her back to my place to have some fun exploring. But she wasn't, and I was all right with that. I didn't need to get in her panties to want to be with her.

Of course, I did want to get in her panties. I was hard as concrete for her and the temptation was real. I wanted to get to know that smooth body. Wanted to touch her, feel her. Let her touch me.

Squeezing her leg a little, I took a long breath. We'd get there.

"Do we want dessert?" Bowie asked.

Cassidy groaned. "I'm too full. That rigatoni was amazing."

"I'm satisfied with the meal as well," June said.

Despite Bowie's protests, I paid for the four of us. Then I helped June into her coat, and we all walked down to the Bootleg Springs Theater.

Like all things in this town, it wasn't your ordinary movie theater. It had been refurbished to look like something from the twenties. An art deco sign hung over the ticket booth, casting a soft glow over the sidewalk. Inside, the lobby was decorated in black and gold. They'd somehow managed to make it glamorous without seeming out of place in Bootleg. Maybe it was the smell of buttered popcorn or the moonshine selection served in mason jars, but it fit in perfectly.

We paid for our tickets but skipped the snacks. I could have gone for a bucket of popcorn, but I was trying to pace myself. And the lasagna I'd eaten had about done me in.

Bowie chose a spot near the back of the theater. I had a flashback to my high school days. This was exactly where I would have taken a date as a sixteen-year old kid. Perfect for a little mid-movie make-out session.

I gently tugged June's arm as we made our way down the row. "Leave a seat between us and them. Give us some space to spread out."

In other words, put some room between you and your sister so I can get a little naughty with you when the lights are low.

Bowie gave me a subtle chin tip. He knew how it was done.

We took off our coats, putting them in the extra chair, and sat.

"I'm not familiar with this movie," June said. "What is it?"

"It's supposed to be romantic," Cassidy said.

Bowie and I shared a look. Not our cup of tea. But neither of us were really here for the movie.

"Oh good," June said, her voice brightening. "I've been working on exploring my emotions through romantic fiction. Film is another medium for that."

"Good for you, Juney," Cassidy said.

After a few minutes, the lights dimmed. I slipped June's hand in mine and stroked the back with my thumb. She watched the previews, her eyes intent on the screen. I watched her face, admiring the way the glow of light highlighted her upturned nose. Her soft lips. Her neck.

Leaning closer, I took a deep breath, smelling her hair. God, she smelled good. Fresh and clean, but still warm and inviting.

The movie began and from the first note of the opening song, I had a strange feeling. Cassidy had said romantic, and it certainly began that way. But a warning was going off in the back of my mind as we watched. I just wasn't sure why.

Despite my intention to have a little make-out fun with June, an hour into the movie, I couldn't stop watching. It was a love story, following a girl and boy who'd grown up together. Life kept pulling them apart, then bringing them tantalizingly close, only to pull them apart again. It was heart-wrenching.

I glanced at June. The glow from the screen illuminated her features, and I suddenly realized why that alarm in my head wouldn't quit. This movie was making my chest ache—I sniffed hard—and it was clear it was doing the same to her.

Her brow creased and her eyes were wide. She chewed her thumbnail and squirmed in her seat, as if her body was having a hard time containing all the emotions she was experiencing.

My attention was only half on the movie now. I wanted to know what would happen—I had a strong suspicion it wasn't going to end happily—but I was captivated by June. Her feelings shone through in her expression in a way I'd never seen before. She gazed at the screen with hope, then worry, then fear. She clutched her hands together and held them to her chest. Touched her mouth. Covered her eyes.

When she looked again, the story had taken a turn for the tragic. I was having a hard time not letting my eyes leak. A quick glance at Cass and Bow showed Cassidy quietly sobbing with Bowie's arm around her shoulders.

June shook her head a few times, as if trying to come to terms with what had just happened in the movie. Death, grief, loss, tragedy. It was all there on that big screen. Her body shuddered, she took a shaky breath, and tears flowed down her cheeks.

"Oh, Juney," Cassidy whispered, reaching out for her sister.

I met Cassidy's eyes and mouthed, *I've got her.*

Cass nodded.

I slipped June out of her seat and coaxed her into my lap. She melted into me, burying her face against my shoulder while she cried. Her body shook with deep sobs as I rubbed her back with slow circles. No one paid us any mind. Half the people in here were crying, the other half comforting them.

147

Even Bowie did a quick swipe at the corner of one eye. I pretended like I didn't notice, even as I cleared my throat and sniffed hard again. Guy courtesy.

The movie ended with enough hope that we didn't all want to walk into oncoming traffic when we left. But it had been bittersweet at best. I tucked June against me, keeping an arm firmly around her. She wrapped her arms around my waist and leaned her face into my chest. She still hadn't stopped crying.

"I'm so sorry," Cassidy said when we walked out of the theater onto the street. She wiped her eyes and sniffed. "I had no idea that movie would be so sad. I'd heard it was sweet and romantic. It sounded like a date movie."

Bowie cleared his throat. "I'm picking next time."

"I can't even argue with that," she said.

I tipped June's chin up with one finger. "You okay, June Bug?"

She sniffed hard and blinked her puffy, bloodshot eyes. "I don't know."

Her eyes welled up with tears again. I wrapped both arms around her and let her wet my shirt.

I've never seen her cry like that, Cassidy mouthed.

I stroked June's hair and kissed the top of her head. "It's okay. I've got her."

Cassidy gave me a warm smile. Bowie took her hand and they said goodbye. June didn't unbury her face from my sweater.

"Come on, June Bug." I ran my hands through her hair again. "As much as I love having you this close to me, I can't walk with you clinging to my front like this. And we're still standing in front of the theater."

"I don't know what's wrong with me." Her voice shook and she sniffed again. "The movie wasn't even based on a true story. It was entirely fictional. Why did it make me feel this way?"

I put my arm around her shoulders and led her up the street toward my car. "Because it touched something in you. And maybe you already had a lot of feelings brewing. They just needed to come out."

June just nodded.

We got to my car and I opened the passenger door for her. She turned toward me, popped up on her tip toes, and gave me a good, solid kiss.

"Thank you," she said.

"For what?"

"For understanding."

I brushed her hair back from her face and placed a soft kiss on her sweet lips. "You're welcome."

Chapter Twenty

June

After the most horrible, awful, heart-breaking, wonderful movie I'd ever seen, George took me to get ice cream.

He was basically a genius. There was definitely something to the *eating our feelings* theory.

We sat in Moo-Shine Ice Cream and Cheese and licked our cones. I didn't want to talk about the movie. The film had been excellent, even though it had made me cry. I didn't much want to talk about anything, but George seemed to understand. He sat with me quietly, letting me process.

Genius.

The chaotic whirlwind of emotions dissipated. I felt better. Cleansed. By the time we finished our ice cream, I no longer felt the need to cry. I was in control of myself. Calm, and happy.

When he took me home, I sensed something from him. There was tension between us. Not negative tension, as if we'd had another disagreement. Physical tension. He kissed me goodnight, and didn't ask to come in. But I felt the question hanging between us nonetheless.

Over the next two weeks, I felt it every time we were together.

He touched me, held me, kissed me. And beneath the surface, I could feel his desire for more. He didn't push. He wasn't putting pressure on me. But it was there.

Our relationship was progressing—developing. And I liked that. I liked that we saw each other almost daily. That he greeted me with kisses and smiles. That I missed him when we were apart and got to experience the sweetness of seeing him again each time we were together.

I liked him. Not only did I like him, I respected him. His physicality and background in athletics were only the surface. George Thompson had played football—and been one of the best during his ten years in the league—but football wasn't who he was. He was intelligent, and kind, and often amusing. I enjoyed his presence and found myself craving his company.

But when it came to the place I knew our relationship was heading, I was scared.

My body wanted things with him—from him. I felt the heat between us as keenly as he must have. Still, I held back from it. I tried to push it aside the way I did with my emotions when they were too strong. That physical yearning—that desire to be with him—terrified me.

I knew it was coming. I just didn't want to face it. Because if there was one thing I knew about myself and relationships— sex meant the end. And I didn't want to lose him.

Friday night, he invited me over to his rental for an evening in. We'd been out in public doing a lot of socializing over the previous few days—dinner with my parents, another movie with my sister and Bowie—and George seemed to realize I was at my limit. A night in with him and his bunny sounded perfect.

We ate dinner, then got cozy on the couch to watch ESPN. Mellow hopped over, so he scooped her up and set her gently in my lap. Her tiny nose wiggled as her eyes slowly closed.

"She sure likes you." He ran his finger between her ears, then tilted my face toward his. "I sure like you, too."

His kiss was familiar, his lips so inviting. He touched my face and put his hands in my hair. This wasn't the first time we'd kissed on his couch—or mine. But this time, I could feel the difference. There was a hunger, simmering just below the surface. He wanted me.

The truth was, I wanted him too. I kissed him back eagerly, enjoying the way this felt, even though fear warred with my physical desire.

He scooped Mellow out of my lap and set her carefully on the floor. She hopped over to her little pillow, as if deciding her nap wasn't over.

And then he was leading me into the bedroom.

I followed, licking my lips, holding his hand. He brought me into his bedroom and laid me down on the bed.

He leaned over me and kissed me again, deeper than before. His tongue caressed mine in a slow dance and his weight was tantalizing.

This was good. I could do this.

But that fear was still there. I wasn't afraid of George. I knew, without a shadow of a doubt, that if I said no, he would stop. That wasn't the problem.

He pulled my shirt over my head and palmed my breast, his mouth tasting mine. He'd been patient. His weight on top of me and his deep, hungry kisses were very enticing. Everything pointed to this being right.

I couldn't understand what was holding me back.

He kissed down my neck and slipped my bra down. His tongue ran over my nipple and it did feel extraordinary. The velvety texture of his tongue sent sparks running through me, making my skin prickle.

Closing my eyes, I tried to relax—tried to tell myself George was different.

He pulled off his shirt and tossed it aside. Unbuttoned my pants and slid them down my legs. As the clothing came off, my anxiety grew. I was at war with myself, indecision distracting me from the feel of his hands on my body.

Stop it, June. Stop thinking and feel.

George hooked his thumb into the waistband of my panties while his other hand cupped my face. "Are you with me?"

He was asking permission. I needed to give him an answer.

"Yes." The word escaped my lips on a sigh. I hoped saying it aloud—making a firm choice—would calm the storm of anxiety swirling in my brain.

It did. For a few moments, at least.

Closing my eyes again, I let him touch and taste me. He kissed my neck and sucked on my nipples. Those hands that were so appealing caressed my skin.

He paused to roll on a condom and settled on top of me, between my legs. I felt him thrust in, not too hard, checking in with me to be sure I was okay.

"Yes." I said it again. Because I wanted that yes to be true.

The mad cascade of thoughts in my brain didn't stop. It continued on, relentlessly reminding me of what this meant. Questions bubbled up through the chaos in my head. Was he really different? Was I capable of this? Had I made a terrible mistake?

Why couldn't I just be *normal*?

He moved and thrust into me. Somewhere, beneath the noise of my thoughts, I knew my body was responding. I knew this felt good—that the physical sensations were pleasurable. I should have been losing myself in this experience. He moved with expert grace, with sensual strength that should have had me mindlessly calling his name.

But I wasn't. Because I wasn't normal. I was June Tucker, and I'd never understood how to do this right. How to get out of my head long enough to be intimate with another person. I'd come as close as I ever had with George. But now that we were crossing the line into physical intimacy, I was lost.

I couldn't do it.

Sadness poured through me as I felt his climax build. I clung to his back and buried my face in his neck. He murmured and groaned and I tried to be there with him. I didn't want him to know.

"Yes," I said. "Yes, come."

He held me tight as his body went rigid. I felt the deep pulsing of his cock inside me. I didn't make a show of faking—I wouldn't have known how—but I rode his orgasm with him. I wanted him to enjoy it. To be happy. To feel good.

But I didn't.

I couldn't. Something inside me didn't work right. I was weird. Everyone knew it. I wasn't built for human relationships, and I'd been wrong to think I could have this with George. Sexual intercourse didn't leave any room to hide, and he was going to feel my failure.

He rolled off me, his brow furrowed. "Baby, what happened?"

"Nothing," I said, trying to hold back the tide of emotion. Mentally, I stepped away. Separated myself. "Nothing happened. It was perfectly satisfactory."

"Why are you doing that?" he asked.

"Doing what?"

"Shutting me out."

"I'm hardly shutting you out. I'm completely naked in your bed."

"You didn't come."

The words flew at me, an accusation I couldn't deny. "You don't know that."

"Uh, yeah I do. Are you okay? Did I do something?"

"I'm fine. You didn't do anything wrong." I needed to go. This was scary and uncomfortable—making me feel inept and inadequate. I didn't like it. I got out of bed, scooping up my clothes.

"June."

I tugged on my underwear and turned away from him to put on my bra. He said my name again, but I didn't answer.

"June, please."

I'd managed to quickly pull on my pants, but the emotion in his voice made me pause. I slowly slid my arm through my shirt sleeve.

"What?"

"Talk to me."

I turned to look him in the eye. "You didn't do anything wrong. I swear."

Tears burned my eyes. I couldn't keep standing here in his room. I pulled my shirt down and walked away. Out the door. To my car. Away from him. Away from the inevitable end.

Chapter Twenty-One

George

This was some messed-up shit.

I gaped at the empty doorway June had just gone through. If I stared hard enough, maybe she'd reappear, and I'd realize the last five minutes had been some kind of crazy hallucination.

She didn't come back.

My stomach turned over, a wave of sickness surging through me as I got up to deal with the condom. I cleaned up in the bathroom, tugged on a pair of sweats, then hit the couch. Mellow bounded over, so I scooped her up into my lap.

What the fuck had just happened?

I replayed everything in my mind, looking for where I'd failed. Where I'd gone wrong. We'd been kissing on the couch, things getting hot and heavy. I hadn't sensed any problems. When I'd led her to the bedroom, she'd come along willingly. It wasn't like I'd picked her up and tossed her on my bed. Granted, there were times when that was called for, but I'd known our first time wasn't it.

I'd taken things slow. Made sure we were on the same page. She'd said yes. *Twice.* I'd given her every opportunity to tell me to slow down. To let me know if she wasn't ready. I'd thought she trusted me enough. That she knew I would have stopped if she said no.

Why had she done that? Why had she *let me* do that to her?

I stroked Mellow's soft fur, feeling the barely-there weight of her in my lap. The way June had walked out left me gutted. I felt hollow, staring at the floor because I couldn't think of anything else to do.

———

I didn't remember falling asleep, but I woke up the next morning with my neck jacked up from sleeping cockeyed on the couch. Mellow snoozed on my chest. I pet her a few times and she cracked one of those blue eyes open.

"Hey, little one. Are things still shit?"

She closed her eye.

"Figured." I got up and set her on her pillow, then went to get her breakfast.

I had enough food in the house that I didn't have to leave for a couple of days. No word from June, which I took as a bad sign. I didn't call her either, but what was I supposed to say after that? We'd slept together and she'd left like the room was on fire.

Another day and I had to drag myself into town. I was out of groceries, and more importantly, I was out of alcohol. That wasn't going to fly. I figured I'd stop at Build-A-Shine and mix up as potent a concoction as Sonny Fullson could come up with. It might taste like gasoline when I was finished, but all I needed was something that would get my tall ass good and shit-faced.

Unfortunately, when I walked into the Pop In to grab some groceries, who should be there but Sheriff Tucker. *Of course* I'd run into her father. This damn town was too small to avoid anyone.

"Hey there, GT," he said. The friendliness in his tone suggested he didn't want to shoot me, but I couldn't tell if he knew that June and I had essentially broken up.

I nodded. "Sheriff."

"You all right, son?"

I rubbed the back of my neck. I wasn't all right, and I was a terrible liar. But it wasn't like I could talk to her *dad* about this.

"Yeah, just fine. How's Mrs. Tucker?"

"Oh, Nadine's good."

An awkward silence hung between us. I was just about to tell him to have a good afternoon and get on with my shopping, when he spoke. This time, his voice was serious.

"Let's go have a drink."

I tried not to groan. I didn't want to have a drink with June's father. Not after I'd slept with his daughter and sent her running. He clearly knew something was going on. Why did he want to sit down and have a beer?

But I also felt like I couldn't say no.

"All right."

We went outside and for a second, I was afraid he was going to put me in his patrol car. Thankfully he just mumbled something about seeing me at the Lookout.

When we got there, I followed him inside. We ordered drinks from Nicolette, but didn't sit at the bar. She handed us two beers and Sheriff Tucker led me to a table off to the side.

Alone. Where there would be fewer witnesses.

I sank into the chair and took a drink of my beer.

"June seems upset," he said after a long moment. "You know anything about that?"

"I suppose it's because of me. But I have to be honest, I don't really know what happened."

He nodded slowly, like my answer hadn't surprised him. "My June Bug is…different."

I wasn't sure what to say to that, so I waited for him to continue.

"She's whip smart. I'm sure you know that."

"She's incredibly smart," I said. "It's one of the things I like about her."

He smoothed down his mustache. "But she has a big ole blind spot."

"A blind spot?"

"Sure. There are things that baffle even that big brain of hers."

I traced my thumb through the moisture on my beer bottle. "You're saying she's smart when it comes to certain things, but other things she doesn't understand."

"Right," he said. "How do I put this... You see...well..."

I waited while Sheriff Tucker stumbled over his words.

"You know," he said, gesturing with one hand. "You must have noticed she's not the best at relating to others."

"She was doing just fine with me." I took another drink. "At least, I thought so."

"I reckon she was. The problem is... She missed things. Cassidy always did a good job helping her out. But relationships were... Oh, how do I explain this?"

I had a feeling at least some of what made people think of June as different came directly from her dad.

"I think you mean she's smart when it comes to math, and statistics, and her job. But she's not very experienced when it comes to relationships."

"Yes," he said with a definitive nod. "There are so few people who understand her. She's too smart for half of 'em, and too...unique for the other half."

"I have to be honest with you, Sheriff. I'm not sure why you're telling me this. June..." I glanced away, feeling the tug of pain in my chest when I said her name. "She walked out on me a few days ago and I haven't heard from her since."

"Hmm." His eyes were on his beer. "I had a feeling something of the sort had happened."

"I'm not sure what I did. But whatever it was, I didn't mean to hurt her."

"That's what I'm trying to say, son."

"I don't understand."

"Damn girl gets it from me, most like. I'm no good at this either," he muttered, more to himself than to me. "She's never been with anyone who thought she was worth the trouble."

Something about June was coalescing in my mind. A realization I couldn't quite pin down. I didn't know much about her past relationships, but I had a feeling this was important.

"You're saying she's been hurt? Did guys she dated in the past treat her badly?"

"First one did," he said, and there was no mistaking the heat in his tone. "There were a couple others, when she got older. But I think that first one set the tone. Didn't court her properly. Hurt her in the end."

She's never been with anyone who thought she was worth the trouble.

The sheriff's words ran through my head on repeat. I knew he was right—I could feel it. And it broke my fucking heart.

"I think what you're trying to tell me is that I need to be the one to reach out to her," I said. "If I think she's…worth the trouble."

He sighed, his shoulders relaxing, like he was relieved I'd figured out what he'd been trying to say. "That's right."

I nodded slowly and took a drink of my beer. Damn straight she was worth the trouble. I still didn't know what I'd done wrong. But it seemed to me that her daddy was trying to send me back onto the field. Maybe the game wasn't over yet.

Chapter Twenty-Two

June

Even the distraction of SportsCenter couldn't pull me from my malaise. I sat on my parents' couch, the game ticker rolling across the bottom of the TV screen, and felt miserable.

I'd been miserable since the day I'd walked out of George's house. And it wasn't getting better.

My parents had invited me, along with Cassidy and Bowie, for Sunday dinner. On a Wednesday. Which usually would have irritated me to no end, but today I didn't care. I hadn't felt like cooking anyway.

The meal had been fine, as these things went. My dad had made half-hearted attempts to pull me into the conversation. My mom had asked me nosy questions. Suspicious sister that she was, Cassidy had eyed me across the table. I hadn't said a word about George, but I could tell she knew something. It was only a matter of time before she stopped making out with Bowie on the back porch—thinking none of us knew—and came inside to force me into talking.

I couldn't decide if I hoped she did or hoped she didn't.

She made the decision for me. I heard her attempt at quietly sneaking in through the back door, and she said something to Bowie. He stayed in the kitchen, presumably to help my mom with the dishes.

"Juney, what's going on with you?" she asked when she came into the living room. "I've never seen you so upset."

"I'm not upset, I'm getting a cold."

She raised an eyebrow and plopped down on the couch next to me. "Don't lie to me. You're no good at lying, and you shouldn't lie to your sister anyway. Talk to me. Maybe I can help."

I cleared my throat, trying to find the right words. How did one express things they didn't understand? I couldn't sort out what I was feeling. How could I tell Cassidy?

"I slept with George."

Cassidy stiffened. "I can't tell how you feel about that by the way you said it. Did you *want* to sleep with him?"

I nodded, then shook my head. "Yes, but no, but I don't know."

"He didn't force you, did he?"

"No," I said, surprising myself with my own vehemence. "No, it wasn't like that at all."

"Okay, so what was it like?"

"I think it was nice. There were things about it that I enjoyed, physically." I paused, twisting my hands together in my lap. "I don't know how to talk about this, Cassidy."

Her expression softened and she reached over to grab my hand. "Oh, June Bug. It's okay. You don't have to tell me the details if you don't want to. I just want to know why sleeping with George made you upset. What did he do to you?"

I shook my head. "It's not what he did to me. It's what I did to him. I don't understand how to do this part. I like George. I'm intensely attracted to him in a way I've never experienced before. He makes me want to be with him all the time, and you know how I feel about other humans."

"I sure do."

162

"But Cassidy…men don't like me after they've slept with me."

"What? What are you going on about? What men?"

I swallowed hard. "You know about Hank Preston, in high school. We dated for a while. And then he wanted to have intercourse. I thought it was what I should do—what a normal girl would do. Many teenagers were having sex by then. But after we did, he broke up with me."

Cassidy's face reddened as I spoke. "Hank Preston was a no-good, dick-licking son of a motherless goat. He treated you terribly and if I wasn't such an upstanding citizen, I'd have burned his house down a long time ago. Or at least, I wouldn't have stopped Scarlett from doing it."

"The point is, I'm not made for intimacy," I said. "I don't understand it, or how to return it. Especially the physical kind."

"One asshole kid who slept with you and broke up with you right after doesn't mean there's something wrong with you, June Bug. It means he was garbage."

"He's not the only one."

Cassidy's eyebrows shot upward. "What?"

"I've dated other men since high school," I said. "Twice, I've had a relationship progress to the point of sleeping together. Both times they broke up with me afterward."

"Hold on. First of all, I didn't know you'd slept with anyone besides Hank. Why didn't you tell me? And second, what do you mean they broke up with you afterward? Do you mean *right* after?"

"To answer your second question, in one case it was the next day. The other was a few days later, but essentially the same thing. To answer your first, I don't know why I kept it from you. I felt very rejected when those men ended our relationships. Especially because I knew why they had done it."

"And why was that?"

I looked down at my hands. "Because I'm ill-equipped for an intimate physical relationship."

"You think they dumped you because you were bad at sex?" she whisper-yelled.

"That's an oversimplification, but yes. It's not that I'm uneducated in the act itself. I understand how it works. But forging a proper intimate physical relationship is beyond my capabilities."

"Juney, that's not true. You don't think like other people, but that doesn't mean you can't have an intimate relationship with someone."

"What if it does?"

Her back straightened and I recognized her expression—her Deputy Tucker face. Equal parts authoritative and stubborn. "It doesn't. It just means you need to find someone who understands the way you work."

Tears stung my eyes. I almost never cried, but this hurt deep enough to elicit a response from my tear ducts. "I don't know if that's possible."

"Okay, let's back up. Tell me what happened with George."

"We'd had a nice evening together. And when the time came, I gave him no reason to believe I didn't want to be with him. I'd resigned myself to it, because our relationship had naturally progressed to a point where intercourse seemed appropriate. Or it would have if I was normal."

"Stop with the *not normal* shit, Juney."

I ignored her comment and kept talking. "It was physically enjoyable at first. But I was anxious. As he got closer to his climax, all I could think was that this was going to be the end."

"You really have that lodged deep in your brain, don't you?" Cassidy asked. "The idea that once you sleep with a guy, they're going to leave you."

"Past experience is the best predictor of future behavior," I said.

"Yeah, if you kept dating jackasses. But you didn't."

"No. I didn't date anyone."

"Because you didn't want to get hurt?"

I thought about that. Was that why I'd withdrawn? I'd never craved human companionship in the way most people seemed to. My sister had insisted I learn to socialize with others

164

and she'd always put a lot of effort into keeping me an active member of society. But my natural tendency had never been to seek out relationships with members of the opposite sex.

Until George.

"Yes, but that's another oversimplification. It wasn't just a desire to avoid emotional pain. I learned from my dating experiences that I'm not like other women. I don't have whatever it is that makes them want to connect with a mate and bond with them. I don't know how to form a pair-bond, Cassidy."

"I'm reading between the lines a little bit here, so correct me if I'm wrong," Cassidy said. "But after you slept with George, did you assume he'd break up with you, so you walked out on him first?"

"In a manner of speaking."

"June, you are the most straightforward, no-bullshit person I know. Don't give me that *in a manner of speaking* crap. Did you leave because you thought you needed to break up with him before he could break up with you, or not?"

"Yes. That's what I did."

The tears came now, as if I had no control over my emotions. Cassidy wrapped her arms around me and pulled me close. I allowed it. In fact, I welcomed it. The solace of my sister's arms as I cried was extremely comforting.

"You can fix this, you know," Cassidy said when I'd stopped sobbing.

"No, I can't."

She pulled away and pushed my now-messy hair back from my face. "Of course you can. Just go talk to him."

"I can't fix what I am, Cassidy. He's passionate and full of emotion. He needs someone who can nurture that. Not a June Bot."

"You stop that right now," she said. "You're not a robot, and fuck Misty Lynn forever for calling you that. Fuck anyone who's ever said it."

"They're right," I said. "You just don't see it because you're my sister."

"No, I see that she's wrong because I'm your sister. Because I know you. You're not emotionless. You just don't know how to process what you're feeling. Hell, most people don't know how to process what they're feeling, they're just not as logical about it as you are."

"Regardless, the root of the problem isn't fixable." The tears started to build again. "I don't know how to be what he needs. And he deserves better than that."

Cassidy sighed. "I'm telling you, right here, right now, that you're wrong. But if you don't believe me, at least consider this. Maybe he should get to make that call. Why do you get to decide what he deserves? You wouldn't want someone making that decision for you."

I leaned back against the couch. I was essentially pouting at this point, which was very unlike me. But it was easier if I shut George out and hid behind my shortcomings. A lot easier than facing them. But Cassidy had always made me face my shortcomings head-on.

"Maybe."

"Well that's something. I'll take it for now." She patted my knee and turned toward the kitchen. "Hey Mama, we have ourselves a situation out here. One that's going to require some special treatment."

"What does that mean?" I asked.

"It means we're getting you drunk tonight, Juney. That's what."

Chapter Twenty-Three
George

My phone buzzing on my nightstand woke me with a start. I sucked in a quick breath and grabbed it. It was Gibson. Why in the hell was Gibson Bodine texting me in the middle of the night? It was one in the damn morning.

Gibson: you might want to come down to the Lookout
Me: what's going on?
Gibson: kinda have to see this for yourself

He sent me a photo. The light was dim, and I was still trying to wake up. It was hard to tell what I was looking at. I squinted at the screen.

Wait. Was that June?

Me: Be right there.

I threw on some sweats and a t-shirt, stepped into my shoes, and didn't bother grabbing a coat. I regretted that half-awake decision the second I stepped outside into the cold night. Despite the fact that it was early spring, it was still freezing. But I wasn't going to pause to take care of my bodily needs. I was a big guy. Muscle would keep me warm.

Noise spilled out into the parking lot at the Lookout. Music and voices carried, even with the door shut. I went inside, and sure enough, there she was, just like the picture Gibson had sent.

June stood on a table in the middle of the bar, drunk as a fish in a barrel of whiskey. She teetered to one side, then the other, like she might fall right over. But she took a breath, held out her arms, and stayed standing—to a chorus of cheers and clapping from the crowd gathered around her.

What in the hell was she doing?

Her voice rose above the din. "All right, y'all, ready for the next one?"

More cheers. Fists, beer bottles, and mason jars raised in the air.

"Okay." She held out her hands, motioning for quiet, although she already had the rapt attention of everyone in here. "Simon says—"

The crowd collectively gasped.

"Rub your stomach in a circle and pat your head."

Everyone standing around her table attempted to do what she'd said. Most appeared too drunk to manage it. A pair of old ladies burst into laughter as they stumbled into a man with a barrel chest wearing a Bootleg Cock Spurs t-shirt. A girl about June's age laughed so hard she had to sit down. An older lady I remembered as being called Granny Louisa was the steadiest on her feet, and she giggled as she rubbed her stomach and patted her head.

Front and center, leaning into each other like they might fall otherwise, were Cassidy and Nadine Tucker.

I knew who I had to thank for tonight's shenanigans. I glanced around for Sheriff Tucker or Bowie Bodine, but I didn't see either of them. Maybe the girls had given them the slip tonight.

June clapped to get everyone's attention. "Simon says stop. Y'all are terrible at that. Okay, listen up. Jump on one leg."

A guy with a trucker hat on backwards was the only one to jump. Everyone else pointed and yelled for him to be out. He slunk off to a table and sat down with a few other dejected players.

"Simon says..." She paused for dramatic effect. "Touch your knees."

Everyone did what she said. Her speech wasn't slurring much but I could tell by the glassy look in her eyes and the way she swayed that she was three sheets to the wind. That, and the fact that I doubted sober-June would be standing on a table in a bar leading *Simon Says*.

"Simon says stop. Simon says turn in a circle."

That one proved to be the undoing of several tipsy players, including Cassidy Tucker. Turned out Bowie *was* here. He appeared out of nowhere to grab a wildly spinning Cassidy and guide her out of the way before she could collide with anyone.

I spotted Gibson by the bar. Gave him a chin tip in thanks. He returned it.

"Simon says stop," June said through a fit of laughter. Her eyes met mine and her smile disappeared. "Hey everybody, look who's here. It's GT Thompson."

Her use of my initials hit me hard. Drunk or not, she was sending me a message. Trying to shut me out.

Too bad for her, I wasn't having it.

I marched over to her table, through a crowd of people trying to say hi. Ignoring the greetings and pats on the back— at least she hadn't said *Simon says attack George*—I put my hands on my hips.

"Hey, you."

She mimicked my stance, resting her hands on her hips. "Hey, yourself."

"What are you doing up there?"

"We're playing a game," she said. "And you're interrupting."

The crowd of tipsy Bootleggers started to turn on me. I

heard a few boos. I needed to tread carefully. They might have been playing a kids' game, but I knew how quickly this town could start a brawl. I didn't want to be at the center of one.

"All right, then, carry on."

She scrunched up her nose and glared at me. "I will. Simon says reach for the sky."

I raised my hands in the air along with everyone else.

"Simon says put them down. Run to the bar and back."

No one took the bait.

"Simon says…" She leaned to the side. I reached out to catch her, but she kept her feet. "Simon says you all win. Go take a shot."

Cheers rose up behind me and someone put their hand on my arm. I looked down to see Nadine Tucker give me a quick smile before ducking behind me.

"Good boy," she said.

June was still standing, her eyelids heavy.

"Come on down from there before you fall."

She waved me off. "I've got it."

"You don't got it."

For a second, I debated taking the time to coax her down and help her walk out of here on her own two feet. The last thing I wanted after the other night was any notion that I'd force her to do *anything*. But I could tell by the way she swayed that she was on the downhill side of drunk, liable to puke or pass out—or both—any minute. I wanted to get her somewhere safe now, not wait until her drunk ass decided to cooperate with me.

I grabbed her by the waist and tossed her over my shoulder. "Let's go, June Bug."

"Wait, no! We're playing a game! They're having fun playing a game with me!"

"Game's over, honey," I said. "Time to go home."

"I don't want to go home." She beat on my back a few times, her blows only one step shy of useless.

"I know, but you're drunk and I don't want you hurting yourself."

"You're drunk."

"Sure, June Bug, whatever you say."

I hauled her outside to my car. If she was going to puke, there wasn't much I could do about it. My rental was closer than her place, so I went straight there. I'd deal with the ramifications later. For now, I just wanted to get her settled for the night.

She didn't puke in the car, but I could tell it was coming as soon as I parked. I got her out before whatever she'd been drinking started to come up.

"That's it, honey, let it out."

I held her hair back as she doubled over. It was freezing cold, and I was dressed in nothing but a t-shirt and sweats. I shivered while I tried to keep June from tossing up a night's worth of heavy drinking into her hair.

She stopped and straightened.

"You think you're done?"

She smoothed down her shirt in what looked like a drunken attempt to regain her dignity. "Yes, I believe so."

Wrong. She doubled over again. I shivered in the night air. My teeth started chattering.

Finally, she seemed to be done. I led her inside, figuring I'd hose down the path to the front door tomorrow.

June looked worse in the light of my cabin. Her hair was matted, bits of it stuck to the sheen of sweat on her forehead. And she had a big, reddish stain across the front of her shirt. I hadn't noticed it in the dim light of the bar. She looked like someone had thrown a drink on her.

"What happened?" I asked, pointing to her shirt.

She tugged on the hem and looked down. "Oh, this? Cassidy drinked a spill on me."

"Cassidy spilled a drink on you?"

"That's what I said."

I looked her up and down. She was a mess. Sticky and dirty. I couldn't put her to bed like that.

"Come on, June Bug, you need a shower. Then bedtime."

171

"Where are we?" she asked as I led her to the bathroom.

"My place. That okay?"

She stumbled and I kept my hands on her waist to steady her. "No."

"No? June, it's the middle of the night and you're drunk as all get-out. Do you really want me to drive you home?"

"I'm a terrible girlfriend," she said.

"No, you're not, and we can talk about this tomorrow after you sober up."

"I never get drunk."

"You did tonight. You need a shower. Can you do that?"

I got her into the bathroom, but she just stood there.

"That depends." She narrowed her eyes and tapped her lips with her fingertip. "Which shower do I use?"

"How many do you see?"

She jabbed her finger at the air in front of her several times. "Three."

I sighed. There was no way around this. "I'm going to undress you and help you in, but only so you can get clean, okay?"

"Why are you so nice to me?"

I was running out of reasons for that real fast, so I ignored her question and took off her shirt. Beautiful as she was, there was nothing sexy about peeling sticky clothes off a drunk June. She stumbled and almost fell no less than six times.

Once I got the water running, I hoped she'd step in the shower and at least rinse off by herself. She could wash her hair properly tomorrow. But she just leaned her hand against the edge of the shower and didn't get in.

"June, honey, can you get in the shower please?"

"George, I think I consumed too much alcohol."

"Yeah, you did."

She didn't reply. I was losing her. I needed to get her cleaned off and hopefully some water in her before she passed out for the night.

"Fuck."

I stripped off my clothes, willing my stupid dick to calm down. Yes, June was naked, and yes, she looked very good that way. But this was no time for an erection. There was no version of this where I touched June tonight. Not a chance in hell.

"Get in there, honey." I stepped in the shower with her. "Turn around, let's rinse your hair."

She stood in front of me and let me run my fingers through her hair, wetting it. Rather than risk her sleeping with puke or the remnants of whatever Cassidy had spilled in her hair, I washed it for her. Her head leaned back as I massaged her scalp.

That hard-on of mine was going absolutely nowhere, which made me feel like a giant asshole.

I rinsed her off and thankfully she took the initiative to wash the rest of herself. I stood back and turned to the side to give her what privacy I could.

Goddamn, she was beautiful. Her wet hair hung down her back and water ran over her soft curves. She was on the tall side for a woman, but little next to me. Most people were. I stole quick glances at her as she washed herself off, admiring the tapering of her waist. The curve of her hips. And that ass. Damn, that ass.

She stumbled and I caught her, which reminded me how drunk she was. Even though her naked wet body was now plastered against mine.

"Why are we naked?"

I groaned. "Bedtime, June Bug. Now."

She didn't protest. Her eyes were heavy and she leaned into me. I practically had to drag her out of the shower. As quickly as I could, I toweled her off. Her hair was still wet but I had to leave it. She needed to lie down.

I got her on the bed and tugged a t-shirt on her so she wouldn't be completely undressed. I'd already decided I was sleeping on the couch, but I didn't want her waking up naked in my bed. I had no idea how much of this she'd remember in the morning.

"Lie down now. I'll get you some water."

"Okay," she said, her voice dreamy.

The t-shirt bunched up to her waist as she scooted onto the bed. I rolled my eyes and got a pair of boxers out of a drawer. Tugged those up her legs. They were too big—as was the shirt—but I needed to cover what she had between those gorgeous legs of hers. I'd be up all night just thinking about it, her pussy tormenting me from afar.

I got her some water and helped her take a long drink. Then she collapsed, her head just missing my pillow.

"Thank god," I muttered, setting the water glass on the night stand next to her. Hopefully she'd sleep the rest of the night.

"Stay." Her face was smooshed into the mattress, so I wasn't sure I'd heard her correctly.

"What?"

"Stay with me," she said. "I'm too inebriated to be alone."

"June Bug, you're just going to sleep. I'll be right out there if you need anything."

Her eyes stayed shut as she talked. "Intoxication can lead to vomiting and there's a danger of pulmonary aspiration."

Even drunk June was smart. "All right. I'll stay. But you better remember this was your idea in the morning. I don't want a hungover June yelling at me for sleeping with her."

"Do you mean that literally or as a euphemism for sexual relations?"

"I mean sleeping literally. No one is having sex in this bed tonight." God, I was tired. I went around to the other side of the bed and sank down. "Let's go to sleep now, okay? I'll be right here."

"Okay, George."

At least she was calling me George again. That seemed like progress, even though she was passing out drunk.

"Night, June Bug."

The only answer was her soft breathing as she slept.

174

Chapter Twenty-Four
June

A sharp pain stabbed me behind the eyes and my stomach felt like it had been scraped out like a pumpkin. I groaned, tucking my knees up. Why had I let Cassidy talk me into drinking so much? I never drank to excess. I knew the precise ratios of alcohol, food, and water my body required to avoid the misery of a hangover. Why had I tossed that all aside and poured blackberry moonshine down my throat last night?

To be fair, it had been fun while it lasted.

Now it was decidedly not fun. I groaned again and rubbed my eyes before taking a chance and opening them.

This wasn't my room.

I sat up and everything started spinning. My stomach roiled, protesting the sudden movement. I clutched my belly and closed my eyes.

"You all right?"

That soft low voice nearly undid me.

I took a shaky breath, my eyes still closed. George. I was in George's bedroom. He'd come to get me last night. I'd been…

had I really been standing on a table? Embarrassment washed over me. I'd made a complete spectacle of myself. And George had brought me here.

I'd walked out on him. And he'd still taken care of me.

Pulling my legs up, I rested my forehead on my knees. "Why?"

"Because you needed me."

"That's all?"

The sheets rustled and I felt the mattress shift with his weight. His large hand rested against my back, warm and comforting. "That's all."

I sniffed and risked a peek at him. He was dressed in a rumpled t-shirt and sweats, his hair disheveled. His eyelids drooped a little, like he wasn't fully awake, and one corner of his mouth hooked in a slight grin.

He was the most beautiful thing I'd ever seen.

"Men don't like me after we've had sex," I said.

"Then you were with the wrong men."

I sat up a little straighter. That hadn't ever occurred to me as a possible explanation. But I was still convinced the root of the problem was me. "That's why I left the other night. In the past, when a relationship progressed to intercourse, it ended shortly thereafter. I came to the conclusion that I'm unsuitable for that type of intimacy."

"Ah hell, June, why didn't you talk to me about this?" There was a touch of heat in his voice and I could tell he was angry. Or hurt. It was hard for me to tell the difference. "If you'd have told me how you felt, we could have figured it out. I wouldn't have…"

"You seemed to find satisfaction in our activities."

"No, I didn't. It was terrible."

My heart sank and the rawness in my stomach clawed at me. "That's what I'm trying to point out. I'm ill-equipped for this."

"June, look at me." He spun me around so I was facing him. "It wasn't terrible because you weren't good at it. It was terrible because you didn't want to be there. Because I thought we were ready to share that with each other, and it turns out that readiness was awfully one-sided. It was terrible because before I could catch my breath, you were running out the door."

"I apologize for the way I left."

"Apology accepted," he said. "But June, that was not what I wanted from you. If you weren't ready—"

"I should be ready," I said, frustration leaking into my voice. "I care about you, and I'm attracted to you. And I don't fully comprehend why, but you're attracted to me, too. I want to understand how to do this right, but I just don't. I can tell you the square root of three hundred twenty-four, but I can't manage to be truly intimate with someone. Even someone as amazing as you."

"What is the square root of three hundred twenty-four?"

"Eighteen."

"Jesus." He scrubbed his hands over his face. "June Bug, I have no idea why you being a human calculator is such a turn-on, but hell if it isn't."

That made me crack the tiniest of smiles.

He studied my face for a long moment, narrowing his eyes, as if he were thinking deeply. "Do you remember when we danced at the Lookout?"

"Yes."

"You said you didn't understand dancing."

"That's correct."

"Did you understand it by the time we were finished?"

I thought back to that night. The way his hands had felt. His body pressed against mine. The rhythm and movement as we swayed to the music. It had been arousing and enjoyable.

"Yes, I did understand dancing by the time we finished."

"Good. I'm going to do the same thing again."

"But you already explained dancing. I don't need another lesson. Unless you're interested in another style, in which case—"

He touched a finger to my lips. "No, not dancing. I'm going to show you how to develop an intimate physical relationship."

I furrowed my brow. "But we've already had sex."

"Only technically. As far as I'm concerned, it doesn't count."

"Just because I didn't achieve orgasm doesn't mean the act didn't occur."

"This is what I'm talking about, June Bug. Physical intimacy isn't just putting your dick in someone's vagina. That's all well and good, and I admit, I've had that and nothing more with a woman before. It was all right. But that's not what I want with you. Call me old fashioned, but sex means something to me."

"George, I keep trying to tell you. I don't understand that part of it."

He smiled. That slow sexy grin that made me ache. "I know you don't. That's why I'm going to show you."

"Physical intimacy?"

He nodded.

"Like you did with dancing?"

He nodded again.

I glanced around the room, my eyes darting back and forth. "Now?"

"No. With baseball."

"You played football."

He laughed softly. "I played football professionally, but I played all the sports, June Bug. Besides, I don't mean that literally. I'm going to take you around the bases, one by one."

Realization dawned on me. I was familiar with the use of baseball as an analogy for the progression of physical intimacy. "Oh, I think I understand."

He reached over and took my hand. Even now, his touch felt so good. So safe and comforting.

"We're going to take it nice and slow," he said. "I'm going old school with this. I'll court you properly, like a good Bootleg girl deserves. No moving to a new base until you're ready. We take as much time as you need."

"So, for example, first base…"

"That's kissing."

"We've already had intercourse once, but you're willing to not have sex again and just do…first-base activities?"

"That's exactly what I'm saying. If you're fine with first base, we do first base. When you're ready for the next pitch, we'll head for second."

"And second is…" I glanced down at my chest. "Above the waist."

"Right. Then, when you decide you're ready for another pitch, we try third. That's below the waist, for one or both of us. I vote both, but I'll follow your lead."

"And then?"

"Home base." He reached out and ran his thumb down my cheek. "Unlike a baseball game, there's no rush to make it home. We can stay at each base as long as you want. Hell, we can go backwards if we have to."

This made sense to me. It was orderly, with a progressive sequence of events, each building on the previous step. If I could become proficient at each base, I could move on to the next, ready to take on a new challenge. By the time we went all the way home—if he was patient enough to stick with me—maybe I'd be ready. Maybe I'd be able to connect with him.

"I think this has the potential to be successful."

He grinned. "Of course it does. You can't be the only genius around here."

But why would he do this? George Thompson was an attractive man. A former professional football player. Financially secure. Sexy. Fun to be around. He could have any woman he wanted. Why would he go to all this trouble for me?

"What are you thinking now?" he asked. "You looked excited for a second, but now you seem upset again. Or is that just the hangover?"

"The hangover is decidedly unpleasant, but no, that's not it." I took a deep breath. "There's a piece of this I don't understand."

"What's that?"

"Why would you do this? Why go to so much trouble?"

He held my gaze, his brown eyes looking deep into mine. "Because I'm in love with you."

Emotion surged through me, crashing like an ocean wave. "Love?"

"Yes, June Bug. I am crazy, stupid in love with you. And I'll do just about anything if it gets you there with me."

"Run the bases," I said.

"Run them, walk them—hell, we can crawl. As long as you're not running off in the other direction, trying to get away from me."

I looked at him in awe. This man loved me. We'd slept together. And he loved me. This piece of information was going to take some time to process. But for now, I let the happiness of it bubble to the surface as another realization dawned on me.

"George. My feelings of fondness for you have grown to a state of committed affection, punctuated by tenderness and infatuation."

He grinned and touched my cheek. "You mean you're in love with me, too?"

"Yes, I'm in love with you, too."

Chapter Twenty-Five
George

First base would have felt good, right then and there. Of course, with June dressed in nothing but one of my t-shirts and a pair of boxers, resisting the desire to steal second—or third—would have taken some superhuman willpower.

But rehabbing June's hangover was more important than my desire to get my hands—and my mouth—on her. She wouldn't let me anywhere near her until she brushed her teeth, and even then, she wasn't feeling well enough for me to kiss her properly.

So instead of asking her to throw my first pitch, I took her home for clean clothes, then bought her breakfast at Moonshine. We medicated with eggs, waffles, and coffee. By the time we were done, I think we both felt better.

I know I did.

June was a woman who challenged me at every turn. Her uniqueness put some people off, but it drew me right in. I loved her intelligence and her no-nonsense attitude. And there was a softness to her, just beneath the surface. She saw me for more than being GT Thompson, and I saw more than the June Tucker her friends and neighbors assumed her to be.

I knew she came by her fear of intimacy honestly. But she wasn't nearly as bad at human interaction as she thought. Like I'd told her father, she'd been doing just fine with me. I understood her, as much as a man can understand a woman.

I loved her. I was in this for the long game. I just needed to convince her she belonged out on the field with me.

While June went back to her home office to work—it was a Thursday, after all—I headed to my rental to get in my PT. My knee was getting stronger. Whether it was the hot springs, my physical therapy exercises, or time—probably a combination of all three—I was healing. My balance and strength were both improving, and I was regaining some of the knee mobility I'd lost.

I was drying off after a shower when my phone rang. I wrapped the towel around my waist and answered. It was Andrea.

"Hey, GT. Do you have a second?"

"Sure, what's up?" I sank down on the couch. Mellow hopped over, so I scooped her up and set her on my thigh.

"I have everything ready to file your taxes. Just a heads up on that."

"Thanks. Anything important in the mail lately?"

"Um, no, not really." She paused for a second and it sounded like she was thumbing through paperwork. "Just the usual stuff. Speaking of mail, when are you coming back to Philly?"

"Not anytime soon," I said.

"So, you're just…staying out there?"

"Yeah."

"Hmm."

This was odd. Andrea didn't usually have much to say about where I went or what I did with my time. Not unless it required travel arrangements or dinner reservations. Those were part of her job. But my staying in Bootleg didn't require her to do anything new.

"What are you hmm-ing about?" I asked.

"Oh, nothing. I'm just surprised you haven't gone home."

I petted Mellow, running my hand over her impossibly soft fur. "I like where things are going out here. And it's not like I have to get in shape for training camp."

"True. Well, I just wanted to touch base, and let you know I'm going out of town this weekend."

"Have a nice time."

"Thanks," she said. "I will."

What June had said about Andrea before poked at me. She had worked for me for a long time, but I also didn't follow-up on things very often. I just let her do her thing and assumed everything was fine. And it should have been. I'd have heard about it if Andrea was messing up somewhere, wouldn't I?

I told myself I was worrying over nothing. Andrea was good at her job. It was one thing I didn't need to be concerned about.

———

Saturday, I picked June up for a late breakfast. Afterward, we decided to walk off the meal. We wandered hand-in-hand through town, both of us quiet. Hints of spring were in the early April air, the cool breeze fresh, rather than biting.

We got all the way to Bootleg Springs High School and walked past the main building. The ball fields were in the back. June stopped in front of the chain link fence.

"My dad used to coach baseball here."

"Did he?"

She nodded. "He only retired as coach a few years ago. He still goes to all the games."

"I take it your dad got you into sports."

"Yes. At first I just wanted to know what the numbers meant. But it gave us something to do together. Something to talk about."

"Did you come to the games here?" I asked.

"All the time."

"Were you crushing on any of the players?" I nudged her gently.

I meant it as a tease, a chance for me to joke about football players being better than baseball, but her expression grew serious.

"Yes. Unfortunately."

"Uh-oh. What happened?"

She held onto the chain link fence and looked out at the field. "Senior year, I liked a boy on the team. Hank Preston. I'd never paid a lot of attention to boys before that. Cassidy and Scarlett did, but I could take them or leave them. But I went to all the games, and he started paying attention to me. I liked that. He asked me to the prom, but…"

I stroked her hair. "But what?"

"We didn't go. A few days before, we were together after practice. I went with him to his house. We had…we had sex. And then he took Tanya Varney to the prom and didn't talk to me anymore."

"Oh my god, June."

"I heard later that he told his friends he just wanted to find out if I was a robot, like people said."

Anger coursed through me, searing me from the inside. "Does he still live in town? Because I would love to pay him a visit."

She sighed. "No, and anyway, it was a long time ago."

"I hope you let your sister and Scarlett go after him."

"Oh, they did. Scarlett flattened his tires with a screwdriver and Cassidy spread a rumor that he hadn't been able to keep an erection long enough to have intercourse with me."

I ran my hand down her back. "I would have done worse. Broke his nose, for starters."

"Do you want to know what doesn't make any sense?"

"Sure."

"I really wanted to go to my prom."

"Why doesn't that make sense?"

"It was a dance," she said with a shrug. "I'd never cared about going to a dance before that one. But Mom took me into

Perrinville to get a dress and Cassidy was going to do my hair. I actually wanted to go. And even though what Hank did to me before that night was arguably worse, sitting home on prom night was when it hurt the most."

I gathered her in my arms and held her close. "I'm sorry, June Bug."

She threaded her arms around my waist and rested her head against my chest. "Did you go to prom?"

"I did." I didn't want to say prom had been great. I'd been crowned prom king, and my girlfriend at the time—a cheerleader—had been queen. High school had been like that for me—fun and easy. I'd been the football star. Everyone had loved me.

They'd loved GT, anyway. I wasn't so sure about George.

"You had a perfect prom, didn't you?" she asked.

"It was…yeah, it was pretty great."

"I bet you were prom king."

I laughed. "Can you read minds, too?"

"It doesn't take a genius to know you must have been popular in high school. You're terribly attractive, and fun, and clearly you were the star of your football team."

"I'm *terribly attractive*, am I?"

"You must be aware of your substantial physical advantages. You're tall, and your athletic prowess makes your body undeniably appealing." She nibbled her bottom lip and her speech slowed. "You have those dimples in your cheeks when you smile. And those hands."

I grinned down at her. "June Tucker, are you telling me you think I'm cute?"

"I very much enjoy looking at you, yes."

Brushing her hair back from her face, I leaned down and kissed her forehead. "I think you're beautiful. And I very much enjoy looking at you."

I wanted to lean in and kiss her, like I'd done so many times before. But there was a right way to do this. If I wanted a base hit, I needed her to throw the pitch.

So instead of leaning in to capture her lips—taking what I wanted—I paused, raising my eyebrows.

"Oh," she said. "First base?"

"It can be if you're ready."

"Yes. I'm ready. I've missed kissing you."

"Oh my sweet June," I said, touching her cheek and sliding my hand into her hair. "I have missed kissing you something fierce."

Moving in close, I let my lips brush hers. Although this wasn't our first kiss, it was *a* first. And I wanted to make it count.

I held the back of her head and slipped my other hand around her waist. Her lips were parted, open for me, her chin tipped up. I captured her mouth with mine, delving in with my tongue.

Our lips pressed together, tongues tangling. She tilted her head to the side and I slanted my mouth over hers. For a single heartbeat, she seemed hesitant, like she might pull away. But her body relaxed and the way she melted into me felt like huge win.

I held her head in my hand, my fingers tangled in her hair, and kissed the hell out of her.

Deep and slow, I savored that kiss. Savored the minty taste of her. The way she slid her hands along my shoulders and around my neck. I pressed her body closer and held her tight, heedless of who might see.

The breeze was no match for the heat between us. Her tongue was velvety soft, her lips warm and full. I kissed her until I wasn't sure where I ended and she began.

It was, hands down, the best kiss I'd ever given. Or received.

We pulled back and her eyelids were heavy.

"Kissing you makes me feel like magic exists," she said.

I touched her face, tracing my fingers across her cheek. "Kissing you is magic."

So I kissed her again.

On the walk back to my car, I kept replaying what she'd

said about her high school prom. I really did want to break that Hank Preston piece of shit's nose. Or maybe his kneecaps.

But more than that, I thought about June missing out on things. That dance had mattered to her—it had meant something. I wondered if I could do something about that.

What would Bootleg Springs do?

And then it hit me. I knew exactly what Bootleg Springs would do. It wouldn't be easy—this would take some work. I had some people to talk to—maybe bribe—so I could make it happen. But I was determined. I was going to make this up to June in a way she'd never forget.

Chapter Twenty-Six

June

My timer went off with a loud *bing* and I tapped my phone's screen to turn it off. I'd given myself one hour to update my research into the Callie Kendall case. Time was up.

I'd found my relationship with George—as well as my other responsibilities and social encounters with my family—had taken precedence over my Callie Kendall research. I hadn't made much progress, which was frustrating.

It made me wonder how my father had balanced his career in law enforcement with the responsibilities of a family. Had there been times he'd wanted to continue his work, but he'd come home to be with us instead?

Regardless, my timer had gone off, so I saved my work and closed my laptop. Jonah glanced over at me from the kitchen. I'd been so focused, I'd forgotten he was home.

"Hungry?" he asked. "I made extra."

"As a matter of fact, yes," I said.

He dished up two plates and brought them over to the table. "Chicken and roasted broccoli."

"It smells delicious," I said. "You certainly have a talent for cooking."

"Thanks," he said. "I like doing it. This is pretty simple, but hopefully the flavors are good."

I took a bite of chicken. It was perfectly cooked—tender and juicy. "The flavor is excellent."

We ate our meal in silence for a few minutes before a thought occurred to me.

"Jonah, you're a man."

He blinked at me. "Yes, I am."

"Are you a straight man, or are you gay?"

"I'm straight," he said, drawing his eyebrows together. "Is it not obvious? Why would you ask?"

"Well, the fact that you don't seem to be interested in dating when most of the people around you are participating in long-term and committed relationships does raise the question of your sexuality."

"I guess that's fair. Yes, I'm straight. I like women. But, to be honest, I don't know if I'm sticking around. Not sure dating is the best idea right now."

"Then I can understand your hesitation to pursue a romantic relationship. Although that's not why I brought up the subject of your gender."

"Oh, okay," he said. "Why did you bring it up, then?"

"I need to know more about pleasing a man in bed. And by that, I mean sexually." If George and I were going to go all the way around the bases, it would benefit me to learn more. And who better to ask than a man?

He blinked at me again. "Um…"

"You're a male with the requisite male anatomy. And I would assume you've had sexual relationships with women."

"Well, yeah, of course."

"So what should I know about sexually satisfying a man?"

"Are you sure I'm the best person to ask? I thought women talked to each other about this stuff. Shouldn't you ask Cassidy?"

"I could. But she's female. She lacks the male perspective."

"True," he said. "Okay. Have you...had sex before?"

"Yes, of course," I said. "But those experiences were less than satisfactory."

"That's too bad." He paused, leaning back in his chair, as if he were thinking it through. "On the surface, men are pretty simple. You know how our anatomy works when it comes to sex."

"You're referring to the male erection."

"Right." He cleared his throat. "For most men, simply getting an erection isn't too difficult. Hell, we can get them when we don't want them."

"I've observed this phenomenon."

He smiled. "Yeah, I'm sure you have. An orgasm isn't that different. From a physical standpoint, as long as the guy is healthy and functioning normally, it's not difficult. But I don't think that's what makes sex really satisfying."

"You're saying good sex requires more than achieving climax."

"Absolutely. The orgasm is just the final note. The crescendo at the end. Don't get me wrong, that part is great. And some guys think that's all there is to it. But they're missing out."

"Missing out on what?"

He took a deep breath and his eyes seemed to focus on something behind me. "They're missing out on the way her skin feels. Women are soft and pliable. They feel like silk when their body slides against yours. They're missing the way her eyelids get heavy. How she moves with you, her body aligning with yours."

I swallowed, my meal forgotten as I listened.

"Good sex isn't just about the last thirty seconds," he said. "It's about the build-up. The anticipation. The touching and kissing. The need. It's about connecting with that person in the most intimate way. You're as close as two people can get, sharing an amazing experience together."

My heart beat a little faster, the way it did when I was reading an erotic scene in one of the novels I'd borrowed from the library.

"If all a guy cares about is getting off, he misses the flush in her cheeks when she's close," he continued, still looking past me. "The way that pink will creep down her neck to her chest. He misses her taste, and the way she sounds when she moans his name. He's missing the heat between her legs. The way she pulses and throbs around you."

"Wow."

Jonah blinked and cleared his throat again, his face flushing slightly. "Sorry."

"Don't apologize. That was very informative."

He chuckled, pulling the collar of his shirt away from his neck. "This is just a little awkward."

"This is helpful. Please continue."

"Look, if you really care about someone, you'll figure out the physical logistics together. Every person is a little different, and they like different things. But part of the fun of it is learning those things with each other."

"You mean, it's typical to spend time learning the specific physical preferences of my sexual partner."

"Yeah and tell him yours. Communicate with him. Most guys love feedback."

I tilted my head. "Do you mean during the act of intercourse?"

"Sure. Tell him what feels good. He'll love hearing you tell him what you like. And he'll do more of it, which is good for both of you."

"Should I expect him to reciprocate with this kind of communication?"

"I think so." He shifted in his chair. "Here's the thing, Juney. If you're worried you don't know what to do, feel for how he responds. If he's moaning or telling you it's good or…" He cleared his throat again. "If he's thrusting his hips harder, that kind of thing? Keep doing it."

"The logic of that makes sense to me."

"But don't only concern yourself with making *him* feel good," he said. "Sex is something you're doing, and experiencing,

191

together. If you're too focused on pleasing him, you won't enjoy it. And if he's any kind of man at all, your pleasure will be a priority to him."

I thought back to my physical encounters with George. That definitely held true. "So you're saying good sex doesn't require a specific set of skills. It requires both a desire to please the other person, and to participate fully in the act so you experience pleasure as well."

"You have a way with making that sound very un-sexy, but yes, that's basically it," he said with a smile.

I nodded slowly, letting Jonah's information sink in. "Thank you, Jonah. This was an informative discussion."

"Sure, Juney. Just…maybe ask your sister if you have more sex questions?"

I went back to my dinner, still processing what Jonah had said. It did make sense. And it dovetailed with what I already knew about intimacy and sexual relationships. Even the fictional relationships I'd read in books showcased many of the characteristics he'd mentioned.

I still wasn't sure if I was capable of that kind of intimacy. But now, more than ever, I wanted to try. Not just for George, but for myself as well.

Chapter Twenty-Seven
George

June Tucker was nothing if not single-minded. Whether it was dealing with a challenge at work or negotiating a deal for one of her Bootleg Springs business partners, she zeroed in on her objective and would not be swayed.

The same could have been said for her determination to find out the truth about Callie Kendall. She was convinced Callie's story about living with a cult in a compound outside of Hollis Corner was a lie. And she was hellbent on proving it.

We'd looked at the possibilities from different angles. Was there another town with the same name? Had Callie been mistaken about where she'd been? From what we could tell, that didn't seem to be the case. And the search for answers started to occupy more and more of that big brain of hers.

I understood. Callie Kendall's disappearance had rocked her small community to its core. The satisfaction of the mystery ending had been tainted for June. It was an equation that didn't add up, and she couldn't let it go.

Which was why I found myself driving five hours out of

Bootleg Springs on a Sunday, so June could see Hollis Corner for herself.

Following my GPS, I turned off the main highway and headed east. We drove for miles through nothing. Some farmland. Open fields. Empty space. An occasional homestead.

"I have to be honest, June Bug," I said after yet another mile passed without seeing any sign of human habitation. "Callie's cult might have been way out here. It's isolated enough for a group that wanted to stay secret."

"We'll see."

"What exactly are we looking for?"

"I want to see if there's really a compound where Callie could have been living for the last twelve years. She said they moved, but the buildings must still be there."

"And that's going to tell you what?"

She shrugged. "I'll know when we investigate."

We got to Hollis Corner and drove around. It didn't take long. There were houses, some in better repair than others. A bank, and a general store. A few other shops and a handful of restaurants.

June pointed out the window, a satisfied smile on her face. "There."

On a corner, next to a dilapidated bowling alley, was a bar. Not just any bar. A biker bar.

Dozens of motorcycles were parked out front in rows. Glancing around, I saw bikes parked at other businesses, too. Some cars as well, but this was definitely biker territory. No question.

"Looks like you were right about the Free Renegades," I said.

"Of course I was."

"Where to now?"

"Let's circle around outside town to see what we find."

"Will do," I said.

About ten minutes outside town we came upon a turn. June and I shared a look—I think we both had a feeling—and I followed the side road. It led past what looked like an

194

abandoned farmstead to a gated gravel driveway. Up ahead, we could see a tall fence and the hints of a rooftop behind it.

"Do you think this is it?" I asked.

June narrowed her eyes. "Maybe. We need to take a closer look."

We got out and I helped her climb over the rusty gate. It was secured by a chain and padlock that looked newer than the gate itself. But that didn't tell us much of anything.

A fence surrounded the perimeter of the property. The gravel drive ended at a double-wide gate, but it was locked up with a padlock and chain, just like the gate at the entrance. June walked around, taking pictures with her phone.

"It's impossible to tell if anyone has been here recently," she said. "Those might be tire tracks, but there's been too much precipitation. Are you tall enough to see over the fence?"

I jumped, grabbing the top edge of the fence, and pulled myself up. "Looks deserted."

"No people?"

I lowered myself down, then brushed my hands together. "Not that I could see. Seems empty."

She put her hands on her hips and looked up at the fence. "I need to get in."

"What?"

"Lift me up so I can climb over," she said. "I need to get in and look around."

"Has it occurred to you that this is private property? Those locks make it pretty clear whoever owns this place isn't interested in people wandering around."

"The likelihood of us getting caught is extremely low," she said. "There's no outward sign of habitation."

I didn't particularly like this, but she had a point. We hadn't seen a soul for miles, and it was dead quiet out here.

"Okay." I crouched so she could climb on my shoulders. "Just be careful."

I stood, getting her close enough to the fence so she could scramble up and over. I heard her feet drop on the other side.

"You okay?"

"I'm fine. Are you coming?"

I did another pull up on the fence, then hoisted a leg over. Careful of my knee, I popped over the top and dropped down to the ground.

June brushed her hands together. "Ready?"

"Lead the way, Scooby-June."

Inside the fence were a series of worn buildings with saggy porches and peeling paint. It certainly looked like the sort of place a cult might live. There were multiple buildings in various sizes. Some could have been living quarters, and others larger communal areas. Raised garden beds and empty chicken coops were on the far side.

We wandered around, but didn't see any signs of recent habitation. One of the buildings was unlocked, so we ventured inside, but it was empty. Bare wood floors, no curtains or blinds on the windows. Nothing hanging from the walls or left behind in a cupboard or closet.

If Callie's cult had been living here, they'd cleared out every last scrap they owned.

"What do you think?" I asked.

"It doesn't look like anyone's lived here for years," she said. "But the yard and garden beds aren't overgrown, either."

"I noticed that, too. Still, doesn't tell us much."

June stood in the center of the courtyard, hands on her hips, and looked around. "Callie said she hid during the chaos of them leaving. If they were that desperate to get out quickly, do you think they would have left it this empty? Wouldn't they have left something behind?"

"You'd think so. But maybe they didn't own much. If they didn't have much to take, maybe they didn't miss anything."

"They missed an entire person, according to her."

I nodded. June was right, this place didn't look like a cult had left it only two months before. But that didn't *prove* anything.

"We need more information," June said, heading for the fence.

"How do you propose we do that?"

"Go back to town, of course."

I crouched so she could get on my shoulders. I didn't like where this was going. "And what are we going to do in town?"

"Talk to the bikers."

Ah, hell.

————

Not a shred of fear showed on June's face as we walked in the biker bar. It was dimly lit by a few exposed light bulbs on the ceiling and the glow of neon signs. A big screen TV showed a baseball game in the back. The walls were covered in old posters, bumper stickers, and vintage license plates. One had a huge painted mural of the Free Renegades logo.

Seated along the bar and at some of the tables were some of the scariest motherfuckers I'd ever seen. Thick beards, thicker bodies, grizzled scowls. Most wore leather—the women and the men—and every one of them looked up with suspicion on their faces when we walked in the door.

"You need something, sweetheart?" the bartender asked, his voice low and raspy. He had a long gray beard and a patch over one eye.

I went to grab June's elbow and get her the hell out of here, but she was already walking toward the bar.

"June," I hissed.

She marched over, head held high. "Good evening. Yes, I'm looking for some information."

Oh god. All eyes were on her and most of them looked like they were gauging her height and weight so they could decide where to stash her body. I rushed to get behind her.

The bartender raised an eyebrow—the one over his good eye—but didn't answer.

"I'm trying to find out—"

"What do we have here?" A guy with a leather vest and full sleeve tattoos on both arms—some looked homemade—turned on his stool. "A little girl asking questions?"

"Yes, and if you'll let me finish, I can explain—"

"We don't like questions," the bartender growled.

"And we don't like little girls," the guy on the stool said.

The attention of the entire bar was on June. The men playing pool abandoned their games, and drinks sat untouched on tables. All eyes on her. Men cracked knuckles and women gave each other knowing looks. She stuck out worse than a sore thumb. Blond ponytail, blouse and cardigan. She also seemed to be the only person in the room who didn't realize how much danger she was in.

"I realize my appearance compared to that of many people in this establishment might suggest youthfulness, but I'm twenty-nine, which does not fit the standard definition of *little girl*."

I grabbed her arm to steer her out of here.

"George, I have a few simple questions for them that have nothing to do with any alleged criminal activity."

"What did you say?" the guy on the stool asked.

"I'm not here to ask about your alleged criminal activities. I have questions about—"

"Let's go," I said, pulling her arm.

"Hey, is that GT Thompson?" a voice called from deeper in the bar.

I froze. *Please let them be fans.*

"Holy shit, it is."

"GT Thompson?"

"Didn't he retire?"

"Best receiver in the league."

"Damn straight he's the best."

I let out a breath, but kept my hand on June's arm. The mood of the room shifted so suddenly it made my heart race. The scowls turned to interest, and a few guys even smiled at me.

"Well holy shit," the bartender said, his demeanor suddenly friendly. "GT Thompson. What are you doing way out here?"

"Y'all Philly fans?"

"Hell yes," the bartender said, and there were nods of agreement all around.

Oh thank god. "Awesome. Sorry I couldn't make it another season."

"You had a great run," the bartender said. "Tell you what, drinks are on the house. What can I get you and your lady friend?"

As much as I didn't want to stay and have a drink in a bar full of bikers that had looked like they might murder my girlfriend thirty seconds ago, I didn't think I had much choice.

"A beer would be great," I said. "Appreciate it."

A guy in a black shirt with the sleeves torn off moved, offering his stool. I motioned for June to sit and the bartender slid two frothy beers across the bar.

"How 'bout an autograph?" the bartender asked.

"Absolutely."

"Be right back."

"George, I need to ask about the compound," June said.

"Shh. I know."

"But we're not here for you to give autographs."

"June," I said, softly into her ear. "They were about five seconds from murdering you and dumping your body out back."

"I admit, most appear rough around the edges, but—"

"Trust me, June Bug."

She took a deep breath and mercifully stayed quiet.

The bartender came back with one of my jerseys. He passed it across along with a Sharpie.

I made sure the bar was dry, then laid the jersey out so I could sign the front. My heart was still pounding from the rush of adrenaline and I could feel the eyes of everyone in here, boring into me.

"There you go." I gave the jersey back to the bartender. "Thanks for your support."

The bartender gave me a nod. "Now what was it that brought you two in here?"

I put an arm around June's shoulders, showing them she was mine. "My girlfriend wants to know about a piece of property about ten minutes northeast of town. There's an old gate and the whole thing is fenced in."

"What about it?"

"Anyone lived there recently?"

The bartender shook his head. "No. It's been empty for years."

June almost shot off her stool, but I held her down.

"Huh, okay. So there wasn't a group living out there? A religious group?"

He looked at me like that was a stupid question. "Religious group?"

"A cult," June said.

There was some grumbling from the patrons closest to us.

"You talking about that Kendall girl on the news?" the bartender asked. "Nope. No cults around here."

"Because you wouldn't allow that in your territory, would you?" June asked.

I was realizing very quickly that the guy behind the bar wasn't the bartender. Or if he was, that was not all he was. I'd grown up playing sports. I knew the way players looked at their coach. And every guy in this bar, old or young, was looking to him.

He was no bartender. He was the gang leader.

"Smart girl," he said.

I decided we should cut out while they were still acting friendly. They couldn't be happy about the police out here investigating Callie's story, and I didn't want him to think we were a part of that. "Thanks. We appreciate the information."

"Thanks for the autograph," he said.

Transaction complete.

I pulled June off the stool and guided her, somewhat forcibly, toward the door. She started to say something but I hushed her. "They're letting us leave. We need to go."

We got outside and into my car and I blew out a long breath.

"Most of those men were carrying guns," June said, her tone matter-of-fact.

"Yes. Yes, they were. That didn't bother you at all?"

"They're members of a criminal biker gang. I expected they'd have weapons."

"And you didn't think about whether or not they'd turn those weapons on you?" I asked.

"Of course I thought about it," she said. "I weighed the risks and deemed our chances of success high enough to make the attempt."

"You're a little bit badass, June Tucker."

The corner of her mouth turned up in a smile. "Good thing they were fans."

I shook my head. "No shit."

"You know what this means?" June asked, her voice tinged with excitement. Her eyes were big and bright. "Callie Kendall's story is a lie."

Chapter Twenty-Eight
June

After the trip to Hollis Corner, I was left with as many questions as answers. It was clear Callie's cult—if there had been a cult at all—hadn't been where she'd said it was. But what that meant in the grand scheme of things was still a mystery.

George reminded me that the simplest explanation was that she'd gotten the town's name wrong. Maybe she'd believed she was somewhere else, and we'd been looking in the wrong town.

However, I argued that she'd been found on the highway just outside Hollis Corner. He had to concede my point.

So if she hadn't been living in a compound outside Hollis Corner, where had she been? And why had she lied? Was she covering for the cult she'd left? Did the cult exist at all?

The questions tormented me. I ran through the options again and again, jotting down notes in a spiral notebook. The clues. The little bit of evidence I had.

The Kendalls had been silent in the media since their one public statement. There were a few straggling stories about

Callie, mostly on conspiracy blogs, but for the most part, the attention had died down. The reporters and bloggers were busy chasing the next sensation.

My dad seemed to have decided he didn't wish to talk about Callie's case. I'd made attempts at engaging him in conversation, but he always changed the subject. Cassidy was similarly tight-lipped, with me at least.

That didn't leave me much to work with.

I sat at my desk with my laptop, going through the fourteen—and counting—browser tabs I had open. Most of what I could find was information I'd been through before. Until I got to tab number eleven.

It was yet another story about Callie's miraculous reappearance, but this one had a photo of her on a sidewalk. I saved the photo and opened it in another program so I could zoom in and study the details.

As I scrolled across the enlarged photo, Callie herself came into view, taking up most of the screen. I moved the photo to see her face. She didn't appear to be aware she was being photographed. I zoomed out again so I could see her from head to toe. Nothing out of the ordinary. It looked like she'd come outside to check the mail or perform some other menial task.

And then I realized something. Her sleeves were rolled up.

Callie had always worn long sleeves. As teens, we hadn't thought much about that. I hadn't, at least, although I'd never paid attention to what other people wore in general. But after discovering Callie's sweater, it had been mentioned that she'd always worn long sleeves, even in the summer.

Cassidy had discovered why. Mrs. Kendall had given her photos of Callie's arms. According to her mother, she'd been cutting—harming herself. She'd worn long sleeves to hide the wounds and scars. But that information had never made it into the media.

I zoomed in on the photo, centering on her arms. It was hard to be certain, but I didn't think I could see any scars.

Tempting as it was to slam my laptop closed and dash out

the door with my newfound revelation, I wanted to be thorough. I spent another several hours doing further research. Solidifying my position. Double- and triple-checking. Following the trail of possibilities and looking for additional confirmation.

When I finished, I closed my laptop and scooped it under my arm. Jonah was in the kitchen and he said something—probably *where are you going*—but I was already out the door.

It wasn't until I pulled up outside the sheriff's office that I realized I'd forgotten shoes. I decided this was no time to worry about proper footwear. I grabbed my laptop from the passenger seat and went inside.

Bex gave me a friendly smile. "Well, hey there June. What can I do you for?"

"I need to see Cassidy." My sister's voice ran through my head, reminding me to have manners. "Please."

"Sure thing." She disappeared for a moment and returned with Cassidy.

"Juney, is something wrong?" Cassidy asked.

"Yes," I said. Her eyes widened and I realized my error. "No, nothing is wrong with any of our family members or friends. This is an emergency, but a different kind."

"Let's go in the conference room. And why aren't you wearing shoes?"

"I forgot."

She led me in and closed the door behind us. I wasted no time opening my laptop.

"Should I get Dad?" she asked.

"Not yet." My screen came to life and I turned it so she could see. "This isn't Callie Kendall."

"Wait. You're going to have to back way up, because I have absolutely no clue what you're talking about."

I took a deep breath. "This woman claims she's Callie Kendall. I think she's lying."

"And why do you think that?"

"She told the police she spent the last twelve years since her disappearance living with a cult outside Hollis Corner."

"Right."

"There is a compound outside Hollis Corner, but it's been unoccupied for years," I said.

"How do you know?"

"I investigated."

Cassidy crossed her arms. "And how did you do that?"

"We found the location and climbed the—"

"Stop." She held up a hand. "I think it's better if I don't know the details. Juney, what were you thinking?"

"That's fine, the compound didn't reveal any solid evidence. It was empty, but that didn't tell us enough."

"All right, so…" She made a circular motion with her hand, gesturing for me to continue.

"Hollis Corner is under the control of the Free Renegades. They confirmed there was no religious cult living in their territory."

"I don't even want to know how you confirmed that with a biker gang."

I waved my hand. "It was fine. George was there. So I already knew her story about the cult was a fabrication."

"But—" She tilted her head, staring at my computer screen, as if something had caught her attention. "Wait a second."

"Do you see it too?"

"Are her sleeves rolled up? Can you zoom in?"

I enlarged the photo, centering it on her arms. Cassidy stared for a long moment, shaking her head. "No scars."

"Precisely."

"I'll be right back," Cassidy said. "Stay here."

She was gone for a few minutes. I waited, my brain buzzing. She came back with a plain manila envelope and shut the door behind her again.

"These are Callie." She pulled a set of photos out of the envelope and set them on the table next to my laptop.

A wave of discomfort rolled through me. They were difficult to view. She'd told me about these photos, but I hadn't seen them for myself. Bloody cuts ran across Callie's forearms, deep slices that seeped thick, red blood.

"These injuries would scar," Cassidy said. "You can actually see scars from previous wounds beneath the fresh ones."

I pointed to the photo on my laptop. "Then I'm right. This can't be the same person."

Cassidy took a deep breath, like she was considering the evidence. That was like her. She didn't jump to conclusions. "Based on this, I'd say there's reason to question Callie's identity."

"Then you need to reopen the investigation."

"It's not that simple. She's not a missing person anymore. Her father positively identified her."

"I took that into account," I said, navigating to a different tab. "This kind of thing has happened before. Three years ago, a young man was arrested for impersonating a missing boy from Kansas. The child had disappeared at the age of thirteen. Two years later, he supposedly turned up in Europe. He claimed to have been kidnapped and sold into sex trafficking. He came back to the States and lived with the family for three months before his real identity was discovered. He'd researched the details of the boy's case and obtained enough information to convince them, at least temporarily."

"Are you serious?" Cassidy asked, squinting at my screen. "It took them three months to realize he wasn't their son?"

"He didn't even have the same hair or eye color, and the family still believed him."

"I suppose they wanted it to be him pretty badly," she said.

"Maybe the Kendalls want this woman to be Callie. Maybe they're willing to overlook the facts so their reality aligns with their fantasy of having their daughter back."

"It's possible," she said. "But why would someone impersonate Callie Kendall?"

"Many reasons. Perhaps greed. Judge and Mrs. Kendall are people of considerable means. Or attention. It's hard to say. The man who impersonated the missing boy in Kansas had done it multiple times. He'd even served jail time in France for a similar offense."

"I've come across a lot of strange criminal activity, but this is something else," she said. "But…how can this woman look enough like her that she's fooled the Kendalls?"

"I researched that aspect as well," I said, clicking to yet another tab. "This website is called *Find My Twin*. There's a theory that among the seven billion people on the planet, there are always duplicate faces, even without shared genetics."

I scrolled through some of the matches on the homepage. There were dozens of them—people who appeared identical, but weren't related to each other.

"Wow, that's…eerie," she said. "I wonder if there's someone else out there with my face."

"One can only hope," I said.

She raised her eyebrows. "Why would one hope?"

"Two reasons. One, I'm fascinated by the fact that such enormous genetic diversity among our species can randomly produce these results. And two, you're very pretty, so another woman would be fortunate to look like you."

"Aw, thanks, Juney."

I clicked back to the photo of not-Callie. "What do we need to do?"

"I'll tell Dad," she said. "But I can't promise this will reopen the investigation. Not if the Kendalls believe she's Callie. One grainy internet photo isn't proof that she's not who she says she is."

"Okay." I stood and closed my laptop. "Thank you for confirming my suspicions."

"Juney, leave this to the authorities."

I nodded. I didn't like lying to my sister, so I decided not to do so verbally.

"And no more talking to people in biker gangs. Unless it's the Dirt Hogs." Bootleg's own biker gang was a group of octogenarians who wore leather jackets and sat on their motorcycles outside the Still on Tuesday nights while their wives played bingo over at the Lookout.

"Thank you, Cassidy. I'll see you at dinner tomorrow evening."

"Bye, Juney."

I left, my mind still buzzing with questions and possibilities. I didn't have the answers. But I knew I was right about one thing. That woman was *not* Callie Kendall.

And I was going to prove it.

Chapter Twenty-Nine
George

Nadine Tucker's famous chicken and dumplings smelled like heaven. I sat in the living room of June's childhood home, beer in hand, with her dad and Bowie Bodine. The TV was on, the sound turned low. June and her sister chatted with their mom in the kitchen while dinner simmered on the stove.

June's parents had invited us over for Sunday dinner. Their house was cozy, with photos of June and Cassidy as kids on the walls. An old wedding photo showed a much younger Harlan and Nadine Tucker. June looked like her dad.

I took a drink of my beer and glanced around, suddenly having an odd flashback to earlier this year. Sitting in a club with music bumping through the walls, an overpriced drink on the table. People showing off their designer labels. Expensive shoes. What a show that had been. A shit-show. Groupies and hangers-on, people who only wanted a piece of your fame.

This was a world apart, and I loved every bit of it. Reminded me of where I'd come from, and where I wanted to be.

"All right, boys," Nadine said, peeking her head into the living room. "Dinner's ready."

We gathered around the table Bowie and I had helped set. Harlan and Nadine at each end, Cassidy and Bowie on one side, June and I on the other.

"Well, isn't this nice," Nadine said, smiling at her daughters.

"Dinner looks delicious," Harlan said as he ladled the thick chicken stew into his bowl.

Bowie looked like there couldn't possibly be a happier man anywhere on earth. He smiled at Cassidy, giving her a quick kiss on her temple.

We all dished up, and the food tasted even better than it smelled.

"Mrs. Tucker—" I said, but she stopped me before I could compliment the meal.

"Call me Nadine. And do you prefer GT, or George?"

I thought about that for a second. "You know, I'll answer to either. I've been GT since I was in middle school or thereabouts. By high school, even my parents called me by my initials. But I like my name. It's old fashioned, but I guess that's why I've always liked it."

"Were you named for someone?" Nadine asked.

"My grandfather," I said. "I guess he was the original George Thompson."

"You live in Philadelphia, is that right?" Nadine asked. "Is that where you're from?"

"I do have a house there, but no," I said. "I grew up in Charlotte. My folks still live there. I was in Philly because of football."

"Shame about that knee," Harlan said.

I nodded. "I only had a season or two left, at most. In football years, I'm old."

"So your parents still live in Charlotte, you say?" Nadine asked.

"Dear, give the man a break," Harlan said. "We don't need his life story."

"Of course we do," Nadine said, as if Harlan had just suggested something outrageous.

"It's fine," I said. "I don't mind. Yes, my parents, James and Darlene Thompson, still live in Charlotte. I also have a sister, Shelby. My parents adopted her when I was five. She was almost a year old. Shelby's the one who told me about Bootleg Springs, actually. She was out here for a while, but had to go home to Pittsburgh."

"Hmm, interesting," Cassidy said.

"George began playing football at the age of five," June said. "He was a starting receiver for his high school varsity team all four years. He played for University of Alabama, and was drafted by San Francisco. After two years with San Francisco, he was traded to Seattle. Then he accepted a contract with Philadelphia where he played for the duration of his career."

"Thanks for the recap," Bowie said, and winked at me.

"She's right," I said. "That about covers it."

"And what are you going to do now that you're no longer playing football?" Nadine asked.

"That's an excellent question." I put my spoon down. "I'm fortunate I have the ability to take some time to figure that out."

"He means he has the financial security to support himself without additional income," June said.

"That is fortunate," Nadine said with a smile.

The conversation turned to other topics while we finished our dinner. June didn't bring up Callie Kendall, which surprised me. It had been all she could talk about after we'd been to Hollis Corner.

After dinner, and the best pecan pie I'd ever had, we said goodnight. June's parents thanked me for coming. I shook her father's hand and kissed her mom on the cheek. Then they stood on the porch, their arms around each other, and waved as we all left.

It was so damn wholesome, I wished my parents had been here to see it. My mother would have fainted with joy to see me dating a girl from a family like the Tuckers.

I held June's hand on the short drive to her house. It fit so nicely in mine. She looked delicious in her collared blouse and brown pants. So very June. I glanced at her from the corner of my eye, and got an idea.

Instead of turning onto her street, I kept going and took another road out of town.

"Where are we going?" she asked.

"It's a nice night. I thought we might take a little drive."

"Okay."

I drove around the lake and pulled off near a deserted beach. It wasn't time to swing for a home run, but maybe she was ready for some second base action. And something about having dinner with her family put me in a mind to make-out with her in the back seat of my car, like we were a couple of teenagers with no other place to be alone.

"Ever made out in the back seat of a car before?"

"No."

"Oh god, that's even better. Get your ass back there."

We both got out and slipped into the back seat, shutting the doors behind us.

I wasted no time, pulling June close and finding her mouth with mine. At first, I just kissed her. I kept my hands on her waist, her face. Slid my fingers through her hair. Felt her soft lips.

"Lips and fingertips are the most sensitive areas of the body," June said, then leaned in to kiss me again.

"Is that so?" I slid my tongue along her lower lip. "Is that why kissing you feels so damn good?"

"Yes. A high proportion of the brain is dedicated to receiving and processing sensory input from the lips. That's why they're classified as an erogenous zone."

I growled, holding her head as I kissed her deeply. "Good god, it's hot when you get all sciencey on me."

"You know what else kissing is good for?" she asked.

It took us a long moment to get back to her question. I sucked on her lower lip, then delved in with my tongue. I needed her closer, so I pulled her into my lap. She straddled her legs on either side of me, her arms draped around my shoulders.

"What else is kissing good for?" I asked.

"Bonding."

"Mm-hmm." I nipped at her bottom lip, then slid my tongue along it. "The flood of dopamine and oxytocin create good feelings and encourage people to form or strengthen their pair-bond."

"Yes, that's correct," she said, excitement in her voice.

"You're not the only one who can get sciencey." I kissed her again.

"Should we be concerned about being seen?"

"It's dark. No one's around. And that's part of what makes it fun." I brushed her hair back and met her eyes. "I want you to do something for me."

"What?"

"Stop thinking. Just feel."

She nodded and I grabbed her ass with one hand, the back of her head with the other. I drew her in for a deep kiss, feeling the satisfaction of her body relaxing. My dick ached with the desire to be inside her again, but I ignored the discomfort. I was determined to bring her along with me and show her she was capable of intimacy, no matter how long it took.

Besides, making out in a car on a deserted road was hot, even if it wasn't going to end with sex.

The more she relaxed, the more she moved, her body's instincts seeming to take over. Her legs widened and she pressed herself closer. I could feel the heat between her legs through our clothes and it drove me fucking crazy.

Our kisses went from slow and sensual to hot and messy. Tongues lapped against each other, teeth nipped at lips. I groaned, deep in my throat, as she pressed against my solid erection.

I slid my hand up her waist toward her chest and paused, breathing hard. "Second?"

"Yes."

Palming her breast over top of her shirt, I squeezed. She moaned into my mouth as I gently kneaded.

"Nipples are another erogenous zone," she said, her voice breathy.

"Hell yes they are."

I unbuttoned her shirt, resisting the urge to rip it open and send her buttons flying. Her bra was plain white, without an inch of lace. It was so practical, and so *her*, nothing could have been sexier.

She slipped the shirt off and I kissed across her shoulder, sliding her bra strap down as I went. Her skin tasted so good, I wanted to lick her all over. I pulled the cup down and she gasped as I brushed my fingertips across her nipple. It hardened at my touch.

I licked her hard peak and she rubbed herself against me. Grabbing her hips, I encouraged her rhythmic motion. Let her know she could grind against my dick all she wanted while I lavished her tits with attention.

Her soft moans were more exciting than the roar of a crowd. I licked and sucked, flicking her nipple, enjoying her taste. She moved faster, thrusting those sexy hips, sliding up and down against my erection.

I didn't say a word—didn't want to interrupt. She was right where I wanted her. In the moment. Enjoying the sensations I was giving her. I thrust my hips into her just enough to give her the friction and pressure she needed. Sucked her nipples until she was breathing hard, writhing against me.

With a sharp intake of breath, her movements slowed. She dragged herself up my erection in one long, hard stroke. I watched in awe as the orgasm overtook her. Eyes closed. Lips parted. Cheeks flushed.

God, she was beautiful.

Her eyes fluttered open. "Oh my god."

I drew her in close and held her. Stroked her soft hair. Her body was liquid against mine, relaxed and languid.

"Did that feel good?"

She nodded and sat up. "It felt very good. But what about you?"

"It's all right. We're not keeping score on orgasms here, June Bug. I'm pretty damn thrilled I could make you feel good like that."

"Me too. And I'm feeling a great deal of affection for you right now."

I touched her face and kissed her softly. "I love you too, June Bug."

Chapter Thirty

June

The afternoon sun was bright when George and I left his house in Philadelphia. He was putting it up for sale and moving to Bootleg Springs officially. I found that arrangement decidedly satisfactory. What I didn't like was the fact that he'd done nothing more than put in a call to Andrea to have her take care of it. There was still something about her that didn't sit right with me. I hadn't brought it up again—I wanted to trust his judgment—but I'd also encouraged him to take a trip out to his house to meet the real estate agent in person.

He'd agreed, and he'd been happy to have me come with him. I'd also talked him into taking me on a little detour. The woman claiming to be Callie Kendall had moved to Philadelphia, and I wanted to find her.

One of the largest publishers in the world had announced a book deal to publish her memoir next year. The Callie Kendall story was already being called one of the most highly antici-pated autobiographies in years.

It meant she was once again newsworthy. She'd been

interviewed by several reporters, telling them she'd moved to Philadelphia to start a new life. I'd done some digging, cross-referencing what I could find in photos online with information in her most recent interviews, and located her neighborhood.

No one seemed to be questioning the fact that she'd chosen to live over four hours from Richmond, where Judge and Mrs. Kendall lived. Nor that she had yet to go anywhere near Bootleg Springs since her reappearance. I found those facts highly suspicious, and although they didn't prove she was an impostor, they did support my theory.

But before I could do anything else, I needed proof. Solid, scientific proof that this woman wasn't Callie Kendall.

"Do you feel better now that you had a chance to negotiate with the real estate agent?" George asked when we got into his car. He reached behind to set a stack of mail on the back seat.

"I got you a much better deal," I said. "He was going to overcharge you."

He smiled. "Thanks, June Bug. Where to now?"

I plugged the address in the GPS app on George's phone. "There."

"All right, Scooby-June. But please tell me we're not driving over there so you can knock on her door and ask for ID."

"Not at all," I said. "I think at this stage of my investigation, speaking to her directly would be a mistake."

"So what are we going to do?"

"Get a DNA sample."

George started coughing. "Excuse me, what now?"

"As part of the original missing persons and potential homicide investigation, they obtained DNA evidence. If I can get a DNA sample, I'll have a genetics lab run it against the known DNA from Callie Kendall. Then it won't matter what she looks like or what parts of her story are questionable. DNA evidence won't lie."

"Okay, I'm with you in theory. But how are you going to get DNA?"

"According to the laboratory technician I spoke with, the

three best sources would be a toothbrush, underwear, or a hair sample."

"June, I am *not* going to steal this woman's toothbrush or panties. Especially panties."

I glanced at him with a smile. He was so cute when he got worked up. "I wouldn't ask you to touch her panties."

"That's good to hear. The only panties I want to make off with are yours."

His comment sent a little tingle rushing through me. But we were here on a mission, so I just smiled at him again. "Let's see if we can locate her."

Following the GPS, we drove across town and pulled into a quiet neighborhood. The sidewalks were clean and the manicured landscaping was tidy.

In my digging, I'd also discovered that the apartment Callie was living in had been rented by Mrs. Kendall. That was a fact I hadn't cataloged yet in terms of what it meant. Did it lend credence that she really was Callie? Were the Kendalls simply as fooled as the rest of the world? Or were they cooperating with her for reasons of their own? I wasn't sure, so I kept that information in the neutral column.

"That's her building," I said, pointing to the large brick structure on the left. "There's a spot up ahead."

George parked and I dug into my handbag, pulling out a pair of oversize sunglasses and a scarf.

"What's that for?" he asked.

"I'm going incognito."

"Are we supposed to just sit here until she comes out? This is pretty stalkery."

"According to what little I could glean from the most recent blog posts about her, I calculated the most likely time for her to emerge from her building as three in the afternoon."

"Which is right about now. Imagine that."

"I didn't imagine it, I used—"

"Just an expression, June Bug."

"Oh, of course." I slipped the sunglasses on and put the

scarf around my neck. I could pull it over my hair if I needed to, or use it to cover the lower part of my face. Then I got a second pair of sunglasses out of my bag and passed them to George. "For you."

"Don't these just make us look suspicious?"

"It's spring. Sunglasses are an appropriate accessory, given the clear sky today."

He took the black aviators and slipped them on. "Indeed."

We waited in comfortable silence for a while. I watched Callie's building. George traced his fingers along the back of my hand, as if he were mapping the shape of my bones. It was very distracting, but I had no intention of asking him to stop. Physical contact with George had become one of my favorite things.

Out of the corner of my eye, I noticed a man across the street. The feel of George's fingers along my skin held my attention. But something tickled at the edge of my awareness.

"Wait, is that…"

I turned to look, but he was gone. Had I imagined him? Or had he turned down the gap between two buildings?

"Is that what?" George asked. "Did you see her?"

"No." I looked again, but I didn't see anyone. "For a second, I thought I saw Gibson Bodine."

"Gibson? What would he be doing out here?"

"I don't know. I must be mistaken."

George rubbed his chin. "Did he know Callie?"

"I'd assume as well as any of us did. Although Gibson was twenty to her sixteen when she disappeared. I don't recall him hanging around with the teenage crowd then."

"Hmm," George said. "I was just wondering if maybe he was here doing what we're doing. Trying to figure out if it's really her."

"I suppose it's possible. But more likely that I saw someone similar and my brain filled in the missing pieces, constructing a likeness I recognized."

He grinned at me. "Fair enough."

Just then, Callie left her building.

"Duck!" I tried to push his head down as I scrunched low in my seat.

"I think ducking is more conspicuous than just sitting here like we belong."

"That's a valid point." Now that I was down-low, I couldn't see, but it seemed prudent to remain where I was so my movement didn't attract additional attention. "Did she look?"

"Nope."

"What's she doing? I need you to be my eyes, George."

"She's getting in a car."

"Is she leaving?"

"Not yet, but I think it's safe to assume that's why she got in."

"Follow her. But not too close." I paused, hearing Cassidy's chastisement in my mind. *Manners, June.* "I mean, please follow her. But not too close."

"Will do, Scooby-June."

He pulled out onto the street. I stayed low, watching the tops of buildings, trees, and bits of sky. Eventually, I deemed it safe to sit up, which was decidedly more comfortable. And certainly safer in the event of an accident.

Callie parked in front of a restaurant and got out. George found a spot a block away and we got out to follow.

"Act natural," I whispered to George as we walked toward the restaurant.

He paused and his eyes flicked up and down. "Are you going to wear those glasses inside?"

I considered that for a second. It seemed as if concealing my identity was the prudent choice. But if this woman wasn't Callie—and I was convinced she wasn't—she wouldn't recognize me. And wearing sunglasses indoors might appear unnecessarily conspicuous.

"No, I suppose that isn't necessary." I took them off and put them in my bag. "You go first and we'll pretend we're not together."

"Why?"

"Because you're going to talk to her."

"Hold on, Scooby-June. You mean you want me to distract her, don't you?"

"Yes, of course. You should flirt with her. I suspect a flirtatious encounter will be particularly distracting."

"Flirt with her." He hadn't phrased it as a question.

I answered anyway. "Yes."

"And you're going to try to get something with her DNA." Again, not phrased as a question.

"Yes."

He shook his head. "All right. I guess I signed on for this crazy when I agreed to come out here. At least it's not a biker bar this time."

"Agreed. The level of danger we're encountering must be at least seventy-two percent less than in Hollis Corner."

"Is that so?" He bit his bottom lip. "Careful, June Bug. You keep talking statistics like that and I'll be dragging you back to my car and making another run at second base."

It took considerable effort to ignore the rush of heat between my legs. "This is important. We need to focus."

The corner of his mouth hooked in a smile. "Okay, but I make no promises once we're done here."

My heart fluttered and my cheeks warmed at the thought of all the things George and I could do in his car. I blew out a breath to stay focused and gestured toward the door. "You first. I'll wait before entering."

"Okay. Just…be careful."

"I'm not a reckless person by nature."

"You're a Bootlegger, June. Reckless is in your blood."

He walked into the restaurant, letting the door shut behind him. I waited several minutes before following him inside.

About half of the tables were full and the buzz of conversation filled the air. It was small, almost cramped, with two- or four-person tables placed too close together for my taste. A harried-looking waitress dressed all in black navigated the small spaces between the tables. A *seat yourself* sign stood just inside the door, which was perfect for our purposes.

I picked a table near the entrance and slipped into the chair. George was already sitting at a table next to Callie. He was so tall, he dwarfed the small table, his right leg spilling out into the aisle. Yet his demeanor was casual, as if he didn't have a care in the world. It made his size less intimidating than it might have been otherwise.

It was fascinating to watch him strike up a conversation with her. He simply leaned slightly in her direction and spoke. He was so natural, so confident in his ability to interact with others, I didn't see even a hint of anxiety in his expression.

I couldn't see Callie's face, nor could I hear what they were saying. George's eyes flicked to me for the briefest second and I remembered I was here on a mission.

I'd considered waiting until she left and taking the straw from her drink. But that might not contain enough DNA for the lab to get an accurate result. I was here now, I wanted to ensure I took full advantage of this opportunity.

That meant hair. The laboratory technician had said it was important that the root of the hair be intact. The best way to ensure I had a usable sample was to pluck several strands directly from her head.

The table behind her was taken, but only by a single occupant. I met George's eyes again and nodded for him to keep talking. He shifted his body weight so he was angled toward her. She did the same. That seemed to indicate she was engrossed in their conversation. Now was my chance.

I moved to the table behind Callie and slipped into the empty seat. The other occupant looked up at me, his eyebrows raised. Clearly he didn't understand why I'd just helped myself to a spot at his table. I needed to keep him quiet before he attracted Callie's attention.

"Sorry. Are you alone?" I asked.

His mouth hung open for a second before he replied. "Uh, yeah."

"May I join you?"

"Oh." He closed the book he'd been reading and adjusted his glasses. "Um, yeah, I mean yes. I mean sure."

"Thank you."

I glanced over my shoulder. Callie and I were back to back, our chairs almost touching.

"I'm Luke," he said. "I haven't ordered yet, if you want to... you know..."

"What?" Something Cassidy had once told me suddenly sprang to mind. *You need to pay attention so you can see when guys are flirting with you.* Had that been an attempt at flirtation? "I'm June, but I'm in a committed relationship."

"Oh, sure," he said. "That's...yeah, I'm not surprised."

"However, you're quite attractive and the fact that you're reading increases your appeal. I suggest frequenting local bookstores if you're interested in finding a date. If you see a girl you're attracted to, offer to buy her a book. Better yet, buy the same book and ask her to have coffee with you later to discuss what you've read."

He looked at me as if I'd just unlocked the secrets of the universe. "That's a brilliant idea. Thank you."

"You're welcome. Now if you'll excuse me."

I twisted around and reached. George's voice rose slightly, and I could hear what might have been the punch line of a joke. I only meant to pluck a few hairs. But right as I grabbed, she flipped her hair over her shoulder, and I wound up with a fistful instead.

Already mid-tug, there was nothing I could do. I yanked a handful of Callie's hair right out of her head.

In a panic, I dove beneath the table. By some miracle I didn't bump into the table legs, but I wound up practically sitting on Luke's feet.

"Ouch." Callie's voice. I couldn't see her—which was good because that meant she couldn't see me—but by the view I had of her legs, she'd whipped around. "What was that?"

George's voice rose in pitch—whether in fear of getting caught, or because he couldn't see where I'd gone, I wasn't sure. "Um, I don't know. Are you okay?"

"Yeah," she said. "I think so."

I hesitated, but George continued talking to her. A second later, I decided the best course of action would be to leave immediately. As quickly as I could, I stuffed her hair in the plastic bag I'd brought to contain the DNA sample.

Glancing up, I caught Luke's gaze. His eyes were wide, his expression full of alarm.

"It's better if you don't know," I whispered.

Staying on my hands and knees, I crawled quickly for the door.

Chapter Thirty-One
George

The door opened and shut, but I didn't see anyone. Was that June? Jesus. She'd practically ripped a handful of hair out of Callie's head. Thankfully, no one seemed to notice her leave.

"My name's George, by the way," I said, trying to keep Callie's attention.

"Callie." She reached up and smoothed the back of her hair down.

The waitress came to my table and asked if I was ready to order. I didn't want to stay and have a meal, but it would look odd if I got up and left now. I ordered a coffee and a bagel. That wouldn't take too long.

I figured June would want me to see what I could find out about Callie while I was in here. So, I kept talking. "Are you from Philly?"

"No, I moved here recently," she said. "I grew up in Virginia. What about you?"

"I'm from Charlotte originally. But I've been in Philly for a while."

"It's a beautiful city," she said. "I've always loved it here. What do you do for a living?"

The way she asked that question set me on edge—something in her tone. It reminded me of girls trying to pretend they didn't know who I was, so I'd think they weren't typical groupies.

"I used to play professional football. But I retired last season after an injury."

"That's terrible," she said. "I'm sorry, I haven't exactly been following…well, anything for a while now."

Was she fishing for me to ask why? Or was she trying to avoid the topic of her supposed imprisonment by a cult? I decided to take the bait and see what she said.

"Pardon me if this is forward, but you look familiar," I said. "Do I know you from somewhere?"

She batted her eyelashes and looked down. "Maybe. I guess I was a little bit newsworthy recently. I'm Callie Kendall."

"Right," I said. "The girl who reappeared after going missing all those years ago. Wow. It sounds like you had quite an experience."

She nodded, tucking her hair behind her ear. "Yeah, I did. I'm just glad to be free."

The waitress brought my coffee and bagel, then set a sandwich down on Callie's table. She glanced at me again, her eyes widening with an expression I knew well. Recognition.

"Oh my god, I can't believe I missed it before," the waitress said. "You're GT Thompson."

"Yes, ma'am."

She practically giggled. "It's really you. I'm sorry, I'm just such a big fan. I literally cried when you got hurt last season."

A few other patrons were glancing my direction. Great. I hoped June hadn't expected me to stay incognito. Now the whole place knew GT Thompson was here.

"Thanks for your concern," I said with a smile. "But I'm doing just fine."

Callie was watching me with what appeared to be mild

curiosity. The waitress asked for an autograph, and the next thing I knew, I had a line of half a dozen people asking me to sign something.

Callie was still eating when the attention on me faded, and everyone went back to their meals. I decided I needed to get out of there. I didn't think June would come in looking for me, but you never knew with that girl. She was ballsy enough, she just might.

I stood and nodded to Callie. "Nice to meet you."

"You too."

I tossed some money on the table to cover the coffee and bagel I'd barely touched, then walked out the door.

Outside, I found June standing next to my car.

"Jesus," I said under my breath. That had been stressful.

"What took you so long?" June asked. "Did you have lunch?"

"Sort of. I couldn't walk out right after you, so I had to order something. And then the waitress recognized me. I had to sign a bunch of autographs before I could get out of there. If there was any reason to keep me being here a secret, I blew that one."

"You are very tall. And you're well known, especially here. It would have been difficult to remain inconspicuous."

"No shit. Did you crawl out of there?"

She waved a hand, like it was of no importance. "Of course. I needed to get away without attracting undue attention."

Since it had apparently worked—no one had remarked on a woman crawling out the door—I decided to let that drop. "Please tell me you got what you need."

She grinned and held up a small plastic bag. "I believe I did."

"Good job, Scooby-June. Now let's go before she comes out."

We got in my car, and I drove away quickly. That had been nerve-wracking. June was many things, but subtle wasn't one of them. I couldn't believe Callie hadn't caught her grabbing her hair.

"What did she talk about?" June asked. "Did you get anything incriminating?"

"Not really. She said she was a recent Philly transplant, but she'd grown up in Virginia."

June tapped her finger against her lips. "Grew up in Virginia is consistent with Callie Kendall. But she must have researched the case thoroughly to be able to pull this off. She'd know where the real Callie grew up. Anything else?"

"I got the sense that she was pretending she didn't know who I was. I could be wrong about that, but I've seen it before. Some girls try to get close to players by acting like they don't know who we are. She gave me that vibe."

"Interesting."

"Tell me something. What are you going to do if you're wrong and she *is* the real Callie?"

She shrugged. "Nothing."

"Nothing? Just let it go?"

"I'll still wonder about the inconsistencies in her story. At that point, the most plausible explanation will be that she made errors when she was interviewed by police. But I'm confident that my theory is correct. And soon, I'll have proof."

"I suppose you will."

———

The next day, I had phone calls to make. Secretly planning a big event was proving to be a lot of work. I'd already gotten Bowie to let me use the high school gym, and Gibson and his band had agreed to provide the entertainment. I still needed to have posters made and I wanted to get a banner to string up across Lake Drive. I was hoping to keep my involvement on the down-low until after the event had been announced, and I could ask June to be my date. I'd let her know I was behind it later.

Andrea had sent me the names of some local printers, so I called to get pricing. I also needed to get my tux. I'd thought about renting one, but I was hard to fit for normal clothes, let alone a tuxedo. I'd either have Andrea bring mine out, or I'd take another trip to Philly before the big night.

With my checklist taken care of for the time being, I turned my attention to the stack of mail I'd picked up at my house. Usually Andrea sorted it for me first, then sent me anything I needed. Since I was there, I'd just grabbed the stack.

I thumbed through the envelopes, tossing the junk mail in the recycling. There was a card from my mom with a little white bunny on the front. She had an honest-to-goodness greeting card addiction. She sent about one a month, whether there was a holiday or not, and she had shoeboxes full of them at home.

At the bottom of the pile was a nondescript white envelope. But the return address caught my eye. It was from the IRS.

Normally I would have sent anything tax-related to Andrea. But something about this made me wonder. If it was time sensitive, it might be better if I opened it.

I slipped my finger beneath the flap and tore it open. The crisp paper crinkled as I unfolded it. Scanning the letter, I stopped short.

…nonpayment…

…back taxes owed…

…applicable fines…

…investigation for tax evasion…

…will be prosecuted to the fullest extent of the law…

What the fuck was this?

I read through it again, letting the details sink in. It had to be a mistake. According to this letter, I not only owed back taxes for the last five years, they were threatening to investigate for tax evasion.

Tax evasion meant *prison*.

I grabbed my phone and tried to call Andrea, but she didn't answer. I paced around the room, reading the letter again. This was bad. Really bad. A guy I'd played with in San Francisco had been caught cheating on his taxes. He'd lied about the income from his endorsement deals and tried to hide the money. They'd come after him hard core. He'd only avoided prison by paying an enormous amount in interest and penalties. It had nearly ruined him.

The urgency had me dialing my lawyer, Marc White. After waiting on hold for several minutes, his assistant put me through.

"Hi, GT. What can I do for you?"

"Marc, I have a problem. I got a notice from the IRS, and I'm not gonna lie, it's kinda scary."

"They always sound scary," he said, his voice even. "Tell me what it says."

I read it to him, then waited, hoping he was about to tell me I was overreacting.

"You're right, that's not good. I'm going to need you to level with me here, GT. We have attorney-client privilege, so be honest. Have you been lying on your taxes?"

"No," I said, vehement. "No, Marc, I swear. This has to be a mistake."

"All right. The first thing they're going to do is an audit. We'll need to pull together all your records—tax returns and every scrap of supporting documentation. Who's your accountant?"

"My assistant Andrea does my accounting."

"She does your taxes?"

"Yeah."

Marc paused. "You don't have a third-party accountant handle your taxes?"

"No. Andrea has an accounting degree. She's always handled it for me."

"That's raising a red flag for me, GT."

"You think Andrea made a mistake on my taxes?"

"If this is all due to an honest mistake, it's more than one. An audit is one thing. Tax evasion is another. That means they have reason to believe you've falsified information to get out of paying what you owe. That's not a mistake, GT. That's either multiple mistakes over several years, or it's something worse."

June's warning ran through my mind. She thought I trusted Andrea with too much. I'd figured she was overreacting—letting unnecessary jealousy cloud her judgment. Now I wasn't so sure.

"What do we need to do to find out?" I asked.

"Does Andrea keep your files and records somewhere I can access without her knowing?"

"Yeah, I can give you my password."

"Send it. I'll do some digging and see what I can find."

"Thanks, Marc."

"Sure. Don't panic yet. I'll get back to you."

While I waited to hear back from Marc, I decided to do my own digging. I almost never looked at my financial records. That was a lot of what I had Andrea do. She was more than an average assistant, and I paid her accordingly. It had always seemed so much easier to have one person who could do everything from make dinner reservations to oversee my investments. Andrea was good. She was on my team.

Wasn't she?

I spent two days poring over tax returns and bank statements. I didn't know what I was looking for. At first it all seemed like Greek to me. I couldn't make heads or tails of anything. How would I know if the numbers were wrong? And more importantly, would I be able to find the cause of any discrepancies?

After a while, things started to make sense. I could see where some of the numbers were coming from—matched them to my sources of income. My football salary was straightforward. I knew what that had been, and the numbers all added up.

But when I got to the ancillary income sources, especially a few of the smaller endorsement deals, something seemed off. I had to look up the contracts to be sure, and then I had a hard time finding them. My files looked to be meticulously organized, but there were key things missing. I'd done a commercial for a car dealership a couple of years back, and I couldn't find a record of it anywhere. And it didn't look like it had been reported on my taxes. That wasn't good.

My tax payments didn't make sense either. What Andrea was reporting on my tax returns as having been paid didn't match what had come out of my bank account each quarter.

It looked like I'd been overpaying, not underpaying, at least compared to the amounts Andrea had calculated. So if that money hadn't been going to pay my taxes, where had it gone?

I called the bank and my sense of dread grew. My tax payments were all routed through a second account—an account that didn't have my name on it.

There was no reason for Andrea to filter my money through another account. No *good* reason, at least.

When Marc called the next day, we compared notes. We'd both come to the same conclusion. Andrea hadn't made a mistake on my taxes. She'd been stealing from me.

She'd underreported my income to the IRS, but still pulled the full amount of my tax payments from my bank account. We hadn't been able to trace exactly where that money had gone, but it seemed clear that Andrea was pocketing the extra.

Marc advised me not to tell Andrea I knew the truth. He needed more time to prepare before we moved on this. He gave me a list of records and documentation to find, and we set up a meeting for the following week.

He also advised I keep the details of my predicament to myself for the time being. He didn't want word getting back to Andrea that we were onto her—giving her time to cover her tracks, or get rid of evidence.

And I didn't want June to know. I felt like the world's biggest idiot for letting this happen. Just when I was getting settled—finding a new direction, a new place in the world—this had to knock me on my ass. And it was my own damn fault. I'd been acting like a spoiled athlete, letting someone else handle my shit, assuming it was fine. Assuming I could trust her.

I didn't understand why Andrea had done this. I thought I'd been a good boss. I paid her well. Didn't make ridiculous demands or act inappropriately with her. Was this retaliation for something? Or was she just an opportunist with a low moral code? From what Marc and I had found so far, it didn't look like she'd been stealing for the first year she'd worked for me. The second year, there were a few numbers that looked wrong, but nothing on a large scale. Maybe she'd been testing me, seeing if I'd notice. When I hadn't—because I just let her do her thing without checking on any of it—she'd gone further. Taken more.

I texted her to say I was going dark for a little while. I needed time to get my head together, so I wouldn't be reachable. In reality, I didn't trust myself to speak to her. If this all turned out to be true, she'd betrayed me. And I didn't think I'd ever be able to forgive her.

I didn't know if I'd be able to forgive myself, either.

Chapter Thirty-Two

June

I stood on the sidewalk with Cassidy, Scarlett, and Leah Mae after meeting them for Saturday brunch. All three of us stared up at the banner strung across Lake Drive. It was white with black lettering and silver and gold starbursts that were reminiscent of fireworks.

Bootleg Springs Do-Over Prom
Saturday, May 7th

"All I know is, Devlin better ask me," Scarlett said.

"To the prom?" Cassidy asked.

"Yep," Scarlett said. "A do-over prom for grown-ups? I'm going and he's bringing me."

Leah Mae looked up, shielding her eyes from the sun. "I'm so excited."

"Why are you even worried about it, Scar?" Cassidy asked. "It's not like he'll ask someone else."

Scarlett put her hands on her hips, her head tilting up toward the sign. "He better not if he knows what's good for him."

Cassidy laughed. "Bowie already asked me."

"He did?" Scarlett asked. "I mean, that's good, he better. Did Jameson ask you, Leah Mae?"

Leah Mae nodded, then clutched her hands to her chest. "We should all go shopping for dresses. And I'll do our accessories."

"Sounds fun," Cassidy said. "What about you, Juney? Did George ask you to the dance?"

"This entire conversation is oddly juvenile," I said. "You sound like you're in high school."

"Aw, don't be grumpy because you don't have a date yet," Cassidy said, nudging me with her arm. "I bet he's planning on asking you."

"He's my boyfriend."

"That's my point," Cassidy said.

By the looks the girls were sharing, I got the impression they knew something—or understood something—that I didn't. The truth was, I was experiencing a strange surge of jealousy toward Cassidy and Leah Mae. They had prom dates. I did not. It stood to reason that if George wished to attend the Do-Over Prom, he'd ask me to accompany him. But he hadn't. What did that mean?

I hadn't seen much of George in the last week. Since we'd returned from Philadelphia, he'd been busier than normal. I'd been busy with work as well as continuing my quest to uncover more information about the supposed Callie Kendall.

I'd spent my evenings reading more of the books Piper had recommended. But I was beginning to wonder if exploring my emotions through reading romantic fiction was as good an idea as I'd originally thought. I'd found myself alternatively laughing, crying, and feeling inexplicably aroused, depending on the content of the stories. Each book was like an emotional roller coaster. I couldn't decide if I liked the ride, or if it had been better when I'd pushed my feelings aside, only observing them occasionally.

"Don't worry, Juney, I'm sure he's going to ask you," Leah Mae said.

As if on cue, George turned the corner, appearing in front of us. He was dressed in a gray waffle knit shirt and jeans. His dark hair was delightfully combed back and in his hands—those hands that I still found inexplicably fascinating—was a large…something wrapped in crisp brown paper.

"Ladies," he said, then met my eyes. "June Bug."

He handed the something to me. At first glance, it looked as if it was going to be a bouquet of flowers. But it wasn't flowers. It was a Romanesco broccoli.

I stared at the beautiful chartreuse flower bud. It resembled a cross between cauliflower and broccoli, but what made it amazing was its natural approximation of a fractal. "This is so beautiful."

"I'm sorry if this is a silly question, but what is that?" Scarlett asked.

"Romanesco broccoli," George said. "Its buds form a natural fractal, the branches making a logarithmic spiral."

"It's math in flower form," I said, my voice awed.

"Wow," Scarlett said. "He's good."

Cassidy, Scarlett, and Leah Mae started backing up slowly, leaving me and George somewhat alone on the sidewalk.

"Thank you," I said. "This is one of the nicest things anyone has ever given me. It's very visually pleasing."

"So are you," he said, and I heard a muffled *aw* from behind me. Apparently the girls hadn't gone far. "I have something to ask you."

My eyes flicked up to the banner, then back to him. There was no reason my heart should have been racing the way it was, nor that I should have been experiencing such a rush of excitement. It made no sense for my bloodstream to suddenly fill with adrenaline, as if this was a crucial life moment. If he was about to ask what I thought he was about to ask, it was just a dance—and an odd dance at that.

But in that moment, I really wanted him to ask.

"I was wondering if you'd be my date for the Do-Over Prom?"

My brain flooded with endorphins and I couldn't keep the smile off my face. "Yes. I would love to be your date."

He stepped in, slipping a hand around my waist, and leaned down to kiss me.

"They're so cute, I can't stand it."

"I know, they really are."

"That's it. I'm going to find Devlin and he better be ready to ask me to this dance."

"Do you have plans tonight?" George asked. "I thought we might have a stay-in date night, if you're not busy. I've missed you this week."

"I've missed you too. I'd love a stay-in date night."

"My place or yours?"

"I think yours is the better choice. Mine has Jonah, who is a perfectly decent roommate, but is also home tonight as far as I'm aware."

"Mm," he said. "A night alone with my June Bug. Whatever will I do with you?"

A tingle rushed down my spine. "That was a rhetorical question meant to be suggestive, wasn't it?"

"Indeed it was."

"Then given that the definition of a rhetorical question is one for which the asker doesn't expect an answer, I'll just say... I can think of several things."

He kissed the tip of my nose. "Me too."

———

Mellow hopped over to George as soon as we arrived. I had to admit, she was extremely cute. Her diminutive size, soft white fur, and light blue eyes were quite appealing. She ran around us in a circle, her little nose twitching. George picked her up and brought her close to his face, touching their noses together.

Every time I saw him do that it made me think of babies.

We'd brought dinner with us, so we dished up onto plates. We sat together and ate, chatting about how our weeks had gone. Mellow was content, nibbling a treat of fresh greens.

After dinner, we decided on a movie. George turned it on, then sprawled out on the couch. He was so tall, he took up every inch.

"Where am I supposed to sit?" I asked.

He reached for me. "Come here."

I settled down between his legs with my back against his front, my head resting against his chest. He leaned his cheek against my head, slid an arm around my waist, and pressed play.

Lying with him like this felt good. His body was warm, the firmness of his athletic frame both comforting and arousing. He traced little circles across my belly with his fingers and nuzzled his face against my hair.

His masculine scent deepened my relaxation, as did the feel of his chest as he breathed. His other hand slid up my ribcage to cup my breast over my shirt. He massaged it gently and a low groan emanated from his throat.

I shifted slightly, the hardness of his erection pressing into my back. I loved the way that felt. Up until now, the male anatomy had been somewhat alarming to me. My experiences with it hadn't been entirely positive.

But I felt safe with George. The framework he'd created to gradually increase the intimacy of our interactions was working. I could feel the change happening inside me. My affection for him was growing, my desire to be close to him increasing. I was not only comfortable with his touch, I craved it—found myself wanting more.

He groaned into my ear as I moved again, pressing against his hard length. "Mm, June Bug. You feel so good."

His hand slipped beneath my shirt. He teased my nipple while he kissed my ear. Waves of sensation shot through my body, traveling across my skin, in my veins, through my bones. His breath on my neck was warm, and he kept murmuring softly in my ear.

That exquisite pressure built between my legs. I rolled my hips, instinct taking over. I needed friction. Contact. Movement.

George slid his other hand down my belly, to the waist-band of my pants. "I want to touch you, baby."

"Yes. Please."

He groaned, pushing his hips up so his erection dug into my backside. He wasted no time unfastening my pants and slid his hand into my panties.

"You want me to touch your pussy?" he asked softly in my ear. His fingers brushed lower, closer to where I needed him.

"Yes."

"That's my girl."

A delicious wave of pleasure stole through me as his fingers delved lower. His hands. His large, glorious hands. One slipped beneath my bra to cup my breast. I glanced down to see the other disappearing between my legs. I was still mostly clothed, and yet the image of his hands on me this way was intensely erotic. I loved those hands and I loved what he was doing with them.

His finger traced the seam at my center, his touch still soft and gentle. "Is your pussy wet, baby? Do you want my fingers inside you?"

"Oh my god, yes."

"That's my beautiful girl," he murmured. "I want to touch that perfect pussy."

I closed my eyes, surrendering to the sound of his voice in my ear, the feel of his fingers teasing me. My nipples were so sensitive every brush of his hand and the feel of fabric against them made me tingle.

He dipped a fingertip inside and I gasped at the intense rush of feeling.

"Is that what you need, baby?"

I nodded.

His finger slid in further, moving easily through my wetness. In and out, his palm pressing against my clit, his finger giving me the friction I needed so badly.

I bucked my hips against his hand, seeking more.

"Fuck, June, I love making you feel good. Your pussy is so hot. So wet. Do you want more?"

"Yes."

He growled low in his throat and slid two fingers inside me. My legs opened wider, my head falling back against his shoulder. He thrust his fingers in, moving faster now, and ground his cock against me in a matching rhythm.

"That's it, my beautiful girl," he said. "You like that? You like my fingers inside you?"

He was stirring me into a frenzy. My cheeks flushed and tension built in my core. I kept my eyes closed, focusing on nothing but the way this felt. His palm rubbing my clit. His fingers moving in and out of me. The wetness, the heat, the delicious pressure.

"George," I whispered.

"Yes, my sweet June Bug," he said. "Yes, fuck, your pussy feels so good."

The pressure in my core rose to a peak, a tight, hot bundle of tension that had me whimpering, begging for more. Begging him to keep going.

"Don't stop. Don't stop."

And then I came apart.

The orgasm rolled through me as dozens of tiny explosions fired off. I clenched around his fingers. Once. Twice. Again. Shuddering and pulsing as I rode his hand through my climax.

When it subsided, he slid his hand out of my panties and threaded his arms around my waist, holding me tight.

I needed more than that. I needed to hold him, too.

He loosened his grip on me as I spun around so I was facing him. I straddled him, letting my legs slide down either side of his waist, and wrapped my arms around his shoulders.

His erection pressed between my legs as we embraced. I moved against him, rubbing up and down a few times. He groaned. That low growl emanating from his throat was so masculine. So erotic.

I sat up and met his eyes, licking my lips as I unfastened his pants.

"June Bug, you don't have to."

"I know. I want to."

Like the rest of George Thompson, his cock was impressively large. It strained against his pants, springing free when I lowered his underwear. I took a moment to admire it. The smooth head. The thick shaft. It was a thing of beauty.

As I wrapped my hand around the base, a bead of moisture glistened on the tip. I applied pressure, testing his reaction. He sucked in a breath. I took that as a sign to continue.

"I'm so amped up right now, I'm ready to shoot off like a rocket," he said.

The strain in his voice was sensual. I liked being able to do this to him. I stroked up and down, swiping the moisture with my thumb. We both watched, our eyes locked on his manhood.

"Holy shit," he breathed.

He thickened even more, his cock harder than ever. He growled again, his brow furrowing, and his muscles flexed.

"June, I'm gonna come."

It was like he could barely get the words out. I didn't stop. I stroked him faster, reveling at the feel of his cock pulsing in my hand. He grunted as a thick rope of come spurted out the tip. I kept going, nearly frantic at the heady rush of watching him come. Another pulse, and more come. Yet another. He grunted and groaned, his abs flexing, his body going rigid as he thrust against me.

I could feel when it was over, his cock softening slightly. I let go, realizing I was breathing as hard as he was.

"Fuck." He leaned his head back against the couch. "I didn't expect that."

"Did that feel good?"

He grabbed me, pulling me close, and captured my mouth with his.

"That felt so good," he said. "You?"

"So good."

We glanced down between our still-clothed bodies.

"Sorry about the mess," he said.

"I don't mind if you don't mind."

A wide grin stole across his features. "I don't mind a bit. How'd you like third base?"

"Third base is good."

Chapter Thirty-Three

June

I expected to hear from the genetics lab about the DNA sample any day. But so far, no news. Not that I had any doubt what the results would show. Seeing the so-called Callie Kendall in person had only increased my confidence in my theory.

She did look remarkably like the Callie I remembered. Even I had to admit the resemblance was striking. But the doppelganger phenomenon was very real. Statistically speaking, most people on earth had at least one person who looked remarkably like them without sharing a close genetic relationship. I found it fascinating, and had even posted my picture on the *Find My Twin* website to see if my doppelganger could be found.

Despite the resemblance, I was certain I was right. And when I had proof, I'd be able to expose her.

Wednesday afternoon, I finished with work early. I decided to surprise George with his favorite meal—meatloaf and mashed potatoes with gravy. I got to work in the kitchen, preparing the meatloaf mixture and putting it in the oven to bake. Then I got started on the potatoes and gravy.

Jonah came into the kitchen while I was cooking.

"Hey June. That smells good."

"Thank you. I'm sorry to say I won't be able to share. I'm bringing the meal to George."

"No big deal." He opened the fridge and pulled out a container. "I meal prepped, so I'm good."

"Your organizational skills are admirable, especially when it comes to your nutrition habits."

"Thanks." He plated his dinner and put it in the micro-wave. "So, the Do-Over Prom. That's something else, huh? Is George taking you?"

I smiled as I stirred the gravy. "Yes, he asked me to accom-pany him. Do you plan to attend?"

He leaned against the kitchen counter and shrugged. "Maybe. I was thinking about asking Lacey Dickerson."

"You don't sound terribly enthusiastic."

"Well, I'm not sure about dating right now. But it seems like everyone else is, so maybe I should give it a shot."

"If you're feeling left out, I can identify with that," I said. "I suppose you've noticed I'm a little different from most people in Bootleg Springs. I know what it's like to be a bit on the outside."

"Yeah. Don't get me wrong, my siblings are great. I expected a lot more resistance when I first came here. But… I don't know if this is where I'm meant to be."

"And dating would complicate matters, especially if you found yourself in what you'd like to be a long-term relationship."

"Yep, exactly." He rubbed the back of his neck.

Jonah and Lacey Dickerson. It was hard to picture. She was the right age, certainly, just a year younger than me. Pretty, with blond hair and blue eyes. And single, which was an obvious prerequisite. But something about the notion of Jonah dating her sat wrong with me. I couldn't pinpoint why. I didn't typically have strong instincts when it came to human relationships.

Perhaps I was learning.

I was also learning that it wasn't always best to say everything that came into my mind. This seemed like an instance when keeping my thoughts to myself would be prudent. I didn't think Jonah should date Lacey. But it was likely that he needed to figure that out for himself.

"If you decide to move forward with your request, I hope she answers in the affirmative."

"Thanks, Juney." He took a deep breath through his nose. "That really does smell good. George is going to love it."

"Thank you." I turned off the heat and whisked the gravy a few more times. "I think so, too."

When dinner was finished and packed in containers for transport, I went to George's rental. I paused outside, looking at the small cabin. The location was excellent for a rental. Close to town. Partial view of the lake. But it was more vacation rental than permanent home.

He was making preparations to move to Bootleg, and when he did, I doubted he'd live here. I'd kept my eyes open for a suitable piece of real estate. A house, perhaps. Or maybe he'd want to do what Scarlett and Devlin were doing—buy land and build something to his particular taste.

I also wondered something else. What if he lived with me?

There was no doubt in my mind his decision to relocate to Bootleg Springs was at least eighty-seven percent due to my presence here. The other thirteen was a mix of the food at Moonshine Diner and the hot springs. But in large part, George was moving here for me.

It was a heady thought, that this man I admired—and was falling deeply in love with—wished to relocate to continue our relationship without the strain of distance.

His financial security seemed well-assured, so even in post-football retirement, I assumed he would live comfortably, whether or not he pursued another full-time career. And if he asked, I could help with his finances and investments. I was highly adept at it, having secured myself a number of lucrative assets and endeavors.

His move here made sense. Perhaps moving in with me made sense as well.

Was our relationship ready for that level of commitment? It wasn't something I'd ever considered before. Generally, I preferred living alone. Jonah had proved to be a good roommate. He was quiet and kept to himself. But living with George would not be the same as living with a roommate. It would be truly sharing my space with another person. Opening up my life in a way I'd never done before.

I found I very much liked the idea.

Feeling a hint of euphoria at my daydreams of cohabitation, I gathered up the dinner I'd cooked and went to George's door. Perhaps tonight I'd broach the subject.

George answered dressed in a white t-shirt and gray sweatpants. Scarlett had once told me that you could discover everything you needed to know about a man by looking at him in a pair of gray sweats. I hadn't understood what she meant—until this moment. He looked spectacular. The crisp t-shirt molded to his athletic frame, hinting at the lean, muscular body underneath. And those sweats. They sat low on his hips and showed the bulge of his manhood in a most enticing fashion.

"Oh, hey June."

I gasped and snapped my gaze back to his face. "Hello."

His expression was tense, his brow furrowed, but his eyes lit up as his nostrils flared. "Do I smell gravy?"

I held up the containers. "I brought dinner."

"Wow, thanks, June Bug." He stepped aside so I could enter and shut the door behind me. "That's very sweet of you."

Mellow hopped over, bouncing across the wood floor. "Hi, Marshmellow. Are you taking good care of George?"

She sniffed my foot.

"Here, let me take all that." He grabbed our dinner and brought it into the kitchen.

I took off my cardigan and draped it over a chair. From

where I was standing, I had a clear view into the single bedroom. George's suitcase was on the bed.

"Are you going somewhere?"

"Yeah, I am. I was going to call you tonight and talk to you about it. I have to go back to Philly for a while."

"You're already packing." I gestured toward the bedroom. "Is this trip imminent?"

"I leave in the morning."

"Oh? How long do you think you'll be gone?"

He rubbed the back of his neck. "I'm not sure. A couple of weeks. Maybe longer. It depends."

I felt a dip, as if my stomach had suddenly dropped. "That's a significant amount of time. Where will you stay?"

"At my house. I pulled it off the market for the time being."

"You're not selling?"

He took a deep breath. "I will, eventually. I just can't right now. I have to take care of some things first."

"What things?"

"Just some things. Financial stuff."

I didn't like the turn this conversation had taken. George seemed hesitant, like he didn't want to talk to me about this. But finances were one of my areas of expertise.

"George, if you're having financial trouble, I could help."

"Yeah, I know. There are just some things I need to handle."

His tone of voice didn't match his words. He was brushing the subject aside, but I could sense that there was more. It was as if something lurked beneath the surface, causing that shadow behind his eyes.

"Are you keeping your rental here?" I asked.

"No."

"So you're moving." It wasn't a question. "You're moving back to Philadelphia."

"No, that's not what I said."

"You're giving up the rental, not selling your house, and going to live there for an indeterminate amount of time. That sounds like moving."

"It's not permanent," he said. "Once I get things squared away, I'll be in a position to come back to Bootleg. And I can come visit on the weekends. I'll be here for the dance and everything."

"The dance isn't my biggest concern, I just…" I trailed off, unsure of what to say. I didn't know how this was supposed to work. "What things do you need to handle? Why won't you elaborate?"

He put his hands on his hips, still facing the window. "I'm fucked, June. That's the problem. I'm good and fucked."

"What are you talking about?"

"I'm in trouble with the IRS."

"What kind of trouble?"

"The tax evasion kind."

"Tax evasion," I said, more to myself than to him.

"I don't want you getting wrapped up in this," he said. "Turns out Andrea was fudging the numbers. She was underreporting my income, so it looked like I owed less. But she was taking the full amounts out of my bank account and pocketing the difference. To the IRS, it looks like I was lying on my taxes to get out of paying. In reality, I think Andrea's been stealing."

White hot anger snaked out from my chest, filling my veins with fire. I clenched my hands into fists, digging my fingernails into my palms. "She what?"

"Yeah. And my dumb ass had no clue. I have to meet with my lawyer, and there's going to be an audit. We're trying to keep this out of the press, but a reporter called me this morning. My lawyer thinks someone at the IRS leaked the story. This is turning into a shitstorm. That's why I have to go."

"Indictment for tax evasion requires that the taxpayer knowingly and willfully committed errors over a period of time."

"I'm well aware of the definition at this point."

"And the error amounts would need to be significant," I said. "There has to be a way to track where Andrea was putting the money."

"Yes, June, I know that. And we're working on it."

"How long have you known about this?"

"Does it matter? A while. Look, I'll handle it. My life is in chaos right now and I need to get my shit together."

"But why didn't you tell me?"

That was what really bothered me. This was a problem I could have helped him through. I wasn't a tax accountant, but I understood more than the average person.

"I didn't want you to be involved," he said. "This is serious shit, June."

"I thought we were serious."

"We are." He turned to me and there was no mistaking the frustration in his voice. "I can't fix this overnight. I have to get this squared away before I can move forward with you."

I could feel the wall he'd erected between us as sure as if I was standing in front of actual brick. He'd kept this from me, didn't want my help. And now he was leaving.

"I could have helped," I said, although true as it was, the sentiment seemed useless now. "I have a better-than-average understanding of—"

"Damn it, June, I don't need another accountant."

I pinched my lips closed and stepped backward. "All right. I'll let you handle it."

"Good."

I no longer wanted to sit and have dinner with him. I was confused, but more than that, I was angry. He didn't need another accountant? Was that all I was good for?

"I'm sure you're very busy packing. I'll just leave the meal and let you get back to what you were doing."

He didn't argue, or try to get me to stay. So I left.

Chapter Thirty-Four

George

I wasn't used to being lonely and bored, but sitting in my house in Philly, I was both. For a decade, I'd had practices and workouts. Training sessions and PT appointments. Team meetings, game film, training camp. I'd had media appearances and charity events. Photo or commercial shoots for endorsements. I'd had plenty to keep me busy, even in the off-season.

Now I had too much time. Too much quiet. One day back in Philly and I was pacing the floors, wishing my meeting with Marc was earlier.

My house here felt so impersonal. It was nice, I supposed. Stylish. But I hadn't chosen much of the furniture. It looked like some designer's take on what a man's house should be. Lots of gray and blue. Pieces of my career—jerseys, awards, photos—hung on the walls. But even those things didn't feel like me. Not anymore.

Maybe I should have stayed in Bootleg.

I brushed that thought aside. Staying wasn't an option. Not when my life was in shambles. But I couldn't get the memory of June's face out of my head. When I'd told her what was happening—and that I had to leave—she'd looked devastated. And coming from a woman who didn't wear her heart on her sleeve, that look of raw hurt on her face had been like a punch to the gut.

It wasn't that I wanted to leave her. Not even temporarily. But what I wanted and the reality of my messed-up life were two different things.

Shelby texted around noon, demanding to know what was going on. Turned out, she was in Philly for the week. When I told her where I was, she answered with I'm coming over.

Although I had a feeling my sister was going to lay into me for being such an idiot, I didn't tell her no. Even a lecture about Andrea was better than being lost in my own head, driving myself crazy.

She arrived about half an hour later. With cookies. I really did love my sister.

"Here," she said, shoving the box of snickerdoodles at me. "They're from the store, so not as good as Mom's. But I figured you could use some cookie love right about now."

"Thanks."

She took off her jacket and hung it up by the door. "You really need to tell me what's going on, though. You're in the news, Mom's in a panic, and Dad decided to remodel the guest bath again."

"That's not good."

Our father was many things, but handy was not one of them. Unfortunately for our mom, when he was stressed, he tended to try to remodel their house.

"No, it's not. I think I talked him out of trying to take out a wall, though."

"I'll call him," I said. When I'd spoken to my parents a few days ago, I'd tried to minimize the situation so they wouldn't worry. But the story had hit the press. I couldn't keep this quiet now even if I tried.

I walked into the kitchen and set down the cookies. Shelby

followed. Grateful as I was for her to bring something to cheer me up, I wasn't in the mood.

"Can I get you anything?" I asked.

She pulled out a chair at the dining room table I'd hardly used. "Nope. Just tell me what's going on."

"All right." I took the seat across from her. "So I guess you know I'm in trouble with the IRS."

"That's true?" she asked, her voice tinged with shock. "I thought it had to be a rumor."

"Nope, not a rumor. I'm being investigated for tax evasion."

"This has to be a mistake."

"Thank you for not assuming I actually did lie on my taxes," I said. "Because I didn't. Not on purpose, at least. Andrea did, though."

"Wait, Andrea lied on your taxes? The press is saying your assistant might be involved, but I thought it had to be someone else."

"It was Andrea. She underreported my income so it looked like I owed less. Then she pocketed the difference from the tax payments."

"Holy shit, GT."

"I know. And I don't need to hear that I'm a dumbass for letting it happen. I realize that."

"I wasn't going to say you're a dumbass," she said. "Andrea worked for you for years. You obviously thought you could trust her."

"And I was dead wrong. I'm fucked, Shelby."

"Okay, what's the plan?" She sat up straighter. "What's your first step?"

"I'm meeting with my lawyer today."

"You fired Andrea already, I assume."

"Yeah, but it gets worse. I don't have proof she did it yet. It looks like she did from everything my attorney and I have found so far. But we don't have enough to nail her. And since the story leaked to the press the other day, and they're mentioning her, she's suing me."

"What?" she practically shrieked.

"Yeah. She hasn't served the lawsuit yet, but her lawyer sent what he called a *courtesy warning* to my lawyer this morning."

"This is unreal. She steals from you, completely screws you over, and now she thinks she can sue you?"

I pinched the bridge of my nose, wincing at the headache I'd been fighting for days. "Yep. That's where my life is right now. Aren't you glad you came over?"

"Come on, don't be like that. You don't have to deal with this alone. You have a family, and friends. You have a community behind you."

"I kinda do have to do this alone. I'm paying the price for trusting someone else too much."

"But that doesn't mean you don't have people in your corner."

Mellow hopped into the kitchen, so I scooped her up and set her in my lap.

"Why is Mellow here?" she asked. "I thought you had her at your place in Bootleg."

"No, I moved back here until I get this mess straightened out."

She narrowed her eyes at me. "You were about to sell this house and move out there. I get that this is a big deal, but do you really need to be in Philly to handle it?"

"My lawyer is here."

"Sure, but it's not like you'll be in his office every day."

"Why are you grilling me about where I live? I have to put things on hold until I get through this."

"Like your relationship with June?"

"How did you…" I glanced away. It drove me crazy how my sister could read me.

I wasn't sure where things stood between me and June. I knew she hadn't wanted me to leave Bootleg. And she was upset that I hadn't told her what was going on. We hadn't exactly parted on good terms. "Yes, like my relationship with June. I can't pull her into this."

"But she knows, right? You were honest with her about what was going on and why you had to leave?"

"Yeah. I mean, eventually. I told her yesterday."

She closed her eyes and shook her head. "Oh, GT."

"What?"

"You just told her yesterday? I thought you two were serious."

"We are. Or we were."

"If you were serious, why did you keep this from her?"

I blew out a long breath and pet Mellow between the ears. "I told you, I didn't want her getting mixed up in my shit."

"That's a relationship, GT. You get mixed up in each other's shit."

"It's not like there's anything she could do."

"That's not the point," she said. "Look, the fact that Andrea screwed you over is horrible. But that's not a reason to push everyone else away. And don't even tell me that's not what you're doing."

"It's not what I'm doing."

"Yes, it is. You're going through the biggest crisis of your life on the heels of your football career ending prematurely. And you come back here, where you have no support? Why would you do that?"

"Because it's *my* problem," I said. "This isn't June's fight, or my family's fight. It's not Bootleg's fight. It's mine."

"GT, don't even get me started on our family. We love you. You don't need to shut us out. And as for Bootleg, I've seen that town come together to protect their own. From everything you've told me, they embraced you. Those friends you made would have your back right now if you let them. And if June is a woman who deserves you, she would too."

"Her deserving me is not the issue," I said. "It's the other way around."

"Don't do that. Don't assume that because you made a mistake that you're not good enough. Everyone makes mistakes, GT."

I shook my head. "Not everyone makes mistakes that could land them in prison."

"Well, you're not in prison now. If June is the one, she'll stand by your side through this."

I knew she would. That wasn't even a question. I just didn't want her to have to. "I know."

"So let her."

"You don't understand," I said. "June's the smartest woman I've ever met. She even had suspicions about Andrea, and I ignored her. I don't know why I thought I could keep up with her. I'm just a dumb guy who used to be able to catch a ball."

Shelby's eyes looked stormy. "Do not talk about yourself that way, GT. You're not dumb, and you never were."

I *felt* dumb. How much intelligence did a guy need to play a game? And would a smart man have let himself get in trouble with the IRS like this? I doubted it.

Shelby's expression softened. "I'm sorry, GT, I didn't come over here to get bossy with you. But I'm looking from the outside in. Just a couple of weeks ago, you were calling me all excited because things were getting serious with June. You'd put your house on the market and were moving to be close to her. Your voice… It was amazing. I don't remember the last time you sounded so happy."

"I was."

"So lean into that," she said. "If she's as good for you as you seemed to believe before this happened, you need her by your side right now."

I rubbed my finger between Mellow's ears again. Damn it, she was right. Everything seemed exponentially worse since I'd left Bootleg Springs. Since I'd told June I didn't need another accountant. Guilt washed over me. She'd been trying to help and I'd thrown it back in her face. Again. That had been a shitty thing to do.

"Maybe I do need her. But I didn't exactly part with her on good terms before I left."

"Are you still trying to convince yourself you aren't pushing people away?" she asked, her tone wry. "Call her. Let her in."

"All right." I stared at the table. "I'll call her after my appointment with Marc."

"Fair enough. And call me, too. I want to know how it goes."

"I'll keep you updated, don't worry."

"I'm your sister, of course I'm going to worry," she said. "But GT, I really believe this is going to be okay."

"Thanks, Shelby."

"Plus, I liked the idea of you moving out to Bootleg Springs. It'll give me a more permanent place to stay when I come back. I like that crazy little town."

"Me too."

Chapter Thirty-Five

June

The sound from the TV drifted past me, largely unnoticed. Even ESPN couldn't hold my attention. The usual comfort I got from sitting on my parents' couch, watching sports with my dad, was noticeably missing. Instead of focusing on the latest news in the sports world, my mind drifted, replaying what had happened with George.

I didn't know what to do with my feelings. There were so many of them. Bright, their colors harsh and glaring. They bounced through my head, leaving messy splotches all over my brain, like splashes of neon paint.

I'd thought about eating my feelings this morning. But Jonah had come downstairs and told me about a new study that had recently been published in the *Journal of Sports Nutrition*. Hearing about macronutrient ratios and intermittent fasting while Jonah made himself a protein shake had dampened my craving for carbs and fat. So I'd decided to go to my parents' house.

It was my dad's day off, so he was dressed in civilian clothing.

In fact, it was early enough in the day that he hadn't yet changed out of his shirt and pajama pants. My mom wore the matching pajama top as she walked around the house, watering her plants, humming to herself. She walked by Dad and gave him a little caress on the cheek before moving on to the next room.

My parents were the picture of a happy marriage. I'd always taken their relationship for granted—never put much thought into what made it special. Or even the fact that it *was* special. Looking back, it was an odd thing to have missed. I'd grown up with the Bodines, their family dynamic a sharp contrast to the life Cassidy and I had lived within these walls.

But I hadn't been paying attention. Relationships had confused me, made me uncomfortable. So I'd ignored them unless forced otherwise. I'd always loved my parents, and cared about them. My sister as well. But I felt a twinge of guilt, now, at how easily I'd taken them for granted. Their place in my life was important—vital, even. It had taken meeting, loving, and possibly losing George to make me see it.

I supposed it was better late than never.

"You and Mom have always set a very positive example as to what a healthy marriage should be," I said. "Thank you."

Dad looked at me, his brow furrowed, his white mustache twitching. "You're welcome?"

"I've never told you what a good role model you've been. So I'm telling you now."

He smiled, his eyes crinkling at the corners. "Well, thank you, June Bug. Truth is, your mama makes it easy. I'm just lucky she's put up with me all these years."

I was about to reply when something on TV caught my attention. Had they just said GT Thompson?

"The former all-pro receiver could be facing charges of tax evasion. Thompson retired after his second ACL tear midway through last season. Now, he's being investigated by the IRS, and his assistant, Andrea Wilson, is allegedly complicit in the fraud."

Dad muted the TV and looked at me, his eyebrows lifting. "Did you know about this?"

"It's not his fault," I said. "His assistant was underreporting his income and stealing the money she should have been using to pay his taxes."

Mom stood in the doorway, still holding her green plastic watering can. "Oh dear. June Bug, invite him over for dinner tonight. He probably needs a good meal."

"He's not here. He went to Philadelphia."

"Well, when he gets back, then," Mom said.

I nodded, looking down at my hands clasped in my lap.

"Is there more to this?" Dad asked, his voice soft.

"I believe him. I'm not upset because he could be facing criminal charges."

"Then what is it?"

"I could have helped," I said. "Only he didn't tell me until yesterday."

Mom set her watering can on the side table and sat in the armchair next to the couch. "Pride makes men do stupid things. Like not asking for help when they need it."

"So you'd consider this within the realm of typical male behavior?"

"Sure," Mom said, and I caught the little wink she gave my dad.

"But it was more than simply failing to ask for help," I said. "When he told me about his predicament, I was given the very distinct impression that he didn't *want* my help. He said he doesn't need another accountant."

"Maybe that's not the sort of help he needs," Mom said. "Sometimes a man doesn't need you to fix things for him. He just needs you to love him through the hard times."

Mom and Dad shared a tender look. I'd seen those expressions on their faces when they looked at each other more times than I could count. But the meaning finally clicked into place. That was love. Real, true love that had lasted decades.

A feeling surged through my chest, making all the other

conflicting emotions pale in comparison. It was warm and certain. A sense of clarity amid the confusion.

I loved George. That wasn't new information. I'd known I loved him for some time. Even said those words to him. But I finally understood what that meant. And more importantly, I knew how to behave in light of that fact.

He was right; he didn't need another accountant. He very likely had a competent attorney who would help him through this process. They would hire the appropriate people—accountants and otherwise—to work on his case.

What he needed was his girlfriend. A partner to be with him and support him emotionally during a difficult time. To love him through it, as my mother had said.

"Thank you," I said, standing up abruptly. "I think I understand now."

"Understand what?" Dad asked.

"How to have a true intimate relationship with another human." I grabbed my coat and paused near the front door. "I have to go. I love you both."

"Love you too, June Bug."

————

When I got to Philadelphia, George wasn't home. His car was nowhere to be seen, and there was no answer at his door. I peeked through the front window and saw Mellow sound asleep on her bunny bed. He must have already gone to his meeting.

I knew the name of his attorney, so it was simple enough to locate his office. Inside, I stopped at the receptionist's desk.

"Hello," I said. "I'm June Tucker, here to see Marc White with George Thompson."

"Are they expecting you?" she asked.

"Yes," I lied without blinking.

"One moment." She glanced at her computer screen. "Mr. Thompson is already in Mr. White's office. I can take you back."

I followed the woman down a hallway to a plain brown door. She knocked twice, then opened it.

"Ms. Tucker is here."

George looked up at me, his eyes widening. He sat on one side of a large mahogany desk. On the other side sat a man dressed in a button-down shirt and tie. He had salt and pepper hair, and more gray than brown in his neatly trimmed beard.

"I apologize for my tardiness." I'd dressed for the occasion, donning a crisp white blouse, pencil skirt, and black pumps. I stepped past the receptionist, into the room, and took the seat next to George.

"What are you doing here?" George asked quietly.

The door clicked closed behind the receptionist.

"I'm here to support you."

"What?"

I patted his knee and settled back in my seat. "I'm June, George's significant other. Please forgive the interruption. Carry on."

Marc looked at George, his eyebrows raised, but George was looking at me, a slow smile spreading across his features.

"Thank you, June Bug."

I nodded, keeping my lips pressed together, trying to show him I wasn't here to intervene. I wasn't his accountant. I was his partner. When he needed me, I'd be here.

He dipped his chin, a subtle gesture I recognized. He understood. That was one of the amazing things about George Thompson. He understood me.

"Sorry," he said to Marc and took my hand, lacing our fingers together. "We can continue."

I sat in silence while they discussed George's case. Since I'd clearly arrived midway through their meeting, I hadn't heard all the relevant information. But it didn't take long for me to catch up. George had provided Marc with the entirety of his financial records from the last ten years. Marc had a team of skilled accountants and attorneys sorting through the documentation. They were preparing for the IRS audit, and seeking evidence of Andrea's theft and fraud.

Marc cleared his throat. "Ms. Wilson's lawsuit is an

261

unwelcome distraction. And it doesn't help your case. The IRS is going to be investigating before a judge has a chance to look at the civil suit. But the IRS will be well aware you're being sued. Put simply, it doesn't look good."

"No, it doesn't," George said. "Is there anything I can do about it at this point?"

"Not really. I'd be willing to bet she knows she can't win. She's just trying to scare you away from implicating her."

George squeezed my hand. "It won't work."

Marc shook his head. "No. But it makes my job more complicated. Anyway, I think we've covered everything. Do you have any questions?"

"No." George looked at me. "What about you, June? Any questions for Marc?"

I squeezed George's hand. "No. If you have everything you need, that's what matters."

We both stood and said our goodbyes to Marc. He promised to contact George within a week with an update, or sooner if there were any significant findings.

Neither of us spoke much when we left the office. There was much to say, but we both seemed to realize the parking lot of a law office wasn't the best place for the conversation. Instead, we each drove back to George's house and went inside.

Mellow greeted me by hopping in a circle around my feet. I knelt on the floor to pick her up.

"Hello, little one."

George took off his coat and collapsed onto the couch. I put Mellow down and sat next to him. An instinct I hadn't realized I possessed made me draw his head gently into my lap. He lay on his side, one hand tucked beneath my leg, the other draped over my thighs.

I ran my fingers through his hair, sitting with him in comfortable silence. Feeling his body slowly relax. This felt good. It felt right. Despite the crisis in his life, we were together. This was where I was supposed to be.

This was love.

"Thank you," he said, his voice soft.

"You're welcome."

"I didn't expect to see you."

"I know. But you needed me."

He nodded against my lap. "I'm sorry I didn't talk to you about everything sooner. I should have. And I'm sorry for what I said last night."

"I forgive you. I'm sorry I didn't fully understand what you needed."

He turned over onto his back, his head still in my lap. "June Bug, you don't need to apologize. I'm sorry you have to go through this. I didn't want to make this your problem."

I brushed his hair off his forehead. "But this is intimacy, isn't it? If I only wanted to be with you when things were good, what kind of a partner would I be?"

His mouth hooked in a grin. "That's a good point."

"And if I were in similar trouble, you would do the same for me."

"Of course I would." He reached up to touch my cheek, brushing his fingers against my skin. "I love you, June Bug."

I pressed my palm against the side of his face. "I love you too. And I'm fully convinced that despite the obvious challenges, justice will prevail for you."

"Thanks. I hope you're right."

"I'm quite certain."

And maybe a little Bootleg Justice would help.

Chapter Thirty-Six
June

Often, Bootleg Justice was swift, delivered immediately and without hesitation. People settled differences themselves in our town, only involving the law when absolutely necessary. As a result, there weren't a lot of lawsuits in Bootleg Springs. Secret town meetings, bar fights, justice committees, and other less-than-official means were our way.

It was a fact of life I'd understood to be outside the norm, but accepted as the way things were done here. Misty Lynn Prosser had cheated on Gibson Bodine, so Scarlett had broken her nose. Bootleg Justice. Earl Wilkins had ridden his lawn mower through Adeline Porter's fence and refused to fix it, so Adeline had done the fixing and painted Earl's side rainbow. Bootleg Justice. Leah Mae Larkin's ex had engaged in public assholery, so the Bodines had tossed him in a dumpster. Bootleg Justice.

But sometimes, Bootleg Justice was quieter. It didn't always involve dumpsters and bar fights. Sometimes it was simply a way to encourage a person to quit being a dick-licking douche-nozzle, as Scarlett would say.

Andrea Wilson most definitely needed a dose of Bootleg Justice.

I wasn't going to try to step in and be George's accountant to fix his tax problems. But his assistant? By Bootleg standards, she was fair game.

So I went to Cassidy for help. Her research skills proved to be immensely helpful. She dug up some very interesting information on Ms. Andrea Wilson. And we came up with a plan.

Of course, George knew nothing about this. I had no qualms about that. My mom and I had been organizing secret town meetings—only when absolutely necessary, of course—without my father's knowledge for years. She'd always said what he didn't know wouldn't hurt him, and now I truly understood what she'd meant. Because he was the sheriff, he *couldn't* know when the town came together to do something that was slightly outside the confines of the law. Even when it was the right thing to do.

And it was always only *slightly* outside the law. Nadine Tucker was a law-abiding woman, and she'd raised us right.

Much like my dad, George couldn't know that I was planning to treat Andrea to a dose of Bootleg Justice. This was something that needed to happen, and although I suspected he'd understand, it was better for him if he had no knowledge of it. The legalities were simpler that way.

With that in mind, I used George's phone while he was in the shower to text Andrea, asking her to come to Bootleg Springs to meet as soon as possible. I was surprised—and suspicious—at how quickly she agreed. I'd expected her to refuse, or possibly not reply at all. But she did, and once the meeting was set, I quickly deleted the texts.

I'd tell George when it was done. For now, my plan required secrecy.

George had come back to Bootleg Springs with me, and for the time being, was staying in my house. I was surprised at how comfortable I felt having him here. My personal space was important to me. Having Jonah for a roommate had proven to be minimally intrusive. But this was far more than another person living in the same house. This was a very large man sharing my room. My bed.

I loved it.

The first night, when we'd climbed in bed together, first base had quickly turned to second. Then George had stolen third. It had been satisfying for us both, although I was surprised he hadn't suggested we go for home. Perhaps after our one and only experience with intercourse, he was reluctant to make another attempt. Or perhaps he was waiting for me to suggest it.

Regardless, I'd gone to sleep tucked against his large body, his hand splayed across my stomach. It was hard to imagine anything more wonderful.

My blissful nights with George sleeping in my bed had hardened my resolve to handle the Andrea situation. The thought of George going to prison was abhorrent. Mostly because of his innocence. But also because then I'd have to give him up.

That was unacceptable.

The next day, I told George I had some things to see to. Without revealing why, I'd asked Jonah to keep him busy. The two of them were going for a run—George's knee had healed to the point that he was able to run without pain—then coming home to grill steaks. That would give me adequate time for what I needed to do, and keep George out of the way while I did it.

Shortly before the appointed time, I went to the Lookout, the designated location for the meeting. Cassidy and Scarlett were there, seated at the table next to me, with drinks and a plate of garlic fries—adding to the pretense that they weren't there with me.

The door opened. My blood froze with icy cold anger when Andrea walked inside. She was dressed in a stylish blouse and slacks, holding a designer bag. My eye twitched in irritation. She'd probably bought that with stolen money.

She looked around, believing she was meeting George. Her eyes landed on me and recognition showed on her face. I folded my hands in front of me and met her gaze, keeping my expression carefully neutral.

"June?" she asked, coming over to my table. "I'm Andrea, GT's assistant. We met once before. Is GT here?"

"No, *George* is not present," I said, emphasizing his full name. "But please take a seat."

"What's going on?"

Cassidy and Scarlett had first suggested I appear friendly, lulling Andrea into a false sense of security. Then we'd all acknowledged that acting was not on my list of skills. Straightforward was our best option.

"George doesn't know you're here," I said. "I asked you to come so we could discuss the issue at hand. Woman to woman."

She pressed her lips together, her eyes narrowing, as she slowly lowered into the seat across from me. "I don't have anything to discuss with you."

Her words didn't match her actions. She claimed she had nothing to say while simultaneously sitting down, as if she meant to stay. But instead of confusing me, this contradiction spurred me on.

"I disagree."

"You've been banging GT for a few months, and you think that means you can speak on his behalf? I've been working for him for the better part of a decade."

"Stealing from him, you mean."

"I've been loyal to him. You have no idea what it's like to work for a professional athlete."

"I don't suppose I do, yet I fail to see how that has any bearing on the current situation."

She sat back and crossed her arms. "He's going to drop you. Whatever points you think you'll score here won't matter. I've seen it plenty of times. You're not special. Trust me."

Andrea was trying to bait me, as she might any other woman. Ignite sparks of jealousy so I'd focus on defending myself and my relationship with George. For the first time in my life, I was grateful for whatever it was that made me June Tucker. June Bot indeed. Robots didn't get jealous.

I wasn't here to prove to her that George loved me. I was here to negotiate.

"We both know there are discrepancies on George's tax returns, as well as in the amounts paid to the IRS," I said. "It's my understanding that you're the one who has been responsible for George's finances, including his taxes, for a number of years."

"Are you accusing me of something?"

"Not yet."

She licked her lips. "All I ever had to work with was the documentation GT provided me. If he underpaid, it's because he was trying to hide things."

"So you claim you acted in good faith."

"Of course I did."

Cassidy stood from the table behind us, dressed in her sheriff's deputy uniform, and came over to lean her hip against the table. "June."

"Deputy."

Scarlett wandered over and leaned against the table next to us. She was dressed in street clothes, but had a lanyard around her neck with some sort of ID card, turned backwards so I couldn't read it. She crossed her arms and leveled Andrea with a fiery stare.

"Ms. Wilson, are you familiar with an online forum called *Jersey Chaser*?" Cassidy asked.

Andrea paled. "What about it?"

"It's interesting," Cassidy said. "It's a subscription service for women to share information and get tips on how to land a pro-athlete."

"So? There are lots of sites out there like that," Andrea said.

"That's probably true," Cassidy said. "But this one is special. It has to be, in order to demand a monthly fee to gain access."

"This site is run by someone with insider information," I said. "Someone with access to players' personal details. Who has a network of contacts—other assistants—who appear happy to share similar information with subscribers. For a fee, I'd assume."

Andrea's spine was stick straight, her jaw set in a hard line. "It's just a way to connect with colleagues and other people in the industry. Most of us don't work in an office environment where we see our counterparts on a regular basis. It's like…a virtual water cooler."

"A water cooler where you share player's locations so groupies can find them?" I asked.

"It's a private forum," she said.

"Nothing on the internet is truly private," I said. "For all your attention to detail, you couldn't hide the fact that you own this website."

"Like I said, it's a place for people in the industry to connect," she said.

"People in your industry sure have interesting topics to discuss," Scarlett said. "One of your most upvoted posts was called *Ten Surefire Ways to Fuck a Football Player*."

"The matchmaking section was particularly fascinating," Cassidy said. "It looked a hell of a lot like a prostitution ring."

"But even if it isn't," I said. "You've been using your position as George's assistant to gain access to player schedules and travel plans. You know exactly where to direct women to find players, wherever they are. Clubs, parties, hotel rooms."

Andrea huffed out a breath. "Look, I don't make those guys hook up with these women. They're looking for it. So okay, yes, I make a little side cash. I refuse to take responsibility for who players decide to bang when they're on the road."

"You give explicit, step-by-step instructions for how to extort the most money out of different players," I said. "Including married men and men in relationships. You instruct these women on how to get past their defenses, how to convince them to have sex, and what to do afterward to make sure they receive high-caliber gifts. You even have an entire section on unplanned pregnancies."

Scarlett rolled her eyes and groaned.

"What is this?" Andrea asked. "Are you all cops? What do you want from me?"

"I want you to withdraw your lawsuit," I said.

Andrea stared at me. "My reputation in this industry is everything. He already fucking fired me. That's bad enough. I have to do this to protect myself."

I didn't say a word. Just stared at her, my expression blank.

"What's this all about?" she asked. "To tell me you found a forum where groupies trade secrets? That's not illegal. Players want a certain type of woman. I'm simply making those connections happen. There's nothing wrong with that."

"The way you go about it, there are about a million things wrong with it," Cassidy said.

"What's your point?" Andrea said, her expression smug.

"Ms. Wilson, we both know you're responsible for George's current predicament. But resolving that isn't my responsibility. I'll leave that to the lawyers and accountants. As I stated, I'm here to ask you to drop the civil lawsuit you've filed."

"Or what?" she asked.

I didn't answer her question. I wasn't going to threaten her. Not openly. And often in a negotiation, people came up with their own answers to their questions if you gave them a little silence to work with.

"That forum is supposed to be private," she said. "People say things there that they wouldn't say in an open setting. You have to keep it in context."

I waited, letting her stew over the implications of her posts becoming public knowledge. What would happen if she was exposed. I watched her glance up at my uniformed sister. At Scarlett, who looked like she could be law enforcement or an investigator of some kind. The ID card around her neck was a nice touch.

Andrea met my eyes again and I let my gaze drift to the window, to where Bowie stood outside a car, wearing a black jacket and dark sunglasses.

"Who is that outside?" she asked. "Are you going to arrest me? You don't even have jurisdiction."

I intentionally refrained from answering her question. "I wonder what would happen if word got out that an athlete's assistant has been using private information about her client and his teammates for personal profit. That same assistant who's allegedly involved in her client's tax evasion case."

"It's a good story," Scarlett said. "Lies, money, sex."

"So blackmail?" Andrea asked. "Is that it? I drop my lawsuit, and you stay quiet about *Jersey Chaser*?"

"No," I said, shaking my head. Here was where I took the risk, but if anyone had an excellent poker face, it was June Bot. "I'm not going to blackmail you. That's far too complicated. But you are going to drop your lawsuit against George."

Her eye twitched again. "Then why even make me drive out here? Why not just go to the press?"

I glanced out the window at Bowie. Gibson walked by and ruffled his hair. I almost winced. *Damn it, Gibson, you're going to ruin it.*

By the time Andrea looked out the window, Gibson was gone. Bowie almost looked a little scary, standing out there dressed in black, his chiseled jaw clenched.

Once again, I didn't say a word. I let Andrea make up a story in her mind about what was happening. Obviously we weren't going to arrest her, nor was Bowie some sort of federal agent who was ready to take her in. He was a high school vice principal. The worst he could do was give her detention.

But she didn't know that. And if I waited long enough, let a few more seconds tick by, she might just—

"Is he FBI? Or something worse? What is this, some kind of mafia?" she asked. I still didn't reply. "Oh my god, fine. I'll drop the lawsuit. Just let me go. Please."

"Call your lawyer," I said.

"Now?"

I nodded.

Her hand trembled as she took out her phone and made

a call. I watched with a blank expression while she talked to her lawyer, requesting that they drop the lawsuit against GT Thompson.

"Happy now?" she asked, slipping her phone back in her purse.

"I'm satisfied with your decision to withdraw the lawsuit."

"So, is that it?" she asked, her eyes flicking to Cassidy and Scarlett. They both acted as if they were bored. "Are you going to let me go?"

"Yes," I said. "You're free to leave."

She hesitated, narrowing her eyes. "Are you going to go to the press about my website?"

"No."

With another wary look at all three of us, then at Bowie outside, she stood and gathered her things.

I watched her go without saying a word. She cast a glance at me over her shoulder and stumbled, almost tripping. Barely keeping her feet, she hurried outside.

After the door closed behind her, Cassidy and Scarlett both burst into laughter. I couldn't help myself. I laughed too.

"Did you see the look on her face?" Scarlett asked. "She was about to pee her pants."

Bowie came in and slipped an arm around Cassidy. "She's gone. Is that it?"

"Yes, we achieved our desired aim," I said.

"But why did you tell her you won't go to the press about her website?" Cassidy asked. "You had her by the lady balls. Why back down like that?"

"I said *I* wouldn't go to the press," I said. "I didn't say what George will do. As she so helpfully reminded me, I haven't been with him very long, so I certainly don't speak for him."

"You're a little bit evil, Juney," Bowie said. "But I like it."

"Why didn't you make her admit she stole George's money?" Scarlett asked.

"I estimated the chances of getting a confession at less than twenty percent. And even if we did, there would be a high probability that it wouldn't be admissible in court. So I determined the best course of action would be to use the leverage at our disposal to convince her to drop the lawsuit."

"I'm in awe," Cassidy said. "You assured me you weren't going to threaten her with anything you couldn't back up, and you weren't kidding."

"I took a risk and it paid off," I said.

"What is this?" Cassidy asked Scarlett, tucking her finger beneath the lanyard around her neck. "You realize that impersonating a law enforcement officer is illegal, right?"

"It's just my gym card," Scarlett said, her eyes going big and round in an expression of mock innocence. "It's not my fault if Ms. Skankson thought I was FBI or something."

Cassidy shook her head, smiling. "You gonna tell George?"

It was my turn to smile. "In time. For now, what he doesn't know won't hurt him."

Chapter Thirty-Seven

George

The news that Andrea had dropped her lawsuit lifted a weight from my shoulders. I still had the IRS breathing down my neck, but at least I wasn't trying to fight a war on two fronts.

And then, not two days later, I got even better news. Marc and his team had clear, undeniable evidence of Andrea's theft. They'd put together a paper trail that was not only admissible in court, it would prove I hadn't intentionally defrauded the IRS.

Andrea was arrested. Charges were filed.

Marc warned me that I would probably still owe back taxes, interest, and maybe even fines. But I wouldn't go to prison. The rest? It was just money. It sucked, but it wouldn't ruin me. I'd come out on the other side, whole, free, and a hell of a lot wiser than I'd been before. Even if my bank account took a hit.

The first thing I did was call my real estate agent and tell him to put my house back on the market. I wanted to make this move to Bootleg Springs official.

The second thing I did was make sure everything was good to go for the Do-Over Prom. June still didn't know I was behind the dance. It was just days away, and now more than ever, I wanted to give her a night she'd never forget.

Who knew I'd be hoping to get lucky on prom night again?

Plans were in place. We had the venue, thanks to Bowie. Entertainment, thanks to Gibson and his band. Leah Mae was heading up the decorating committee. Cassidy and Jonah had volunteered to organize refreshments, along with Sonny Fullson, who was bringing the moonshine. When the prom was for grown-ups, spiked punch wasn't optional—it was expected.

Everything was falling in line. Until June threw one last curve ball at me, just two days before the prom.

"I knew it," she said, staring at her laptop screen.

She sat at the dining table with a neat stack of romance novels, her laptop, and a steaming mug of tea.

"You knew what?"

Looking up from the screen, she met my eyes. "Callie Kendall is a fake. It's not her."

I let that sink in for a moment while I slid into the chair across from her. "No shit?"

"I just got the results from the genetics lab. The sample I supplied is not a match for Callie Kendall. It's not her, George. I was right."

"Wow." I wasn't sure what else to say. June had taken the hair right off that woman's head. Like she'd said, DNA evidence wouldn't lie.

"Yes, wow, and many other exclamations of surprise and triumph."

"Are you going to pass that on to Cassidy?"

"Yes, but…"

"But what?"

I could see the wheels turning, something going on in that big brain of hers. I wasn't sure if that was a good thing or a bad thing in this particular case.

"DNA evidence is conclusive, but…it's not enough."

"Not enough? You said DNA won't lie. This proves she's not Callie. You were right. You can turn this into the police and they can reopen the investigation into the real Callie's disappearance. What more do you want?"

"I want to talk to her."

"Talk to who?" I asked.

"The Callie impostor."

"Oh, June Bug," I said. "Are you sure that's a good idea? She's a woman pretending to be a missing girl. She's obviously not right. What if she's dangerous?"

"That's why I'm bringing you."

"Whoa, slow down there, Sherlock," I said. "Maybe it's time you hang up your cap and trench coat and let the law handle it."

"I can't."

"Why not?"

"Because people cared."

"Of course people cared," I said, still not comprehending what she meant.

She took a deep breath. "I didn't understand it before. Why did we keep those posters up for so many years? Why bother? The chance of Callie ever being found alive diminished with every passing year, but that didn't matter to Bootleg. We still held out hope. I never realized how important that was. How deeply these events are woven into the fabric of who we are."

"All right, I'm with you."

"Bootleg is made up of people who won't stop caring, no matter the odds. And this woman stomped all over that. I have to know why. I don't understand what could have motivated her to do this."

"It's an equation that doesn't add up."

"Yes," she said, her voice excited. "Exactly."

I shook my head. Sometimes this woman was infuriating. Her need to understand the intricacies of every problem, math or otherwise, was maddening.

I fucking loved it.

"You're determined to get me into trouble, aren't you?" I asked.

"You talked to her. Did she seem crazy?"

"No, but that doesn't mean she *isn't* crazy. Especially if you're going to confront her with DNA evidence that she's not who she says she is."

"I understand the implications of what I'm proposing," she said. "But I need this. If I turn in the DNA results, yes, they'll reopen Callie's investigation and maybe someday we'll have the truth. But it won't be the same. I need to look this woman in the eyes and ask her why she did this."

"What if she won't explain?"

"At least I will have tried."

I had a feeling that wasn't precisely what June meant. She could acknowledge there was a possibility that this woman wouldn't talk to her—wouldn't tell her what she wanted to know. But June was confident she would. I could see it in her eyes. In the determination she wore like some women wore jewelry.

My sweet June Bug wasn't asking me for expensive things. She didn't want a flashy car, designer shoes, or a fancy condo. She wanted me to help her right a wrong.

I reached across the table and enveloped her hand in mine. "Okay, June Bug. We'll track her down one last time."

———

Since we knew where Impostor Callie lived, we simply drove out to Philly and camped in front of her building until she came out. We followed, parked two blocks away when she stopped, and watched her go into a nail salon. That wasn't exactly ideal for a confrontation of this nature, so we waited.

After coming out of the nail salon, she did us an unintentional favor, heading into the coffee shop next door. We got out of my car and followed her in.

The rich scent of coffee beans filled the air. Impostor Callie stood to the side, her attention on her phone. She appeared to have ordered and was waiting for her coffee.

June walked in as if she owned the place, back straight, all

277

confidence. She went right up to the woman, never breaking stride.

"Callie Kendall?" June asked.

The woman looked up. "Oh. Um, yes. Do I know you?"

"You should, but no, you don't."

She glanced around, seeming to notice me. Her eyes widened slightly—did she recognize me?—but moved back to June.

"Do you need something? I'm not doing any more interviews."

"I'm not here for an interview," June said. "But I do need to speak to you."

The barista called Callie's name and she took her coffee from the counter. "What's this about?"

June gestured toward a table in the back. Wordlessly, I followed the two women and the three of us sat down.

"I'm June. This is George."

"We've met before," she said to me. "At the restaurant."

"You did," June said. "We're here because we know you aren't Callie Kendall."

I held back a wince. Holy shit, she'd just come right out and said it. No games with this one. God, I loved her.

"Excuse me?" the woman said.

"You're not Callie."

"Of course I am." Her brow creased and she leaned away. "What are you talking about?"

June pulled a sheet of paper out of her bag. "I took a sample of your hair and had it tested against Callie Kendall's DNA. It was not a match."

"What? When?"

June gestured toward me. "I took a hair sample while you were talking to him in the restaurant that day."

Her mouth dropped open and she smoothed the back of her hair down with one hand. "What the hell?"

My muscles tensed, the instinct to protect June sending a surge of adrenaline through my system. This woman was getting angry—no surprise there. I'd toss June over my shoulder and carry her out of here before I let this get ugly.

The woman touched the paper with one finger, drawing it closer, her eyes scanning the text. "You have got to be kidding me."

"My sense of humor is not well-developed enough to pull off a prank of this magnitude," June said.

She looked at the paper for a long moment, but she no longer seemed to be reading. Probably deciding what to do.

"What do you want?" she asked, finally.

"I want to know the truth," June said. "Who are you, and why are you impersonating a missing girl?"

Her posture changed. She'd gone from wary and alert to defensive. Back and shoulders stiff, jaw tight.

"My real name is Abbie Gilbert."

"Why are you pretending to be Callie?"

Abbie let out a breath and her shoulders slumped. "It's a long story."

June didn't reply. Just kept watching her.

"Callie's story was in the news and people kept joking about me being her. I'm a year younger, but obviously I look just like her. It got me curious. So I started reading everything I could find about her case. It was fascinating. That whole town kept her memory alive for so long."

I put my arm over the back of June's chair. This Abbie person seemed to have relaxed, but I still felt like a coiled spring, ready to strike if she turned out to be the dangerous kind of crazy.

"Anyway, I'm not hurting anyone," Abbie said. "If anything, I'm doing something good. I gave the Kendalls their daughter back."

"But you're not their daughter," June said. "Pretending to be her means no one is looking for the real Callie anymore. They closed the investigation."

Abbie rolled her eyes. "Callie Kendall is dead."

"You seem overly confident, stating that as a fact," June said.

"It is a fact."

"Do you have proof?"

"No, I don't have proof," Abbie said. "No one does. I know this case inside and out. Even without a body it was being treated like a homicide investigation. Everything points to her being dead."

"And you think that gives you the right to impersonate her? To lie to her family? To the public?"

"Why does it matter?"

I almost cut in with *because it's illegal and insane*. But I kept my mouth shut. This was June's conversation to have. I was just here as backup.

"It matters because people still care about her," June said. "And whatever happened to her, people deserve the truth, not some impostor who's trying to profit from her tragedy."

"Why are you here?" Abbie asked. "Do you want to threaten me? Blackmail me?"

"I told you already, I want to know why. I want to know why you would go to so much trouble to pretend to be someone you're not. Other than the distinct possibility that you have a serious mental illness."

"Because I did disappear and no one cared," Abbie said, her voice sharp. Her eyes widened with shock, as if she were surprised she'd said that. When she spoke again, her voice was quieter. "I left my family the day I turned eighteen, and no one did a thing. No one reported me missing or tried to find me. So fine, they didn't give a shit. I thought I was over it. And then, last year, Callie Kendall was all over the news. The mystery of the girl who went missing from some stupid town in West Virginia. Those people kept her posters up for over twelve years. All those years, and people still wanted to find her. That girl who looked just like me."

"So you decided to become her?"

"Why not? I created the happy ending everyone wanted for Callie. The Kendalls have a daughter again. That town can move on, knowing the mystery is solved."

"Except it's a lie."

"A lie that doesn't hurt anyone."

"I beg to differ," June said. "It hurts everyone."

A flicker of fear crossed Abbie's face. "What are you going to do?"

"Tell the truth." June stood, her chair scraping across the floor.

I stood and grabbed June's arm, intent on getting us the hell out of here. Abbie didn't move, just sat in her chair, staring at June, open-mouthed. But I wasn't taking any chances.

"Let's go."

I didn't release my grip on June's arm until we got to my car. She got in the passenger's side and I cast a quick glance around, half expecting to see Abbie. My heart raced. It wasn't that I was afraid of her—not physically at least. But who knew what someone like that was capable of doing, especially when backed into a corner. I wasn't taking a single chance with my woman. She'd heard Abbie's explanation. Now we were getting as far away from her as possible.

The scenery went by in a blur as I drove. June was quiet. I could tell she needed a little time to process what she'd heard. I clasped her hand in mine, gently stroking her skin with my thumb.

When we left the city behind, I finally started to relax. We still had a long drive ahead of us, but my heightened sense of danger abated.

"You were concerned she'd hurt me, weren't you?" she asked.

"You just never know. She went to a lot of trouble to convince people that she's Callie. She has the Kendalls fooled. Got a book deal that's worth a lot of money. That woman had everything on the line and we cornered her. Anyone could be dangerous in that situation."

June silently nodded.

"Did you get what you needed?" I asked.

"Yes. The strange thing is, I feel sympathy for her. Or perhaps it's pity. A whole and happy person would never do something like this. I suspect she's very broken."

"No doubt."

"This is going to hurt a lot of people. There was so much relief at Callie being found, and this will take it all away."

"That's true. And I think it means a lot that you recognize it. But I still think people deserve the truth, even if it isn't what they want to hear."

"I agree."

I squeezed her hand. She was right. This was going to hurt a lot of people. The Kendalls. They'd lost their daughter once, and now they were going to have to face that they'd been fooled. The Bodines. Suspicion was going to fall on their late father again, especially because now there was no longer an innocent explanation for the presence of Callie's fingerprints in their mother's car. The entire town of Bootleg. They'd celebrated the happy ending to Callie's story, and now they'd be right back where they started. No closer to finding answers.

But at least now someone would be looking.

Chapter Thirty-Eight

June

"O uch." I reached up to smooth down the little hairs alongside my ear.

"Sorry Juney," Cassidy said. "I'm trying not to pull."

I sat in a chair we'd dragged into my parents' bathroom, facing away from the mirror. I still didn't understand why we were getting ready for the Do-Over Prom at our parents' house, but the other girls had loved the idea. Something about nostalgia and *doing it right this time.*

From a practical standpoint, my parents did have the largest bathroom of any of us. Scarlett's house was bursting at the seams with two people and her psychotic cat. Cassidy and Bowie were still remodeling their duplex into a single residence. The dust alone was a nightmare, not to mention the allergy-inducing dander from her two cats. My house was not tiny, nor was it in a state of construction or contaminated by cat hair. But my two bathrooms weren't large, and the other girls had insisted the primping ritual would be fun this way.

They'd been right. It was fun.

I hadn't turned over my findings about the Callie Kendall impostor. Not yet. There had been a time when I wouldn't have considered waiting. I had the data, it needed to be shared. End of story. But I'd realized that when it came to people, facts and data weren't always the most important thing. There were thoughts and feelings behind every story, every situation. And in this case, my resolve to uncover the truth and expose Abbie Gilbert as the fake she was had to be tempered with compassion.

The news that Callie was still missing—and that we'd been fooled by an impostor—was going to hit my town hard. This was going to affect the lives of people I cared about. My sister. Scarlett and her entire family. So before blurting out what I knew, I'd thought about it. And come to the conclusion that waiting a few days—at least until after the Do-Over Prom— was the kind thing to do.

Cassidy stood behind me, doing something with my hair that involved a curling iron. She had a YouTube tutorial open on her phone and checked it periodically, as if to make sure she was on the right track. Leah Mae had already done my makeup, but they were refusing to let me see the results.

Scarlett sat on the counter, one leg lifted so she could paint her toenails. Leah Mae stood on my other side, leaning toward the mirror as she brushed color across her eyelid.

"Why didn't you just get a pedicure?" Cassidy asked.

"I did, but I didn't like the color," Scarlett said. "Are you almost done? You still need to do mine."

"I know, keep your panties on," Cassidy said. "We have time."

"I'll keep 'em on for now, but they're definitely coming off later tonight," Scarlett said with a wicked grin.

"Preach, sister," Cassidy said. "Knowing we're getting laid on prom night sure does take off some of the pressure, doesn't it?"

"Yep," Scarlett said. "So does knowing my date isn't a jackass. I swear, what were we thinking back in high school?"

"Good question," Cassidy said.

Even I had been burned by a boy in high school. It seemed none of us had come out unscathed.

"Maturity makes a significant difference," I said.

"Isn't that the truth," Leah Mae said. She dipped her mascara wand into the bottle. "My prom date got mad because the heels I wore made us the same height. He wouldn't dance with me unless I took them off. So there I was, barefoot on the dance floor, and I stepped on something sharp."

"Ouch," Cassidy said.

"Yeah, and it gets worse," Leah Mae said. "I yelped and looked down. There was already blood all over. My date took one look at my bleeding foot and fainted."

Scarlett laughed. "You're kidding."

"Nope," Leah Mae said. "He crumpled to the floor and everyone was so busy making sure he was okay, I just stood there, bleeding all over the place. I limped to the bathroom by myself, then called my mom to come pick me up."

"That is an unfortunate turn of events," I said.

"My date didn't faint, but he did get so drunk he spent the entire night puking out back behind the gym," Cassidy said.

"I remember that," Scarlett said. "And I was covered in mud because Freddy Sleeth's tire went flat on the way to the dance, and he didn't know how to change it himself."

"If I recall, you were still crowned prom queen," Cassidy said.

"Course I was," Scarlett said, then she winced. "Aw, dang, Cass, I got drunk that night, too, didn't I? You had to deal with a drunk date and a drunk best friend."

"Mm-hmm," Cassidy hummed, tugging on my hair. "That's okay, though. We did a lot of dumb things back then."

"We're much more mature now," Scarlett said, pointing the nail polish brush at Cassidy. "Although not *too* mature."

"Amen to that, too," Cassidy said. She fluffed my hair. "All right, Juney, I think we're done."

"Wait, don't let her look until she gets dressed," Leah Mae said. "It'll be like a makeover reveal."

"Good idea," Cassidy said.

They blocked me from the mirror and ushered me into my parents' bedroom, where our dresses were laid out in garment bags on the bed.

We'd all gone dress shopping together over in Perrinville—me, Cassidy, Mom, Scarlett, and Leah Mae. The clerks had looked at us funny as we'd tried on dozens of prom dresses, but we hadn't cared. We'd made a day of it, including lunch with mimosas.

I'd chosen a peach dress with a subtle vintage look. Leah Mae had taken it home with her, saying she wanted to add a little flair. Make it *more June*, whatever that meant.

Now she took the garment bag with my dress and lowered the zipper. "I'm so nervous all of a sudden. I hope you love it."

The dress that emerged from the black bag was like something out of a dream. The top still looked similar to its original design—light peach with cap sleeves and a V-shaped dip at the neck. Leah Mae had added a gold ribbon along the neckline that tied in a small bow in the center. The gold set off the peach perfectly, adding a sparkly touch to the dress.

But it was the lower part of the dress that made my breath catch. She'd sewn on dozens of little gold butterflies all over the skirt. Beginning at the waist, they were sparse, growing thicker toward the hem. The bottom swarmed with them, their tiny wings glittering in the light.

I touched my hand to my mouth. "Oh."

"Do you like it?" Leah Mae asked.

"Put it on," Scarlett breathed.

I couldn't find the words to answer—just stood in stunned silence while the girls helped me out of the button-down flannel shirt I'd been wearing, and into the dress.

"Careful of her hair."

"Oh my god."

"Oh, Juney."

Leah Mae zipped up the back. "What do you think?"

I stepped into the bathroom and gazed into the full-length

mirror. I didn't recognize the woman staring back at me. Her dark blond hair was down, soft curls framing her face. Her eyes stood out against her pale skin. Long lashes. Shiny peach lips.

But the dress. It hugged my curves—look at that, I had curves—and the color made my skin look as if I was illuminated from inside. The gold touches at the neckline were lovely, but those butterflies. They sparkled when I moved, making the dress look positively magical.

"I'm almost without words," I said, my voice soft. "Telling you it's the most beautiful thing I've ever seen would be the truth, and still not adequate to describe how much I love it."

Leah Mae clasped her hands at her chest and scrunched her shoulders. "Really? As soon as you tried this on in the store, I had a vision of what it could be. I kept seeing you as a butterfly, emerging from your cocoon."

"Damn it, Leah Mae, now you'll have to fix my makeup," Scarlett said, wiping tears from her cheeks.

"Mine too," Cassidy said, sniffing.

I brushed my hands down my waist and hips. "I can't imagine how much time this took. The workmanship is incredible."

"I had some late nights," Leah Mae said. "But I loved making it. And look at you. It was worth it."

"Thank you," I said. "This means so much."

We finished getting ready together in my parents' bedroom. Cassidy did Scarlett's hair while Leah Mae did hers. My mom came in and burst into tears when she saw me in my dress. She and my dad were attending the dance as well—it seemed just about everyone in Bootleg who was over the age of twenty-one would be there. Cassidy and Leah Mae fussed over Mom's hair and makeup until they were all satisfied.

"Ladies," my dad called from downstairs. "There's a fancy limousine outside. I believe your dates have arrived."

My mom descended the stairs first, dressed in a beautiful blue gown that set off her eyes. Dad, looking dashing in his suit with his mustache neatly trimmed, watched her in awe. He took her hands when she reached the bottom, and stared at her for a long moment.

"You look more beautiful than ever," he said, his voice soft.

The other men congregated near the front door, eyes trained on us. Bowie wore a sleek black tux, complete with a purple bow tie to match Cassidy's purple dress. Devlin looked like a model in a magazine with his slate gray suit and ascot. Even Jameson had dressed for the occasion, in a black tux much like Bowie's. He had a pale pink handkerchief in his jacket pocket, sparkling with tiny sequins, just like Leah Mae's dress.

George waited behind the rest of the men. His dark suit fit his broad shoulders and tall stature perfectly. He had a little gold butterfly—just like the ones on my dress—pinned to his lapel. Leah Mae had thought of everything.

Scarlett took to the stairs. She'd opted for a short red dress with a tulle skirt and cowboy boots. Devlin watched her like he was ready to rip that dress right off her.

Cassidy went next, her deep purple dress rustling around her legs. The way Bowie looked at her made me smile, and I had to bite my lower lip to keep the tears from my eyes. His face practically shone with happiness, like he couldn't imagine anything better in the entire world than my sister.

It struck me how many times I'd seen my dad look at my mom with that same gleam in his eyes.

Jameson chewed his lower lip as Leah Mae walked down in her pale pink dress, the fabric shimmering in the light. Her blond hair was up, emphasizing her tall, willowy frame. He scooped her into his arms and pressed his cheek to hers.

It was my turn. All eyes lifted, waiting for me to descend. My heart fluttered with sudden nervousness, my tummy tingling.

Plucking the skirt of my dress between my thumb and finger so I wouldn't trip, I held it up slightly and walked down the stairs. I rarely wore heels, but I'd found a pair that weren't too high, so I didn't feel like I was in danger of falling.

Everyone watched, but the second I met George's eyes, I

forgot about the rest of them. He was all that existed in the world. His eyes, crinkling at the corners with his smile. The dimples puckering his cheeks. His expression was awed, as if he couldn't quite believe it was me.

When I got to the bottom, George stepped forward and took my hands in his.

"Hi, beautiful," he said softly.

My breath caught in my throat and my skin buzzed with excitement. This was really happening. Me, in a fancy dress, with a handsome date for the prom. For the second time today, I was rendered almost speechless.

"You look remarkable," I said, and it was such a vast understatement, it almost felt like a lie. He looked gorgeous. Delectable. Handsome. Wondrous. Sexy. Too many adjectives burst through my brain. I couldn't keep up with them.

"Oh June Bug," he said, his voice low. "I'm nothing compared to you. You're a vision tonight."

The men had gone all-in with the prom theme, and brought us each a flower corsage to wear on our wrist. George had chosen white and peach flowers with tiny pearls for mine, matching my dress. He slid the band around my wrist, then leaned in to kiss my forehead.

"Are y'all ready?" Dad asked. "Your driver's waiting."

Mom and Dad were driving separately, but the rest of us went outside and piled into the waiting limousine. I'd never been in a limo before, and I wondered where they'd even found one. There wasn't a limo to be found in Bootleg Springs. He must have come from a neighboring town.

The seats were plush leather and there was an ice bucket with a bottle of champagne. Bowie poured for everyone as the driver pulled out onto the street.

"We have another stop to make," Bowie said. "We're picking up Jonah and Lacey, too."

The rest of us waited in the big limo while he stopped at Lacey's house to pick up our last couple. Jonah looked very nice in a dark gray suit and tie. Lacey wore a light blue dress with a long slit up the side. They got in and sat side-by-side. The driver shut the door behind them and once again, we were off.

We were minutes from the high school, so the driver must have taken a longer route, or perhaps driven a loop around town, giving us time to finish our champagne.

By the time we got to the high school, everyone was laughing, cheeks flushed. George helped me out of the car, then offered me his arm. I tucked my hand in the crook of his elbow, took a deep breath, and walked in to my first ever formal dance.

The gym had been transformed into everything I'd imagined a prom to be. Streamers, balloons, twinkle lights. A big banner said *Welcome to the Bootleg Springs Do-Over Prom*. A photographer had a backdrop set up in a corner, and there were snacks and refreshments on folding tables. Colored lights flickered around the dance floor. Gibson, Hung, and Corbin occupied the small stage, already playing a set.

Couples—wearing everything from sequined prom dresses and rented tuxes to vintage outfits that looked like they might have been their original prom attire fifty years ago—danced, ate, drank, and mingled. My parents were there, holding hands near the moonshine fountain. Bernie O'Dell had traded his customary overalls for a hickory shirt and brand-new jeans. Opal Bodine—no relation to Scarlett—wore a black dress and a bow in her hair, rather than a baseball cap.

Granny Louisa and Estelle were there, both wearing silver and black. Wade Zirkel had brought Zadie Rummerfield. He saw our group coming and suddenly turned in the other direction. Bootleg Justice wasn't soon forgotten.

Everywhere I looked, I saw familiar faces. People decked out in their best, dancing, nibbling on snacks, or drinking punch and moonshine. Music filled the air and the lights danced off the decorations. Even the sight of Misty Lynn Prosser making eyes at Gibson Bodine as he sang, although she was here with Rhett Ginsler, didn't dampen my enjoyment of the evening.

It was amazing.

Gibson and his band rolled into a new song. *Tennessee Whiskey*.

"Shall we?" George asked, taking my hand and nudging me toward the dance floor. "I feel like this is our song."

I nodded, and he led me onto the dance floor. One hand went to my lower back, the other tucked my hand against his chest. We swayed to the slow beat of the music, and I closed my eyes, letting myself feel.

"So, what do you think?" George asked.

"About what?" I opened my eyes and looked up at him.

"All this," he said.

"It's wonderful. I need to thank whoever had the idea for this dance."

George grinned. "Can I confess something?"

I raised my eyebrows. "Yes."

"It was me."

It took a second for what he meant to sink in. "You? The dance was your idea?"

He nodded, still smiling.

"Did you…" I almost couldn't utter the words, it was too stunning. "Did you do this for me?"

"Yes, June Bug. I did this for you. I wanted you to have this experience. And I wanted you to have it with me."

Tears burned my eyes and I found myself having the ludicrous thought that if I cried, I'd ruin my makeup. "This is the most wonderful thing anyone has ever done for me."

"I've got a lifetime of wonderfuls in store for you. You're mine, my pretty little butterfly. And I intend to keep you."

Chapter Thirty-Nine

George

I really did like dancing.

My arms around June, holding her close. Her body pressed against me as we moved to the music. We'd had a little moonshine and some cherry cheesecake cups that were to die for. Wandered around and chatted with friends. Posed for pictures. Joked. Laughed. Danced. A damn near perfect evening.

I indulged in a little self-congratulation at having pulled this off. It looked like most people were having a great time. Bootleg residents of all ages, from their early twenties to their nineties, had come—some as couples, some in groups. There were dresses, tuxes, suits, hats, canes, and even someone's dog running around in a little black bow tie.

It felt good to have made this happen for June. I hadn't foisted it off on an assistant. I'd handled most of the details myself. Sure, a lot of people had been in on the planning and execution. I couldn't have done it alone. But I'd had a big idea and I'd made it happen. It shored up my confidence quite a bit, even if it was just a silly dance.

But the way June beamed at me, looking like a dream on wings tonight, made it seem not the least bit silly at all.

We took a break from the dance floor and moved off to the side. The party was still going strong, but I hadn't seen Bowie and Cassidy in quite some time. Scarlett and Devlin had disappeared early as well. Although we'd all taken the limo together, each of us had parked our cars here at the high school so we could leave whenever we wanted.

I happened to know Bowie had rented a hotel room to make the prom night experience complete. I'd thought about doing the same. But I didn't want to put pressure on June. Did I hope to hit a grand slam home run tonight? Of course I did. I was aching for her something fierce. But her being ready was far more important than the pressure of my persistent erection.

"It appears that Jonah is leaving," June said, gesturing toward the door.

I was about to snicker and say something about him getting lucky, but he was alone. "Where's Lacey?"

"Uh-oh." June nodded toward the dance floor.

Lacey was cozied up with a man who was *not* Jonah Bodine. "Who's he?" I asked.

"Amos Sheridan. He's Cassidy's ex-boyfriend."

There was nothing subtle about the way Amos held Lacey. They were pressed close together, her arms tight around his neck, his hands almost too low on her backside to be decent.

I looked back at the door. Jonah paused, casting a glance over his shoulder toward the dance floor. He shook his head and left.

"Ouch," I said. "That sucks. Poor Jonah."

"I knew he shouldn't have taken Lacey Dickerson to the prom," June said. "Maybe I shouldn't have kept my misgivings to myself."

"He'll be all right. Jonah's a good guy. He just needs to meet the right girl."

"I agree. But I have a strong urge to make Lacey pay for ditching Jonah."

"Slow down, tiger." I traced my fingers down the side of her cheek. "Maybe Bootleg Justice can wait this time."

The corner of her mouth tugged upward in a little grin and there was a mischievous sparkle in her eyes. "Speaking of Bootleg Justice…earlier you confessed to all this." She gestured at the decked-out gym. "I have a confession as well."

"Oh yeah?"

"I was the one who got Andrea to drop her lawsuit. Cassidy and I did some research and discovered she owned the *Jersey Chaser* website." She hesitated, chewing her bottom lip. "I confronted her with it and she agreed to drop the suit."

Chuckling, I pulled her against me. "June Bug. What am I going to do with you?"

"Are you angry?" she asked, looking up at me. Her eyes were big and round, but she wasn't trying to play cute to manipulate me. June didn't know how to play cute, and I loved that about her. She was really worried I'd be upset.

"I'm not mad." I leaned down and kissed her forehead. "Just promise me you didn't do anything illegal."

"Cassidy was there."

"That doesn't really answer my question, but…okay." I kissed her again, deciding it was probably best if I didn't know the details. "Thanks for having my back."

"You're welcome."

She trailed her fingers up my forearm. I'd taken off my jacket and rolled up my sleeves. Her touch was warm and tempting.

I leaned down, capturing her lips with mine. I'd kissed her a hundred times tonight—she looked so good, she was impossible to resist—but this kiss was different. It was more. Her tongue lapped against mine hungrily and she grabbed my shirt, tugging me closer.

There were too many people around for me to kiss her the way I wanted. Taking her hand, I led her through a set of double doors.

We emerged into a dark hallway lined with lockers.

Something primal roared to life inside me. I pushed June up against one of the metal locker doors and delved into her mouth. She grabbed the back of my neck, pulling me to her, like she needed me as much as I needed her.

Her hands traced a path down my chest, over my abs, to the waistband of my pants. I was already hard, but her hands near my dick made me groan.

"Maybe we should go," I said between kisses.

"Mm-hmm."

Neither of us made a move to stop making out. But we seemed to be alone, so a few more minutes wouldn't hurt anything.

Her hand slid down and she grabbed my cock through my pants.

I growled. "June."

She squeezed. "I want this."

A red haze of lust tinted my vision. I kissed down her neck while she rubbed my dick. My hands roamed across her body, but there was too much dress. It was getting in my way.

I wasn't sure how I was going to make it home. My blood boiled, my erection throbbing as she rubbed and squeezed. She was driving me absolutely out of my mind.

"We should go," I said against her neck, then slid my tongue along her skin.

"Where?" she breathed.

"Home."

"Too far."

I'd never heard so much need in her voice. So much desperation. She literally had me by the balls. I would have done anything she asked. But…here?

"Where do you wanna go, baby?" I asked.

"Come on."

She took my hand and led me down the hallway, practically running in her heels. The first door she tried was locked. The second opened to a dark, empty classroom. Rows of desks faced a white board and the blinds were drawn on the windows.

As soon as the door shut, June grabbed my shirt and started unbuttoning.

"Whoa, June Bug." I was breathing hard, aching for her, and totally into whatever was about to go down. But I wanted to make sure she knew what she was doing. "We running for second or third in here?"

She stopped on the last button and looked up at me. In the dim light her eyes almost glowed. "I want you to hit a home run, George."

Oh, fuck.

I swallowed as she yanked my sleeves down my arms, working hard to get me undressed. "You're sure?"

"Yes." She attacked my belt, but paused, meeting my eyes. "Don't think. Just feel."

"Fuck yes, baby."

Grabbing her by the arms, I kissed her hard. Then zippers came down, she shrugged out of her dress, and I kicked my pants off. I fumbled for the condom in my wallet while June practically ripped her panties down.

I picked her up and set her on the edge of a desk. She freed my cock from my underwear and stroked it a few times while I tore open the foil packet. Her tongue danced across her lips as she watched me roll on the condom.

Her legs widened, and I stepped in close. Held my cock and rubbed it against her, teasing her clit.

She leaned her head back, closing her eyes, and let out a sigh. "Oh, George."

"You want this?" I asked, my voice rough and low.

"Yes."

"Look at me." My dick still in one hand, I slid my fingers through her hair, holding the back of her head. I wanted her to look me in the eyes and say it. "Tell me what you want."

Her voice was breathy and full of desire. "I want to have intercourse with you."

Only June Tucker could take the unsexiest word in history and make it hot as fuck.

I grabbed her ass, lined up the tip of my cock with her entrance, and slowly pushed inside. Her legs wrapped around me as I sank in deep.

"Yes, George," she whispered. "Yes, yes, yes."

I needed those yeses. Needed to hear them and know they were true.

Her pussy was hot and tight around me. I pulled out halfway and thrust back in, reveling in her moan of pleasure. Out, then in again. She held my shoulders, her eyes closed, her hair falling in sweet curls around her face.

"You're so beautiful," I said.

She smiled. "This feels so good."

"Baby, we're just getting started."

I got a good grip on her ass and used my hips to drive into her. Every thrust sent a shock wave of sensation through me. I pounded into her, increasing my pace, her little whimpers and moans better than the roar of a Superbowl crowd.

"You still with me, baby?" I asked.

"Yes. So good."

She was heating up, her walls tightening around my erection. A flush of pink crept down her neck, across her tits.

"Yes, George," she said again. "More."

I tightened my grip and pounded her harder. Faster. Grunting with every thrust. The desk scraped against the floor.

She leaned back, still holding my shoulders, and looked down between us. I watched my glistening shaft disappear inside her and it almost undid me right then and there.

"Oh, I felt that," she said. "Your erection pulsed."

"I could come in you right now," I said. "But I'm making you come first."

The only answer was her rapid breathing. Her nipples were hard, her skin pink. I reached in between us to stroke her clit while I drove into her.

"Oh my god, George. That's…yes. Oh, yes please more."

Her body moved with mine, her hips bucking in time with my thrusts. I lost myself in the feel of her. In her fingers digging into my shoulders. In the heat of her body and the sweet caress of her most intimate places.

Our eyes locked. I felt a primal connection to her. This was so much more than sex. It was as if she reached inside me as I fucked her, wrapping herself around my soul.

I'd loved her before this moment. But this sealed the deal. I was hers, forever.

"I love you, June."

"I love you, too," she whispered.

"Does my baby need to come?" I stroked her clit again, keeping up my rhythmic thrusts. It was hard to hold back. I wanted to explode inside her.

"Yes. Please, George."

I pounded her harder, flexing my glutes to sink my cock in deep. Her pussy clenched—hard—and she threw her head back.

"Yes. Oh god, yes."

One more thrust and I came undone. I held her hips tight and drove into her, over and over. Grunting, growling, the desk scraping across the floor. All that hot tension erupted as I spilled into her, my vision going blurry.

My orgasm subsided, and I pulled June close. She held me tight, breathing hard against me. I wanted to wrap my body around her and never let go.

But we were in a classroom in her old high school…

I pulled back, reluctant to sever contact, and touched her face. "June, that was amazing."

The look of pure bliss on her face was better than anything I could ever imagine. Better than catching the game-winning touchdown with thousands of fans cheering my name. It was everything.

"George, I did it."

"You sure did, baby. How do you feel?"

Her eyelashes fluttered. "So good. So…warm and relaxed. That was so much better than a third base orgasm. I don't know if my legs work."

I chuckled and pulled out, then took off the condom.

The awkwardness of having to dispose of it here was totally outweighed by the orgasm-high I was swimming in.

Still in a daze, we quickly dressed. I made a brief stop in the bathroom, then came out and scooped her up into my arms.

I leaned down to plant a kiss on her nose. "You ready to go now?"

"Yes," she said, her mouth turning up in a sexy smile. "I want more."

Chapter Forty

June

George had unlocked something deep inside of me. A long-repressed sexual beast. Despite the incredible sex we'd just had, I wasn't sated.

My insides were molten—all heat and pressure and burning need. I walked to his car, my hand clasped in his, completely preoccupied by the idea of having him inside me again. I hadn't realized how much I wanted him. How much I wanted this. And now that I did, I needed more.

So much more.

I could barely contain myself on the drive to my house. It was only minutes, but I wanted to reach over and unzip his pants. I settled for stroking his erection through his clothes, happy to note he was hard again.

An empty classroom in my old high school wasn't the location I'd have predicted I'd finally experience mutually satisfying sexual intercourse. But there was an odd sort of logic to it—something my subconscious had understood. My previous sexual experiences had all been in traditional locations. In a bed, behind a closed door.

Something about the danger and excitement of having sex in a forbidden place—I'd taken English in that room—had helped break me out of my shell. Eased my fear that I couldn't have this with someone. If I could have an orgasm while George fucked me on top of a desk, I could certainly enjoy a sexual experience in a more typical setting.

And I fully planned to.

George groaned while he parked the car. My hand squeezing his manhood might have had something to do with that.

"June Bug, you're driving me crazy tonight."

"I'm also feeling somewhat unhinged."

He leaned over and kissed me, his tongue lapping over my lower lip. "I like you unhinged."

Sex in the car was enormously tempting, but next I wanted a bed. I wanted to stretch out on the sheets and let him touch me, the way it should have been the first time.

We got out and went inside. Jonah had changed into regular clothes—a long-sleeved t-shirt and track pants—and had his keys out.

"Hi, Jonah," I said. "I'm sorry Lacey ditched you for Amos Sheridan, although I didn't like the idea of you dating her. You can do better, I'm quite certain of it."

"Um, thanks, Juney."

George's hand slid down to cup my backside.

I gasped, then gestured to Jonah's keys. "It's probably best that you're leaving. George and I are going upstairs to have lots of sex."

George squeezed.

Jonah's face flushed and he shook his head. "Yeah, then I'm definitely going out. Have a good time."

I wasted no time waiting for Jonah to leave. I took George's hand—although it did feel nice grabbing my ass like that—and led him straight to my bedroom.

George kicked the door closed and tore off his jacket,

tossing it to the floor. He lowered the zipper on my dress while I once again unbuttoned his shirt.

My dress pooled on the floor at my feet. We stepped out of our shoes and peeled off the rest of our clothes. He pulled me against him, the skin on skin contact electrifying.

His lips caressed mine while his hands roamed over my body. I was relaxed, attentive, fully in the moment. I could feel every sensation, every subtle shift and movement.

"I need to taste you," he growled.

He dropped to his knees and pushed my legs apart. Suddenly his mouth was on me and it was like I'd reached a new level of bliss. His tongue lapped against my clit, the warmth and wetness stimulating me in ways I'd never imagined possible.

My legs shook and I wasn't sure if I'd be able to remain standing. But I did *not* want him to stop. I gasped, moving against his mouth, feeling his tongue work strange and incredible magic.

He slipped a finger inside, growling against me. A moan escaped my lips, my head rolling back. God, he was so good at this. I'd never felt anything like it.

The second finger nearly undid me. They curled and stroked, moving in sync with his tongue. It felt so good I thought I might die right there. Tension heightened—a hot whirlpool of feeling—swirling, building, bringing me to the brink.

Without warning, he stopped. In one fluid motion, he stood, grabbed me, and tossed me to the bed. I lay there panting as he got out another condom and rolled it on.

He didn't thrust in immediately. He started low, licking between my legs again. Murmuring about how good I tasted. Then he worked his way up, licking and kissing my skin. Feeling me with his hands. I closed my eyes, losing myself completely. This. This was what I'd wanted with him. Surrender. No walls between us. Just our bodies responding, connecting. Loving.

This was intimacy.

"You still with me, baby?" he asked, licking his way up my belly.

"I'm with you, George. I'm right here with you."

He moved up to my breasts, lavishing them with attention. He settled his thigh between my legs, letting me rub up against him. It wasn't enough—I needed more—but it gave me pressure where I needed it while he licked and sucked my nipples. I bucked against his leg, rubbing my clit across his skin.

"George, I need more."

"Mm, me too, baby."

He got to my neck and nibbled on the sensitive skin at the base of my throat. His cock was between my legs, teasing my opening. He groaned while he kissed and licked me. The scrape of his teeth had me writhing beneath him.

I'd never been so frantic and out of control. I was desperate for him, ready to beg him to fuck me. I'd never felt so shamelessly sexual—never felt so alive.

"Fuck me, please," I whispered.

He groaned into my neck and thrust inside me—hard. I clutched his back, my eyes closed, all thought gone from my mind. His thick erection stretched me open, the pressure exquisitely satisfying.

"Tell me again," he said.

"Fuck me, George."

"Oh my god."

He drove into me, again and again, growling with every thrust. His body on mine, his sheer size, was overwhelming in the best way. I was consumed, completely taken. He had every bit of me, and I gave it to him willingly.

"June, your pussy feels so good," he said, low in my ear.

His words added fuel to my fire. I wrapped my legs around his waist and held tight, every thrust a magnificent journey into pleasure. My bed frame slammed against the wall, George growled, I moaned and whimpered.

My climax built—again—my insides turning molten. I was hot, the pressure so intense I could barely stand it.

"More," I said. "Give me more."

"I love you, June Bug."

"I love you, too."

His back stiffened and I felt the telltale pulse of his cock inside me. It was as if he'd grown thicker, his shaft lengthening and expanding. It felt amazing.

"Yes," I said. "I'm with you."

"Come with me, baby," he said. "I want to feel you."

The tension built, my hot bundle of nerves pulsing with feeling. He drove in and out, giving me everything I needed. Everything I craved. It was hard and rough and intense, and I loved every second of it.

My walls clenched around his erection, the first wave of my orgasm washing over me. The rush of pleasure left me crying out, clutching onto him, as if it would sweep me away. My climax triggered his and he drove into me hard, his body releasing.

We moved in sync, clutching each other, letting go. The ripples of pleasure spread through my body, leaving me trembling in his arms. His muscles flexed and tightened as he rode out his orgasm inside me. The pulses of his cock nearly had me coming again, his low growls erotic and satisfying.

He pushed into me one last time, holding me tight. When he pulled out, he left me breathing hard, my eyes still closed.

A minute later, he was back, gathering me in his arms. My eyes fluttered open. I traced circles across his chest while I caught my breath.

"That was fucking incredible," he said, his voice awed. "June Bug, I've never… I don't even know what to say."

I nestled against him, loving the way I felt. Drifting in bliss. "Me neither."

He kissed my forehead and squeezed.

This was it. I'd done it. Not only had I engaged in mutually satisfying sex with George, I'd broken through the barrier I'd erected in my mind. I could have an intimate relationship with him—both emotionally and physically. We'd just had an amazing sexual experience, but it had gone so far beyond that. We'd connected.

We'd bonded.

This was what I'd been so afraid I couldn't have. But it had just taken the right man—this wonderful, beautiful man—to have enough patience to show me the way.

Chapter Forty-One

June

Hundreds of candles flickered in the cool night air. Most of Bootleg Springs filled Lake Drive, from the beach all the way to the library. It had been closed to traffic, although that had been an unnecessary precaution. No one was around to drive. They were all here, standing side-by-side, candles in hand.

Candles to honor Callie Kendall.

I'd gone to Cassidy with the DNA evidence that proved Abbie Gilbert wasn't Callie. At first, Cassidy had lectured me on leaving things to the authorities, proper evidence gathering, and admissibility in court. But she'd also acknowledged that it was best the truth came out.

Our dad had been the one to break the news to Judge and Mrs. Kendall. He'd said they'd been understandably shocked. The next day, they'd issued a statement, saying they were deeply wounded by Abbie Gilbert's actions. We hadn't yet heard if they planned to press charges, and so far, they hadn't been seen in public.

Once the story had gotten out, the news sites and blogs had eaten it up. There were as many theories about how Abbie had pulled it off as theories about what had happened to Callie.

Mom had called a public town meeting where she stood with my dad and they told the town the truth. The news that someone had impersonated Callie had been met with gasps of shock and calls for Bootleg Justice. But peacemaker that my father was, he'd calmed the crowd. He'd channeled the anger everyone felt toward Abbie into compassion and hope for Callie Kendall.

Her missing persons case was officially reopened. The Bodines seemed unsurprised, but resolute, at the news. Questions about their late father's involvement were still unanswered, thrusting them once again in the middle of the mystery.

The next day, Millie Waggle and Dottie Leigh had blanketed the town with fliers. *Candles for Callie*, they called it, and tonight everyone was here.

Pride in my town filled me as I stood next to George, holding my candle. This was who we were. We had a free-range chicken roaming our streets, our town pastime involved home-brewed liquor, and bar fights were as common as rain. But we stood by each other. Cared for each other. This was home. A home where even the weird girl had a place, among people who believed the best, and always held out hope.

The Bodines were all together, showing a unified front. Bowie stood with his arm around Cassidy. Scarlett and Devlin held hands, Scarlett's usual fire subdued. Leah Mae had her arms around Jameson's waist, her head on his chest. Jonah had a candle in one hand, his other stuffed in his pocket. He stood next to Gibson, who looked angrier than usual. He glowered at anyone who made eye contact, as if daring people to bring up the fact that his father was still a person of interest in Callie's case.

George and I stood with the Bodines. More than ever, I felt the connection between our families. Not just because my sister was on her way to becoming a Bodine in the not-too-distant future. Because, more than any other two families in this town, we were linked, the Tuckers and the Bodines. Linked by shared history and friendship, and by a belief that the past didn't have to write our futures for us.

Shelby, George's sister, was on his other side. She'd been here, in Bootleg Springs, last year at the tail end of the media circus. She'd come back this morning. I hadn't had a chance to speak to her much, past our initial introductions. But she was here doing research of some kind. I was interested to find out more.

Scarlett and Jonah both gave her the side-eye, but I wasn't sure what that was about. In fact, a few people eyed her with suspicion. Perhaps they didn't remember her, and they wondered why she was here, on a night that was so personal to our town.

I glanced across the street and noticed Henrietta VanSickle. She glanced across our group, her gaze intense. I hadn't seen her in town in months. She was a hermit who lived outside Bootleg Springs. Rumor had it that she'd taken a vow of silence. I'd certainly never heard her speak. There'd always been something slightly appealing about Henrietta's life, quiet and alone in the mountains.

But imagine the things I would have missed if I'd have withdrawn so completely like she had. I'd have missed George. And that would have been a tragedy.

When the vigil was over, the crowd started to break up. George and I said goodbye to his sister, who was staying in a B&B down by the lake. Cassidy asked the rest of us to meet her at the Red House in half an hour.

I directed George to the little rental house Scarlett owned. It was a cute little cottage, secluded from most of the other rental properties around the lake. The long drive was lined with cars when we arrived.

Everyone shuffled inside. The businesses in town had all been closed, but someone had managed to rustle up pepperoni rolls and sandwiches. Someone else had brought beer and lemonade.

Everyone who wanted food or a drink got it, and we settled in the small living room. Jameson and Scarlett sat at the tiny table, picking at a donut. Leah Mae sat on the couch next to Gibson. Jonah stood, and I wondered if he was subconsciously keeping himself separate from his half-siblings. Devlin sat on the hearth in front of the cold fireplace, and Bowie sat in an armchair.

George and I found a spot on the floor. He put his arm around me and scooted me closer.

Cassidy stood and glanced around the room. "Thanks for coming. I figured we were all in one place, so might as well get things out in the open."

George shifted next to me. "I can go if…"

"He can stay," Gibson said, his voice gruff.

"Agreed," Bowie said. "We're all involved, now."

Cassidy crossed her arms, her expression serious. Her Deputy Tucker face. "For now, none of this leaves this room. We clear?"

Everyone nodded in agreement.

"Okay, here's where we are. Callie is still missing. We all know Jonah Sr. had her cardigan. DNA evidence shows it was her blood on it. We also know her fingerprints were in Connie's car. Abbie Gilbert's story of Jonah giving her a ride out of town seemed to explain all that. But of course, none of it was true. So we still don't know why they had the sweater, or why her fingerprints were in the car."

Everyone shifted uncomfortably.

"Y'all, it gets worse." Cassidy took a deep breath. "The remains of a teenage girl were found in upstate New York a week ago. It used to be a rural area, but now it's a construction site. New houses going in. One of the crews came across a body."

"Oh god," someone muttered. I wasn't sure who.

"The remains are a partial skeleton. There's not enough to get a DNA sample or dental records for a positive identification. But they were able to determine it's been out there for twelve or thirteen years. Gender and approximate age are a match for Callie. And it was found about twenty miles from where Jonah Sr. got that speeding ticket. We got the call shortly after we reopened Callie's case. It's a close enough match, they alerted us."

Gibson's face reddened and he clenched his fists. Bowie scrubbed his hands up and down his face. Jonah rubbed the back of his neck—a gesture I remembered his father engaging in. Leah Mae reached over and rubbed Jameson's leg. He looked a bit green. Scarlett's eyes glistened with tears and Devlin stood to put his arm around her.

"God, I just…" Scarlett said, her voice uncharacteristically shaky. "I thought Callie was alive, and now…"

"Jesus," Bowie muttered.

Gibson stared at the floor, his jaw tight. I wondered if he was about to lose his temper, but he remained still.

"So that's it, then," Jameson said. "Dad must have—"

"The evidence isn't conclusive," I said, interrupting him.

"It's pretty fucking conclusive, Juney," Gibson said.

"Until there's a positive identification of the remains in question—"

"He took her out there and dumped her fucking body," Gibson said. His voice was thick with anger, his ice-blue eyes like cold steel.

I shrank back against George.

"Easy, Gibs," George said.

"Fuck this." Gibson stood, pushed his way past Jonah, and marched out the door, slamming it behind him.

Everyone shifted in the uncomfortable silence, the sound of the slamming door echoing through the room. Or maybe it just echoed in my head.

"Why does he always have to make things worse?" Scarlett muttered.

"I'll give him time to cool off, then go talk to him," Jameson said.

Scarlett gave him a weak smile. "Thanks, Jame."

"Y'all, I'm so sorry about all this," Cassidy said. "I wish the news was different. It was such a relief when we thought she was alive and your dad's role in it was explained."

"It's not your fault." Bowie stepped in next to her and put his arm around her shoulders. "We need answers, Cass. We need to find out what really happened, for better or worse, so we can all move on."

"There's one more thing," Cassidy said. "Y'all know Bowie and I found your mom's old GPS. It had the location she'd been to on the day she died—the Four Seasons Hotel in Baltimore."

"Why would she have gone out there?" Jameson asked.

"I didn't think it meant anything at first," Cassidy said. "With the Callie mystery supposedly solved, I didn't think there was any connection between your mom's accident and Callie's case. But after June told me the woman was an impostor, I got to thinking. I did some research and there was a charity event that day at the Four Seasons. I'm sure Connie had a good heart, but I don't recall her attending a lot of fancy charity luncheons in the city."

"No," Bowie said.

"Fortunately, they keep lots of records, so I was able to drum up a guest list from the event," Cassidy said. "Y'all, Mrs. Kendall was there that day."

"You think our mama went there to see Mrs. Kendall?" Scarlett asked.

"It seems likely," Cassidy said. "It doesn't prove anything, and without talking to Mrs. Kendall, we don't know why. But it sure looks like she went out there to talk to Mrs. Kendall, and got in an accident on the way home."

"Let's be logical about this," Bowie said. "Let's say Dad did something. Maybe he didn't kill Callie on purpose. Maybe it was an accident. What if he tried to hide what had happened and Mom found out? If Mom discovered the truth, she could have decided to tell Mrs. Kendall."

"Would she have done that first?" Jonah asked. "Or gone to the police?"

"And if she told Mrs. Kendall, why didn't the Kendalls do anything?" Jameson asked. "If they had the truth from Mom, why didn't *they* tell the police? They've said they wish the investigation was over. If they could end it with evidence from Mom, why stay quiet about it?"

"Because Mom died?" Scarlett asked. "She wasn't around to confirm the story?"

"I suppose," Bowie said. "Or maybe Mrs. Kendall didn't believe Mom. Or hell, maybe Mom changed her mind and didn't tell."

"She could have decided to protect Dad," Jameson said, his voice quiet. "Maybe she drove all the way out there and turned around before she talked to Mrs. Kendall."

Cassidy glanced at Bowie, and he gave her a nod. "I have to be honest with y'all. I don't know if your mom's accident was an accident. There weren't any brake marks on the road."

"What?" Scarlett shrieked. "Are you saying someone might have run her off the road?"

"It's a possibility," Cassidy said.

"Did the forensics lab find anything when they reexamined the car?" Devlin asked. "Something that would tell us whether she was forced off the road?"

"Their results were *inconclusive*," Cassidy said, emphasizing the word.

"I hate to even say this out loud," Jameson said, his voice quiet. "But could Mom have driven off the road on purpose?"

"Mom wouldn't have done that," Scarlett said. "I know she had her frustrations, but she never would have left us like that."

"I think Scarlett's right," Bowie said. "Mom was too stubborn to give up on life. Hell, she never even gave up on Dad. Not entirely."

Bowie raised an important point. Jonah and Connie Bodine hadn't exhibited the traits of a happy marriage. But they'd seemed to do their best to hold their family together.

"No, she didn't give up on him," Scarlett said. "She didn't give up on our family."

"Y'all are right," Jameson said. "But that means…"

"Could it have still been an accident?" Devlin asked. "A hit and run?"

"That's possible," Cassidy said.

Scarlett narrowed her eyes. "But you don't think so."

"There's something about this whole thing that doesn't add up," Cassidy said. "She went to Baltimore, where she might have had contact with Mrs. Kendall, and then she got in a car accident on the way home. When you add in the sweater, and the fingerprints in her car…"

"It's suspicious at best," Bowie said.

"I hate leaving y'all with more questions and no answers," Cassidy said. "But I'm going to do everything I can to find out the truth—about Callie, and your parents."

There were mutters of, "Thanks, Cass," from around the room.

I leaned against George, turning the facts over in my mind. The sweater and the fingerprints pointed to Jonah Bodine's involvement. But what about Connie? It was her car. Had she done something and Jonah had been covering for her? Was it the other way around?

Connie Bodine could have given Callie a ride somewhere on another day. We were a small town, a close-knit community. It wasn't uncommon for Bootleggers to parent other people's kids.

But why had they kept her sweater? And why had Connie gone to Baltimore that day, a year later? And the biggest question of all—had Callie's body finally been found?

Cassidy was right, there were still more questions than answers. It seemed as if every new clue only muddied the waters. That bothered me deeply and I vowed I'd do everything I could to help the Bodines find out what had really happened. I'd exposed Abbie Gilbert. Maybe I could help discover the truth about Callie Kendall, too.

Chapter Forty-Two

George

It was the perfect day for moving. The sun was out, but it wasn't hot. Traffic from Philly had been minimal. I'd spent the last week packing and getting rid of things I wouldn't need. Today, on a bright day in May, the movers loaded up what was left and drove it out to my new home in Bootleg Springs.

The home I was sharing with my June Bug.

Her house already had plenty of furniture, so I'd gotten rid of most of mine. I had some memorabilia from my years playing football that she was champing at the bit to put on display. She'd also decided she liked my couch better than hers, so we were switching that out. But all in all, it was an easy move, as moves went.

My career was over, my house sold, and I couldn't have been happier about any of it. If I'd played another season, I might never have come to Bootleg Springs. I might never have met June Tucker. And that would have been a damn shame.

I paused on the grass in front of her house—or rather, *our* house—to watch her. She directed the movers with her no-nonsense brand of confidence, making sure they knew exactly where to put things. Back straight, arms at her sides, expression neutral. She was strange and beautiful and oddly hypnotic. I loved her.

I was an absolute goner for June Tucker. Seven billion people on this planet, and I couldn't imagine there was another one like her. She was logical, blunt, and so smart she made my head spin. But she was also passionate and determined. She challenged me, made me want to be better than I was, and I loved the hell out of her for it.

That woman was mine, and she was going to be mine forever. I wasn't sure if she knew it yet, and I wasn't going to rush her. But I was going to marry June Tucker someday.

"Why don't you take a break?" I asked, walking up next to her. "They've got this under control."

"It's a more efficient use of everyone's time if I ensure they put boxes in the correct locations. Otherwise we'll have to move them a second time."

"Everything's labeled."

"That's true, but I'm not completely confident they're reading the labels."

I slid my arms around her, pulling her in for a kiss. "You're cute when you're insisting on maximum organization and efficiency."

"I can't tell if that's a serious statement."

"Of course I'm serious," I said. "You're adorable."

Jonah came out the front door, just as the two movers took a load in. "How's it going down here?"

"Almost unloaded," I said.

"Thanks. I'm all packed and ready for them."

Although June and I had offered to let Jonah stay—we didn't need the extra bedroom—he'd decided to move out. When June had announced to everyone that we were officially *engaging in a living arrangement of mutually agreed upon cohabitation*—and I'd explained that she meant we were moving in together—everyone had looked at Gibson, as if expecting him to offer to let Jonah move in with him. Gibson had said nothing, just raised one eyebrow, and Jonah had quickly said he'd decided to find his own place.

Shelby pulled up in her little blue sedan. Her hair was in a bouncy ponytail and she waved at me from the street.

"Hey, big giant brother," she said as she walked over. "Hey, June."

"Hello, Shelby," June said.

I knew it could take a little while for June to warm up to people—not to mention the other way around—but she and my sister seemed to get along. June had even suggested we offer the soon-to-be vacant bedroom to Shelby after Jonah moved out. Shelby had thanked us, but decided to stay in her B&B for the time being. I got the feeling that she was grateful for the offer, but didn't want to intrude on our privacy.

To be honest, I was glad. I loved my sister, but I didn't really want her sleeping one room away. Not when June had only recently discovered her sex kitten side. We'd been having a hell of a lot of fun exploring her sexuality. I wasn't too keen on anything that would put a damper on that.

"Hey Jonah, have you met my sister, Shelby?" I asked.

Jonah hesitated, and when he spoke, there was coldness in his tone. "Yeah, we've met."

"Hi," Shelby said, flashing him a smile. "Nice to see you again, Jonah."

"You too," he said. "Um, I have to get going. Moving out and everything."

"Right," Shelby said. Oh shit, I knew that little spark in her eye. Maybe Jonah didn't know it, but he'd just thrown down a gauntlet, and Shelby loved nothing more than a challenge. "Good luck with the move. Maybe I'll see you around."

"Sure." He went back inside.

Shelby crossed her arms. "Well that was weird."

"Jonah recently experienced an unfortunate public rejection at the Do-Over Prom," June said. "Perhaps his present mood is due to lingering feelings of resentment toward his date."

316

"Oh, that's too bad," Shelby said.

Bowie and Cassidy pulled up in Bowie's car, distracting us from Jonah's abrupt departure. He parked behind Shelby and they both got out.

"Sorry we're late," Bowie said. "But we brought beer, so hopefully that's better than lifting heavy furniture."

"The movers handled most of it," I said. "And beer is always appreciated."

I introduced Bowie and Cass to my sister. They'd also met her before, but this felt like an important moment. These two were going to be family to me, once I married June. I couldn't come out and say that, of course, but I was thinking it. Made me smile.

It also made me excited to introduce June to my parents. We'd had several video chats with them already. My father was enamored with June's mental database of sports statistics. They'd started chatting over text, and she'd invited him to be a part of her fantasy football league next season. I'd warned him that June almost never lost, but like Shelby, he loved a challenge.

I couldn't blame him. So did I. Ran in the family, apparently.

Shelby offered to make a run into town to get food for everyone. By the time she got back, the movers had taken Jonah's stuff to his new place. We spent a bit of time moving boxes into corners and unpacking a few things, then sat down to pizza and beer.

And damn, it felt good.

Cassidy and Bowie lounged comfortably on the couch that had barely been used in my old place. I hadn't been home enough to use it. Shelby sat on the floor, her paper plate in her lap, and scratched Mellow's tiny head.

June sat with me in the oversized arm chair that had been hers. The two of us barely fit, which was exactly why I liked sharing it with her. She was halfway on my lap, the warmth of her body soothing and comfortable. Her attention shifted from the TV—I'd turned on ESPN—to the conversations around her.

317

I held her tight, enjoying the closeness. The intimacy we shared, even here, among our family. She'd let me in her life—in her space. Trusted me with her body, and her heart. She'd helped me see that I was more than a guy who could catch a ball. That I was worth more.

Maybe we weren't the likeliest pair. But sometimes, possibility is stronger than probability. And with June Bug by my side, the possibilities were endless.

Epilogue
June

One year later

Steam rose from the surface of the hot spring. The air was warm, and I closed my eyes, letting the heat from the water relax me.

George sat next to me, idly playing with my hair. "I'm glad y'all keep this spot secret."

"There are a number of reasons secrecy is beneficial," I said. "How's your knee?"

He shifted next to me, stretching his leg out. "Good as new."

By the time fall—and football season—had rolled around last year, George had started feeling the pangs of missing his sport. But opportunity had come in the form of an opening for head coach of the Bootleg Springs High School football team. Not many small-town high schools could boast a former professional football star as a head coach. But Bootleg Springs wasn't just any small town.

He'd taken to his new job with enthusiasm, although I'd had to remind him not to get too involved in the team's scrimmages. His knee was healed, but after two ACL tears, the chance of re-injury was higher than average. For the most part, he listened.

George was an amazing coach. I loved to attend practices and watch him work his magic with those kids. He was the perfect blend of supportive and challenging—expecting his players to work hard, but giving them the positive reinforcement they needed to rise to his expectations. They'd made it to the playoffs, and although they hadn't gone all the way, there was always next year.

Apparently coaching high school in the fall hadn't been enough for him. He'd organized a Pee-Wee league for the younger kids in the spring. Watching him coach little boys and girls in their small helmets and pads was one of the cutest things I'd ever seen.

It made me think of babies. His babies.

I let out a long breath, enjoying the warmth of the water. There was plenty of time to think about having babies with George. I wasn't in a rush.

"I forgot to mention, my parents called this morning," he said. "They'd like to come visit this summer. What do you think?"

"I think that sounds very nice," I said. "We can finally introduce them to my parents."

"Exactly," he said. "I figured you'd be on board."

I loved James and Darlene, George's parents. We'd taken a trip to Charlotte so I could meet them several months ago. Fortunately, James hadn't held a grudge about me beating him at fantasy football. Much like my own father, I'd found common ground in sports statistics with James Thompson. We'd had an excellent visit, and I was excited for them to come see us. To see Bootleg Springs.

"So June Bug, I've been thinking about something."

I opened my eyes. He grabbed me by the waist and pulled

me around, so I faced him, straddling his lap. I let my legs rest on either side of him and wrapped my arms around his neck.

"What have you been thinking about?"

"Do you remember the first time we met out here?" he asked.

"Of course I do. That's not something a girl is likely to forget."

He smiled. "You liked what you saw that day?"

"It was very impressive."

"Why, thank you," he said with a wink. "I've just been thinking about the first time I saw you in Moonshine. And then when we sat in this hot spring together. How I had no idea I'd just met the love of my life."

I slid my fingers through the back of his wet hair. "I'm the love of your life?"

"You bet you are. I've been crazy stupid in love with you almost from the start."

"I can't say that my love has rendered me stupid, in a literal sense, but I'm very much in love with you as well."

He smiled again. "I think it's time I asked you something."

My heart skipped and my breath caught in my throat. I understood the subtext behind his words. There was only one question he could be referring to.

"Yes," I said quickly.

"I didn't ask you anything yet."

"Oh, I'm sorry," I said. "I jumped ahead."

"That's okay, I know your brain moves fast." He laid his large palm against my cheek. "But I'm still going to do this right and ask you properly. I already spoke to your parents."

"Okay."

"June Tucker, will you do me the honor of marrying me?"

I looked into his brown eyes, feeling the deep connection between us. "Yes."

He brought me in for a kiss. Slow and sweet and delicious. His hands moved up and down my back and the warm water lapped around us.

My heart felt so full, I almost didn't know how to contain it. This man was everything. Intelligent, steady, easygoing, and fun. And he understood me in a way no one ever had. Not my parents, or my sister. He didn't see the weird girl. He just saw June. And he liked what he saw.

It was an amazing thing.

He'd taught me to unlock a part of myself I'd been convinced I didn't have. How to handle the emotions that had often felt foreign and confusing. His love and patience had guided me into a mutually satisfying relationship, the likes of which I'd been convinced I'd never have.

I loved him so much.

"Oh no," I said, pulling away.

"What's wrong?"

"This means the girls are going to want us to have a wedding."

He laughed. "What's wrong with a wedding?"

"A wedding means a fancy dress, and guests, and flowers, and decorations. My sister is going to get very worked up over this."

"Should we just take a trip to Vegas?"

I tilted my head to the side, considering. "That is a tempting suggestion."

"How about we take this one step at a time," he said.

"Like baseball again?"

"Little bit," he said. "First, I'll give you a ring. Then we'll announce our news to our families. After that…maybe we just see what happens. The important thing to me isn't how we get married, just that we do."

I nodded. "That, I can do."

"Speaking of the ring." He reached for his pants, sitting on the side of the pool, and pulled a small ring box out of the pocket. He opened it slowly.

"Oh, George."

It was a silver band with two wavy lines engraved around the outside. In the space where each wave met, there was a small stone embedded in the band. It was simple, yet profoundly beautiful.

"They're sinusoidal waves," he said.

"Oh George," I breathed. "Sine waves keep their shape even when another wave of the same frequency is added to them."

"Exactly." He took the ring and gently slipped it onto my finger. "It symbolizes eternity, of course. But also two things coming together and still retaining who they are."

"Like us." I held out my hand to admire the ring. It shone in the sunlight. "And it's math."

"It's math in ring form," he said with a smile.

"You understand me so well."

He touched my face again and kissed me softly. My whole body tingled with happiness and love. The weight of the ring felt good on my finger. It felt right. Like it had always been meant to be there.

I still didn't understand most people. Not in general. And maybe I never would. But George understood me, and that was much more important.

What we had together made sense. I'd found a person who appreciated me for who I was. I loved and respected him in return. It was like my parents, or my sister and Bowie. George and I made each other better. We made each other happy. We supported each other when things were tough, and gave each other space to be ourselves. He'd never wanted to change me. He accepted me for who I was, quirks and all. And I loved him for the good man he was.

We'd found love. True love. And there wasn't a force in the universe that was bigger, or better, than that.

Afterword

Dear Reader,

I hope you enjoyed another trip to Bootleg Springs! To say Lucy and I have enjoyed working on this series together would be a vast understatement. It's been one of the highlights of the last year or so.

Quirky heroines are one of my favorite things, and June is probably the quirkiest character I've ever written. She's intelligent, blunt, and often unfiltered. And she lacks an understanding of the complexities of emotion and human relationships.

But like many characters we meet in Bootleg Springs, June is more than meets the eye. She's not just a math genius who lacks social skills. She cares deeply about the people in her life, even if she's not always adept at expressing her feelings.

Enter George Thompson. A superstar athlete is an unlikely match for June Tucker, but George is also more than meets the eye. He's smart and sensitive, and his easygoing nature makes him a good counterpoint to June's logic.

I really enjoy writing characters who get each other,

especially when the other people in their lives don't. George understands June from the start. He doesn't think of her as the weird girl. He loves her quirks and all the things that make her June Bug.

I hope you're enjoying the series! We're having a blast, and there are more shenanigans to come.

If you enjoyed *Bourbon Bliss*, please consider leaving a review on Amazon and Goodreads.

Thanks and happy reading!
CK

Acknowledgments

Thank you for the millionth time to my Lucy-Lou-Who for writing this series with me. This has been the BEST experience. I love your face!

To my beta readers, Christine, Jodi, and Nikki: thank you for your honest feedback and criticisms. I appreciate the time you take to help me make my books better.

To Christine: thank you for all your behind the scenes work on this launch, and everything else.

To Adrian: thanks for letting me pick your brain and helping with some of the finer details of this book.

To Cassy: thank you again for another beautiful cover.

To Elayne: thanks for calling me out on my bullshit and not letting me mess this up.

To David and my family for putting up with my weirdness and never giving up on me.

To all my readers: thank you a million times over for your love and support. I love your guts!

About the Author

Claire Kingsley is a #1 Amazon bestselling author of heartwarming, sexy romance, including contemporary romance, romantic comedies, and small-town romantic suspense. She writes fun, quirky heroines, swoony heroes who love big, romantic happily ever afters, and lots of big feels.

She can't imagine life without coffee, great books, and all the crazy characters who inhabit her imagination. She lives in the inland Pacific Northwest with her three kids.

Website: clairekingsleybooks.com
Facebook: Claire Kingsley
Instagram/TikTok: @clairekingsleybooks

Printed in the USA
CPSIA information can be obtained
at www.ICGtesting.com
LVHW050055101024
793434LV00034B/614